Jewel

OF THE

Pacific

THE
DAWN *of* HAWAII
SERIES

Book Three

Jewel

OF THE *Pacific*

LINDA LEE CHAIKIN

MOODY PUBLISHERS
CHICAGO

Scripture taken from The Holy Bible: New King James Version. Copyright ©
1982,1992 by Thomas Nelson, Inc. Used by permission. All rights reserved.

This is a work of fiction. Names, characters, places, and incidents either are the prod-
uct of the author's imagination or are used fictitiously, and any resemblance to actual per-
sons, living or dead, businesses, companies, events, or locales is entirely coincidental.

Edited by Jeanette Littleton
Interior design: Ragont Design
Cover design: Studio Gearbox
Cover image: Woman on front / Bigstockphoto
             Man on front / Getty images
             Background imagery / Thinkstock

Library of Congress Cataloging-in-Publication Data

Chaikin, L. L., 1943-
    Jewel of the Pacific / Linda Lee Chaikin.
       pages cm -- (The dawn of Hawaii series ; book 3)
    ISBN 978-0-8024-3751-8
    1. Life change events—Fiction. 2. Blindness—Fiction. 3. Hawaii—History—
19th century—Fiction. I. Title.
    PS3553.H2427J49 2013
    813'.54—dc23

                                                          2012046387

We hope you enjoy this book from River North Fiction by Moody Publishers. Our goal
is to provide high-quality, thought-provoking books and products that connect truth
to your real needs and challenges. For more information on other books and products
written and produced from a biblical perspective, go to www.moodypublishers.com or
write to:

River North Fiction
Imprint of Moody Publishers
820 N. LaSalle Boulevard
Chicago, IL 60610

1 3 5 7 9 10 8 6 4 2

Printed in the United States of America

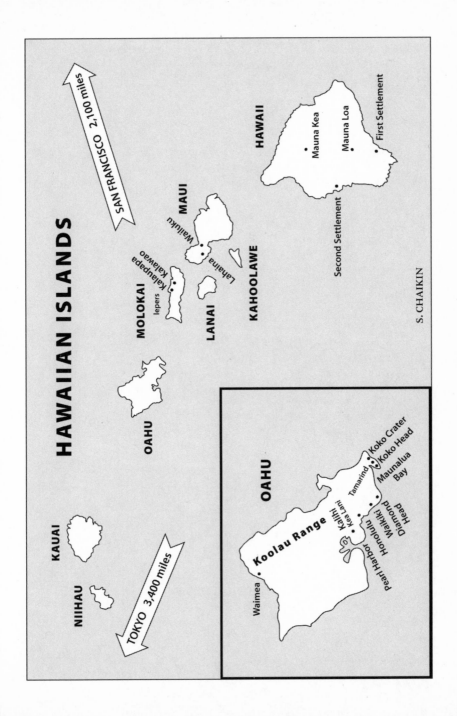

HAWAIIAN ISLANDS

SAN FRANCISCO 2,100 miles

TOKYO 3,400 miles

KAUAI

NIIHAU

OAHU

MOLOKAI
Kalaupapa
Kalawao
lepers

MAUI
Wailuku
Lahaina

LANAI

KAHOOLAWE

HAWAII
Mauna Kea
Mauna Loa
First Settlement

Second Settlement

S. CHAIKIN

OAHU

Koolau Range

Waimea

Pearl Harbor
Honolulu
Kalihi
Kea Lani
Tamarind
Waikiki
Diamond Head

Koko Crater
Koko Head
Maunalua Bay

Contents

Part 3: Stars and Stripes Forever

Historical Characters and Terms

Many of the characters who appear in *Jewel of the Pacific* are not fictional. Woven into the story of the Derrington and Easton families are real people who played an important role in the history of nineteenth-century Hawaii. The following lists include several of the more important characters and terms from Hawaii's colorful past. (Not listed are historical locations, buildings, and objects.)

Characters

Claus Spreckels — the sugar king from California.

Hiram Bingham — one of the first missionaries to Hawaii who helped create the Hawaiian alphabet, which was used to translate the Bible into Hawaiian.

John L. Stevens — American Foreign Minister (political) to Hawaii.

Kamehameha I monarchy — Kamehameha the Great conquered the other independent island kingdoms around him to form one kingdom, which he named after his island, Hawaii.

King David Kalakaua — who ruled over Hawaii for seventeen years until his death in 1891; the second elected monarch and the first to visit the United States.

Lorrin Thurston — member of the Hawaiian league and a grandson of pioneer missionary Asa Thurston.

Priest Damian — a Belgian priest who was ordained in Honolulu and assigned at his own request to the leper colony on Molokai in 1873, where he died in 1889 after contracting the disease.

Queen Emma Kaleleonalani — who in the 1870s had a cousin who was a leper at Molokai.

Queen Liliuokalani — the last reigning monarch of the kingdom of Hawaii, who was deposed in 1893; a musician and songwriter, she wrote Hawaii's most famous song, "Aloha Oe."

Walter Murray Gibson — King Kalakaua's controversial prime minister, who was eventually run out of Hawaii and died on his way to San Francisco.

TERMS:

alii — chief, princely

aloha — love, hello, good-bye

auwe — an expression of lament; alas!

haole — foreigner, especially white person; Caucasian

hapa-haole — person of mixed race; Hawaiian-Caucasian

hoolaulei — festive celebration

kahu — caregiver or nurse

kahuna — sorcerer or priest of the ancient native religion

kokua — helper; a person who would live with and assist a leper

lanai — porch, terrace, veranda

luna — overseer

makua — parent or any relative of one's parents

muumuu — gown, Mother Hubbard gown

Pake — Chinese

wahine — woman

Derrington Family Tree (Fictional Characters)

Ezra Derrington ======= Amabel
(missionary doctor)

Jedaiah ======= Sarah Wilcox
(minister)

Ainsworth (sugar & politics)   Nora

Douglas   Townsend   Jerome ======= Rebecca Stanhope   Lana Stanhope
                                    (Doctor)   (missionary teacher)   (Rebecca's sister)

Candace   Zachary   Silas   Eden

Easton Family Tree (Fictional Characters)

Daniel Easton ======= Naomi
(missionary)   (missionary)

Nathan ======= Laura
(sugar grower)

Ambrose ======= Noelani   Mathew ======= Celestine
                                 (Matt)

Keno   Rafe
(Noelani's nephew)

Part One

The Gathering Storm

Chapter One
The Devil-Lion Prowls

*T*he flames sputtered and fumed as lashing rain struck the front of the Great House of Hanalei Kona coffee plantation on the Big Island of Hawaii.

Rafe Easton held his fiancée, Eden Derrington, one arm around her shoulders and the other about her waist. Rafe had just pulled Eden from the burning inferno and now they stood on the soggy lawn, drenched to the skin in warm rain. But now a safe distance from the flames.

Eden shivered. It had all happened so fast. First her own uncle, Townsend Derrington, had abducted Eden from Honolulu, where she lived in her grandfather's house.

Next Townsend Derrington had commanded his son, Zachary, to take him and his hostage on a journey aboard Zachary's boat, *Lilly of the Stars*. When Zach had refused, Townsend had struck his son, and left him tied in the hold. Then, at gunpoint, he had commandeered a boat, the *Princess Kaiulani*, from the cousin of an extended family member, and had brought Eden to the Big Island, here to Hanalei.

If that hadn't been dastardly enough, he'd left her incapacitated in the home built by his own stepson, Rafe, the home she would soon oversee as Rafe's wife. Then he had set the house on fire . . . to destroy his stepson's future, fortune . . . and life.

Fortunately, Rafe, in pursuit, had found Zachary aboard the *Lilly of the Stars*. He had untied Zachary and left him to rest in the boat while Rafe rushed to Eden's rescue, barely reaching her before the room where she was tied completely blazed into an inferno.

The downpour continued its heavenly blessing, keeping the blaze from spreading from the front of the house to the rest of the lanai. The acrid smell of smoke clung in the night air, filled with hissing and sizzling of burning wood.

Rafe glanced at Eden and her gaze answered him with the same steady love he possessed for her.

As he held Eden a little tighter, trying to steady her shaking body, Rafe's thoughts about Townsend kindled a fury that burned as intensely as the fire. His heart yearned for revenge. *If I could get my hands on him—*

But did not God spare Eden for you? Was not His rain quenching the flames? Then be still!

What if Eden *had* met her death tonight? What if Hanalei *had* burned down, what then?

Even then, the desire for revenge should be stilled. That hour belonged to God's wise timing. *Vengeance is Mine, I will repay, says the Lord.*

Rafe tightened his jaw, trying not to think of his stepfather.

A rider on horseback burst through the palm foliage, abruptly drew the reins, then saw Rafe on the lawn and rode toward him.

Townsend returning for more trouble? Rafe wondered, not clearly seeing the rider through the smoke and rain. He thrust Eden behind him and then relaxed a bit as he recognized the rider. Liho, the owner of the *Princess Kaiulani* that Townsend had shanghaied. Liho was also the cousin of one of Rafe's closest friends, Keno, who was also Rafe's cousin by marriage.

Liho rode up to where Rafe and Eden stood drenched in rain. He was hatless with his dark hair clinging to his forehead. His broad face was split by a fresh cut across his cheekbone. His wrists were raw, an injury incurred as he escaped from the ropes Townsend had used to tie him to the steerage.

Frantically, Liho rattled off information to Rafe in a mixture of Hawaiian and English.

Keno, in his saddle a short distance away with Rafe's uncle, Ambrose Easton, edged his horse forward, with Ambrose coming behind.

"I saw Townsend Derrington down at dock!" Liho explained.

"When?" Rafe demanded to know.

"Little time ago."

"You saw him? You're certain it was Townsend?"

"He didn't come back to my boat this time. I hid, and see him move toward *Lilly of the Stars*."

Rafe gestured to one of his *kanakas* for his horse. The young Hawaiian hurried forward, leading the horse by the reins. Rafe reached for the bridle, placed a boot in the stirrup, and swiftly mounted. He exchanged an angry look with Keno.

"I'm going to stop him," he said through gritted teeth.

Eden rushed to Rafe's horse. "Don't go, Rafe!"

Rafe gazed at her, but he did not answer. He swiftly turned his horse toward the road and Ambrose caught her shoulder, to keep her from grasping Rafe's leg as he started to speed off.

"Too late I fear, lass," he stated.

Eden looked at the older man. Ambrose was not only Rafe's uncle, but he'd been like a father to Eden. He and his wife Noelani had done much to raise Eden since her parents were not around— her father, Jerome, was an acclaimed doctor who spent much time in the East, searching cures for leprosy, so Eden seldom had seen him while she was growing up. And she could barely remember her mother, Rebecca. For some time she'd thought that her father's family, the Derringtons, had murdered her mother because they'd always refused to talk about her. Recently, though, she'd learned that her mother was indeed alive, but was a victim of leprosy and was living in a leper colony on a distant island.

Eden had lived with Ambrose and Noelani until her early teens, when her grandfather had taken her to live in his home.

As a pastor, Ambrose had also been her spiritual father throughout the years. And now she naturally turned to him. "He mustn't be alone with Townsend."

"Yes," Ambrose agreed. "Keno!" he called to his wife's nephew, "we best go with Rafe."

Keno knew his childhood friend and ally, Rafe, only too well, and was already starting after him. The thudding hoofs sounded ominously on the wind.

"Let us hope the law will reach the harbor first." Ambrose mounted his horse and motioned for Liho to follow him. They too, rode into the dark.

Eden stood in the rain, miserable and wet, fearing what might take place. She understood Rafe's anger. She trembled, knowing her uncle had planned for her to die.

Thoughts of the past twenty-four hours hovered around her like grimacing ghosts fretting over denied prey—and she had been the prey. *But, no,* she had proven the pawn for Townsend to lure Rafe to the cliff's edge. Rafe was the prey, the one Townsend wished to destroy. And why? Because of envy, pride, and resentment.

She was also angry. And there was just cause! Even so, anger too easily grew into a sin of its own making: *The wrath of man worketh not the righteousness of God.*

She was suddenly more afraid than she had ever been—not for herself but for Rafe. A breath of wind slid through the wet, fringed palm fronds, causing a rustle.

Lord, she pleaded, *protect Rafe from self-destruction through his own fury!*

A dark lion seemed to crouch nearby—as though sensing a victory. Its mouth anticipating the taste of blood. She could almost hear a deep-throated grumble as it prepared to roar, as though it were beginning to move faster in the shadows along the road, toward the harbor, toward the *Lilly of the Stars*.

She sank to the soggy lawn and lowered her head.

A moment later she felt a hand gently touch her shoulder. She raised her face to see a young Hawaiian boy, Koko, looking at her with sympathetic eyes.

"Ling comes," he whispered. "He looks for you."

Eden turned her head and saw the friendly figure of Ling Li. She had known Ling from his first early days in Honolulu as a sugar worker under contract to leave China and work at Kea Lani. She'd helped him get his wife and children out of China to join him on Kea Lani, just as she and her cousin Candace had done for many other workers serving the Derrington enterprise.

After fulfilling his work contract, Ling had started his own hackney business while his wife and children had stayed on at Kea Lani.

Nearly two months earlier, Rafe had brought Ling to the safety of Hanalei. And Ling needed a refuge, for he, too, was in Townsend Derrington's sights. Ling had finally told authorities that he'd seen Townsend at one of his evil deeds. Ling had witnessed the struggle between Townsend and Rafe's father, Matt Easton, on Hanalei. He told how the two men had fought and then how Matt had fallen— or perhaps been pushed—from a rocky ledge. When the severely injured Matt had called for help, Townsend had hurried away.

Ling had gone for help, but his English was so poor that he could not explain the problem. By the time he had convinced Eden's Great-aunt Nora that Matt needed help, it was too late. When the marshal looked into Matt Easton's death, Townsend had claimed he'd not even been on Hanalei that day.

Later, when Nora decided to write a book on the history of the Derringtons, including Matt Easton's *accidental* death, Townsend began fearing Ling's witness and set fire to Ling's hut to frighten him. Ling had fled to Rafe for safety and had been working on Hanalei as Rafe's cook ever since.

"You come with me, Miss Eden," Ling urged. "Mr. Rafe be very upset you out here in rain and mud. I check rest of rooms already. Some very good. You come now. Many rooms all right. You close door, you not smell smoke. Wife bring you to good room. You rest; you eat. Mr. Rafe come back. You see."

──── ⋙⋘ ────

The fire, except for God's mercy, would have reduced the Hanalei plantation house to a few surviving bricks. The rainstorm had quelled the flames. As it was, the front parlor with its roof, and a section of the breathtaking dark wood staircase were charred and ruined. The smell of smoke hung in the air.

Ling showed Eden to the rooms that Celestine, Rafe's mother, used when she was at home in their lovely residence. Celestine had lived here on Hanalei from the time Rafe was born. This had been the home she'd shared with Rafe's father, Matt. After Matt's father had died, she had married Townsend Derrington. She'd been the Lady of the Estate until she had recently ignored Townsend's protests and had arranged for the legal rights of Hanalei to be signed over to her son, Rafe—the act that had solidified Townsend's hatred of his stepson.

The lovely area Celestine lived in was untouched by the fire and included a private sitting room, dressing room, and bedroom.

The closet even held a significant wardrobe Eden could use until she returned to Kea Lani. All she had were the garments she was wearing when Townsend had shanghaied her. Eden knew Rafe's generous mother, Celestine, would be pleased to have helped her.

Eden quickly rid herself of her smoke-stained, grimy clothes. While she cleaned her appearance, however, the day's grim events kept overtaking her mind.

After setting fire to the downstairs parlor, Townsend had fled toward the boat to head for Honolulu and Kea Lani. Rafe intended to stop him, but what if Townsend got away? Then Townsend would go directly to his father, Ainsworth Derrington, who was also Eden's grandfather.

Ambrose had said that Grandfather Ainsworth was in Honolulu with Dr. Jerome, Eden's father. The two men had departed Kea Lani at the same time as Rafe, in order to alert the marshal of her abduction. Ainsworth intended to pressure the marshal to authorize a civilian posse to hunt for Townsend. Whether this had occurred, she had no idea, but the authorities might even now be on their way to the Big Island in chartered boats.

Eden sat at the desk to write a message to her cousin Candace Derrington, who was also her dearest friend. As soon as Liho returned to Honolulu, she would ask him to deliver it to Candace. She wanted to warn Candace about the situation.

"If Townsend should elude capture he will go to Kea Lani before leaving the Islands, thinking Grandfather will give him money to flee to the Caribbean. He is also seeking jewels from you and Great-aunt Nora, so beware. He believes the Derringtons will do most anything to protect their name—so he's expecting everyone to take care of him rather than letting information get out about his treachery."

⸻ ❧ ⸻

The *Lilly of the Stars* was still in harbor. Rafe tied his horse, and headed toward the dock, keeping in the shadows of the palms. Rafe passed several dark, still boats tied along the shore. He passed cabins with lamps flickering through reed window blinds. He moved on silently.

Rafe heard an oar creak at the stern. The *Lilly of the Stars*. He paused and then approached the side of the boat. Arguing voices cut through the night.

"No! You're not taking my boat. What did you do with Eden?" Zachary's voice was shrill with helpless indignation as he argued with his father, Townsend.

"You'll do as I say, or I'll break your disobedient neck!"

Rafe's heart thudded like the cadence of a military drumbeat. Instantly Rafe was over the rail, his feet landing softly on the wet wooden deck.

As Rafe quietly opened the cabin door, Townsend swung round, shock carved on his sweating face.

"You," he said, his eyes cold and hard. "You've ruined my life."

"You've ruined your own. Eden is safe. Hanalei is safe. The rain put the fire out."

"I'll kill you."

"I was hoping you'd try," Rafe challenged.

Zach's right arm was in a sling from his father's earlier rage. But the brave young man still grabbed a bookend and hurled it at Townsend's head—it missed.

Townsend barely noticed. His weathered face with its high cheekbones and steely silvery eyes leered at Refe. "I'll do more than 'try.' I'll beat you. Then I'll tie you up and dump you at sea."

"Think so? Not this time. I'm going to kick your face in. I'll give you a licking you'll long remember, while you sit in your prison cell awaiting execution for my father's death."

For a moment Townsend showed surprise, even uncertainty, but then charged Rafe.

Rafe smashed his fist into Townsend's face.

Townsend gasped as he flew backward, thudding against the cabin wall. He grunted, and slipped down the wall, landing on his seat, legs stretched out before him. He shook his head as if something were out of place.

Zachary laughed hysterically as he held his injured arm.

"Too easy, Townsend." Rafe shook his head sadly. "Where's the bluster you tormented Eden with—and my mother? You've had this coming for a long time. Get up."

Zachary sobered. He wiped his palm on his shirt, glancing from Rafe to Townsend. "Caution, Rafe. Take it easy, now."

"That first blow was for my father and to begin to pay for your pushing him off that cliff and leaving him to die," Rafe said coldly. "I have a few more to go to pay for the way you tricked my mother into marrying you and then abused her. And for the way you tried to kill the woman I love—your own niece. Say goodbye to your teeth, Townsend because when I'm through, you'll have to eat mush while you wait for a hangman to drop a rope around your neck."

Townsend spat blood and wiped his mouth on the back of his sleeve. He rose to his feet and rushed at Rafe, striking out with his fist. His swing was wild but it caught Rafe on the side of the head. Townsend smashed his fist a second time on the back of Rafe's neck as Rafe staggered. Townsend's horrible laughter filled the cabin.

Townsend viciously kicked. But Rafe rolled aside and jumped to his feet. His fist sent Townsend again stumbling back against the wall. Townsend reached into his belt and came at Rafe, knife in his hand.

Rafe heard Townsend's breath and saw the light gleam along the blade. Rafe stopped, poised for attack. Townsend lunged but Rafe sidestepped, extending his leg and catching Townsend's toe, tripping him as Rafe swung upward.

The blow caught Townsend off guard, but Rafe felt the knife rip his sleeve. Townsend came back up and ran toward Rafe again, jabbing. Rafe caught Townsend's wrist and twisted fiercely, causing Townsend to lose his grip on the knife. He threw his weight into Rafe. The force pushed Rafe backward, but his forearm caught Townsend's chin. Rafe landed on his back and Townsend tumbled over him. They both panted fiercely.

From the deck footsteps pounded and someone yelled.

Keno burst through the cabin doorway and stood there, looking from Rafe to Townsend.

"Back off!" Keno warned. "Both of you!"

Rafe's head was buzzing. "Stay back, Keno," he warned, eyes on Townsend. Townsend was up again and Rafe struck with his left fist. Townsend stepped back and Rafe stepped in, his thrust low and hard.

He grabbed Townsend and slammed him back against the bulkhead as the cabin rumbled.

Rafe picked up the blade and threw it across the cabin. Zach hobbled forward and snatched it. Rafe grabbed Townsend's blond head and began smacking it against the cabin wall.

"Stop! It's enough, Rafe! You'll kill him!" Keno demanded.

Rafe continued the merciless attack.

Keno threw himself against Rafe's back, grabbing his arms and wrestling him away from Townsend, his voice fierce. "Rafe stop!"

Zach lunged as Townsend grabbed the heavy brass bookend on the floor. Townsend pushed himself to his feet, shoving Zach aside.

Rafe broke Keno's hold, shoving him backward.

"Rafe! Watch it!" Zach threw himself against his father, but went down easily as Townsend kicked him.

Rafe turned and saw Townsend behind him, arms raised, teeth bared, his face bloodied, the brass bookend in his hands. Townsend brought the bookend down with a grunting blow that smashed Rafe's forehead.

Rafe's brain filled with sparks, and his ears roared. He reached for something to grasp and found nothing as he spun into searing blackness. He heard shouting voices as he felt something warm running into his eyes, and then tasted blood.

Tiny flames appeared in his vision. He ran a hand across his eyes. Nothing. He imagined a voice cackling with demonic laughter. His head throbbed. Sweat stung the abrasions on his face, and his knuckles were stiff and swollen.

Rafe's vision grew as dark as rolling clouds. He closed his eyes tightly, trying to refocus, to think. . . . He half-consciously realized that Keno was shouting madly.

Thud!

Rafe had fallen to the floor unable to move.

───✦───

Ambrose Easton clambered aboard the *Lilly of the Stars* a short time later with Liho just behind. Ambrose burst through the cabin doorway and gasped at seeing Rafe unconscious. He dropped to his nephew's side.

"I was afraid of this." He bowed his head as his groans of dismay and prayers blended together.

Keno gazed at Rafe's blood-splattered face. "It's my fault. I distracted him."

Zachary, pale and in pain hobbled to the cabin door. He ranted at Liho: "Why are you just standing there! Go! Go for a doctor! Hurry—!"

Liho rushed into the windy night.

Zachary glanced uneasily at his father, Townsend, crumpled on the floor amid broken furniture. His eyes opened slowly, like a lizard's, then closed again.

Zachary stepped toward Ambrose and Keno and looked down at Rafe with anguish.

"This wouldn't have happened if I hadn't distracted him," Keno tried to explain. "Rafe turned toward me—and Townsend took advantage—" Keno picked up the bronze bookend and stared at it. "He smashed him in the forehead. Rafe must have a concussion."

"Then don't lift his head!" Zach shouted as Keno moved a hand toward Rafe.

Keno stifled a sob.

"You were right to try to stop him," Ambrose murmured, putting his strong, steadying hand on Keno's shoulder. "Rafe might have killed Townsend and what then? He crossed the line tonight. Eden and the burning of Hanalei were as much as Rafe could take without exploding, and Satan knew it would be so. If Rafe had killed Townsend his future would end in rubble!"

"But look at him now. Is it any better for him? Rafe's dying."

"The Almighty will decide that. Remember who is in ultimate control. Both of you lads, steady yourselves."

Rain began to splatter on the deck of the *Lilly of the Stars*.

Zachary opened the cabin door and stepped onto the deck. He strode to the side of the boat and looked toward the darkened quay, clutching his arm against his chest. "Why doesn't that miserable doctor get here!"

Thump!

Zachary whipped around to face his father steadying himself with both hands on the frame of the cabin doorway.

Zachary lunged toward him. Townsend thrust out his arm, shoving Zachary out of his path.

Zachary's knee buckled and he grabbed the rail. Townsend rushed past him and jumped over the side of the boat with a splash.

"Stop him!" Zachary shouted, as he stared into the dark water.

Keno came from the cabin door.

"He leaped over the side. He's out there. Somewhere in the water," Zachary explained.

Keno ripped off his shirt and dove over the side with another splash.

Zachary fumbled down the gangplank to the wooden wharf, and limped into the night.

*T*he long uncertain hours of the night provided Eden with little sleep. She was dressed with the dawning of the eastern sky over Hanalei. She strained her ears to hear any distant horse hoofs galloping up the road. She cheered herself by imagining the arrival of good news: *"All is well, darling,"* Rafe would say, embracing her joyfully. *"Townsend yielded without any trouble."* *"Yes, and he's repented,"* Keno would add. *"We left him kneeling in prayer with Ambrose."*

Sobering, Eden paced across the lovely pale blue carpet to the lanai. Then she walked back again, and heard the ominous clock ticking. With each minute her belief that something had gone dreadfully awry took command of the struggle she fought to keep her mind free of chains.

God is on the throne. Whatever may have happened, He is in control.

And, still . . . Rafe should have returned by now, or sent me a message. And Ambrose—where is he?

She went to the lanai again, and again looked toward the road— nothing.

She would at least have expected Liho to come back. She had intended to ask him to deliver her letter to Candace. But by now, Noelani and Candace must also be wearing out the carpet at Kea Lani as she was here at Hanalei.

The clock in the hall struck noon. She drew in a breath and turned at the sound of Ling rapping on the door and entering with fresh fruit and broiled chicken. "You mebbe eat something, or you faint. Here—you eat this."

"Ling," she said firmly, "I know something must have gone horribly wrong or one of them would have returned by now."

"You right." He set the tray down. "Police don't catch Mr. Townsend quick, I think. Pardon, we both know he very evil man. Very bad fellow, that one. Burn down my house, this house! Try to kill people."

"At least this house wasn't totally ruined," she said, though the rooms in the front were devastated. Feeling as if she needed to be optimistic, she added: "Rafe can rebuild better than ever."

He nodded. "He can. But no rest for tired hands. Always work."

"Well, God's mercy did provide rain just when we needed it to put out the fire. And no one can convince me it wasn't the gracious Lord who answered many prayers. Ambrose agrees."

"I agree. Great God can do anything He want to do."

She tried to smile.

"Rafe been after me," he admitted. "Keno, too. Always telling me I need Son of God, Jesus. After all I hear, I become humble fellow. I believe. Soon, be baptized to tell all my people." He smiled at her.

Her heart lightened. "Ling, now we're all in the same family, all members of God's family."

He patted his thin chest beneath the white tunic.

Christ's words when He was about to be betrayed came to her mind. *In the world you will have tribulation, but be of good cheer, I have overcome the world.*

It was 2:30 in the afternoon.

As time slipped by, Eden's emotions raced. *Lord, I believe—help me to trust You—I'm so afraid.* She couldn't endure not knowing any longer.

"Ling!" she called toward the kitchen. "I'm taking a horse from the stables and riding to the wharf. I'll be back when I've learned something."

He rushed out of the kitchen with his hands dusted with flour, crying out words of warning in Chinese. But Eden was already out the door, not caring if it was improper or dangerous for a woman to go to the wharf alone. She called to Koko to saddle the mare, and hurry: "*Wiki!*"

When she arrived at the beach and the small quay the wind had begun to gain strength. She looked all around for the *Lilly of the Stars*, Zachary's boat, or Liho's *Princess Kaiulani*.

Her heart sank. Neither vessel was docked, nor was either anchored farther in the harbor.

She curled her fist. *Too late. I should have acted as soon as it was light!*

She saw some Hawaiian fishermen on the landing wharf tying down their boats. She asked if they knew what had happened to the two boats and their passengers.

"Both boats left last night, miss."

"Was there trouble last night?"

"Ho! Much trouble. Very bloody fighting."

Her heart beat so fast she was breathless. "Who was hurt, do you know?"

"Several haole men were hurt."

Several!

"Did the police take anyone away?"

The talker pursed his lips and shook his head. "Don't know."

Another fisherman said, "There was talk of a missing man, no, two missing men."

Two! Eden shaded her eyes and looked at the rough blue-gray waters. She might be able to hire a boat to take her to Honolulu. She mentioned this to the fishermen but they shook their dark heads apologetically. They knew of no boatmen willing to risk the choppy sea. An older Hawaiian pointed. "New storm coming. Rain—and strong wind."

Eden turned her horse around and started back to Hanalei. If a storm was brewing she probably wouldn't get to go to Honolulu until tomorrow, or even the following day.

Two missing men? What did it mean?

Her mind trembled to explore the idea, afraid of where it might lead.

⌒⊙⌒

Ling opened the front door and Ambrose entered, drenched with rain. He handed his dripping dark coat and hat to Ling with an apology.

Ambrose was a tall and solid man of sixty, with piercing deep-set eyes beneath a swath of silver-gray hair that in some places remained dark. His suntanned jaw was square and his stance resolute. He had always been there for her, Rafe, Keno, Zachary, and even her cousin Candace, so he seemed to never need anything.

Even in his wearied condition, Ambrose's presence brought a feeling of security into the room. Eden rushed toward Ambrose and grasped his arm.

"Ambrose, I rode to the wharf earlier. One of the fishermen told me *two* men were missing last night after a terrible brawl. Where is Rafe, and Keno?"

Ambrose was somber. "Keno is safe. So is Zachary. There is distressing news, though. We need to talk about it, lass."

She met his sympathetic gaze. She was seized with an uncomfortable notion that "something more" had entered the door behind Ambrose. *Something* spiritual trailing after his steps. Some dark, slippery "thing" she couldn't see, but *sensed*, tracking in slime, and then backing into a shadowy corner, searching for an opportunity to strike.

Eden must have paled because Ambrose laid a firm hand on her shoulder. "Now lass you must be strong. Let's find a place to sit so we can talk sensibly."

"Not in there," she said as he started for the parlor, "the room is in rubble."

Like everything, she wanted to add.

She took him to the luncheon room. When they were seated at the square, wood table, Eden looked straight at Ambrose.

"Is he . . . is . . . Rafe dead?"

Ambrose reached across the table and patted her hand. "He was alive when I left him. He's in Honolulu, at the medical ward, seriously injured. Your father is the physician and is in touch with Dr. Bolton and others. Dr. Bolton is now a declared leper, unable to enter the ward where Rafe is being watched. Jerome tells me Rafe will be unconscious for at least 24 hours, and perhaps days." His sober gaze fixed on her. "Being a nurse, Eden, you would understand comas."

Eden frowned as she recalled what she knew about comas from her work at Kalihi hospital.

"Townsend shot him, is that it? And my father isn't sure Rafe will survive."

"Rafe wasn't shot. There was a fight. Rafe was caught off guard, and Townsend struck him on the forehead with a brass bookend."

She closed her eyes, as if that would make everything painful fade away. Her heart reached out to God in prayer.

She considered Ambrose's words, "Alive when I left him."

The news that Rafe was in a coma turned her hands cold, and she knew this was not his first. He might not awaken from a *second* concussion. Although Rafe had never given the details, he did tell her a year ago that he'd suffered a head injury on a voyage he'd made to French Guiana. As a result, he had frequent headaches.

Ambrose looked at her kindly. "I see you understand. We know, as does Keno, that Rafe is not a man to live in a chair or on his back. And yet, *what if life demands it?* Can we not say this outcome, too, is in God's hand? We must rest in God's character, in His wisdom, and sovereign purposes."

The penetrating question *what if life demands it?* echoed in her mind. The answer Ambrose hoped she would see was clear: *many* chosen Christians had these demands placed upon their lives, or on the lives of loved ones.

"This is bitter," she choked, swallowing the urge to weep. "Whether Rafe lives or dies, the outcome may bring little but the promise of tears . . . for all of us."

"And bitter situations often bring no instant blessing to be seen within our earthly eyes. We are such people of clay that if we cannot soon know the purpose of our trials we quickly believe there is no meaningful reason for them. Most likely our understanding may not come until when we are in His presence. Even so, our Redeemer is merciful. So we will pray, and hope."

Would she ever be Rafe's wife now?

When Ling brought in the coffee and fruit, he paused. "May ask question?"

"Certainly, Ling," Ambrose said.

Ling looked from Ambrose to Eden then back. "What of *Makua* Townsend? Evil man escape?"

Eden turned to Ambrose. "Yes, what about Townsend?"

Frowning, Ambrose admitted he had not been seen since he'd jumped overboard. Keno had gone after him, but Townsend had eluded him. Zachary, too, had searched the wharf, but then Zachary, too, had disappeared.

"Keno admits he didn't search long for Townsend," Ambrose said. "Rafe's condition was on all our minds. It was urgent to get him to a doctor. Thankfully, by the time Keno returned to the boat, Liho arrived with a doctor from the village."

"He told me earlier that he was going to Kea Lani to get money from Grandfather so he can escape to the Caribbean," she explained. "He will already be there if he kept his plan."

"The authorities have been alerted. The docks are being watched," Ambrose said. Neither he nor Ling looked satisfied.

"I won't say what I think of him and all he's done," she said tensely.

"I understand. My carnal nature growls that he's the one who deserves to be in a coma. Don't think this is easier for me because I'm a minister. That old sin nature we inherit in Adam is nothing to ignore. It's dangerous, deadly, and evil. That's why we're told not to let it reign over us, not to yield the members of our body and mind to it. Townsend is responsible for Matt's death," he said of his younger brother, Rafe's father. "That was a great loss to me. When I saw Celestine marry Townsend and subject Rafe to his bullying— well, I spent many long walks on the beach in prayer."

Eden reached over to him. "I know—"

"Rafe became the son I always wanted. Rafe and Keno, both." Ambrose shook his head. "Unfortunately, Rafe let his old nature reign for just an hour! Your abduction, the burning of Hanalei, and Matt's death sought its pound of flesh. I'm not making excuses for Rafe, for this has produced a miserable harvest."

"Townsend is the one who should reap the harvest," she said. "He's done more hurt and evil than Rafe ever could!"

"Ah, my lass, that somber time will come, as it will for all men rejecting God's mercy. We leave Townsend's verdict to the great Lord alone. Rafe, we know, is a true Christian. He can be chastened for his disobedience, but never condemned. Townsend, on the other hand . . . I have long prayed for Townsend."

He glanced kindly at Ling. "Will you come with us to Kea Lani, or will you remain here at Hanalei?"

"I stay. Lock all doors. As you say, I not alone ever when Son of true God knows me."

Ambrose threw a strong arm around Ling's thin shoulders and smiled. "Well said."

He turned to Eden. "Come, lass, I'll bring you to Honolulu, to
Noelani. She's waiting for you at Kea Lani with your grandfather
and Candace. Keno and the boys are holding an all-day, all-night
prayer vigil for Rafe at the mission church. If there is a solution to
all this sinful harvest, lass, we will find it there."

"Can we make it to Honolulu in this rainstorm?" Eden asked.

"Liho is confident we can. He's waiting for us."

"Your prayers for Rafe are just as acceptable here as in the
church in Honolulu," Ambrose told Ling. "So you gather the others
to pray together."

"Next time you see me you bring the Holy Book in Chinese, like
you say?"

"I'll have it next week from the printer in San Francisco. I sent
for more Chinese Bibles two weeks ago."

"One longer week. I wait."

The thought of intercession for Rafe, and the knowledge that
she was not the only one who cared for him strengthened her confidence. She followed Ambrose to Liho's boat, and boarded quietly
for the excursion through the dark, choppy waters to Honolulu.

awn broke in the eastern sky, as Eden and Ambrose arrived at Kea Lani House at the Derrington sugar plantation. The sun glowed above the white-pillared structure with three stories, a replica of Eden's great-grandmother Amabel's house in Vicksburg, Mississippi.

Grandfather Ainsworth walked the floor of the large parlor. His face was drawn, his cheek twitching with tension, and his pallor gray.

Eden stopped abruptly. "Grandfather!"

Only in seeing how ill he now looked over this unsettled tragedy with his middle son, Townsend, did she consider how deeply he'd been affected.

Townsend had retained his powerful position in the family and boasted his rightful sonship, aided, Eden often thought, on account of what Ainsworth considered Jerome's wasted dedication to his medical work rather than to the Derrington family sugar enterprise and its political influence on the Islands.

Now, Grandfather Ainsworth hurried to her. "My dear child! Thank God! Then you are all right?"

His concern pleased Eden.

"Yes, Grandfather, I'm unhurt."

"A terrible, terrible tragedy." He shook his head with more distress than she'd ever seen him show. "I blame myself for what has happened to Rafe. The injustice he put up with at the hand of my wayward son went on for too long, and I foolishly did little about it."

His words fueled her emotional fire, but she refused to unleash tears.

"Rafe arrived in time to rescue me from the fire Townsend set. Rafe risked his life to save me."

"Then Townsend *deliberately* left you in the house." His dignified features revealed his shock.

Her grandfather held her protectively. She heard his groan of sorrow for his wasted son Townsend, as well as for her.

"What has the Derrington family become in this last generation that we, the sons and daughters of the first Christian missionaries, could produce a man who would stoop so low. Anger, revenge, greed—murder."

Ambrose entered the parlor, followed by Keno and his aunt Noelani. Grandfather Ainsworth continued speaking. "And he was granted so much to use for good and godliness in this life! Now look at him, a would-be murderer! Oh how I've failed Him!"

"Townsend has failed *you*, Ainsworth," Ambrose stated.

Ainsworth sank into a chair as though his strength had drained out of him. His eyes trailed to a painting high on the wall, and Eden followed his gaze. The painting was of her great-grandfather Jedaiah Derrington with silver hair, high cheekbones, and alert, kind eyes. He had left New England in the late 1820s to serve as a missionary. His firstborn son, Ainsworth, had been born in Honolulu.

"I was not thinking of my failure to Townsend," Ainsworth said tiredly, "but *my* failure to God."

"Who has not failed Him?" Ambrose said. "The most pious offspring of Adam has stumbled into the quicksand. We struggle to climb out on our own. We promise to do better tomorrow. We rely on good works, on religious rituals—yet, we remain where we fell, sinking deeper with each hour. The strong arm of Christ alone can lift us out of the mire to stand before God, spotless and complete in His righteousness."

Ainsworth bowed his silver head, nodding.

"You haven't prayed with me in a long time, Ainsworth. Why not now? Then go upstairs and rest," Ambrose said.

Eden, Noelani, and Keno bowed their heads along with Ainsworth and Ambrose. When the prayer ended, Eden slipped out of the room with Noelani and Keno, and went down the stairs. Eden stopped on the bottom stair and turned to Keno.

His sympathy was plain. He said in a low voice: "I'm sorry, Eden."

He used her first name as he always did in private, something he wouldn't have done in parlor society, but they knew each other well, having been in each other's company often with Rafe and Candace. She knew he had a nickname for her that he used with Rafe—"Miss Green Eyes." She managed a smile and laid a hand on his arm.

"I shall be all right, but did Rafe say anything at all on the way to Honolulu, to the medical ward?"

"No. He was not conscious. Look, Eden, we've begun a 24-hour prayer vigil at the mission church for him. Maybe there's some real hope. All things in God's will are possible. So don't give up yet."

She squeezed his arm. "Yes it's possible. As you so well put it, everything in God's will is possible. I won't give up yet, especially if you won't."

"You can be sure. And neither will Noelani." He put a strong arm around the older woman's shoulder.

"Rafe is like a son to me," Noelani admitted. "Just like my Keno. Ambrose and I have been praying much."

Keno turned to leave. "Get some rest, both of you. I'm going to the church now. All my cousins are there—even Silas," he said with a note of surprise about Townsend's illegitimate son.

"You mean Silas was at the church *praying?*" she asked, surprised.

"Well." Keno rubbed his chin. "Whether he was praying is questionable since I don't believe he's reconciled to God yet—but he has been coming to church to see Ambrose recently. Isn't that right, Noelani?"

"Silas is a rascal," she said. "Ambrose says Silas likes to come to his office and argue about the Bible. It doesn't worry Ambrose any."

"Well, maybe some of it is getting through," Keno said. "Anyway, Eden, he was there earlier, but he suddenly left."

"Oh? Why was that?"

"I don't know. Liho said a coach passed by slowly but didn't stop. He recognized the driver as his friend who works at the Royal Hotel. Silas slipped out after that."

"He didn't come home here," Noelani said. "I've been here all evening. I'd have heard him."

"Then he must have gone into Honolulu," Eden suggested.

"Well, good night Eden, Aunt Noelani. I'll see you both later at the vigil. Aloha."

Noelani urged Eden up the stairs. "One day with its troubles is enough. You need sleep," she said.

"I'll stay with you," Noelani said. "Just like I used to do when you were small, to make sure you don't wake up with a nightmare."

Upstairs in her own familiar bedroom, Eden was able to put down some of the burdens weighing on her heart. She stretched out on clean, crisp sheets, hoping for a few hours of sleep before going to the prayer vigil.

Noelani sat in a rocking chair across the room, near the open windows. Soon she began humming hymns and island melodies, as if Eden were a child again. Eden smiled. *Thank You, Lord, for people like Noelani and Ambrose.* Townsend's violent face faded into the dimness of her mind as Noelani's soft voice prevailed.

～⌒～

Eden looked across the bedroom at the clock. "Noelani, why didn't you wake me sooner? I must get to the church."

"You needed sleep even more. Here, drink this."

The statuesque woman brought her a cup of tea and stood until Eden drank it.

This woman who had helped raise Eden was a dignified older woman with white hair and a pleasantly creased round face. She was a *hapa*-haole—her white, haole father had worked on a New Bedford whaling ship.

"Any news from Dr. Jerome?" Eden asked.

"Nothing yet. Mr. Ainsworth left with Ambrose earlier."

"He was supposed to sleep."

Like me, she thought with self-incrimination as she rushed to get dressed.

"And Candace?"

"She's gone to the hospital to bring your cousin Zachary home." Noelani shook her head. "I always knew the Derrington matters would end badly when it came to your uncle. Townsend brought trouble wherever he walked. I can almost see the grass withering beneath his footsteps. When I think what might have happened to you if Rafe hadn't arrived when he did." She placed the palms of her hands against her temples and closed her eyes.

There was no carriage out front to suggest that Candace and Zachary had arrived, though the groom might have brought the horses back to the stable.

Great-aunt Nora had arrived a week earlier from Tamarind house on Koko Head, but she had preferred a room at the Royal Hotel. She was at harmless odds with her brother, Ainsworth, over a loan she needed to keep her newspaper, the *Gazette*, financially stable. Eden was convinced that Nora had gone to the hotel to appeal to Rafe for a loan.

If things weren't so tragic Eden could have laughed at the turn-around of events. With possession of Hanalei, owning half of the pineapple plantation called Hawaiiana, and the Easton pearl beds under his rightful control, Rafe Easton had unexpectedly become the man the Derringtons looked to. Before acquiring control of all things Easton, Rafe was merely the adventurous son of Matt and Celestine, respected for his abilities, but not seen as someone either Grandfather Ainsworth or Great-aunt Nora would have approached for help.

Ainsworth had always taken favorably to Rafe, but in earlier times when Rafe had supported the queen's rule rather than annexation, Rafe had practically been told to leave Honolulu and not come back.

As for Great-aunt Nora, ever since Rafe had promised to loan Dr. Jerome the money to build his research clinic on the island called Molokai, where the leper settlement was, Nora had realized that she might turn to him for help with the *Gazette*. She'd come to the hotel, but then the tragedy at Hanalei had occurred—and Rafe was in a coma, and . . .

Eden worried. The marshal hadn't brought any new information on Townsend. If he'd tried to slip away on a steamer, wouldn't someone have noticed his condition?

Voices came from the direction of the parlor. However, the room furnished with magnificent native woods and green potted ferns was empty.

Eden swept across the room and out onto the lanai. She hoped she'd see her father, Dr. Jerome. He could explain everything so much more clearly than anyone else. She'd been disappointed on arriving at Kea Lani to be told again that Dr. Clifford Bolton could not continue as Rafe's physician since he'd been pronounced a leper.

Naturally she was confident in her father's ability to care for Rafe, but he must be told about Rafe's severe headaches from an earlier injury. Perhaps Dr. Bolton had sent Jerome the information, but she wanted to make certain

She leaned over the railing and scanned the garden below. She could see no one amid the thick banana plants, white orchids, and black lava rocks. The voices, however, continued even louder than before.

She couldn't distinguish the precise words being flung in disagreement, but the voices were not Dr. Jerome and Grandfather Ainsworth. One was a woman, the other a man—no, there were *two* men's voices.

Eden recognized the southern accent of her cousin Silas Derrington. Silas claimed to have grown up in Louisiana, and his accent confirmed that.

Zachary resented his father's preference for the illegitimate Silas, but Grandfather Ainsworth and even Great-aunt Nora with her stolid principles had readily accepted Silas. Grandfather thought Silas would prove an asset to the family sugar enterprise and had recently placed Silas in a position of authority—suggesting to Zachary that Silas might be appointed heir above him.

Eden worried of further misunderstandings and growing trouble between the two half brothers. She imagined the shame and heartbreak the Derringtons would face when Townsend was put on trial. It was Grandfather Ainsworth's family pride that had caused her family to not reveal to Eden that her mother, Rebecca, was a leper on Molokai. Ainsworth and Great-aunt Nora had feared certain people in society would shun the Derrington name, afraid the disease loitered within the premises.

Grandfather Ainsworth's ambition for the family name had also driven him to want to marry Eden into another powerful island family, and he was displeased when she became a nurse at Kalihi hospital working with her Aunt Lana in leprosy research.

From the garden, Silas's voice rose above the others. "So that's the way it is."

A moment later Silas emerged from behind the banana plants, followed by a man and woman.

Eden stood motionless. *I've seen them recently . . . somewhere.*

The man was tall, thin, and gloomy looking in black clothing and a sleek top hat. The woman wore a scarf rather than a stylish hat. She also wore gloves, and a satiny black dress. Were they in mourning?

Silas climbed the steps to the lanai. Eden expected the couple to follow, but they turned toward the front gate. Eden didn't recall seeing a carriage parked nearby.

Suddenly Eden could hear familiar voices in the entryway and footsteps coming into the parlor. She turned and looked at Silas again. He saw her standing there, and his eyes flickered with something like surprise.

Silas was a pleasant-looking young man with wavy chestnut-brown hair and the same light blue eyes as his father and Zachary. Recently he'd received as many invitations to picnics, dinners, and balls as Zachary.

Silas, while of a husky build, showed little interest in outdoor activities, and did not care for breeding thoroughbred horses as Rafe and Zachary did. Silas once commented that if they'd race their horses against each other, then he'd be interested. Such talk only bolstered Zachary's claim that Silas was an "untrustworthy gambler from New Orleans."

One of Silas' walking sticks had a heavy silver handle designed like a wolf's head. Zachary had recently accused Silas of "bashing me on the side of the head" with that stick. The head injury had occurred weeks earlier in the darkened Hunnewell garden. Eden was there that night, and so were Silas and Rafe, but the culprit had proven to be someone else. The accusation, though, did show Zachary's suspicion of Silas.

Candace and Zachary Derrington entered the parlor with Great-aunt Nora. Eden went into Great-aunt Nora, anxious for the latest news on Rafe.

"My dearest child!" Nora's face was etched with worry. "How could such a horrid thing happen! Are you well, my dear? That rapscallion nephew didn't hurt you?"

Eden forced a smile and they embraced. Eden planted a kiss on her cheek. "I'm safe, Aunt Nora. And what's the news of Rafe?"

"No change, my dear. Your father remains nearby. He is in contact with other doctors. Everything possible is being done."

Zachary stepped forward and hugged Eden.

"Poor little cousin," he said emotionally. "It must have been wickedly evil for you."

Eden patted his shoulder. "And you! Are you badly injured? I was horrified when I saw him attack you on the *Lilly of the Star*."

"Just bruises and probably a sprained arm." His light blue eyes turned icy with anger. "Sprained where 'dear old Dad' kicked me with his boot."

"Let's forget that now," Candace said, stepping forward.

Silas had entered the parlor just behind Eden. Caution flamed his eyes when he met Zachary's glower.

"Well," Silas said with forced cheerfulness, shoving his hands into his pockets and rocking on his heels, "you look as though you'll be right as rain in another day or two, Zach, old boy."

"Disappointed?" Zachary sniped.

"Not at all, little brother."

Zachary smirked. He moved to the parlor door. "I'm going to my room."

"I'll bring up some tea," Great-aunt Nora told him. "Get into bed, my boy, just as the doctor advised."

Great-aunt Nora recently had begun to show Zachary more attention and sympathy than she had before. Perhaps their growing closeness was due to his working for her at the *Gazette*, and his hints at the dinner table recently that he might just change his mind and decide to support the queen rather than annexation. Any political change was obviously meant to get even with Grandfather Ainsworth for favoring Silas in the Derrington enterprises.

Silas watched Zachary leave, and then excused himself and left the parlor.

Eden stayed for tea with Candace. When Candace left to meet

Keno at the mission church, Eden slipped out of the house. Commandeering her private horse and buggy, she rode to downtown Honolulu to meet with her father, Dr. Jerome.

Chapter Four
Reap the Whirlwind

*R*afe awoke at the chatter of birds in the branches. *Strange;*
they're singing before the sun is up.

He stirred in the bed and winced. Every muscle in his body
hurt, and his head felt swollen. He brushed his arm across his face.
Why couldn't he see?

He felt bandages around his forehead, covering his eyes—so
that was it. Where was he? He felt the stiff bedsheets. He wasn't on
the boat. Then the scene flashed in his mind—Townsend—the
boat. His hands were wrapped—he must have given Townsend a
work-over. As he moved, his head felt ready to burst.

Rafe listened to the wind rattling the bamboo blinds. He was
frustrated. After years of struggle, he had finally gained legal control
of Hanalei, the plantation his father, Matt, had begun, only to have
Townsend set fire to the house. True, the Great House hadn't
burned down and the Kona coffee plantings had never been in jeop-
ardy, but he faced a great deal of work to rebuild the burned-out section. And then, there was Eden. . . .

He heard footsteps hurry to his side and a man gripped his arm. "Stay calm, or your pain will increase."

The voice belonged to Dr. Jerome Derrington, Eden's father. Rafe felt Dr. Jerome's cold stethoscope on his chest.

"I don't need these bandages over my face. I feel like a mummy."

A smile sounded in Jerome's voice. "It's not quite as bad as all that. The bandages protect you from infection."

"Where am I?" Rafe asked. But hadn't he asked that question before? Had he been awake before this? How long had he been here?

The sheets smelled white and sun-bleached, and he'd heard garden birds.

"Where am I?" he repeated.

"You're in a Honolulu medical ward, young man. You've been here five days—and 36 hours of that in a deep coma. You've been coming around to wakefulness since yesterday. The mission church has held a round-the-clock prayer vigil for you. Hopefully, you'll soon be ready for Zachary and Keno to take you home to Hawaiiana pineapple plantation. They'll take care of you there."

"I don't *need* to be taken care of!" He didn't want to be dependent on others, not even Keno.

"I'm afraid you'll have little say about it."

Silence.

As quickly as his emotions had roared, they sank. Rafe would rather forget about Townsend. His head was swollen and painful. He felt disgusted with himself. Nausea washed over him.

Years earlier Rafe vowed to God that he'd never lay angry hands on his stepfather. Even back then he had wanted to destroy Townsend, knowing that he'd been responsible for his father's death. The way Townsend had bullied Rafe's mother, Celestine, had only fed his loathing.

Now he'd broken that vow, giving in to his rage. He had deliberately gone to Zach's boat to find Townsend. Laying his fists into Townsend had brought momentary vengeful pleasure.

But now. Now he felt spiritual misery and physical pain.

He tried to throw aside the covers, tear the bandages from his head and face, and get to his feet.

Dr. Jerome gasped and rushed at him.

"Rafe! No! Do you want me to call a guard? I will if you don't keep quiet! You have a severe concussion. Another brain hemorrhage and you could end up immobilized. You must be inactive and let your internal injuries heal."

The concern in Jerome's voice convinced Rafe to restrain himself.

"That's better," Dr. Jerome said.

Rafe remembered the boat; how after he'd been struck his vision dimmed in and out. He felt that way now and wondered if his vision was affected.

"You're remembering?"

"Everything," Rafe murmured.

"Thank God. This is excellent. There may be no permanent damage to the brain."

"What about my eyesight?"

Dr. Jerome spoke too casually, "We won't know for certain for a while. For now the bandages remain in place, and you must rest your head." Jerome paused. "Something else has me concerned, Rafe—the head injury you received two years ago. I fear this may have compounded your previous injury."

Rafe touched the bandages across his eyes. "You know about the frequent headaches, then?"

"When Dr. Bolton first learned what happened he sent word that you have suffered in the past from blackouts and frequent headaches. Dr. Bolton's prognosis is that the condition will be temporary."

"How temporary?"

Dr. Jerome cleared his throat. "He mentioned cases lasting anywhere from 48 hours to several weeks, and in some cases, months or longer."

What if it lasted for a year or longer? He could survive that.

And though Rafe didn't want sympathy, he did want the truth. He tried to smother his concern. *This will go away. It must.*

Then the thought flashed: *Suppose I never see again?*

Blindness meant dependence on others. He'd always had difficulty trusting others. Except for a very few—Uncle Ambrose, Keno . . .

For years he hadn't even trusted Eden with his heart, so reluctant was he to admit he needed her and wanted her for his own.

He experienced an icy grip of panic. Blindness meant vulnerability. It made him feel trapped, restricted to a dark narrow tunnel.

He tested the waters: "So, I may already be permanently blind."

"We don't know, and we can't be certain for some time. So we will carry on with hope and faith."

All of this merely reminded Rafe how much misery was interwoven throughout the twisting journey of life. Because a man was a Christian and redeemed from his sin did not mean he was liberated from the consequences of living in a fallen world. The thorns of nature, and the viper's poison were still prevalent, and a fall from the cliff's edge remained treacherous, should a Christian think he was exempt from suffering.

Only Christ could return to set up His Kingdom on earth, as promised, so the viper's den becomes safe for a child. Until then . . .

"I'm urging you to choose a wise course of action," Dr. Jerome was telling him.

Rafe asked wearily, "And what is that, sir?"

"Dr. Bolton and I want you to seek medical attention from Dr. Kelly. He's better qualified to monitor your condition. He's a specialist in brain and vision who lives in San Francisco. We were at medical school together for several years. Since then he has gained a well-earned reputation. Our letters of recommendation will go with you. I hear you'd been planning to go to San Francisco anyway. . . ."

That was right. The memory of Rafe's plans made the week before Townsend took Eden hostage came rushing back. He'd been about to board the steamer to San Francisco and some other men who were members of the annexation committee. These third-generation Hawaiians had come around to the political viewpoint that the Hawaiian Islands should become annexed by the United States. He had planned to travel with Eden's grandfather, Ainsworth Derrington, another local leader in the community, Thaddeus Hunnewell, and Lorrin Thurston, the man behind the annexation movement.

Rafe's plans for the immediate future in San Francisco had also included signing adoption papers and taking care of some other legalities concerning Kip, the toddler Rafe was in the process of adopting.

Rafe had discovered Kip on a journey to take Eden's father, Dr. Jerome, to visit the leper settlement on Molokai island. He had found the baby boy on the beach, and had rescued him from the tide that nearly swept him away. Mystery surrounded Kip. Rafe had not been able to find out much about the boy's parentage beyond the fact that he was at least part white, had been born to a leper . . . and had been abandoned.

What would blindness do to my plans to adopt Kip? he suddenly wondered.

"I'll go to San Francisco as planned," Rafe said. "And I'll visit this Dr. Kelly you recommend."

"Ainsworth and Hunnewell plan to proceed with their voyage in two or three weeks and are expecting you to go with them. That should suit your recovery fairly well. Mr. Thurston was going to go along, but he found it necessary to board the earlier steamer and went on to Washington."

Rafe wasn't surprised to learn that Lorrin Thurston had already departed. He knew Thurston was on his way to Washington to meet privately with the secretary of state to discuss what situation in the Islands would move the president to act positively on the annexation question of Hawaii.

Dr. Jerome cleared his voice. Rafe noted that Jerome often made a throaty sound when he was preparing to make a troubling remark.

Now, what?

"I understand from Pastor Ambrose that you and Eden had decided to marry at once."

"Yes."

"With the situation now altered, you may want to reconsider such a serious decision until we know the outcome of your recovery; another reason to seek Dr. Kelly's expertise."

Bringing Rafe's concern for Eden into this situation seemed to add weight to his already heavy dilemma.

"Would you wish to discuss the marriage issue with Eden during your recovery period?"

Anguish cut into him, *recovery period—if I recover.*

"No," Rafe said. "I'm not ready to deal with that. I don't want to marry just so I will be cared for."

Silence filled the room. Finally Dr. Jerome cleared his voice. "Well, you're quite honest, I must say." After another pause he added, "Then what do you suggest we do? Eden is already upset that she's not yet permitted to be with you."

"Then you've told Eden about my condition?"

"Ambrose was the first to speak to her. He brought her from Hanalei to Kea Lani, where she is now. Since then, I've discussed matters with her every day. Being the exceptional nurse she is, one of her first questions was if your sight was affected. My daughter is naturally worried."

His daughter. She'd been about to become my wife. For a reason Rafe couldn't explain, his anger began to simmer.

"Eden's been with the congregation at the mission church in their prayer vigil for you," Jerome said. "It's only fitting she would be there."

Rafe suddenly wanted to be alone. And though he loved Eden, the emotion of talking to her now would overwhelm him. He was too vulnerable to feel the warm, salty tears on her soft face, and to kiss her trembling lips. First, he would need to recover enough to know the verdict on his sight. And if he did not recover his sight—

Rafe would not ruin her life, or his own, by becoming a burden to her. He was too independent to depend upon someone else to lead him—even if the hand that led him belonged to the beautiful young woman he loved!

Yes, it was best that he leave Honolulu for San Francisco. And Eden? Well, he knew she had wanted to help her father start a clinic on Molokai, where her mother was at the leper colony. Now she would be free to do that.

Yes, pride was getting in the way. And pride always led to more trouble, misunderstanding, and a widening gulf. Rafe already knew a delay of the marriage was necessary.

"I'll send a letter from San Francisco when I know the outcome."

"Perhaps this is best. We'll all have more time to sort out our callings."

Did Jerome sound relieved? Perhaps he was thinking how he needed Eden on Molokai.

Rafe knew he could easily take advantage of Eden's love and her willingness to be consumed by his tragedy. Eden was a *giver*. Rafe jerked the reins on his runaway emotions. *There's nothing I can do about any of this*, he thought bitterly.

"You'll need someone to travel with you," Dr. Jerome pointed out. "Maybe Keno or Zachary? Or one of your Hawaiian friends could go along as your valet."

The thought of Keno playing the part of his valet made Rafe smile. He believed Keno was involved in more advantageous planning right now than of being his valet. Rafe could not remember when Keno was getting married, but thought it was soon. He'd never ask his old pal to set marriage aside to nurse him. Knowing Keno, he would make that sacrifice. Especially after Rafe's plans to get his co-owner of the Hawaiiana pineapple plantation, Parker Judson, to turn over his portion of the plantation to Keno. That was another reason to go to San Francisco. He'd be able to discuss Hawaiiana with Parker, who lived in San Francisco.

He could take Zach. Zach had told Rafe that he wanted to go

to San Francisco to research a story for the *Gazette*, the newspaper his great-aunt Nora owned.

"How is Zach?" Rafe asked

"Nothing serious. Not physically. He will heal. But he's despondent. A voyage to San Francisco may do him good."

"I'll be on the steamer with or without Zach," Rafe told Dr. Jerome. "I'll make it worthwhile for my old friend, Ling, to come along as my valet."

"He's still at Hanalei, isn't he? I'll send a message for him to come here to Honolulu."

Dr. Jerome said nothing else about the wisdom of waiting to marry his daughter. Undoubtedly Jerome knew Eden would agree to help him on Molokai when she learned that Rafe had set sail for San Francisco.

"When you're released from this ward in a few days, Rafe, Ling Li can accompany you to the Royal Hotel. I'll speak to Ainsworth this afternoon about our decisions. You get some rest now."

Jerome's steps left the room. All Rafe heard now was the steady beat of his own heart and the wind on the open lanai.

Rafe had questioned Eden's long-term ability to marry a man who had lost his sight. And what of himself? Could someone so lovely and innocent as she was trust him to maturely accept the ragged loss that so suddenly had changed him?

If I take all this on now she's the one who will lose. Far better to see what the future holds before I ask her to commit to marriage after all the recent turmoil.

What if the Lord permitted permanent blindness? What if losing his sight was God's way of teaching him crucial lessons he had refused to learn when strong and free?

Yet hope cast its flickering light in the dark prison that bound him. After all, he'd not been declared permanently blind. Perhaps this experience was a warning, and the Lord wanted his attention— or was it a chastisement of a son who had gone astray? Rafe had insisted on his revenge to be pounded again and again into

Townsend. Beneath the raging voice that had driven him, the still small voice of God had kept telling him no. Rafe hadn't listened.

Rafe understood he must accept the fact that he could do nothing but wait. Wait and trust that God had a purpose—not only in disappointment but also in potential tragedy.

When the news spread among friends and family that Rafe had awakened from his coma, Pastor Ambrose led a thanksgiving service at the mission church.

Eden was overjoyed. When Keno brought her the news she had literally danced about with him in celebration on the front lawn, only to find Candace watching them afterwards, arms folded, an auburn eyebrow lifted, pretending feminine suspicions.

Eden laughed and ran to her. "Rafe is awake. He can talk and remember everything!"

"Thank God!" Candace hugged her.

Eden realized it was too soon to know if Rafe would be left with any debilitating trials and blindness, but at least her darling wouldn't die.

The celebration ended as Keno, Candace, and Eden saw Ambrose arrive. After the thanksgiving meeting he'd gone into Honolulu to talk to Dr. Jerome. Ambrose stopped his horse and buggy under a large kiawe tree. A breeze blew and the yellow blossoms showered down like snowflakes. Eden hurried to meet him with

Candace and Keno close behind.

"Any further news?" Eden called.

"Well, that depends, lass. Your father asked to see you. You can meet him in Rafe's rooms at the Royal Hawaiian Hotel."

The request startled her. "Is Rafe there?"

"No. Jerome's been spending all his time at the medical ward so Rafe suggested he sleep there instead of going back and forth from Kea Lani. It does show that Rafe is thinking well. Either Keno or I can take you there."

She noticed that Ambrose did not seem as joyful as he'd been at the church before going to see Dr. Jerome.

Candace looped an arm through Eden's. "I'll go with you, Eden," she offered.

"You and Keno are expected for dinner at the Hunnewells' tonight. I don't want to ruin that. No, I'll take my own buggy. I wanted to see Aunt Lana anyway. She sent me a note this morning about Molokai. Is everything all right, Ambrose?" Her eyes searched his.

"We're over one big hurdle," he said. "That is something to be pleased about."

As she caught Keno's eye he looked away.

He knows what Ambrose is concerned about—and he's unhappy about it, Eden realized.

"I'll go and send for your buggy," Keno said. He and Candace hurried toward the house.

Eden turned back to Ambrose. "Something has happened, hasn't it?"

"I'll let your father explain the rest, lass. Stop by the bungalow on the way home tonight. Noelani will have some refreshments." He tried to look cheerful. "I also have some other good news to share with you then."

He turned the horse and rode down the road toward the church.

Eden sat on a rattan chair by her father and hardly tasted the crushed golden-yellow papaya fruit drink her father had ordered.

Eden watched her father slump in his chair, sipping his fruit drink. Dr. Jerome's once dark hair and his long sideburns were tipped with gray. His lean face was tanned, leathery, and haggard from years of traversing the tropics.

Although Rafe was recovering, Eden had learned that Dr. Bolton and her father still didn't know if he'd suffered any permanent physical or mental impairment. Eden knew setbacks were possible. She'd discussed Rafe's condition with both Ambrose and her father.

She was dancing near a cliff's edge where her emotions were concerned.

"I don't understand about Rafe," she said. "He can talk, and you said his memory seems normal. Why would he refuse to see me?"

Especially after we'd decided to marry at once, she thought, frustration igniting her temper.

"Rafe isn't sure about himself or his future. Don't look so upset, my dear. It's only reasonable after what's happened that he should give second thought to what's ahead. We both would do the same."

"I understand, but it's not just his future—it's our future. I told you we'd decided to marry now."

"Yes, you did tell me. But it's rather unwise to marry so hurriedly. Especially now, when Rafe's future is on uncertain ground."

"When can I see him, Father? Tomorrow morning?"

"Rafe remains in critical condition. If anyone can understand how critical, it should be you, dear. His emotional level must be calm. If a blood clot forms . . ."

"I can help him." She leaned forward, setting her glass on a rattan table. "After all, I'm a nurse. I'll look after him. You can marry us—or Ambrose can—and then I'll move here and become his nurse."

Dr. Jerome sighed, stood, and shoved his hands into his white trouser pockets. He paced about, frowning.

"This is painful for me to explain, Daughter, but Rafe has requested I do so."

She looked at him. "Rafe asked you to explain what?"

"I'm getting there. I'd have preferred that Ambrose tell you, but he said no. So, it's left to me." Jerome gazed at her with compassion. "Making you unhappy is the last thing I wish to do!"

Eden stood and walked toward her father. "Ambrose refused to tell me a message from Rafe?"

That just did not sound like Ambrose, and yet earlier at Kea Lani he had acted as if he wasn't telling everything he knew.

"I know you have a wonderful, loving heart to help Rafe," Jerome said. "Even so, the decision is not mine to make. I must respect Rafe's right to discover, on his own initiative, the direction his life should take should he be permanently blind."

She searched his troubled expression. "What did Rafe tell you that he can't—or *won't* tell me?"

"He does not want to discover himself blind, or immobilized, and obligated by marriage plans. He made that quite clear. A man's pride can sometimes prove difficult. Especially Rafe. He's always felt a responsibility to protect you. He cannot accept having the shoe on the other foot. He doesn't want to burden you."

The strange words sent her emotions reeling.

"Burden me?" she finally repeated. "Are you saying Rafe's changed his mind?" She looked into his eyes. "That he doesn't want to marry me?"

Worry filled his tired face. "Rafe does not want to get married *now*. Keep in mind that he remains ill. What he needs now is as little emotional disturbance as possible. He needs rest and time to heal his bewildered feelings."

Eden fought for words. "Doesn't he understand that I love him, no matter what?"

"Oh, I think he does. If he's unsure of anyone, it's himself. He doesn't want to enter marriage as a liability to you. Given time, however, the outlook might change."

"If anyone can take care of him, I'm the most skilled person to do so. If we married now—"

Jerome sighed. "You know Rafe. If he's robbed of his sight, Eden, he won't be an easy man to get on with. He'd rather wait to know what his new calling is."

"I'm beginning to wonder if I know him at all."

"I'm sorry, my dear."

Her father's firm hand rested on her shoulder.

She rubbed her forehead and turned toward the cool breeze from the sea.

"Still, there seems something I can do, or should do," she stated.

"He's made it clear he doesn't want either of you to have the strain of seeing him just now."

So, was that the way he wanted to handle their relationship?

"I should be part of the decision, whatever it is." She grew angry. "So my opinion simply doesn't matter. To exclude me is to assume I have a child's mentality."

Eden walked to the lanai and gripped the rail. Her heart pounded.

"Rafe is a born leader. He can't make peace with the idea of being dependent, even if it's your hand, Eden, he must take to lead him."

"It's just plain pride," she said, frustrated.

"I think he knows that, but it won't change his decision. He needs to go to San Francisco."

She gasped and turned toward him, simply staring at him.

"San Francisco?" Her anger evaporated as fear took the reins. *This is dreadful! I must see him and tell him I will always love him, not for his appearance, nor for his physical abilities, but for whom he is, Rafe Easton.*

"This is for the best, my dear Eden. I've recommended a doctor there, Dr. Kelly. A month or two under his specialized care should give the answer Rafe is looking for. Ling will go as his valet. Rafe will stay at Parker Judson's home on Nob Hill. Celestine will see he's well provided for. Don't worry."

Yes, Celestine was staying at the Judson mansion in San Francisco. And Eden knew that Kip, the young child who would become Rafe's legal son—and whom she'd also welcomed into her heart, mystery about his parentage or not—was with Celestine. Perhaps Rafe wished to explain to Celestine about Townsend. And where was Townsend?

"Zachary will also go with him," Dr. Jerome explained.

So Rafe would be staying in the Judson mansion. Even though she knew Zachary was eager to see Parker Judson's niece, Bernice Judson, Eden suspected the fair "Bunny" was looking at Rafe, admiring, and considering . . .

"In the meantime, it isn't as though you have no calling of your own," her father said. "You have your own mission on Molokai. Your mother wants to see you. I need your assistance, too. You have more than enough to do to find life worth living."

Eden remained silent.

"I'm sure he'll contact you when possible," he said. But it wasn't enough for Eden to be given secondhand assurance, even if it did come through her father. The painful reality that Rafe would not meet with her held her captive. This behavior wasn't like the Rafe Easton she knew—or thought she knew.

She could understand his pain and his inability to put his feelings into words, for she felt the same. But to set aside marriage without speaking to her about it—

Then again, maybe it was her fault, she thought with a sudden self-incrimination. Rafe knew what she would do if they were alone together—*cry*. Yes, she would want to splash warm, salty tears all over the front of his shirt. She would promise her love, and put him in a predicament, and he didn't want to deal with that extra burden.

But I'm mature enough to not cry if he doesn't want tears, she thought irritably. *If he can be unemotional about our relationship, so can I!*

The pain was deeper than she thought she could bear. Far worse than losing Rafe was the truth that he could push her away with that cool determination.

She turned on her father and exclaimed, "If loss of the physical means an end to love, then what do couples do when they grow old together? Do they stop loving each other as the hair turns gray and their strength weakens? Is the 'burden' of failing flesh too much for one to be true and faithful?"

Dr. Jerome's eyes watered. "If so, every marriage would end up on the ash heap of decay. And in answer to your question, my daughter, that is why I've searched so long for some way to save my beloved Rebecca."

She stared at him as if meeting a stranger. Suddenly she understood her father's motivation for traveling to far places searching for a way to rescue his Rebecca from physical corruption.

Her tears gushed, and she threw her arms around him.

After taking her buggy to Honolulu, Eden had not felt up to meeting with Aunt Lana at Kalihi hospital. She needed the emotional support that only Ambrose and Noelani could give.

They warmly welcomed her at the bungalow.

No one mentioned her meeting with Dr. Jerome, so she kept silent. She was sure they already knew Rafe was going to San Francisco and that the marriage was off. The fact that Ambrose preferred not to mention it that morning, and that Keno had looked displeased, told her they were already privy to the information.

"What's the good news you promised?" she asked Ambrose after cake and Kona coffee.

"Ah, the printing press, my lass. I've word from Miss Nora that she's willing to sell us the new one in the *Gazette* warehouse."

Before Rafe's injury, he had arranged with Great-aunt Nora to buy the press ordered almost a year earlier, not by Nora, but by an exuberant Zachary who helped Nora and had "big plans" for the *Gazette*. Nora had expected a smaller and less expensive press to arrive from San Francisco, and already on the verge of losing her paper to spiraling debt, she had been furious with Zachary for buying it. The next best thing to returning the printer was to sell it to Rafe, who had offered her a fair price. Ambrose and Eden had wanted a printing press to use on Molokai to print Sunday school materials and perhaps, even some Bibles. Ambrose would give a young Hawaiian lad from the church training on how to run the press.

"And," Noelani said, "we have permission from the mission board to print some Scripture portions in Hawaiian, isn't that right, Ambrose?"

"Yes, along with some of their Sunday school materials. Your father is anxious to get there and begin work. So as soon as we get things arranged, Keno and his cousins will haul the supplies to Molokai. Rafe is letting Keno captain the *Minoa*."

"As soon as we get ashore, Keno and I can get the boys started on the private bungalows," Ambrose said. "After that's done we'll work on the medical clinic. However, it will be several weeks before we can get all the necessary supplies ready and stored on ship. Then we'll be on our way." He shook his head. "Thankfully, Rafe signed his name to the money draft this morning. We couldn't do this without his support."

Eden felt a lump begin in her throat, and sipped her coffee to hide her emotions. Noelani quickly pushed more cake toward them.

Eden smiled at Noelani, trying to lighten the moment. "You're letting Ambrose go away for a whole month, Noelani?"

"When it comes to God's work, I let him sprout wings. Just as long as he comes back home."

"Oh I'll be back," Ambrose teased. "A wise man would become a fool to go away from a good woman for very long, especially one who can bake coconut cake. Besides, none of us can get along without you for long. Especially me."

"My very words," Eden said. She rose to her feet, looking at the time. "And I'd best get back." She kissed Noelani's cheek.

Ambrose accompanied her to her buggy. She stepped up to the seat and took the horse's reins.

"Did you know Zachary is going with Rafe to San Francisco?" she asked. "So is Ling."

"Yes, I'd heard about Zachary, but not about Ling. I'd better get that Chinese Bible to him soon as I can. Now you go home lass. Get some sleep. Leave the future to the Lord, and know that we're praying for you and Rafe."

Ambrose pulled a folded piece of paper out of his pocket and handed it to her. "Here is your verse. Memorize it. In the days ahead I have a feeling that you, and the rest of us, will need it."

Eden took the folded paper and drove the buggy to Kea Lani.

When she arrived at the plantation she turned the horse and buggy over to the stable boy. She decided to walk back and look at the water to calm her emotions before going into her house. Nearing the bank, she listened to the soothing lap of water. The melancholy call of a night bird echoed from the trees. She saw a small fishing boat tied up. Not far away stood Silas, hands shoved in his trouser pockets.

At the sound of a low voice she looked toward the open doorway of the *halau* that the canoes were stored in. A figure emerged and walked toward Silas.

The slim figure with the tall hat appeared to be the same person she'd seen in the garden yesterday morning talking to Silas. This time the woman wasn't with him, unless she was in the *halau*.

She backed away. When she was sure she was out of hearing range, she sped toward the front lawn and the pleasantly illuminated plantation house.

Inside, she closed the front door, climbed the stairway to her room, and prepared for bed.

          ―◌◌―

The days of preparing for the trip to Molokai trudged on.

She had heard from Zachary that Grandfather Ainsworth, Mr. Hunnewell, and some others in the Annexation Club would also be on board for San Francisco. Zachary would room with Rafe, and Ling was Rafe's valet.

During those last few days before Rafe's departure Eden had thought she would receive a message from him through Ambrose or even Keno, but nothing arrived.

Eden was at Kalihi when the steamer left Honolulu for San Francisco. Watching the departing vessel from the windows overlooking the harbor, she extended her hand and envisioned a moment of unity with Rafe.

"Aloha, my love, and Godspeed." But she found little to link with her empty hand except a cold gray shadow that dimmed the glimmer of her diamond engagement ring.

How ironic, she thought bitterly, watching the departing steamer. When at last she had chosen to put Rafe first in her commitments, above her work with her father, then suddenly he'd been caught away from her.

Eden remained at the window looking toward the harbor when her aunt, Lana Stanhope, Rebecca's younger sister, joined her. She was a tall, willowy woman in her late thirties, with thick honey-colored hair rolled up at the back of her neck. Fatigue lined her hazel-green eyes.

She grasped Eden's hand and her squeeze of understanding imparted courage. If anyone had a right to say, "I understand how you feel," it was Aunt Lana who'd endured a life of hardship and disappointment. During her years of youth and beauty, she had loved Dr. Clifford Bolton and he'd apparently been in love with her, but their feelings had never been declared, and circumstances had separated them. Only after Lana left the nursing school she'd managed in San Francisco to work at Kalihi did she and Dr. Bolton come together again.

"Clifford and I will leave with Dr. Jerome next week for Molokai," Lana said. "We've decided on a quiet, small wedding before we go. After all, it's not exactly what others would call a happy wedding, is it? Not with Clifford in his leprous condition. I shall be, well, his *kokua*."

Dr. Bolton's last sacrificial act was to join her father's medical team to begin the research clinic on Molokai. It had become Lana's sacrifice as well.

"And now you're going back to Molokai," Eden said softly looking out at the harbor.

"I'll go where Clifford goes," Lana said. "He thought I ran away from him when I went to San Francisco years ago, but he misunderstood why I left. I was running away from myself, from my inadequacy. But I didn't know it then, so I couldn't explain. Unfortunately, that took away twenty years in which we could have married, had a family, and been happy. Odd, isn't it? The way things work out sometimes? Though, in everything, if we know Jesus, our circumstances are not left to fate, as some people imagine. He can use ruin in our lives and still bring us to the finish line on time!"

Eden watched the ships in the smoky-blue waters, some leaving, and some coming. "Yes," she said quietly. "Now you'll be together at last."

"Yes, for a little while." Lana's voice was steady, without a suggestion of self-pity.

"The Good Shepherd," Eden said.

Lana looked at her. "Yes?"

"I was thinking that whichever way we go, we have the promise that the Good Shepherd will find His sheep and bring them *home*."

Lana smiled. "Yes. A promise for a troubled mind."

And heart, Eden thought.

"Neither of us are under any romantic illusions about our future," Lana commented. "We never were. Illusions are for the young. If either of us had wanted illusions we surely wouldn't have come to research leprosy. It is an ugly, dangerous work, and few understand our commitment in doing so."

Eden glanced at her.

"Even though Clifford and I pretend that we were not at risk, we knew we were." Lana looked at her. "You know as much, Eden. I confess I was secretly pleased when I first discovered you weren't going to work with us on Molokai because I didn't want you to take chances. But merely meet Rebecca before she dies—and she's very ill. You know that, don't you? Word came in just yesterday that she weakens. Dr. Jerome becomes more determined to go at once. So, we leave next week." She turned to Eden. "Why don't you stay here—"

Eden shook her head. "For years I've sought this opportunity. Until a few days ago I had given up the idea. Then again, here I am. Rafe has left me—" Her voice became tinged with a hardness that surprised her. "He's gone to San Francisco. I don't know when he'll come back, or if he ever will. I'll go on with my life as I planned it. I'm going with the rest of you."

She turned and walked past her aunt and down the hall toward Dr. Jerome's office to tell him that she, too, was leaving next week. She was sure he would be pleased to learn of the change in her decision. Yes, the paths of life led on, twisting and turning, to where only God knew they would lead.

—⟨∾⟩—

During the following rushed days, most common things went unnoticed by Eden. The marriage of her aunt to Dr. Bolton was soon put back in the closet of her mind. During this time the society sections of the newspapers, and societal gossip journals buzzed over the announcement of "Miss Candace D. Derrington's engagement to Mr. Keno P. Hunnewell, a cousin of Miss Claudia and her brother Oliver P. Hunnewell, the gentleman polite society was once mistakenly informed would be the fiancé of Miss Derrington. Meanwhile, the young and sought-after Oliver was said to have recently left the Islands for San Francisco."

Eden overheard Claudia Hunnewell telling Candace, "Life just isn't fair. My engagement to Zachary was on the brink of disclosure, when he ran off to the mainland." Candace had murmured a sympathetic response, but Claudia was not consoled. "I have this horrid feeling he's gone to see that dreadful niece of Mr. Judson."

As Eden prepared to leave, the insistent questions from Candace about the wisdom of Eden's decision darted past her like bees.

"Now that Lana is married and going with Dr. Bolton to Molokai, maybe you'll be offered her position at the hospital. Think of the authority you'd have in the research department, not to mention the better wages."

"I don't think I'd be offered the position. A new physician is coming to take Dr. Bolton's place and he'll choose his own assistant."

"And you're not even going to try?"

"You forget Rebecca. She is my *mother*. I want to meet her before she dies.

"There's an opportunity to come back to Kalihi in the future," she explained. "Dr. Bolton—I guess I can call him Clifford now since he's an uncle by marriage—has requested that I be given a few months to make that decision. By then, I should know what I want to do with the rest of my life. It's either Molokai and one day taking over my father's clinic, or coming back to Kalihi. Time will make clear what the Lord has in store for me."

"Oh, Eden!" Candace dropped into a white wicker chair. "I simply hate the way things have turned out."

Eden smiled and laid an affectionate hand on her shoulder. "Thank you, Candace, for caring."

Candace straightened her shoulders and turned her auburn head away, as if she feared a display of emotion and a gush of tears she so disliked.

"I'll be all right," Eden said, and continued packing. "What of you? You're letting Keno go and serve so gallantly with his cousins."

Candace sighed. "Yes, I know . . . it wasn't an easy decision. Then I saw Great-grandfather Jedaiah's painting on the wall eyeing me with disappointment. 'You have so much,' he seemed to say, 'can you not give back a little?' So I gave in. Keno promised he'd stay far afield of any danger zones."

She got up from the chair. "All right. If you're certain about this,

I'll not bother you with my wailings and laments."

Eden kept her frayed emotions from coming apart. She felt safer hiding behind the suitable demeanor of a professional nurse on a venture of self-sacrifice. One thought alone threatened to break through the facade: Rafe was gone.

Part Two

The Black Cliffs of Molokai

ifty-eight miles east of Honolulu, Rafe Easton's ship, the
Minoa, anchored off the island of Molokai, the isle of exiles.
It was less than a mile from the jagged black cliffs rising from the sea.

Eden was trying to sleep in a corner of the hold behind a cur-
tain she had hung for privacy. She hardly slept a solid hour without
waking from the creaks and groans as the ship rolled and pitched on
the voyage from Honolulu.

The noise of the crew on deck announced that the morning's
activities were under way. Eden emerged and dressed, wanting to
join her father and Ambrose on deck.

Steadying herself against the hull, she arranged her dark hair
into a braided coil at the back of her neck. The reflection of her
sober face in her hand mirror revealed the stressful imprint of the
past month. In the shadows of the cabin her eyes looked darker than
her unusual green and revealed her inner turmoil to those who knew
her best.

Eden wore an older nursing outfit for the rough landing, and
also to identify herself as a representative of the Board of Health.

Lepers always came to the beach to meet the boats rowing in, and in the dark they had probably mistaken the *Minoa* for the monthly steamer that brought them food, mail, and a few new lepers who were being forced to join the settlement.

She gathered her possessions and marched toward the ladder. Grasping the handrail, she mounted the steep, narrow steps to the deck. As she reached the top and pushed against the low door, the wind struck her. She placed her palm to her stomach, feeling nauseated. Never one for the sea, she held on to the casing in the doorway to steady her.

The sun was rising, reflecting on gray-green billows. The wind smelled of brine water. She glanced at crew members on deck getting whaleboats ready for the excursion to the shore. Their sure-footedness and strength impressed her, as did their grins and nods. She suspected they knew she was the girl their Captain Easton had held a strong interest in. They probably knew nothing of the breakup.

Meanwhile the *Minoa* pitched in the rollers coming in from the north. The rugged coastline amazed her, so stark against the morning light. Below the cliffs the sea-beaten rocks and boulders stood their ground refusing to surrender to the attack of the rollers.

Oh Lord, You are my rock, my fortress. Strengthen me.

Dr. Jerome's loud voice burst forth. "There's no time to waste!"

She released her grip on the door and moved toward her father. He was upset over something, and was protesting.

"There is no reason for this delay," he said to Keno. "It's not as though we had an eternity here on earth. I won't stand for it, young man."

Keno calmly shook his head and said something that roused her father more. His voice rose, "I tell you I want *all* of the supplies unloaded from the ship this morning and taken to Kalawao. There's no reason why this must wait until tomorrow."

"I'm sorry, Doctor, but it's too risky," Keno said. "The *kanakas* know what they're doing. They have plenty of experience bringing heavy supplies ashore. They ask that we wait until the wind lowers and the swells ease. And I've agreed."

"There must be a way to avert this delay, Keno! I must get that clinic started."

"Be sensible, Jerome," Ambrose interjected, walking up. "You're no novice about the sea. Look at those waves. Keno's captain for good reason. Think of how you'd feel if supplies were lost before reaching shore."

The wind whipped Eden's long skirt, and blew sea spray against her, prickling her face.

Suddenly, Eden noticed her father's countenance change, and the flesh over his high cheekbones turned a ruddy color. She had been worried about her father's health the last few weeks. He had been over-burdened by attending to Rafe day and night, and then by the task of preparing the medical supplies for this trip. Now that he was finally getting his clinic, he had become irritated with minor hindrances.

Keno grabbed Jerome's shoulders as the doctor started to slump. "Sir?"

Eden hurried past them to the captain's cabin, opening the door. "It's his heart. Keno, bring him in here."

"I'm all right," Dr. Jerome gasped. "I'm all right."

Eden knew he was not.

Keno brought him to the bunk bed in the corner of the cabin, stretched him out, then moved back toward the door as Ambrose entered.

Eden rushed to her father's side and knelt beside him, unbuttoning his shirt collar. He was perspiring and pain was written across his lined face, his eyes staring at the cabin roof.

"His heart?" Ambrose asked, bending over him.

"Yes."

"Father, where did you put the glyceryl trinitrate?" she asked.

"Medical satchel. Desk."

Eden looked toward the desk, where Keno stooped to pick something up from the floor. Ambrose was now kneeling by Jerome as Keno stared at a letter.

"Keno, the satchel—do you see it?" she called.

He slid an envelope into the desk drawer and brought her the medical bag.

Eden swiftly located the familiar bottle. She took a tablet and placed it under his tongue.

She noticed that Ambrose was praying silently.

Twenty minutes passed before she was satisfied with his improving signs. He may have been suffering angina before the attack this morning. If so, why had he not carried his medicine with him? He was becoming lax, even careless in the excitement of coming to Molokai to work on the clinic and see Rebecca.

"He's looking a little better," Ambrose said.

"Yes, I'm feeling better."

Eden took his hand with both of her own. "The last time you had an attack you told me it taught you not to go anywhere without your medicine in your pocket," she scolded. "Oh, Father, you've been much too worried these past weeks."

"Yes, you're right. This was a sober warning to me—both to manage my impatience, and to be reminded from the Lord how short my time here is."

"You'll need to rest all day," she insisted. She expected him to argue, but surprisingly he agreed. He looked at Keno, standing by the foot of the bed. "As the captain says, the weather is against us right now anyway."

Keno smiled at Jerome's humility. "You're right, sir. Those waves are mighty rough. I don't think they'll settle until sunset."

"Yes, we'll be wiser if we wait until morning," Ambrose suggested, and looked toward Keno.

"No argument this time," Jerome said meekly. "Though I do prefer to rest in my own quarters instead of the captain's quarters if you and Ambrose wouldn't mind bringing me to my bunk," he said with a rueful smile.

"Now, Father, you need to rest while I watch your heartbeat. I think you should remain here for a few hours."

Jerome smiled weakly. "You see how blessed I am to have a daughter who's a nurse?" he said to Ambrose and Keno. "Very well, my dear. I'll be an obedient patient."

Eden smiled too, but her heart was sober. She mused about how long it took to locate his medicine. *And what did Keno pick up from the floor that seemed to bother him? He didn't think anyone noticed as he put it in the desk drawer.*

—◦◦—

Dr. Jerome slept comfortably in the captain's cabin. The ship's creaking filled Eden's ears as she gazed at her father's face. She finally stood from the chair and left the cabin to breathe some salty fresh air and quiet her anxiety.

She rested against the ship's rail and looked toward Molokai, which was shrouded with clouds and rolling gray mist. She was troubled about that white envelope in the desk drawer.

Keno had quickly glanced at her after looking up from the letter. It must have something to do with her. After all, the cabin had previously been the place where Rafe, as captain, had lived on the ship.

It's none of your business, she told herself. *Why can't you leave these matters to God whom you say you trust? If His eye is on the sparrow, can't He arrange your circumstances? If an unexpected tidal wave submerges your dreams, there must be a reason. Don't charge ahead, taking disappointments into your own hands.*

Whatever the envelope contained worried Keno, though. And whatever worried Keno when it came to Rafe Easton was usually important.

Eden returned to the captain's cabin. She looked at the bunk bed. Her father remained asleep.

In the glow of the oil lantern heavy, dark beams and shadows confronted Eden. Yes, this had been *Rafe's* cabin. She thought again of Rafe leaving the Islands without seeing her or even sending a letter. True, Dr. Jerome had explained that Rafe was going to San

Francisco to see an expert in vision problems. Even so, in a time of personal crisis, where did Rafe choose to go?

Not to me. To San Francisco. And who was there? Bernice.

As the woman in Rafe's life, she felt put aside by him.

She stared at the desk drawer. It couldn't be locked. She would have seen Keno use a key.

Even if I'm caught looking at the letter what will they do? Nothing.

Yet she simply stood there.

Suddenly she reached forward and pulled the top desk drawer open.

Footsteps sounded outside on deck. She pushed the drawer shut and stepped away from the desk, her heart jumping. She held her breath and stared at the cabin door, expecting Keno to fling it open.

The footsteps passed.

She returned to the desk, looked toward Jerome still asleep, and reopened the drawer.

She sorted through maps and drawings. There was a handwritten drafted agreement between Parker Judson and Rafe creating a partnership for a pineapple plantation on Honolulu.

Besides these she saw business papers concerning the ship, folders stuffed with papers, a small stack of envelopes tied with string, and another folder holding photos and correspondence. A white corner of a newer envelope looked as if it had been quickly shoved in one of these folders. Setting her conscience aside, she leafed through the folder, glancing again toward the door.

There were some pictures of Rafe's parents, including his uncle, Ambrose Easton, as a young man. She saw the resemblance between Matt and his elder brother Ambrose.

Next, she pulled out an envelope addressed to Rafe at the Royal Hawaiian Hotel in San Francisco.

Eden bit her lip. The return address was written in a flowing, feminine hand. It was from Bernice.

Should I?

No.

Don't give in. Flee temptation.

Her heart beat faster.

But I must—because I always suspected something between them. When Bernice had visited Honolulu, she had shown an obvious interest in Rafe, though he did not seem to return her interest. Zachary was the one who had fallen over his feet to win her attention. He still wanted her, and had broken his engagement to Claudia Hunnewell.

Stoically, Eden opened the flap and removed a card. Eden opened the card, and a photograph fluttered onto the desk like a little bird released from its cage. A young woman with gold hair and stunning gray eyes stared at her. Eden turned the photograph over and read the flowery handwriting.

For you, Rafe, always yours, Bernice.

The card was also signed.

Happy birthday, Rafe. When will you again admit that you do love me still?

Eden stood immobile. The creaking wood, the water slapping, the wind, the sounds held her captive. Slowly her heart seemed to die. The surge of raw, angry jealousy and humiliation burned itself out and settled at her feet. Then she saw an ornate box that had been tucked under the folder. Inside was a remarkable jade comb, beautifully crafted. No doubt, for his secret love.

And he never once hinted he'd ever cared for her. At least Bernice claimed in her card that he'd once loved her and perhaps still did.

This implied that Rafe had carried feelings for her all along, and for some unknown reason he'd never acted upon them.

Why? Because Bernice lacked a strong Christian faith? His commitment to Christ meant he would be unwise to marry an unbeliever. So after his travels he'd gone back to Eden Derrington the girl with the missionary heart?

If so, why did he say he loved me? Perhaps he did love me in his own way.

But the fact that he'd kept the photograph and card goaded her to know why they were important to him. And why were they here aboard the *Minoa* and not in his hotel room or at Hawaiiana or Hanalei?

The picture of his parents was here—why not also keep one of a woman who suggested he'd cared for her?

She blinked hard to keep tears from forming. *Everything is ruined between us. Why should I care!*

With numb fingers she replaced the photograph in the card, placed the card in its ivory envelope, and put it back in the drawer.

With his other treasures, she thought bitterly.

She closed the drawer. No one would ever know that she'd discovered this secret. She was cold. She wrapped her arms tightly about herself and sat down.

The cabin door opened quietly and Aunt Lana stepped inside.

"My goodness, Eden, what's happened?" She looked at Jerome asleep in the bunk. "Is Dr. Jerome all right?"

Eden couldn't find her voice for a moment. Lana took over, pouring water into a glass and bringing it to her.

"Here, drink this and clear your throat."

Eden's hand shook as she took the water and drank, spilling some on the front of her pinafore.

"It's no—no good. Everything is destroyed. It's all over this time—"

"What's all over, dear? Jerome looks to be recovering."

"R-Rafe. He doesn't love me anymore—"

"Rafe—oh, come. People can't fall in and out of love that easily."

"It—it's been a long time coming. He said so."

Lana was quiet. She drew her fair brows together. "Did he say that? I thought you hadn't heard from him?"

"I've disappointed him too many times. He's disillusioned."

"This doesn't sound like Rafe Easton."

"Oh, Lana, it's all over between us for certain this time." She burst into tears, trying to keep quiet.

Lana put her arms around her and held her in understanding silence.

After a while Eden, emotionally spent, watched as Lana slipped over to the bed, checked Jerome's pulse, then returned to Eden. "Try not to worry too much."

Eden went to the cabin door, and stepped out.

Outside the cabin door Eden felt the wind blow against her, loosening her dark hair. She hoped her eyes were not red or puffed from tears. *Never again.* Tears were useless.

—❧❧—

If Eden had looked toward her right when she'd come out of the captain's cabin she would have seen Keno emerging from the morning sunlight. He did, however, notice her.

He watched Miss Green Eyes slip out of the cabin, her gray nurse's skirt floating behind her as she went down the steps to the hold. Something in her expression, in the way she held herself, disturbed him.

Had she found the picture? Naturally she had. What else could go wrong for his pal Rafe?

Keno thought of the time he'd told Rafe he'd commandeer the ship to take them and their supplies to Molokai. Rafe had also requested, "When Eden arrives the place will be a shock for her. Keep an eye on her, will you?"

"Sure thing, old pal."

Keno walked to the cabin and entered quietly. He noticed that Dr. Jerome was sleeping and walked to the desk.

Well, I haven't done a very good job of taking care of her. He opened the drawer. *Yep, Miss Green Eyes made a search all right. So she did see me with it. I was sure she hadn't noticed. A lesson, Keno, never underestimate a woman's desire to know her man. Worse thing, though, this will just hurt her and Rafe. Miss Bernice Judson would probably smile.*

He held the envelope with picture and card in hand and murmured, "I should've put it in my pocket. And that's exactly what I can hear Rafe telling me!"

None of us have been too smart lately, including Rafe. What was he thinking of, going off without talking things over with Green Eyes?

Keno shook his dark head. The rift would tear Rafe and Eden asunder, even if going to San Francisco without talking to her didn't.

Keno shoved the drawer closed, just as the cabin door opened again and Mrs. Bolton entered, looking at the bunk where Dr. Jerome was still oblivious to all going on around him. She saw Keno and paused.

"Keno, aloha. Dr. Jerome is doing much better."

"Good news, ma'am. He's still asleep. I'll leave, and let you to your business."

Chapter Eight
Ride the Waves

The following morning Eden was dressed before daybreak. Wearing a hooded cloak, she joined Uncle Ambrose on the upper deck and huddled over a tin mug of hot coffee.

From a distance Molokai looked forlorn with its black cliffs and low gray cloud cover. She tried to imagine being a recently diagnosed leper getting her first view of the lonely settlement where she would be forced to spend the rest of her life. What abandonment to be left here, separated from your loved ones and your plans for a satisfying life.

My poor, godly mother. All of these years, here, all but forgotten. I must write her story and see it published with all its pathos in the Gazette. Perhaps I should write Great-aunt Nora about this. Maybe she'll let me write Rebecca's story for the paper.

Her enthusiasm grew as she contemplated the task. Regardless of her tense state of mind at the moment, she was as ready as she would ever be for the uncharted adventure awaiting her.

"This may be the Hawaiian Islands, but it's outright cold," she told Uncle Ambrose who seemed to be enjoying his mug of coffee.

Ambrose glanced toward the black silhouettes of Molokai's cliffs. "I've heard on some areas of Kalaupapa—one of the areas of Molokai—there's sunlight for just a few hours a day. The cliff overshadows the Kalawao settlement and blocks the sun."

"A dreary place for the lepers," she agreed.

Ambrose gravely nodded his graying head. "Yes. And I've never been much pleased with your decision to come here, lass, even if your father encouraged it. Rafe isn't at peace with it, either."

The mention of Rafe and how he might feel kindled her raw emotions into a flaming irritation. "Rafe? I'm sure he doesn't care one whit. He's laid aside any right to judge my plans. He ran away and didn't even write me a note to explain."

"Yes, my dear girl, but Rafe's merely human. Every knight gets unhorsed sometimes in life you know. He can't bear the thought of being blind."

"So everyone has assured me," she said doubtfully. "Everyone except Rafe himself. He can't become a burden to me."

Tears pricked her eyes and the wind made it worse. "He could at least have told me so. Any goodbye is better than none. I'll be curious to know if he feels as honor bound to another woman about his sight as he claims about me!"

Ambrose raised his brows. "What's this about? You think Rafe is seeing someone else? Now, now! And what's on your hand but an engagement ring."

The ring was back at Kea Lani locked securely away until she could return it to him, but she said nothing. She wore gloves this morning, and Ambrose hadn't noticed its absence.

"You sound bitter today. Surely, lass, he'll write you from the mainland as he said he would."

"Perhaps," she said, and drank from her coffee mug. The coffee was too strong and bitter. Just the way she felt. She understood more about Rafe Easton than anyone seemed to think she did. Even Ambrose didn't appear to know about Rafe's past feelings for Bernice Judson, a secret he'd evidently kept for years. Was this recent injury the proverbial thunderbolt that awakened him to realize he did care for Bernice? Enough to break off his engagement?

She merely said, "Well, he didn't mind going to Parker Judson's house in San Francisco with his injury. He could trust *them*, but not *me*, the woman he *claimed* he loved and wanted to marry? Ambrose, I wonder if Rafe actually does, or did, love me . . . I think there might be someone else. Someone he's afraid to love because of doubts about her faith, and her flirtatious ways."

Ambrose frowned into his coffee. At last he said, "Your point is taken, Eden. You speak of Parker Judson's niece. Unfortunately, if it's true—and I'm not at all certain it is—there will be even more trouble. Zachary is determined to have Parker's niece as his wife. Keno believes that's a main reason he accompanied Rafe to the mainland. But I know Rafe. He won't marry a woman who isn't committed to Christ."

So Uncle Ambrose suspected something. I'm the one who's been unable to see clearly, she thought. *So much for my "womanly intuition." How confident I felt in his love. So confident I thought I could delay marriage until my goals at Molokai were completed.*

"However, lass, I'm not at all convinced Rafe is running to someone else on the mainland, as you might suppose. Knowing Rafe, I'd say he was running from *himself*."

Keno emerged from the captain's cabin followed by her father and Dr. Bolton. Eden didn't need to ask her father how he was faring on this new day. He smiled as he discussed the low tides with Keno and Dr. Clifford Bolton. His cheerfulness showed his enthusiasm for the challenges ahead.

She could not say the same for Dr. Bolton. His fair features had aged considerably in the last six months since the discovery of his leprosy. Nor could she say she was ready to lead the parade, now that the hour was upon them.

At least I'll see Rebecca, she thought, mollified, but uneasy. *What would she say—indeed, what could she say to her mother in so tragic a situation?* Words defied the emotions she was sure they both would experience.

"Keno's decided the waves are calm enough for our landing," her father exclaimed.

Keno gestured to the seamen who were removing the heavy canvas from the whaleboats. "The *kanakas* are confident. They've been handling oars in rough seas since they were boys. The best conditions for landing are from May to September. The rest of the year storms make landings messy, dangerous, and sporadic."

"Look," Eden said, gazing toward the shore, where torches flickered.

"A welcoming committee from the leper exiles," Keno told them. "Lookouts spied the ship yesterday. They must think we're bringing food and mail."

"The steamer isn't due for another week," Eden said. She was well acquainted with the schedule of the Board of Health's supply steamer as was Dr. Bolton who'd led the Board for some years until his recent disease.

Dr. Jerome's mouth tightened. He looked to Dr. Bolton. "I tell you, Clifford, those early days of the settlement were a shame and a disgrace to the Board, and to the Hawaiian throne. The lepers might have starved out here for all anyone cared. Many of the landings were a horrendous debacle."

"All true, not that anyone could do much at the time, with no secure landing wharf."

Eden knew the depressing history of the early settlement, which had lacked sufficient food, adequate personal safety, and medical care.

The tales that had drifted back to Kalihi hospital throughout those years told of overturned boats and deaths by drowning. The steamers would anchor about a half-mile offshore in the deeper water. Both lepers and cargo were sent by rowboat or whaleboat toward the rocky shore beneath the black cliffs. The attempt to land demanded calm waters as well as high tides to catch and roll the boats to shore.

She could imagine the lepers' difficulty after a boat overturned, dumping them into the sea. Even though most—especially the advanced cases—were so weak, they had to swim to catch hold of the strong incoming waves to sweep them to the beach. Often they were swept backward and eventually drowned.

It seemed to her that there should have been a safer landing site, but there was no harbor anywhere along the peninsula's rocky shore. If the sea was calm, the arriving vessels would anchor a half-mile offshore from Kalawao. They would use boats and *kanakas* to ferry passengers and cargo to the narrow beach. This area was located at the mouth of a valley east of the peninsula. The surf was usually treacherous along this stretch of beach, and the boats were often overturned or swamped. Keno assured them his *kanakas* handling the oars knew their "business," as he put it. One glance at their smiling faces and muscled forms convinced Eden.

In the early days many passengers were not so fortunate. A captain might send a loaded whaleboat, then watch helplessly as a great breaker snatched the boat, whacked its steersmen, and fractured the boat on the rocks.

"Sometimes even now, a captain will refuse to attempt a landing," Keno said. "If he's impatient or careless, he might pitch his cargo overboard and claim it was delivered."

On the other hand, if a captain decided to land at the Kalaupapa side of Molokai, the prospects were only slightly improved. To try to land at either shore carried the imminent possibility of loss. The exiles making it to shore, wet and sick would then have to walk two miles inland to Kalawao. When they got there, they had to wander about looking for pieces of wood for a fire to dry their wet clothes and keep them warm through the night. Illness was prevalent. There were a few huts provided, but at times people had to find caves or rocky crevices to settle in until a hut could be added.

At that time, the settlement had no permanent doctor. No one came from the Board of Health to help them, except the appointed superintendent of the settlement, Rudolph Meyer. Eden had heard more than once how he'd been well paid for doing little. The superintendent would assemble the group and march them toward

Kalawao. He rode horseback and the lepers followed on foot.

Dr. Bolton then told them of one captain who encouraged the lepers to leap over the rails and swim. Others were dumped into the water. A few might make it, but most were sucked back by the current. If not, the water swept them toward the shore and they were killed upon sharp lava rocks.

"How like this earthly pilgrimage without the Savior," Ambrose commented. "No safe harbor, no lighthouse to warn heedless arrivals of great dangers ahead. No helping hand, only treacherous rock, and pounding waves to sweep the heedless soul to its final end."

"Well said," Dr. Bolton stated.

"In my opinion Rudolph Meyer and the Board of Health did precious little to alleviate their sufferings," her father said.

"We need to be just in our judgment, Jerome. The problem was then, and remains now, money," Dr. Bolton said. "The Hawaiian government was deeply in debt and simply didn't have the finances to provide food, clothing, and shelter for all those people. Even now there is never enough."

"After the reckless spending by the Kalakaua and Walter Murray Gibson government, I'm not surprised they had no money," Ambrose lamented. "However, I understand your point. The government can hardly provide every need for every individual."

"Matters now are much improved from what they were in the 1860s and '70s," Bolton said. "Even so, I agree with Jerome—much more needs to be done. Now that I'm one of the exiles maybe I can have more influence with the Board. I shall do my best, anyway."

"And your abilities as a doctor, dear friend, cannot be too highly appreciated." Jerome put a hand on his fellow doctor's shoulder. "With you and Lana working at the research clinic, we're bound to make great headway."

The ship weighed anchor and moved a quarter-mile off the coast of Molokai, to the Kalaupapa landing.

When it was time to board the whaleboats, Keno came to Eden, and looking uneasy, ran his hand through his curly dark hair.

Eden smiled. "If you're worried about me, Keno, thank you. But I'll be all right—" She glanced toward the swells. "I think," she added lightly.

"For everyone going ashore, people and cargo are alike, Miss Eden. It's going to be a little risky and very wet. No one arrives dry, or with much dignity intact. We'll all be dumped on shore like baggage, drenched to the skin. You're sure you want to go on with this?"

"Yes. Thanks for your concern. But I'm going."

"I thought so, but your aunt wanted me to ask you one more time."

"There's no turning back for me now."

Keno's brown eyes reflected his understanding of the deeper meaning behind her words.

"No," he said, "I don't suppose there is." He gestured. "That whaleboat is the one you're to ride in. The *kanakas* are experts. I'll join them. There's some canvas inside. Try to keep underneath. I've told Mrs. Bolton the same. Those waves can be mighty intimidating."

He then went off to get Dr. Jerome and Ambrose. Meanwhile, a seasoned *kanaka* picked up her baggage as if it were feather-filled, and grinned. "This way, miss," he said as he walked toward the whaleboat.

To board the small craft Eden and others had to cautiously descend a loosely strung "contraption of rope and wood," as Eden called it. Eden felt tremendous sympathy for the lepers. How difficult this would be in their maimed condition.

Eden was last to go down the rope ladder while Keno and Ambrose held it straight and her father looked on uneasily, calling out to place her feet carefully.

She was finally helped into the boat, breathless from the excitement. She smiled at her father who nodded. While the passengers settled, the four oarsmen, strong and shirtless, pushed off from the ship and began rowing as the steersman turned the bow toward shore.

The cliffs of Kalaupapa appeared to rise, stark and black, from a narrow shore, upon which the waves rolled in with swells of white foam. The cliffs wore a thick layer of cloud which extended for miles along the shore, while below the torches flared and seemed to sway. She imagined lepers gathered, waiting to greet the boats.

Somewhere up there on that promontory of land jutting out over the beach were two villages. At the far side was Kalaupapa. On the other was Kalawao, where the main leper settlement was located. From the beach position beneath the overhang of cliffs, a person could not see the huts. The "village" lay behind the jagged lava rocks and scraggly trees.

An inrushing wave rolled upon them. With shouts in cadence the crewmen pulled in unison upon their oars as the boat moved faster before the wave.

"Pull!" Keno shouted. They gained speed and the swell lifted the entire boat, raising the rear upon the wave's advancing slope.

Eden wanted to scream, terrified of the deep water as the boat tilted downward. The oarsmen yelled and Eden turned her head in alarm, but their glee assured her they were cheering for having caught the huge wave.

Eden buried her face in Ambrose's jacket and felt his arm around her. She heard his laughter rising with Keno's. She remembered then; how it was Ambrose who had taught both Rafe and Keno the ways of surfing the big waves, and diving for pearls.

She groaned, nauseated. Would they ever get there—alive?

*H*aving caught the wave, the *kanaka* oarsmen held the oars above water as the wave speedily carried them through the greenish water. All Eden could see in front of them were sharp black rocks along the beach. A scream died in her throat. There was no sand at their landing site! Only rocks! Big, black rocks washed with white foam.

"It's okay! Don't worry. My cousins are the best of the *kanakas*!" Keno shouted at her.

Eden saw the glow in her father's deep-set eyes. This landing was, for him, a victory long fought for and now close at hand.

The boat sped toward Kalaupapa, landing in the curve of the bay beneath the cliffs.

"Get ready!" Keno shouted. She felt his strong grasp on her shoulders.

Near the beach, the swell turned into a wave that rose from behind the boat to break all around them. At the moment when the boat was between the departing wave and the next incoming, the oarsmen slid over the sides into water above their waists. Avoiding the rocks underfoot, they moved the boat toward shore, and then called out, "Now!"

The muscular *kanakas* were dragging and lifting the heavy boat over rocks to a spot safe from the waves.

Eden lifted the hem of her cape and skirt to keep them from gathering sand. Her skirt, shoes, and stockings were soaked. She was miserable but silenced the inner groan.

When Keno turned back for Eden's father, Ambrose was still beside Jerome, trying to get him out of waist-deep water while another wave rushed upon them. Keno ran out into the water and helped them reach the shore.

Satisfied that everyone was safe so far, Eden looked up toward the overhanging dark lava cliff said to be the highest sea cliff in the world.

Eden dropped her gaze from the lofty heights to the foot of the cliff wall where she saw some of the lepers, who'd come to meet the boat, huddled against the dank rock, away from the incoming waves and loose stones that would come pelting down. Just then a heavier hunk of rock hurtled close to where she stood. Eden darted nearer the cliff, away from the overhang. Here, against the cliff, she took refuge from the damp wind sweeping in from the ocean.

The lepers watched her, noting the red cross on her nursing pinafore, which she wore over the plain gray dress of her uniform. Her clothes were now dripping wet and her hair was stuck like sea-weed to her neck.

These individuals were not badly deformed yet. Because they weren't, they retained some strength and ability to work.

"I'm sorry," she called above a wind that sighed morosely among the cracks and crevices of the cliff. "You mistook the private ship for the government steamer."

"No *poi?*"

"No, I'm so sorry," she repeated, folding her arms tightly about her. She was shivering, perhaps from more than the chilling wind. "The steamer will arrive in a few days. Have you enough to eat? Is anyone going hungry? If so I can come up with something from our supplies."

"We survive," another man answered. "Don't worry about us; no one ever has."

"That isn't so—" She stopped. It was pointless to get into a discourse here and now. From the gruffness of the man's speech she guessed he'd already made up his mind about life and was bitter.

"We're from the Board of Health," she called. "You may have heard of my father, Dr. Jerome Derrington? That's him by the boat —the tall, slim man in white. I'm his daughter, a nurse from Kalihi."

One of the more friendly asked, "Why you come here, to this evil prison?"

"Dr. Derrington and Dr. Bolton will explain. They'll hold a meeting as soon as we're settled into bungalows."

Some made sounds of approval, and two or three tried to smile.

"Did he bring any whiskey or opium?" asked the gruff one with a raspy chortle. "That's the only thing to help the likes of me."

Some of the others joined in the gurgling sounds of laughter from decaying throats.

Even though Eden had experienced some symptoms of leprosy at the Kalihi hospital, she'd never met people in the later stages, when decay and deformity had taken over.

Keno walked forward with the authority of a ship's captain. He stopped beside Eden and, in a stance very much like Rafe Easton, stood with hands on hips looking at them. It was a silent reminder that they were to treat her with respect. They quickly quieted.

As his cousins began to unload the cargo, stashing it upon the rocks out of way of the waves, the lepers began to leave their shelter. They came, some hobbling, over loose stones toward the goods.

Keno raised a palm toward them. "Say, pals, I'm real sorry, but these belong to the medical team. Cheer up, though! Pastor Ambrose, my uncle, has brought you some goods from his mission church. If you line up, he'll see that each of you gets a bag to take back with you."

His words brought smiles and cheers. The cynic called: "Any whiskey from the church pantry?"

"Watch your tongue, pal," Keno warned.

Evidently the quiet tone was convincing, for the leper's mood changed and he hobbled into line with the rest of them.

Ambrose was uncasing his goods with friendly talk, and Keno went to help in the distribution.

Dr. Jerome walked up, wet, with sand stuck to his soggy trousers that flapped around his ankles in the wind.

"I'm Dr. Jerome Derrington from Kalihi hospital. I'm here to open a research clinic. These goods are for my work, and those who will assist me."

"*Oe!*" One of the native Hawaiian men pointed at Dr. Bolton.

"You remember my good colleague, Dr. Bolton?"

Dr. Bolton walked up, looking at ease around the lepers.

"Sure they remember me," Dr. Bolton said with a tired smile.

"We remember," one of them grumbled. "You send us here."

"To protect others. Even your families. And now I'm one of you. Like Dr. Derrington, I want to help others who are not yet lepers from ever coming to this place." He pulled up his trouser and a low murmuring sounded as the men saw the signs of leprosy on his leg.

"So sorry," some said, shaking their heads. "You caught it from us, eh?"

Two or three murmured as they hobbled away, "You get what you deserve for sending us here."

"I remember you," another man said to Jerome. "You try to help us at Kakaako." Kakaako was the holding station center near the entrance to Honolulu's harbor.

Dr. Jerome smiled. "Yes. We, here, are *all* your friends. We want to help all of you. But first my clinic must be built by these men." He gestured toward Keno, Ambrose, and six of Keno's cousins, all from Ambrose's mission church. "I'm asking you to cooperate with anything they may ask of you."

"We all help, *kauka* , no worry."

"Aloha!" a male voice called from behind them.

Eden turned to see a sturdy man in a plain monk's robe seated in a worn, one-seat buggy pulled by a swaybacked horse. He climbed down and strode toward them with a smile.

"Aloha!" Dr. Jerome and the others echoed, smiling in return. "You must be Ira B. Dutton," Dr. Jerome greeted him warmly. "I believe we may have met once in the past."

"It was several years ago I believe, Dr. Derrington. You called at Kalaupapa with several others. I believe a Mr. Hartley was with you also."

Eden, surprised, looked at her father's face. When had her father been here on Molokai? And why had he not told her? Surely he'd seen Rebecca then.

Dr. Jerome showed no concern over the revelation, however. Although Brother Dutton was not an official priest, he had taken the place of the beloved Priest Damien who'd died of leprosy a few years earlier.

Dutton said, "The settlement superintendent told me you were coming. To set up a—what did he call it—a research clinic."

"You assisted Priest Damien in his work, did you not?" Dr. Jerome asked.

"He died a leper, you know," Dutton said of Damien. "In fact, he died not too long before you arrived . . . a true saint, he was. I've taken his place as representative of the Church of Rome, though I haven't been able to fill his saintly sandals."

"Well I'm sure you do well," Eden's father said warmly. "Come to think of it, I did arrive very soon after Damien's death. I remember, now. I'd hoped to meet with him but I arrived too late. Even back then I was trying to gain the Board's approval for my research clinic. I'd hoped Damien might use his favorable reputation to aid the project."

"Most interesting, Dr. Derrington. I look forward to hearing about your plans when you've settled in."

At the sound of horse hooves, they all turned and peered toward what passed for an open road off the curve of the shore. Eden saw a man riding up on a horse, with several others behind him.

"It's Hutchinson," Dutton announced cheerfully. "He's the appointed superintendent—as you would know, Dr. Bolton. You and the Board appointed him."

Eden recognized the government's superintendent of the leper colony. Mr. Hutchinson, too, had leprosy.

"I knew Hutchinson before he was an unfortunate victim of leprosy," Dr. Bolton said. "The settlement is fortunate to have such a man in charge here."

The superintendent was under orders from the Board of Health to meet all new arrivals and escort them to the official place of registry. He would meet the new lepers onshore where he handed over the items the Board of Health had purchased for the exiles. Men received a shovel or an ax, and a single gray wool blanket. Women got only the blanket. Unless the person's family had some money—then all the things needed to make the unfortunate family member comfortable were provided, along with a *kokua*, such as had been provided for her own mother, Rebecca, these many years.

Dr. Bolton and her father walked forward to meet the superintendent who had climbed down from his horse.

"Clifford! Good to see you again, old friend—though not under these conditions. And you, Dr. Jerome! Welcome, friend."

—◌◌—

A half-mile from the rocky shore the *Minoa* rested at anchor. Her boats were still ferrying to and from the ship to offload building supplies. On the beach, Keno, his cousins, and several church workers were busy loading the packhorses and a few donkeys. Eden thought it would take many such trips to complete the haul.

Once the animals were loaded, the cousins would remain on the beach with the boats while Keno and two others would lead the animals to the Settlement. Mr. Hutchinson's job was to lead the parade with the rest of the group following on foot.

"Look, why don't you, Dr. Jerome, and Uncle Ambrose use two of the horses," Keno suggested. "We'll need to make a dozen trips anyway. What's two horses less now?"

Eden declined. She drew her cape about her, but still shivered.

"Rafe will be in a mighty temper with me about not taking care of you."

"Rafe has relinquished any right to judge anything I do," she snapped. Then seeing the hurt look in his eyes, she quickly laid a hand on his arm. "Oh Keno, I'm sorry. It's not you. You've been so helpful and I appreciate it. I'm out of sorts. And I'm tired."

"You don't need to explain. I understand. That's why I suggested the horse. I'll see if I can get your father a mule at least. And Ambrose, too." He left her and went to talk to Dr. Jerome.

Eden loathed her cranky attitude. *I need to watch my tongue.*

But she knew why she felt this way. *Rafe, Rafe, Rafe! He's to blame for this!*

She overheard her father telling Keno—"If we take two mules it will make more work for you and the young men."

Keno's cousins all shook their heads. "No, no," they said, smiling in good humor as always.

"It's far more important to get the supplies to the settlement as quickly and efficiently as possible," Jerome said reluctantly. "I don't know. What do you think, Ambrose? Should we take two mules?"

"We'll take three," Dr. Bolton said wryly, coming up with Lana, who was laughing. "We're not used to long hikes," she confessed.

Ambrose clapped a hand on Jerome's shoulder. "The clinic won't do much good if you're not around to use it." He winked at his nephew, Keno. "Work is good for you, lads. Come along, Jerome, we're commandeering *three* hopefully cooperative mules. You, too, Eden," he called over to her.

Eden folded her arms and smiled but shook her head. "I'm disobedient today, Ambrose. I'm trekking—just the way my patients have to. But you and Father go ahead. I want both of you around when the clinic is in operation. And poor Aunt Lana mustn't get sore feet, or she won't be able to make our tea and coffee tonight," she teased.

"For a ride on a mule? I'll also make dinner," Lana called, smiling.

So Eden walked ahead, not far behind Keno, while the superintendent led the way forward.

At least she was dressed for the walk, Eden thought, with high-button shoes—now sandy and squishy-wet. The hem of her nurse's uniform was sandy and waterlogged. She tried to wring it out but the cloth was uncooperative.

Eden looked about with interest at this desolate section of the island. How heartbreaking it must be for the lepers when first arriving, especially for those whose leprosy had not yet disfigured them! They would be depressed with the change in their lives, and many would have no hope. Heartbreaking! And to think of young girls, women, and even children!

What must Rebecca have gone through so many years ago before the settlement improved with laws and conditions? She could not bear to think about it.

At the foot of the cliff the group encountered a narrow roadway that scaled upward from the shore. The ground here was grassless, brown, dry, and in places, even dusty, which seemed unusual to her, since she'd expected everything to be tropical.

When working at Kalihi hospital she'd always been confused about whether this area was Kalaupapa or Kalawao. Later, when her father had unexpectedly arrived from his travels to work at Kalihi she'd learned that there were two villages, both tiny and insignificant.

Kalawao sat on the eastern shore with some weatherworn thatched huts cloistered against the side of the dark cliff. The cliff's massive shadow shifted with the sun, removing most of the sunlight for the day. Eden had grimaced when Dr. Jerome explained that dusk fell at 3 o'clock in the fall and winter months. "A terrible condition for the weakening lepers, and those sick with consumption.

There's even times when the wet, eastern winds blow across the village year-round. As for Kalaupapa, the village occupies the plain's opposite edge, farther out from the looming cliff and so it enjoys more of the sun's benefits."

Eden noticed the border of the village produced some patches of periwinkle, blue morning glory, and nightshade.

"Look," she called out, "not all is bleak and dead."

"So like God's mercy," Ambrose spoke. "Roses contain thorns, but the rose rewards with fragrance and color."

Eden looked up toward the misty sky of gray. Yes, there was hope. It was never so dark that God could not deliver one's soul from the muck and mire of discouragement, depression, and loss.

Chapter Ten
Isle of Exiles

The serpentine path was hard and stony beneath Eden's feet. It climbed and circled before coming upon the tiny village of Kalaupapa. Then the path looped past the village and continued eastward to the leper settlement of Kalawao. Soon after passing the village, she noted how the huts or bungalows became intermittent.

They had not traversed far when the roadway began to narrow with rough and prickly shrubs, like foes pressing them into a single file. She looked at the horses and mules but they appeared to be at peace with the route and went forward obediently. *If I were as obedient to my God as these animals are to their master,* she thought.

Soon the little huts became scarce. There were ditches, or what Keno told her were "watercourses," lined with stones. All of them dry now, though some grass sparsely grew in places on the dry plain.

Eventually the plain of Kalaupapa surfaced. From the narrow roadway, she could gaze upon the waves rolling toward the rocky shoreline. She drank in the lovely view.

"If I were an artist I'd draw that for Candace," Keno said.

A short while later Mr. Hutchinson stopped his horse and

looked behind him. He called for Ambrose to join him in front of the small procession.

Now what? Eden wondered.

Hutchinson pointed toward the mouth of a dead volcano. "They named it the Given Grave."

The eerie wind whispered across the mouth of the empty volcano, in a low, almost perpetual moan.

"Without hope, many individuals with this incurable disease have hurled themselves down into its blackness rather than continue to leprosy's gruesome end. One person set himself afire instead. They found him some time later, a charred bundle. His remains were hurled below."

A sober silence wrapped about the group.

"If only these had known the One who is victorious over death and the grave," Ambrose said soberly.

"There were Christian leaders here even back then," Dr. Jerome said. "I know, because Rebecca mentioned them. They never received the public attention of the Priest Damien."

"Nor did they receive the help of several nuns brought here by Walter Murray Gibson," Ambrose stated.

One of the nuns was Sister Marianne, now called Mother Marianne, a nurse. Eden remembered reading about her and several others who'd come from the mainland to the Kalihi hospital grounds where Mr. Gibson had a house built for them. After a time they had come to Molokai, where they lived in a cloister.

"In the days of King Kalakaua, Gibson dipped into government funds to build a nuns' home and hospital here on Molokai, but it's up on a nicer slope, overlooking the leper camp," Ambrose said.

When they reached the top of a low bluff, she gazed for the first time on the small, drab collection of huts, small bungalows, and a few houses, all set against a backdrop of gray-blue sea.

"So, *this*, is Kalawao," she murmured.

While she looked at the little center of heartbreak and helplessness for so many, she wondered how she could work up the courage to meet her mother. Now that she was here confronting the brutal reality, her courage seemed to flee.

Now what? These words kept coming to her mind.

She refocused on what Keno told them was a wall twenty feet high and made out of black lava. The cliff wall stood between the settlement and the rolling Pacific Ocean. As she contemplated their isolation, suddenly a huge wave of seawater hurtled against the rock with breathtaking force. Startled, she almost fell.

Keno steadied her. "It's all right, Eden. The waves come in like that every minute or so." Even as he spoke a new swell broke with a glitter of white foam.

"Yes, I just wasn't expecting it."

Aunt Lana, who was no longer riding her donkey, took hold of Eden's arm and pointed. "Look, it's not even midday, and the sunlight is receding."

Keno turned to Dr. Jerome and Ambrose. "Say, if twilight is early, I'll need to have my cousins hold off on another trip from the *Minoa* until dawn."

Jerome reluctantly nodded. "Yes. And fortunately you got us here in one load."

"Then we'd best move along and become settled before we're in darkness," Ambrose said.

"You're right," the superintendent called from the front. He led them forward.

As they moved ahead again Eden overheard Ambrose say quietly to Keno, "I won't join you in the morning. I need to do a few things here."

"Understood," Keno replied.

Did Ambrose expect to look into the arrangements for Eden's meeting with Rebecca? A *kokua* was caring for her now, and Ambrose knew who the person was, but Eden did not. Dr. Jerome may not even know the woman. The first *kokua* her father hired to help his wife had died, Ambrose had told her. Ambrose had arranged to hire the second *kokua* with financial aid from Grandfather Ainsworth.

Until recently Eden had no idea of either her grandfather's or Ambrose's involvement.

Had Rafe known about all this? Perhaps, since he'd been the one to first tell her that her mother was alive, and a leper. Eden couldn't forget how her own family had hushed it up out of embarrassment.

Eden, walking with Aunt Lana, was not prepared for what awaited them. As their small group emerged from the head of the trail to enter Kalawao, they were met by a group of severely deformed lepers.

Eden caught her breath and felt Lana's steadying hand squeezing her arm. Dr. Jerome had also come beside her and spoke in a low voice: "Steady, Daughter. Remember why you have sacrificed to come to this place of the dead."

Eden swallowed and struggled to not turn her head away in horror. She was not prepared to confront the appalling corruption of living human decay.

From behind her she heard Keno's gasp of dismay.

Now, standing here looking upon the end result of leprosy unchecked, Eden recalled the patients at Kakaako who had been in the early stages of leprosy. At the time the mere rising of their flesh here or there did not appear so bad to the afflicted, or to Eden. She had almost felt the Board of Health was cruel and overreacting to keep them isolated and send them to this settlement.

Here at Kalawao it was different. Lepers were in advanced stages of the disease, losing fingers, toes, earlobes, eyes, teeth and gums, lips and throats, even tongues. Throats gurgled because speech was gone. But there was no need for delicacy among the lepers. They felt a part of the group. Here, they lived as the true "normal," the rightful residents, while they might begin to see the healthy as the intruders—putting up with them only because of the supplies and assistance they brought.

"*Oe!* What did you bring us to eat?"

"Got mail?"

"Got new shoes from some fancy lady?"

"Got *okolehao?*" A toothless man, missing part of his nose and upper lip, hoarsely asked for Hawaiian liquor. With a grin, he added in a hissing tone, "Any new *wahines*, eh?" He chortled with foolish merriment. He and the men around him tried to hula, then wheezed with laughter.

"You are making a bad impression on our new guests," Brother Dutton scolded, but added a smile as if they were naughty children.

"Yes, they come from the Board of Health," Superintendent Hutchinson announced, still astride his horse.

"We get our own *kauka* again?" one asked hopefully.

"Doctor, yes." Hutchinson nodded toward Jerome. "Two doctors. This is Dr. Jerome Derrington, from Kalihi hospital in Honolulu. And this good fellow is an old friend of mine from Honolulu —Dr. Clifford Bolton."

"About time get *kauka*," another grumbled.

"This is the *kauka's* daughter, Miss Derrington," Hutchinson went on. "Miss Derrington is her father's *kahu*, nurse. This fine lady over here is Mrs. Bolton, a wonderful and wise nurse married to Dr. Bolton. And this good fellow is Pastor Ambrose Easton from the Christian Mission Church in Honolulu. And this young man is Keno, his nephew. These strong fellows are Keno's cousins. They have come here to Kalawao to help you physically, and spiritually."

"No more missionaries." He held up a charred hand. "We have our own *kahuna*," one hissed.

Some of the Hawaiians had seen the early sober-minded missionaries not as loving representatives from the supreme God, but as taskmasters out to ruin their frivolous way of living, drinking, and gambling.

Eden watched a few of the younger people showing off, refusing to admit that there was any serious difference between them and anyone else. Perhaps it was a bluff, or a challenge to others because of their desperate state. They scampered about like children on a village green. Sadly, they would never be children again, innocent and hopeful.

Lord, help me to love them with Your love. To do them only good. And if I cannot win them with my words, then may I do so with my prayers. At least help me to have compassion.

The group opened before them, allowing the superintendent to lead the way onward into Kalawao.

Dr. Jerome, Ambrose, and Dr. Clifford Bolton followed Superintendent Hutchinson and Brother Dutton into the little village. The path widened to become the main street of the village. There were some huts constructed from inferior lumber, and some of the bungalows were whitewashed.

"Some of these old bungalows built years ago look as dilapidated and sick as the people," Lana remarked to Eden and Keno, who walked beside them as self-appointed escort.

"I say that for the shame of the Hawaiian government," Lana said.

"More should have been done," Eden agreed. "We Christians should have spoken to the churches on the mainland and raised some money for building." She sighed.

Eden noticed that each of the huts in the leper section of Kalawao was not only kept back and separate from the public street, but fences made of rocks separated the huts from each other. Most of these fences had green mildew or slime growing on them.

However, as Christians we have a far better city that awaits us, Eden thought, straightening her shoulders. *There is no power, nor circumstance that can steal it away from us. Though the outward man is perishing, the inward man is being renewed day by day.*

They arrived at the hospital yard, which was as far as possible from the Kalawao village street. It was quieter and more remote, with a few small bungalows kept vacant and ready for visitors from the Honolulu Health Department, or guests like authors Robert Louis Stevenson, who had visited Molokai.

A special bungalow called the "Doctor's House," was for physicians sent to Molokai to live while working at the little Kalawao hospital. Dr. Jerome and Eden were taken to this bungalow.

Although Dr. Clifford Bolton had been in authority at the Board of Health, now that he'd been diagnosed a leper, the Doctor's House was off-limits to him. He and Lana were taken to a different bungalow closer to Brother Dutton's.

The Doctor's House was large enough to hold Eden, her father, Ambrose, and Keno, with his three cousins able to sleep at the back porch.

The house was furnished comfortably with firewood available for the stove.

"Ah, what I'd give for a good cup of coffee." Ambrose sighed. "What do you say, Jerome?"

"If I had a gold piece I'd give it for a cup."

"Sold," Keno said lightly, "one tin cup of coffee for a shiny gold piece."

He cheered everyone by taking it upon himself to see that, not only coffee, but also their supper was prepared.

There were furnished beds, and even though the odor of mildew was prevalent and the thin mattresses were made of straw, Eden accepted them thankfully. She closed her tired eyes and saw nothing but ocean waves, black cliffs, and distorted faces.

But how quiet it was! After the constant roaring of the breakers, suddenly she realized the noise had ceased. She could still hear the ocean of course, but it was distant and subdued. She could hear her heart beating in her ears.

As she settled down into slumber she committed tomorrow and all it would bring into her heavenly Father's safe, strong, and comforting hands.

⁓◌◌⁓

The next morning Eden arose and dressed early. In the kitchen she found some coffee still warm on the stove, and some salty bacon and scrambled eggs. She would tease Candace in a letter by writing that they wanted Keno to stay on Kalawao with them.

With a cup of coffee, she went into Jerome's little office. He was bent over a small desk and sat facing the window. The foliage outside the window was swaying. The winds appeared to be increasing.

"Hard at work, Father? Have you had coffee and something to eat?"

He turned in the chair and frowned at her. Then removed his spectacles and the frown turned into a smile.

"Ah, good morning, my dear. I won't ask how you slept." He put a hand against his back. "Lumpy mattress, indeed. But yes . . . I've eaten, but you can leave that coffee if you will. Thank you, dear. I'm going with Bolton to tour the hospital in a few minutes. You should come with us and get a good idea of what we have and don't have in the way of supplies. We'll need more bandages to be certain."

"I—I said I'd go tomorrow with Lana. This morning I'm meeting with Ambrose about the printing press."

"Oh, that's right. I'd forgotten. Well good! A wonderful idea to print some Scripture portions in Hawaiian."

"He's taking me to meet David, the young boy he's training to run the press."

"Very well, then. I believe Keno stored boxes of printing paper and such on the back porch. They're covered with some canvas from the ship."

"It was different at Kalihi. The inevitable decay and death was not so glaring to me as it is here."

"You'll learn to cope. We must get the clinic constructed and continue with our research." He looked out the window. "Where are Keno and the boys? I wish they'd put more energy into building it."

"I'm certain they're doing all they can, Father, and as quickly as they can."

"From the looks of those clouds they'd better try harder." He turned back to look at her. "When you're busy helping me in my research you'll adjust. It's the moping and thinking that dashes the spirits. As soon as you meet with your dear mother I think your mood will change."

He bent back over his desk, so Eden decided to sample Keno's cooking. While she was munching a crisp bacon slice, Dr. Bolton showed up on the porch and called cheerily. Her father came out of his room with his satchel, put his black hat on, and hurried out the door to join Bolton.

Eden heard them talking about shared interests as their shoes crunched over the path toward the Board of Health's rambling little hospital. Inside the low structure were the lepers who were too sick to care for themselves and had already passed their better days. Most were on the verge of dying. As she thought of them, she could remember the smell of rotting flesh from her nursing days. She put the bacon down unfinished and got up from the table.

She had barely stepped away from the table when Ambrose arrived.

"Breakfast?" she asked.

"I ate earlier with Keno and the boys. They're on the shore, ready to haul more building supplies." Ambrose seemed tired and thoughtful. He looked at her. "I'll have a cup of coffee if it's still warm. Has Jerome gone with Bolton to the hospital?"

"Yes, just ten minutes ago." Eden smoothed her dark braid, coiled behind her head. She felt uneasy.

Ambrose took the coffee and stared into the cup as though it held dark secrets.

"Something's wrong," she murmured. "You weren't able to contact the *kokua?*"

"I met with her. You'll see your mother this morning."

The statement was unexpected. Eden sat down. "This morning?"

He nodded and sipped his coffee, frowning. "Keno always makes the coffee too strong."

He focused on her. She knew something remained wrong; he was not relaxed and smiling as usual. She waited.

"First, I need to make matters as clear as I can, just as Dr. Bolton made it to me." He smiled at her wearily.

She folded her arms. "I'm ready."

"You need to know just how ill Rebecca is, and how short her remaining time is. She's very sick . . . the same symptoms Damien had a couple of weeks before he died—short of breath, tremors, unable to walk. The *kokua* wonders if our visit will be too much for her *and* for you."

Her heart sank. *Oh, no. Too late? After all of this tribulation?* Would life be so cruel as to hurl this disappointment upon her now?

"I told the *kokua* it's extremely important for you to see your mother, even if Jerome must wait another day or two to see her—after she recuperates enough to see him as well. I believe you're up to this. I suggest we see it through, lass."

A breath of relief seeped through her lips. "I can do it. I can handle the moment."

"With God's help."

"Yes, with His help."

"Then we will see her before the noon hour." He looked at the small clock on the table.

Eden, however, wondered if her father would be able to wait to see Rebecca. In his troubled mindset he had come here on the "wing of urgency" to waylay the disease from gaining its final stranglehold and carrying Rebecca away.

"If Rebecca is this close to death it will hit my father hard. He doesn't seem to anticipate that she may expire before he can proceed with his experiments and research."

Daily she'd watched the depletion of his physical strength without being able to do anything about it. She had also seen Ambrose and Dr. Bolton speaking quietly to each other of their concerns. Not that her father would pay heed to any of their suggestions. He refused to acknowledge his decline to anyone, especially to himself.

Even this morning his face showed lines of worry, even while an unrealistic excitement glimmered in his green eyes.

She grew uncomfortable. Did Dr. Bolton's expert medical eye notice her father's gradual decline? She thought that Ambrose had, and that this was the reason for his worry.

"Does Father understand how weak and ill she is?" she asked.

She detected a disquiet he was trying to conceal. She was convinced that he had a brotherly affection for her father. Jerome was the one who had asked Ambrose to pastor the mission church when he'd left the Hawaiian Islands to seek a leprosy cure. And Jerome had worked with Ambrose in the recent ministry to the Chinese sugarcane workers. Ambrose also had a spiritual compassion for Jerome's obsession over Rebecca. Even Rafe had recognized it and mentioned it to her at one time.

"No, Jerome doesn't know how near death is for Rebecca. He wouldn't accept it. He's not a well man, as I think you've already noticed."

"His heart—" she began, but he shook his head.

"We know it's more than his heart, lass, so let's be straightforward. It's too important and far-reaching to disguise. Dr. Bolton told me this morning he thinks Jerome is headed for a breakdown. I believe his assessment is right. If Jerome can't release to God the obsession he has over curing your mother of leprosy, then this breakdown will happen. His emotions are stretched near the breaking point. Dr. Bolton and I fear he's functioning on the edge of fallacy when it comes to curing your mother."

Eden sighed. "Yes. I've noticed it coming for weeks. I guess we all have."

"I think part of his dilemma is from blaming himself for Rebecca's condition. Jerome was anxious to come to Molokai at the time to help a certain doctor with some experiments. When the worst happened to Rebecca during their stay here, Jerome never could forgive himself."

Eden thought of her own mission on Molokai. Rafe had always been concerned for her safety, but why had her father never worried about his daughter following in Rebecca's footsteps? Just this morning when she'd tried to share her concerns with him, he had pushed them aside lightly, as if they were inconsequential to his mission.

"When Rebecca meets you, lass, she'll be hooded and veiled.

That's the only way she'll agree to see you. She wants the memory to be as pleasant as possible under these circumstances, so you can look back on it."

Eden turned away, hands to her face. "I know. I understand."

Ambrose laid a hand on her shoulder. "There's nothing Jerome, in all of his research, can do for her. What Dr. Bolton and I are concerned about is how he will handle her inevitable death. I must go back to Honolulu soon, but of course Bolton will be here. I'll also keep in touch by mail. The steamer comes once every few weeks. You'll have another week to decide to return with me to Honolulu or stay on. Rebecca may have three to four weeks left."

"I'll stay until after her death."

"Then we'll follow this long path to its conclusion. It may be the only solution . . . to finish the course. Some struggles can only be won on our knees," he added. "I believe Jerome's dark obsession is one of those."

Dark obsession . . . Perhaps she had one of her own.

Ambrose shook his head. "In the end, though, each one of us must come to an understanding that life's sorrows and troubles are not always going to be taken from us or solved to our satisfaction. Not in this life. What we want to do as Christians is to learn that we can trust God in the valleys, and that it's perfectly safe to do so because He has promised to be with us."

His words were not only spoken for Jerome, but for her bitterness over Rafe and Bernice.

⚊⚊

When her father returned to the house, he looked consumed with worried thoughts. He didn't seem to realize that his hat was missing. He seemed more troubled than when he'd left with Dr. Bolton. Could he have seen Rebecca after all? Because he was a doctor and her husband, not even a well-meaning *kokua* could keep him from seeing her if he insisted.

When Ambrose took Jerome aside and explained Rebecca's worsening condition, Jerome took the news as expected.

"As soon as word was brought to me in Honolulu of her debility, I did all I could to get here as quickly as possible."

"We know that, Jerome," Ambrose said gently. "So does Rebecca. The *kokua* says she has much peace."

"Thank God for that." Jerome looked at Eden. "The *kokua* is right. It will be best if you see your mother first. It has been a long journey for you. Go, and give her my love."

Eden put her arms around him. She rarely felt close enough to him to embrace him without embarrassment. She felt no discomfort now, only sympathy and affection.

"Explain about the clinic, and let her know I'll visit when she's able to receive me."

"Yes," she said gently. "I'll tell her."

"Tell her there is hope. I have research that may turn the tide."

Eden made no reply and Ambrose said, "We best be going, lass. The wind is rising and clouds are moving in. It looks like we may get a good drenching this afternoon."

Dr. Jerome groaned. "Another delay in the building process. Has Keno brought in another load yet?"

"Early this morning," Ambrose said. "And they've gone for a second load."

"Those young men have more than proven themselves," Jerome said. "I'll be proud to have Keno as a nephew."

He went to the back porch where boxes of medical supplies were stacked. Eden left the house with Uncle Ambrose and they walked together in silence.

"Where are we going to meet her?" she asked, heart thudding. "Isn't she being looked after in the hospital?"

"She isn't in the hospital. You'll see. Her *kokua* will meet us and take us there."

"I should like to know all about the *kokua*," she reflected. "If possible, I'd like to reward her with a special gift. Grandfather

Ainsworth told me he'd set up a special fund for me. He called it an early inheritance."

"Ainsworth holds himself guilty for the trauma you've endured with Townsend. I think something good did come out of it, for you at least. Ainsworth has finally realized how much you mean to him. I think he has been oblivious to his feelings until the fire at Hanalei."

She felt approval, which had long been held from her, and she had no adequate response.

Eden walked with Ambrose, who was deep in thought. Finally he spoke: "Rebecca's first *kokua* died a year ago. Your mother was in serious need and another qualified helper was difficult to find. So we did what we could. A sister at the convent hospital recommended someone from the Bishop Home. When the offer was made, your mother accepted with gratitude, and she affirms she's well satisfied with her."

Eden was not unfamiliar with the history of the Roman Catholic convent and dormitory for orphan girls, called Bishop House. "Ambrose, you're not telling me Rebecca is being cared for in the convent?" she asked again.

"No . . . not in the convent. Just come along, lass. It's better I show you."

They walked up the cliff road to a hill near the boat landing on the beach and stopped at the white fence enclosing the grounds. Some nuns were outside in the yard while a handful of girls played croquet. The sea wind came in strongly, blowing the sisters' black robes like outspread birds' wings.

The compound was comprised of four whitewashed cottages and a white convent house with green shutters, all facing the sea. A tiny bungalow outside the compound with small shrubs growing around it captured her interest.

Ambrose nodded toward the bungalow. "Rebecca is there. She's being cared for by one of the older girls who grew up here in Bishop House. The girl is also a leper," he said.

Eden watched a girl near her own age coming across the yard. She limped on one leg and looked to be of Chinese background, not Hawaiian. She smiled self-consciously when Ambrose introduced her to Eden.

"This young *kokua* is Miss Lotus."

"Aloha," Eden said, "it is pleasant to meet you. You are my mother's *kokua*?"

"Yes, Miss Derrington, thank you. Missus Rebecca is waiting now. She is veiled. She asks you not to touch her . . . perhaps to sit on the porch while she is sitting up in her bed?"

Eden nodded, deeply moved. She looked at Ambrose. He gravely patted her shoulder.

"I'll wait here by the gate," he said.

Lotus smiled at him and turned toward the convent house. "If you please, Mr. Easton, Mother Marianne has asked to meet you in the house. You go ahead, she comes."

Just then the door of the convent house opened and an older nun with a smile stood waiting for him on the porch. Ambrose looked pleased and walked quickly across the yard toward her.

Meantime, Lotus bid Eden to follow her across a dirt and grassy section to the cottage with a small porch. The door was held open by a black lava rock, which was shaped like two praying hands. On closer inspection Eden saw that some gifted artist had chiseled it into shape.

Two pots of dark blue blossoms sat against the outer wall, a bit ragged from the strong winds.

Eden stepped onto the creaking porch and paused in the doorway. The old bed faced the door and had a tiny table beside it. Propped up in bed with several pillows behind her lay a stranger. Her mother.

In one brief overwhelming moment Eden was determined to control her emotions and not burst into sobs.

This is Rebecca. My mother. At last the bewildering path of wondering about her mother came to a quiet end. The long path stopped near a pot of battered blue flowers, a whitewashed shack that creaked with each gust of wind, a simple bed with plain blankets, and a thin figure of a dying woman covered in a pale blue bathrobe. A scarf was draped over her head and face, with two eyeholes. Her hands were wrapped in homemade gloves.

That Rebecca had gone through this trouble to protect Eden from seeing her corruption made the moment even more heart wrenching.

The wind blowing so strongly against her back seemed to push Eden over the threshold. Her gray skirt tangled around her ankles. She held on to either side of the doorjamb. She swallowed, her throat dry.

"Hello Mother. I'm your daughter, Eden."

Silence. Could Rebecca no longer use her diseased vocal cords? But at last a word came, clearly, and with a sigh.

"Beautiful."

"Mother—"

"No! Stay there. Do not come to me, not yet. We will meet again on another day, a better day, in a city whose maker is God."

Eden bit her lip and her heart thudded in her ears.

"I'm going there at last. And I'm so happy about it. Don't grieve, dearest. Our *real* reunion is not now, not here, but *then*. This is a mere moment in time. Not worthy to be compared with the glory that will be revealed in us, when we are in our new bodies with our Savior, the Lord Jesus."

Eden could not talk. She had so much to say and yet, at the same time, nothing worthy to say. So much to ask, yet the questions could sound trivial. So much to explain, to understand and know, and yet . . .

"It is then we will commune," Rebecca whispered, her breathing now difficult. "We will know as we are known."

Eden finally found the words that momentarily expressed her

heart. She repeated, "Yes, we will know as we are known. For now we see through a glass darkly, but *then*, face-to-face. *Now* we know in part. But *then*, we shall know even as we are known."

Lotus brought a chair for Eden to sit on just outside the door. The silence and the words that followed were sporadic, but slowly sentences began to come—and as the minutes went on never to return again, she asked the questions that had always knocked at her heart's door.

"I will give you all the answers to your questions and more, though not now, dearest. I have written them down over the years, always intending to have my journal sent to you on my departure. I've kept a journal from the beginning of my landing here until several years ago when I could no longer use my fingers. Even then my dear *kokua* wrote as I spoke. The last few years have been neglected, but little has happened that Ambrose can't tell you about.

"The one event to shake my small world was the news that you knew about me and intended to see me. I never thought you would wish to see me in this condition. Then all the news began to come to me through Ambrose. Dear brother Ambrose! He told me all about my Eden. Your career in research at Kalihi, your sobriety of purpose, your dignity, your strong belief in the Lord, and your sweetness and charm.

"I was so thrilled, so happy. I can rest now, knowing you are all—perhaps even more—of the young lady I wanted you to be. Others have done my work in answer to my constant prayers for you. Eden, my dearest, I'm so very proud of you!"

he first indication that Rafe's vision showed any hope of improvement had come on the tenth day aboard the steamer after he left Honolulu.

Now, after a month in San Francisco had crawled by, Rafe drummed his fingers. He was bored and miserable. He felt as if he were wandering about on one of San Francisco's foggiest nights. All he could hear was the deep groan of a foghorn. He'd lost Eden, and his sight. His house and plantation were in a state of neglect. What else could go wrong? He may never again see a God-given Hawaiian sunset, or look into Kip's happy face.

"Keep this up and I'll soon be crying in my cup," he mocked himself.

"You say something, Mr. Rafe?" Ling asked.

"Coffee," Rafe repeated.

"I get some. You wait here."

"Yes, Ling. I'll wait right here."

The first month of his stay was spent at the Parker Judson mansion on Nob Hill, where his mother, Celestine, babied him against his wishes and told heroic stories about how wonderful her son was to Miss Bernice Judson, Parker Judson's niece.

Celestine's stories frustrated Zachary, who held his angered tongue in her presence. When alone with Rafe, however, he released his displeasure and put miles of wear on the Judsons' fancy carpet by pacing to and fro.

"Doesn't your mother know I'm in love with Bernice and want to marry her?" Zach complained. "What is your mother trying to do? Marry you to Parker Judson's niece?"

"Why not?" Rafe pricked him, also in a foul mood. "Look at this big mansion I'll inherit on Nob Hill." He spread his arms wide. "Trouble is, I won't be able to see it."

"Very funny."

"Not really. Relax, Zach. Sit down. First, old chap, no one will marry me to any woman unless I decide it's the woman I want. But if you plan on marrying Bernice, you'll first need to break off with Claudia Hunnewell. From the stalwart plans of Ainsworth and her father, Thaddeus, you won't find it all that easy."

"Never mind," Zach grumbled. "I'll handle the Hunnewell family."

"Sure you will. Ainsworth, too, right? You're just fortunate Claudia didn't come along on the steamer to keep an eye on you. She's a determined girl. And she knows about Bunny."

"Look, Rafe, I don't find any of your goads amusing. You knew Bernice in the past," Zach accused.

Rafe had to judge everything from tone of voice. In his vision all he could see was a ghostly figure that he knew to be Zach moving about in grayness. It was frustrating to say the least. From Zach's voice he could *see* that he was upset.

So, then. Bernice must have said something to Zach about having known Rafe. He wished she'd kept silent. Bernice was spending too much time with him. If the circumstances were different he would have avoided her company. Because of his anger with Eden, and perhaps, also, because of boredom and frustration, he'd allowed her to have her way. Now that Zach noticed the camaraderie and was jealous, it was time to leave.

He wished now that he'd gone straight to the Palace Hotel on his arrival as Ainsworth and Hunnewell had done. Rafe had come here to Parker's house because he was a friend and business partner, and P.J. had insisted.

Then, too, Rafe had wanted to discuss the Hawaiiana pineapple plantation with P.J. He remained determined to see that Keno was granted opportunity to take over a portion of Hawaiiana before marrying Candace.

His mother and Kip were also here. They still had a great deal to discuss about the adoption, and whether or not he should sign the papers that would make Kip his son. So he delayed, waiting until he knew more about his future and whether he'd regain his sight.

His eyes had improved some, but not enough. Dr. William Kelly was contemplating surgery, but was in no hurry, even though Rafe was. The wise and calm Dr. Kelly wanted more healing time.

"I continue to believe this is a temporary loss of sight, Rafe," he'd said that afternoon. "We need to be patient, and wait."

Between Celestine commending her son to Bernice and Zach's jealousy flaring up, Rafe decided he'd have Ling make arrangements for him to move to the Palace Hotel the next evening.

"You're quiet about discussing the question," Zach grumbled. "You knew her in the past, so why not admit it?"

"When I was making runs in the Caribbean a few years ago, I met Parker Judson at the Palace Hotel when King Kalakaua was there. You should remember. You, too, were there."

"I remember," Zach said morosely.

"I met Parker there that night. He had me over here to meet the big sugar giants like Claus Spreckels. Parker was interested in my pineapples, and I was interested in his land. So I came. That's where he introduced me to his niece. I knew her casually for a short time. That's all."

"Well, lately you've spent too much time in her company. And don't forget Eden."

The mention of Eden riled Rafe even further. "Then maybe you should spend more time keeping Bunny happy, instead of running off for the day trying to dig up dirt on your brother, poor old Silas."

"I'm not amused about poor old Silas."

"And neither is the woman you're enamored with. I'd prefer she had someone else to sip tea with each day. So don't make things so easy for me by running off."

"I'll keep that in mind," Zach said.

"A wise decision. And, I'm also leaving. That should help."

He heard Zach straighten abruptly. "What! Leaving?"

Rafe heard self-incrimination in Zachary's voice. The pendulum of his emotions had swung from accusation to affection. "What do you mean? You can't go yet! Why, Dr. Kelly isn't through with you. There may be more tests. Even surgery. You can't give up. Your sight will come back—it's got to."

Rafe smiled. "Thanks. I meant to say, I'm going to get rooms at the Palace Hotel. It's less complicated. And I actually prefer the quiet."

"If you go, I'll go too. You'll need help."

"There's Ling."

"We'll both go. Come to think of it, Grandfather Ainsworth's still there, too. He may not go with Mr. Hunnewell to Washington, D.C., after all."

Rafe found that news curious. Ainsworth had been keen to go to Washington to meet with Thurston for the discussion with the Secretary of State on the possibilities of annexation. They wanted to do this before President Harrison left office and Grover Cleveland, who was against annexation of Hawaii, was sworn into office.

"Did Ainsworth say why he'd decided to stay here in the Bay City?"

"No, but I don't think he's feeling well. Hunnewell is going on, though. He's promised to keep me updated by wire on everything important that happens in the meeting. I'll be the first with a big story in the *Gazette*. A personal interview with Hunnewell. Maybe

even old Thurston. Great-aunt Nora will smother me with beautiful *leis* when we get back to Honolulu."

*And you'll be more indebted to not disappoint his daughter Clau-
dia with that big diamond engagement ring*, Rafe thought. The truth
was, Rafe liked Miss Claudia. She was an unpretentious girl. She
was not as beautiful as Bernice, but was attractive, and more importantly, he believed she sincerely loved Zach, and believed the Scriptures to reign in all matters of life. He couldn't say the same about
the troubling Bernice Judson and her determined ways.

———

When Rafe moved to the Palace Hotel his condition unexpectedly changed. It began with a letter from Ambrose Easton, written
from the leper settlement of Kalawao.

Rafe kept Ambrose's letter inside his pocket for a day. Finally
he'd sent Ling to Ainsworth's room to ask Ainsworth to come read
it to him. Having to do such things was a key point of Rafe's frustration. Always independent, the need to "ask" for help was particu-
larly menacing to his peace of mind.

Ainsworth came over at once to see Rafe.

On an earlier occasion Zach had told Rafe that his grandfather
was ill, but as far as Rafe could tell by his voice Ainsworth was as
determined of spirit as ever. He told Rafe of how he was in communication with Thurston and Hunnewell who were hard at work
in Washington, D.C.

"I believe, my boy, that the annexation issue is going our way," he
said after he and Rafe had settled into comfortable chairs. "Thurston
is assured that a revolution to unseat the corrupt monarchy will take
place this year. Naturally, we cannot unseat Queen Liliuokalani
without cause, but if the information we've received of her intentions
to overturn the legal Constitution is true, we will have ample legit-
imacy. Secretary of State Blaine has privately assured Thurston that
the president will back us before he leaves office, if he should lose

this election to Grover Cleveland. I believe he'll call a special meeting of Congress and ask for a vote to annex the Hawaiian Islands."

"If that proves true, sir, it's the best news I've had in months."

"Indeed, indeed . . . and now, this letter from Ambrose you wish me to read."

Ainsworth drew his chair closer and accepted the envelope from Rafe. He opened it and read the contents quietly, showing respect in treading on another's privacy. Rafe didn't mind sharing the letter from Ambrose, but he would have if it were from Eden.

Most of Ambrose's letter was personal, written to Rafe not merely as his blood uncle, but as his spiritual mentor—the decent man and lay pastor who'd brought him to Christ and discipled him through childhood and into Rafe's robust teen years as a pearl diver in the old Easton lagoon. Many times Ambrose had kept him and Keno out of trouble.

As Ainsworth concluded the letter he must have decided Rafe needed to be alone to digest the news. He stood from the chair, returned the letter, and, with a firm but brief pat on Rafe's shoulder said, "I have a meeting with Spreckels and Hunnewell." He left the room for his own suite.

Rafe mulled over what he'd heard.

Ambrose had given Rafe some wise and compassionate advice, as well as affirming they were all well on Molokai, but Ambrose did not mention Eden.

He might at least have discussed how she was responding to Kalawao. Why hadn't he written anything about her? If anyone knew Eden, it was Ambrose. They were *all* well, he wrote, so there was no cause for Rafe to be concerned. What then, had changed about Eden that caused Ambrose to avoid mentioning her, or passing a message she may have had for him?

Rafe could conceive of only one reason—Eden must have no personal thoughts she wished to share. Rafe realized their relationship must be truly broken.

Rafe had written to Eden before he'd left on the steamer for the mainland, and from San Francisco when at Parker Judson's. But neither of his letters had produced a response.

He'd been forthright—perhaps too straightforward about the likelihood of permanently losing his vision. He hadn't told her, however, how her father, at the medical ward in Honolulu, had strongly urged that they end their relationship until the outcome of Rafe's condition could be determined.

The request had put him in an uncomfortable position. If he'd said no, he would have appeared self-centered and inconsiderate of the yoke he'd be placing upon Eden.

In his physical and emotional condition at the time, the test had weighed heavily, and he'd been brief in the message to Eden that her father had written out for him. Rafe had thought she would answer by a return message before he left for the mainland. When she sent no reply, Rafe thought she'd made her decision. She had stepped back from his crisis and run off to Molokai.

Evidently, her decision had pleased Dr. Jerome. This had always been his goal. But perhaps that was somewhat unfair since seeing her mother and helping with the leper settlement had been Eden's goal from the time she was sixteen.

More than six weeks ago now, Rafe had written her a second message, with Ling's help. He'd told her that after two months in San Francisco under the care of the vision specialist, Dr. William Kelly, the problems with his eyesight continued, and that Rafe saw little hope of recovery.

As a gentleman, he'd offered to call off the marriage since he would be unable to fulfill his plans for an independent future. She knew better than anyone how blindness would restrict his activities. And so, if nothing else, he'd expected Ambrose to include her response, or at least some of his impressions about her feelings on the matter.

Rafe admitted to himself that he'd overestimated the gracious Eden Derrington. He thought she would have declined his offer and reaffirmed her love at whatever cost.

How wrong he had been.

And how bitter the rude awakening.

Well, now she had what she wanted, he thought angrily. He'd always been a spoiler for her dreams involving her esteemed father.

And now—now that Rafe Easton was mostly blind, he was no longer important to her . . . no longer the man to make her dreams viable.

As he mulled this over in the gray fog smothering him, he considered how some love, unlike God's love in 1 Corinthians 13, was not faithful and dependable, least of all forever. There was a kind of love which, when tested by circumstances, easily shattered. Those once "in love," now had hearts disillusioned.

The prince on the white horse, they finally discovered was a cripple, and the fairy tale ended with a sigh of disappointment, and a wince for the little princess.

The trial had proven that her commitment to him was shallow. As long as he could finance her father's clinic, could pay for the bungalows, and even bail her Great-aunt Nora's cherished newspaper out of debt, then Rafe Easton was worth her commitment. Now that he'd become blind—well, that was a different story.

He reached for his coffee cup, but in his frustration knocked it onto the rug with a thump. He stooped to pick it up. When he couldn't find either cup or saucer, but bumped into the table and heard something ceramic crash down, his temper broke. His disappointment in Eden and in life in general was becoming so bitter that he almost picked up the table and hurled it across the room into the gray mist.

But he caught himself abruptly, gripping the edge of the table, his dark head lowered. *Forgive me Father. I am thinking as a fool. My anger is like a lion's ravenous appetite! Help me to know both how to be abased, and how to abound . . . to do all things through Christ who strengthens me. I surrender my difficulties and my life to You, to do as You will.*

The door opened and Rafe heard Ling groaning.

"You sit down, Mr. Rafe. I get mess I clean. You rest."

"That's the trouble, old friend. I don't want to sit and look at gray fog all day. What am I going to do, Ling? What if I never see another Hawaiian sunrise, or look at the pages of Scripture, or see a true friend's smile?"

He took the chair Ling pulled forward and sank into it. He leaned his dark head back against the headrest.

"Grace, grace, Mr. Rafe. You tell me so, right? I read in Bible your uncle Ambrose give me. Christ has much grace for you, for me. His strength work strong when man weak!"

Rafe was silent. He rubbed his forehead. Hearing Ling speak as he did brought satisfaction to his soul. Ling had once fled to him for refuge from Townsend, and now, after Rafe had invested time and Scripture in the old Chinese gentleman, Ling was giving back to him a bounty of blessing and true friendship.

"You are a true friend, Ling. I won't forget your loyalty."

"You true friend for me. How else can humble self like me tell to such fine fellow?"

Rafe couldn't help it, he laughed. A fine fellow, was he? Someone should tell that to Eden.

"I get you more coffee," Ling said softly. "Maybe something to eat."

"Neither. Are you certain you took care of that letter I entrusted to you?"

"One to Miss Eden?"

"Yes, Ling, to Miss Eden."

Rafe, rather than asking his mother Celestine, or even Zach to write out his private letter to Eden, had gone so far as to send Ling to Chinatown for someone who knew English well, and who had written it at Rafe's dictation. Afterward Rafe signed the letter, had the envelope addressed, and then paid Ling's friend with a generous tip.

"For sure. Was put to mail many long weeks ago. No mail today either. Maybe tomorrow."

Speak, Lord, in the stillness . . .

Rafe Easton was angry with himself. He recalled yet again how he'd broken the vow to God that he'd made a few years earlier when he was so outraged with the way Townsend treated his mother Celestine that he'd gone to Ambrose to talk it over.

Ambrose had talked Scripture to him, showing him that though it was admirable to protect the weak from danger, another responsibility of being a Christian was in yielding to the Lordship of Christ and leaving vengeance to our just and righteous God.

By the end of that meeting, Rafe had prayed with Ambrose and turned his anger over to the One who judged righteously, and vowed he would not lay a hand on his stepfather, Townsend Derrington.

Now, some years later he'd not only broken the vow, he'd put his life at risk and damaged his reputation. He had come close to killing Townsend with his fists. He'd also left Keno in Honolulu blaming himself for Rafe's loss of sight, though actually, as Rafe had told Parker Judson, "If Keno hadn't drawn my attention from Townsend, I'd likely be in jail with manslaughter on my hands."

The dangerous snare he had wrestled with through the years was the congealed hatred he'd locked away in his heart, knowing, as did Ambrose, even back then, that should he let himself loose he was likely to go too far. He now seriously considered the advice Ambrose had written in the letter from Kalawao:

> *The vow you made to God that night in the bungalow was a good one. Even so, without dealing with the root cause of hatred, you were always walking near the cliff's edge, inches from going off.*
>
> *That's where we both went wrong. With God's strength and grace, we needed to dig out the root of hatred. As long as the root remained, it could grow. No matter how deeply it was buried in the mind, there could come a time, under the right circumstances, when it could yield poisonous fruit. I'm convinced that's what happened.*
>
> *I rebuke myself for not having recognized this earlier. I've told the Lord so. Let us both be humble before Him, being thankful He inter-*

vened when He did. One more thing, my son. We often depend on our own abilities when life seems easy, but when we feel powerless to help ourselves we turn to God. We must recognize that even when life seems easy we depend on God, for He upholds the universe.

Dependence is not defeat, but the realization that God is the source of all life, truth, and value. With this awareness, problems drive us closer to God. Learn how to depend on God daily. And after that, you must forgive yourself, get out of the mire of self-condemnation, and keep trusting in Him.

"Faithful are the wounds of a friend, but the kisses of an enemy are deceitful" (Proverbs 27:6).

Rafe lifted his hands and could just make out their shape. They had healed as strong as ever. Had he kept hitting Townsend, however, he could imagine his conscience creating permanent bloodstains on them.

Thank You, Lord, for stopping me when You did.

Even so, Rafe remained depressed. The harvest of his wrath was indeed bitter.

Making a vow to God, then breaking it, was not to be taken lightly. If God was going to restore his sight, He did not seem to be in a hurry. And though Rafe was impatient, he didn't think God would alter His program to appease Rafe's frustration. Circumstances would come together according to God's good purposes.

Now, he thought, hands on hips, *if I could just rest in that!*

Rafe heard Ling enter the room. "Mr. Zach come back from town minutes ago. Changing in his room. Very agitated. Anxious to talk to you."

Now what? The three of them were sharing a suite in the Palace Hotel—not that good carpet and matching brocade meant anything to Rafe at the moment.

When Zach came into the room his new leather shoes squeaked as he paced back and forth across the carpet.

"Zach, you're like an erupting volcano."

"That's from being around you."

Rafe smiled. "What's up? You're heating the room."

"It's that Honolulu marshal, whatever-his-name-is."

"Harper," Rafe said. "Percy Harper. He's all right."

"Well nice chap or not, Percy Harper's flubbed everything. He's been all over Honolulu with a magnifying glass and hasn't found Townsend. Now, new information came to Grandfather Ainsworth by telegraph just this afternoon. Townsend apparently escaped the Islands. He could be anywhere by now."

Rafe wasn't surprised. He thought all along that Townsend had escaped. He had his own theory of what may have happened once Keno and Townsend entered the water. Rafe hadn't yet discussed the matter with Keno, but he did know Townsend was a strong swimmer. Townsend could have swum underneath the *Lilly of the Stars* to the other side of the hull, and waited while Keno swam farther away, thinking Townsend was making for the wharf. Once things calmed down and Rafe was brought to Honolulu, Townsend could have found a place to recover with one of the immoral women he knew on the Big Island. After recovering from injuries, he would make other plans.

Zach had apparently assumed his father's arrest was imminent.

"It's Harper," he grumbled. "He should have checked every steamer leaving for the mainland—and especially the interisland boats. I doubt if he did."

"If I'd been awake," Rafe said wryly, "I would have suggested the search include the casino. My guess is that he got a boat out of Honolulu through the smuggling cartel. He knew them well enough. He took out a loan to pay them off from his gambling debts using Hanalei as credit when he had control. Where he got money to pay someone to get a boat I don't know, but there were a number of ways he could have done it."

Zachary's leather shoes stopped squeaking. Rafe felt his gaze. "We all should have thought of that. By George, I think you're onto it, Rafe."

The trail was cold by now. The time to have nabbed Townsend was past.

Zach's shoes started again. "You know who's involved, as thick as roaches, with the cartel don't you?"

"Don't tell me. Let me guess . . ."

"Don't be funny. Who else but Silas? Why, he would have helped Townsend escape. I think he's proud of our father's brass neck. Look at all Father did for Silas, since he showed up, *uninvited*, by the way. If either of us inherits anything from being a Derrington it won't be me. Silas's already raked in plenty, so he owes Townsend. I think Townsend's right here in the Bay City," Zachary said in a despondent voice.

"And I wouldn't be able to recognize him from a desert bobcat, even if he stood in this room," Rafe commented.

Zachary's voice came closer to where Rafe was stretched out in a chair, hands interlocked behind his head.

"What if he is planning such a move? Especially if he knows you're temporarily blind!"

Rafe wasn't worried. "I don't believe he will. I think Townsend has one ambition at present: to board a ship for South America."

"You're taking this too lightly."

"Hardly. But consider the facts. For one thing, he didn't plan to confront me, either on Hanalei or your houseboat. If he wanted a face-to-face meeting, he could have had it easily enough. Instead he ran away. The confrontation we had on your boat—by the way, I'll pay for anything broken—"

"Everything in the captain's room is in rubble," Zachary said woefully.

"That confrontation wasn't what Townsend expected, or wanted. If he is here in San Francisco, I don't believe he'll make a midnight call on me."

Zachary did not sound convinced. "What about your mother? She's here with you. Will he want to see his wife for a change? I tell you, Rafe, I don't like any of this. Something is all wrong when he's able to get away so easily."

"I agree that someone helped him escape the Islands. Otherwise Harper should have spotted him. Harper isn't the greatest detective, but he did have the steamship lines watched."

Rafe held his own suspicion, though he couldn't prove it now, in his condition. Nor did he intend to discuss it with Zachary. Rafe was worried about Zachary. Zach's emotions continued to hover at an unhealthy level since the fight aboard his houseboat. Anything might tip the scales—including a discussion of who may have helped Townsend escape.

"I keep telling Great-aunt Nora what the *Gazette* needs, but she won't listen to me," Zach said his shoes squeaking again. "Well, I'm here in the Bay City at last. Zachary A. Derrington! And I have a lot of pokers blazing in the fire."

Rafe groaned inwardly.

"But if I telegraph Nora about the leads I'm working on, will she let me report these facts in the *Gazette*? Not on your life. The *Gazette* could be a great newspaper but she stands in its way without realizing it."

"The *Gazette* is her trumpet, to sound a rallying cry for Queen Liliuokalani," Rafe admitted.

"Sure. That's it. And Nora's bamboozled into believing that Silas has also sworn his loyalty to the monarchy. So she dismisses all the other big stories that might implicate him or the Derringtons. I can't figure out why she defends Silas. He's an annexationist. I'd have expected her to be on to him by now."

"She doesn't believe Silas is an annexationist," Rafe said, calmly. "She believes what pleases her. As for digging up these 'big stories,' I agree they'd likely burn the pages of the *Gazette*, but don't forget she stands with Ainsworth on protecting the Derrington name. That's your answer, Zach. She's not likely to put anything into print about Townsend, or Silas."

"She'll have to in the end. And a lot more than just Townsend and Silas. You just wait. The stories I dig up while *here* in the Bay

City will sink a ship. Why, I'll bring an upheaval in Honolulu.

"I'm going to Sacramento on Monday," Zach announced. "Remember how Silas claimed he worked on a newspaper there? Well! We'll see!"

"Let me guess," Rafe said. "Silas is involved with the drug and gambling cartel."

"Yes," Zachary insisted, "I'm glad you've come round to the truth at last."

Rafe already knew Silas was involved with the cartel. Silas had admitted that much to him. Rafe had encouraged him to go to Ambrose for help from the only One who could change his life.

Rafe had kept the disclosure between them, giving Silas time. Getting out of the trap wouldn't be easy. One of Rafe's former workers, Sen Fong, was dead because he'd wanted out of the cartel after coming to Christ through the Bible teaching that Dr. Jerome and Ambrose had conducted among the Chinese workers on various plantations. Silas might also risk their strong disfavor, depending on how much he knew, and whether they were convinced he would keep silent about what he knew.

The idea that Silas could be in danger—and for that matter, Zach too, since he was digging about where the body of truth about the cartel was buried—added to Rafe's frustration of being shackled by his inability to boldly enter the fray.

You need to learn to pray more, trust Christ more, and lean less on your own abilities, he could imagine Ambrose saying. *"My grace is sufficient for you. For My strength is made perfect in weakness."*

When a man can't solve the world's problems, he thought, *it's best to turn it over to the wisdom and power of the Almighty.*

Rafe decided to spend some time in intercession for Silas. He didn't need his eyesight for that.

"Say what you will, but I'm staying on the lookout for Townsend just the same," Zach was saying. "I've given orders to Ling to make sure each of our room windows are closed and bolted tonight. And today I stopped in a store and bought us each a .38 caliber pistol."

Rafe put a hand on his head and moaned.

"What the *Gazette* needs to bail itself out of the red is some robust reporting that will set the society of Honolulu back on their polished heels. What about a Derrington journalist turning the light of justice on another Derrington by the name of Townsend? With his son doing the job, at that. Not that illegitimate Silas—but me."

"Ling!" Rafe pushed himself up from the chair, reaching to the side of a table to gain his balance. "Ling!" he called.

"And, Mr. Zach, don't forget Sen Fong," Ling said, entering from the connecting room.

"Yes! The body was discovered right in Rafe's own garden at Hawaiiana. What a story!"

"Ling," Rafe snapped, with such emphasis as to make him scurry toward him.

"You call me, Mr. Rafe?" came Ling's apologetic voice.

Rafe stared into the gray misty fog at the vague figures before him.

"What time is it, Ling?" he asked, changing the subject. "There's a dinner tonight at Parker's, isn't there?"

"Yes, Mr. Rafe, at eight o'clock. Almost seven o'clock now. Some big sugar men be there. Mr. Spreckels too."

"Spreckels? Then there should be quite a confab over mashed potatoes and gravy. We'd best get dressed, Zach."

Once Parker Judson and Claus Spreckels got going on the sugar business in Hawaii and California, any other topic went out the window. Not that Rafe minded, especially when Bernice would be trying to overwhelm everyone at the table with her charm and beauty. He felt she was doing everything in her power to stir some old memories he did not want springing to life again.

Another testing, another temptation. And poor old Zach was smitten badly. Bernice was definitely the wrong woman for Zach. Yes, little Claudia Hunnewell could put up with his tirades and soothe his nerves—something Rafe wished he had for himself at the moment.

*R*afe was at the Judson mansion on Nob Hill waiting in the library with his mother, Celestine, for the dinner bell to chime. He wasn't surprised to find her distraught over news about Townsend, and he tried to calm her.

"Yes, it's disappointing about his escape, but he won't come here. He's selfish to the core. Even before the fire he'd planned to go to South America. He's either there now or will be soon enough. He couldn't have hung around the Islands for long or he would have been spotted. Stop worrying, Mother."

"Well, I do hope you're right. However—"

"I don't want to ask this, but I'd better. There is gossip in Honolulu about you and Parker. Some thought it might help Townsend at his trial if he were to bring out that you've been here in Parker Judson's care for several months. Just what are your feelings about him? Is something going on, or—?" He arched a brow. "It doesn't look too good, you know. Regardless of the bum Townsend is, he's your legal husband."

Celestine drew in a deep breath, and sank to the divan, Rafe bowing over toward her.

"Well I guess that's my answer," he said dryly.

"Shame on you. All right, dear. I do love him, but—"

"Not Townsend! Say it isn't so."

"No, silly boy. How could I? He's a murderer."

Rafe felt her shudder and put an arm around her shoulders.

"That he is. But never mind that now. Tell me about good old P.J."

"Absolutely nothing untoward has occurred."

"I'm sure of that."

"I spend most of my time with Kip and with Bernice. Parker and I do care about each other. I was a fool to have married Townsend. Once I knew he was responsible for Matt's death—and now with his diabolical plan against Eden and you, well, I want to be free of him. Even if he is in South America. Frankly, I hope he never returns. When I return to Honolulu I'm going to see a lawyer about legally protecting myself from him."

"You're doing the right thing."

She relaxed. "I'm very relieved. About Eden—" she began.

"What about her?" he asked sharply.

"Now it's my turn," she said. He felt his mother's hand on his sleeve.

"I don't care to upset you," she lowered her voice, "but a letter arrived this afternoon. Bernice was just leaving the house to meet friends for tea when the postman came . . ."

"Where is the letter?" he asked tonelessly.

"That's the difficulty. I can't locate it."

"Can't locate it!"

"I knew you'd be coming to dinner tonight so I put it on the salver in the room you were using. I was going to give it to you after dinner. When I went to the room, it wasn't there. Of course, I wasn't wearing my glasses, but even so, I would surely have noticed an envelope sitting there where I'd placed it."

"One of the servants could have removed it."

"I've asked around the staff. No one has seen it."

His agitation rose.

"I'll ask Bernice if she removed it. If she did, please don't be too stern with her. She's very much taken with you, you know."

"And Zach is very much taken with Bernice. The last thing I want right now is a triangle!"

"I know, dear, I know. It's all so troubling. I found Bernice crying in the garden the other day."

"Crying! Oh, come, Mother, there's been nothing between us for four years."

"Well she seems to think differently."

"And even then it wasn't love. Not on my part."

"She's as upset about poor Zachary as you are. She has no desire to marry him, but he's evidently misled himself into believing so."

"As she's misled herself into believing that she and I are two hearts beating as one?"

"Rafe! You can be so hard sometimes."

"Mother dear, I don't want to marry Bunny. I don't want to become involved with any woman, or any project right now, except Hanalei and annexation. Before I can give myself adequately to these two goals, I'll need my sight recovered. Forget Bernice. In fact, that letter from dear, sweet, faithful Eden can just remain as invisible as my foggy eyesight as far as I care—"

"Dear, you don't mean that. The letter *must* be around somewhere and, I shall find it. Oh, I believe that was the dinner bell—"

"By all means," he said, "let us go hear what the Sugar King genius, Mr. Spreckels himself, will enlighten us with this evening. I'm sure it will aid our digestion."

"Such a naughty boy sometimes. Come, dear."

⁓⌇⁓

Bernice Judson stood near the library door, studying Rafe Easton as he stood leaning against a table, arms folded across his chest. She liked what she saw. He was everything she wanted and she intended to marry him in any way she could manage.

"In this life, short as it is," she had recently told her women friends, "we must collect what we want before our one commodity is spent. Time is a thief and a robber. My grandfather used to tell me, 'A woman can have few things to bargain with in this life. Beauty, wealth, and a name in society.'"

And I, Bernice thought pragmatically as she watched Rafe Easton, *have them all. I am beautiful, I have money galore, and I have the powerful Judson name, respected in San Francisco and the Hawaiian Islands.*

"You sound positively arrogant," one of her friends had said courageously—courageous, for if "Bunny" Judson got angry at a friend it meant the end of that girl as far as society and its entertainments and connections were concerned. Bernice's answer was plain and forthright. What was the use of denying her assets by wearing robes of false humility? Mirrors did not lie, neither did her inheritance, nor the collection of families she associated with on Nob Hill. She was sure she could marry any man she wanted.

Bernice wanted Rafe. She liked his wavy dark hair, his stimulating eyes framed by dark lashes, and his strong build. It amazed her how he'd escaped capture by now. The Derrington girl must be very foolish indeed. Bernice almost felt sorry for Eden.

When her usual tactics hadn't worked—she'd heard he was engaged to Eden—Bernice decided she would need to use a ruse. So before Rafe Easton arrived from Honolulu to see Dr. Kelly, Bernice had planted misleading evidence in clever ways. As fortune smiled on her, events had fallen into her hands.

She had studied him for a year, and learned as much about him as she could through friends in Honolulu, including Zachary Derrington. Naturally, she had to play Zachary along to gain an open door into the arena of life where Rafe moved.

She had also studied the Derrington woman from afar. Bernice did not like her. She was too religious. Too dedicated to unselfishness.

Imagine! Willing to work with vile lepers. To trail after the steps of her father, an old man, and one who was a trifle touched in the head, if her sources were correct. Perhaps Eden, too, was a bit "teched," as the Scotch put it. Imagine! A man like Rafe wanting to marry her while she'd strung him along for years. The girl must be a fool.

And I will win in the end.

Actually, she was delighted Eden was on Molokai.

Bernice had no father to worry about pleasing as Eden did. Uncle Parker was as impressed with Rafe as she, and he also wished for a marriage. He liked Rafe's business head, his abilities, and his energy. Bernice liked Rafe's coolness, his determination—except she wanted it focused on her.

In the last month enough had happened here in San Francisco to convince her he could be taken. She wasn't worried about him regaining his sight. She understood from Uncle Parker and Rafe's mother that Dr. Kelly was pleased with signs of improvement in Rafe's vision, and was gaining confidence in his recovery.

And so she'd made her plans. Rafe's present dependency had worked to her advantage. Rafe had written a letter to Eden, which Ling had placed in the hall for the postman to pick up. She had intercepted that letter, and now she would enjoy "reading" Eden's letter to him.

There actually was no letter from Eden, but knowing what Rafe had written made it a pleasure for Bernice to write the girl's response. It was fortunate that Celestine hadn't been wearing her reading spectacles when she'd taken the envelope and placed it on the salver in Rafe's room. All Bernice had needed to do was go back later and pick it up. If all went as she'd planned, she'd be the one to read it to him, and hopefully tonight. She even had her excuse for taking the letter.

Rafe would then close the door to Eden. This would set him free to give her time to win his commitment. Love would come later in their marriage. She would see to that. She'd never yet lost a man she wanted. Nor would she lose this time.

If only Zachary would cease troubling her . . .

⸺❦⸺

After dinner Rafe returned to the library for his meeting with Bernice Judson. He had managed to speak to her just as they were seated at the table earlier, and she'd agreed to meet him in the library to discuss the letter from Eden.

She came to the silent library as softly as a summer's breeze in the garden. Rafe knew it was Bernice from the fragrance she wore when she was around him. Before he'd become seriously committed to Eden he'd bought Bernice perfume for her birthday. He believed she was intentionally wearing the same fragrance now.

Bernice turned quietly and slid the bolt into place to make certain no one would interrupt.

"Good evening, Rafe."

"Did you bring the letter?"

His tone was quiet and polite.

"Oh, yes. Celestine asked if I'd read it to you. She's still playing hostess. You see, she opened the envelope when it first arrived. Miss Derrington must have thought it more appropriate to address the letter to your mother. I hope I'm not being too bold. I'm a little embarrassed, Rafe."

"Don't be."

"Celestine wasn't wearing her glasses when the postman came. I told her she had a letter from Miss Eden Derrington and, well, she asked me to open it at once. She asks me to do that sort of thing since we've come to trust each other so well."

She continued. "So I do apologize for opening the envelope this afternoon. As soon as we understood it was actually a private letter to you, we ceased reading—"

"You needn't worry about it. Unless she confessed to stealing the crown jewels, I don't think it matters whether you saw her confession."

136

"Oh I'm certain a wonderful girl like Miss Derrington would never steal jewels. She's quite a selfless person, I must say." She sighed. "I'm quite impressed with her courage and spirit of adventure. Giving so much of herself to others in need. And so devoted to Dr. Jerome Derrington."

Bernice saw the reaction she'd hoped for from her words. His jaw flexed. She had heard that Eden's feelings for Dr. Derrington had proven a problem in their relationship.

She walked over to him and laid a hand on his arm. "Shall we sit?"

When seated, she left her hand on his arm a moment, waiting to read his response. She could watch him as carefully as she wanted, but he could not read her expression. He knew what she looked like—"fair as a white rose," was how Zachary liked to put it. Meticulously groomed blond hair and blue eyes.

"Rafe, this is very difficult for me," she said with a rather breathy gentleness. "I'm sorry, but it isn't the news you may have expected from her, a lovely girl you thought you understood so well. It's—it's almost cruel of me to read it to you."

A moment of tense silence hung between them until she feared she'd made an error, and wondered how she was going to recover from the long pause.

"No need for all that," he said. "Go ahead. Read it. Thank you."

Thank you, indeed. She smiled faintly. Then, for a moment she was surprised at how her conscience was pricked by his trust.

"It's a brief message. I suppose she's busy on the island with Dr. Derrington. She sends her best, and—her love, and well, here it is:

Dear Rafe,

My father and Ambrose have both spoken to me about your blindness. They assure me there is a religious reason for your trial, and that you, and all of us, must accept the great changes brought into our lives. God intervenes, altering our plans, and arranging for the best.

I'm deeply hurt that this tragedy has occurred. Blindness will be difficult for you. Therefore, Rafe, after much soul searching, I see that you are correct. Perhaps it is wise you learn to walk your own pathway, before "asking me to walk it with you," as you said. My work here on Kalawao is very important to me. I've come to understand that working at my father's side is the most important purpose in my life, so I believe I should continue here. It will be better for both of us if we forget the decision we made about marriage.

Bernice hesitated, rather proud of the way she wrote with the zeal of someone like Eden believing in religious matters such as "God's will."

Bernice waited a few seconds for effect, and then said softly, "Then she signs her name, *Eden*."

She allowed another minute to slip by and then placed her hand on his, curling her fingers gently around his strong ones. She edged closer against him, making sure their bodies touched. "Rafe . . . I—"

He drew his hand away and abruptly stood.

She too, stood. She narrowed her eyes.

"I'd like to be alone if you don't mind," he stated.

"No, no, of course I don't."

But she did mind. His reaction hadn't been quite as she'd expected. He was angry, not melting with a broken heart. In fact, she could see just how angry he was with Eden by the pulse beat in his throat. She would like to think it was her nearness that affected him, but she knew better.

Bernice turned away toward the door, tightening her mouth, when his terse voice halted her.

"That letter, please. I'd like to keep it." He held out a hand.

She turned and looked at him. His hand was held out to receive it. A steady hand, she noted. He wasn't broken up over this perceived dismissal by Eden Derrington. He was as resolved and formidable as an oncoming duelist. For the first time she feared what she'd done. Suppose he confronted Eden? What if he found out the letter was not real?

I'll think of something.

"Yes, of course," she murmured.

They heard a tap on the door. "Miss Bernice? Are you in there?"

Zachary. Now Rafe would know she'd locked the door.

"The letter," Rafe said his hand still held out.

She laid it on his palm, thinking how she'd like to smack his handsome face with it instead. *Keep calm, Bernice.* She whipped about and went to the door, but before she slid the bolt back, she turned her head and looked over her shoulder.

I need to get that letter again and destroy it, in case he regains his vision soon.

He placed it in the pocket of his dinner jacket.

Well that should be easy enough to retrieve later.

She slid the bolt back and pulled the door open. Her cool gaze met Zachary's even cooler one. He glanced past her and saw Rafe standing with his back toward them.

Bernice took hold of Zachary's arm.

"He doesn't care for company right now," she whispered. "Let's go out into the garden, shall we?" She gave him her sweetest, most promising smile, then pulled the door shut.

Alone, Rafe endured the pain of Eden's rejection. She might as well have thrust a knife into his heart. One thought came to mind. He remembered reading the story of the hymn writer George Matheson who'd been engaged to a lovely young woman from a good family in England. When he told her he was going blind she ended their relationship, saying she did not wish to be married to a blind man. Later, Matheson had written the hymn *O Love that Will Not Let Me Go*, which celebrated the unchanging nature of God.

He felt his way to a chair and sat down. God's love was faithful and steadfast. He would never leave one of His own. God's love did not depend on talent, physical appearance, strength, or goodness.

While we were yet sinners, Christ died for the ungodly.

139

I will never leave you, nor forsake you.

When my father and my mother forsake me, then the Lord will take me up.

The Scriptures filled his mind. But the one woman he loved had betrayed him, because he no longer measured up to her needs.

—⊙⊙—

As Bernice walked with Zachary through the garden, she told him of how Rafe and Eden had broken their relationship permanently.

At first he merely shrugged.

"Oh they're always doing that," he said. "I don't know how many times their engagement was broken and a new marriage date set. I admit, though, that this last one I really thought was going to cross the wedding line."

By the time Bernice ended her tale, she'd not only dampened Zachary's jealousy, but also raised his concern for his "dear brother Rafe."

"Eden always put Molokai and her mother, Rebecca, ahead of Rafe," he said. "I'm surprised she actually came out and told him she no longer loved him, though. Especially at a time like this. It seems cruel. And Eden isn't anything close to being heartless. She was depressed when she couldn't see him," he said as they walked back toward the house. "I've never seen her as depressed as she was when he was in the medical ward in Honolulu. At one point none of us thought he would come out of that coma. If it hadn't been for Ambrose and the mission church holding round-the-clock prayer vigil for him, I don't think Rafe would have awakened."

She looked at him. "Do you actually believe that?"

"Sure I do. There was a time when I didn't . . . but Eden brought me to understand who Christ is, and what He's done for us. His mission when He came to our little earth was awesome."

Bernice almost yawned.

"God gave His Son for us, didn't He? Don't you believe in Christ?" he asked.

She looked at him. Was he this naïve? In the reflection of the garden lamps she could see the sincerity in his face.

"Why of course. I go to church most of the time," she said. Then she changed the subject. "Well, Miss Derrington does seem to be wholly dedicated to her work. Anyway, Zachary, do be kind to Rafe, won't you? And whatever you do, *please* don't let him know I told you Eden no longer wishes to marry him."

"I won't. Rafe has more than enough problems right now."

"Let's go indoors, shall we? The fog is coming in and I forgot my wrap."

Chapter Thirteen
Let Your Heart
Take Courage

*E*den could hardly sleep that night after visiting Rebecca. *Her mother's journal.* A hope was coming to fruition. From the moment she had learned her mother was alive and Eden determined to meet with her and discover and safeguard her story at Kalawao, she had hoped for at least a diary!

The road that brought her to this moment of satisfaction and renewed purpose had been demanding. Even now, it hardly seemed possible that she had been successful. The satisfying meeting with her dear mother, though sad, had fulfilled a greater portion of her goal.

Now, to learn there truly was a substantial journal on hold for her was as rewarding to her heart as a miner finally coming upon a strike of gold.

As acquainted as she was with the writing of histories through Great-aunt Nora, Eden was more than enthusiastic about the opportunity before her. Nora had written several books on the Hawaiian Islands and had begun a book on the Derrington family history. She'd begun with the first Derrington missionary from Connecticut, and had gone on to the present political position of

Ainsworth. Unfortunately that history section had been waylaid by Uncle Townsend who feared Nora would reveal his crime against Matt Easton and cause his death. Nora had not yet been able to find that missing section of her work.

Eden intended to write Rebecca's family history. Now, in her excitement, she decided she'd return to Honolulu to gain Nora's help. The history would contain the pathos of her mother's leprosy discovery, and what it would mean to her marriage to Jerome and to her only child, Eden—a mere five-year-old. Eden would write what it had meant to Rebecca to live the rest of her days as an exile on the leper isle of Molokai during its early years when the misery was compounded.

Eden felt a rebirth of ambition and a driving desire to work. She would remain at Kalawao until her mother died, then she would return to Kea Lani to create the history of Rebecca Stanhope Derrington. She longed to have the journal in her possession now, but for some reason Rebecca would not present it to her yet. Her mother would only say that Eden must wait until after her own departure. Then she would receive the written works.

Eden had not inquired about Kip's parentage. That disclosure must wait for their next visit, arranged for Sunday. Her mother spoke of needing rest to regain strength. Jerome was to visit Rebecca on Friday morning, three days away. He'd already sent her messages, which the *kokua*, Lotus, would read to her.

At last Eden fell asleep thanking God for permitting the impossible meeting to occur.

A storm broke that evening, and rain fell in gushing torrents. The house leaked, and Eden and Keno rushed about placing everything from cooking pans to pails beneath the drips. Eden even set down some cups, only to see them fill to the brim within minutes. She picked up two of them and stood looking about as if wondering where to empty them. Keno opened the front door and pointed. She laughed and tossed out two cups of water while the rain came down in giant bucketsful.

"I give up," she said. "I'm going to bed."

"If the roof doesn't leak over your bed," he called.

It did leak. She dragged the mat and blanket to the other side of the little room and settled down in hope of dry sleep.

She hoped Rebecca was dry. She suspected that she was. Lotus would see to that. *Dear Lord, bless Lotus.* While Rebecca's bungalow was tiny, it had looked to be constructed well enough—better than the leaking Doctor's House.

Dr. Jerome walked alone one evening to see Rebecca in her bungalow near Bishop House. Eden heard him come back to the house with slow, tired feet. He went into his study and shut the door. The candlelight burned long hours that night as she heard him weep. Eden worried, cried with sympathy, and prayed.

Her next visit to her mother was to come on Sunday. Then on Saturday night the *kokua*, Lotus, came to explain that Rebecca was too sick. She would need more time to rest. No more visitors for the next few days.

Regardless, Eden had much to do. With the weather having improved, Keno and the other men went to work building four small bungalows, to be followed by the research clinic.

Eden and Aunt Lana set about to arrange the bedding and furnishings—mostly a few rattan chairs and tables—in their private cottages. Jerome and Clifford were "allowed" to borrow a few pieces of better furniture from the Doctor's House until more suitable furnishings could be hauled in. Eden had no idea how long she would stay here at Kalawao. She was sorry to disappoint her father, but she'd made up her mind she could not stay permanently after her mother died. She supposed she could begin writing the journal into book form in her own bungalow, but something kept pulling her emotions back to Honolulu. After all, her father would have the expertise of both Dr. Bolton and Aunt Lana in the clinic when it was up and running, and their capabilities far exceeded hers.

Finally, after almost two weeks, the bungalows were up, followed several days later by the clinic. The group had as merry a celebration as they could in such circumstances. Dr. Jerome hailed Keno and his cousins for their selfless work.

"And of course," Dr. Jerome said, "although Rafe isn't here, we especially toast him for the generous loan he gave to make this possible, as well as for the supplies he arranged and the use of his ship!"

"Blessings!" they all said. Eden joined the applause, aware of a sympathetic glance from Aunt Lana.

Eden and Dr. Jerome had supper that evening in one of the new bungalows with Lana and Dr. Bolton. The Board of Health strictly ruled against lepers living in the Doctor's House or staying in any guest bungalows. Such bungalows were kept for Board of Health personnel or official visitors who came to Molokai.

But these new bungalows were private, so Eden and Dr. Jerome could intermingle with Lana and Clifford Bolton as much as they had at Kalihi hospital.

The evening included Keno and the young men from the church who were all returning to Honolulu in the morning—which saddened Eden. Keno was such a close ally of Rafe's that when she was around him Rafe seemed near.

Ambrose would remain at Kalawao until he could give further training to the ambitious young Hawaiian boy who would run the printing press.

"A nice lad," Ambrose told everyone. "A Christian, too."

Eden was glad Ambrose was staying longer to get the printing press running. She was enthusiastic about the work of making Christ known. The Hawaiian boy was named David, and he'd already told her and Ambrose about the need for Sunday school booklets for the sick children in the little Bible church. The pastor had died and Ambrose was going to fill his place while at Kalawao. Eden promised to write some simplified Bible stories to be printed. David planned to carve out press picture blocks to go along with the story booklets. She was pleased that it was Rebecca who'd first contacted Ambrose about a printing press.

Keno shook his head and folded his arms across his chest. The mannerism was so like Rafe that she felt a pang. "This makes me mighty proud of all of you. I'm a little nervous, though, about leaving you to this environment." He looked at Eden.

"My dear boy," Dr. Jerome said. "Your concerns are well taken. Yet, is anything or anyplace safe in this uncertain world? If some of us don't take risks, who will ever step forward to do the difficult work that must be done for future generations?"

"Understood," Keno said. "It will take braver men than I am. It will take those who are willing to sacrifice. Right now, sir, I'm looking forward to marriage, a family, and a good portion of Hawaiiana. I guess that's rather selfish."

"Nonsense," Dr. Bolton said. "You're not selfish, Keno, and you've contributed your part toward our success. Isn't that right, Jerome? Each of us sitting around this table wished you the full cup of God's happiness and blessings for the future."

"Thank you, Dr. Bolton." Keno looked across at Eden. As their eyes met, she lowered her gaze to her plate. She knew his discourse was also meant for her benefit, and that in speaking of a happy future he was hinting that she, like Candace, should return to Honolulu and focus on marriage.

The next morning Keno and the young men from Ambrose's church left Kalawao for the beach. Some of the crewmen were waiting ashore with the boats. The weather was windy, and the waves starting to rise, but they rowed out to sea and soon boarded the *Minoa*.

Within an hour Keno gave the order to weigh anchor and the *Minoa* headed for open sea.

Eden had been outside, and went behind her new bungalow to a solitary place she'd discovered. She ascended a hill, and crossed the running brook that provided their water supply. She stood on a mound and viewed the bay and the landing area where their whaleboats had arrived. She viewed the blue-gray vastness of the Pacific and watched the *Minoa* get smaller and smaller, heading toward Oahu and Honolulu.

A lone seabird cried, then disappeared toward the black cliffs.

She turned and, looking past the Doctor's House, could see the neat bungalows recently put up. Her father's research clinic reminded her of a military barrack. Beyond the roof of the clinic, the hospital buildings appeared worn and windswept. Across the single street in Kalawao stood the little Catholic church where Priest Damien had ministered. His bungalow, now occupied by Brother Dutton, was built up from the ground. Nearby was the graveyard with various markers of wood crosses, as well as rocks, and Hawaiian symbols of a religious belief system.

Wind flowed over the mound and shook the brush. A restive spirit settled over Eden's heart as she looked on—first at the ship on the sea, then at the exile settlement amid the beauty of green ferns, wild ginger, and black cliffs. She refused to let her heart dwell on Rafe Easton.

One evening, when Eden was settled in her own little bungalow, Ambrose came to pray with her and to say goodbye.

"David will need more help and training in the next year, but I plan to come and go as necessary. I see you've written the children's stories."

Eden had finished the work that evening, and had planned to bring the stories to David the next day.

"I was remembering Hiram Bingham," she said, "and all he did through God for Hawaii."

"Ah, yes. His most enduring work was his translation. He did the books Luke, Colossians, Hebrews, Leviticus, Ezekiel, and part of Psalms, as well as collaborating on some other books. He also created the Hawaiian alphabet. The missionaries also taught them to read and write as well as creating schools and medical facilities.

How easily the following generations forget!"

"They only seem to remember the things to criticize."

"They're not qualified to criticize. They've inherited all the benefits and some seem to think they were always part of Hawaii. But, lass, the praise of mankind is one thing; but that of God, another. The Good Lord knows whom He will acknowledge with His words, 'Well done, good and faithful servant.'"

Eden was not pleased to see Ambrose leaving Kalawao, but she knew he had to fill the pulpit at the mission church back home. "And Noelani is concerned with some of the changes taking place in Honolulu."

"Changes?" she asked.

"The annexation movement is butting heads with the queen. Liliuokalani seems to have dug her heels in to get rid of the '87 Constitution. Sanford Dole and Thurston are saying if she tries it will bring the revolution we've all heard about for the last two years."

"Noelani firmly supports Queen Liliuokalani," she stated. "You've never actually said what you favor. I suppose you back Rafe and annexation, like Keno does."

"I back whoever gives the most honor and obedience to the Lord," he said. "As for Keno, whatever he prefers is understandable. Though his father was English, I give him more credit than to think he simply sides with whatever ethnicity he feels most reflects himself. He's looking down the long road to future generations when these Islands may make a difference in history. Now," he said, patting her shoulder, "I want to pray with you, and commit you to the Lord before I leave in the morning. It's steamer day you know."

She nodded. "I'm sorry to see you go—"

"Now, now, none of that, lass, or you'll have us both morose."

"When will you actually return?"

"Not for several months. Now, I want you to listen to me," he said gravely. He took hold of her shoulders and peered down into her eyes with a fatherly frown. "Rebecca is likely to pass on before I return."

Eden bit her lip. "Yes, I know."

"If Jerome needs more help and support than any of you can give him, I'll want to know—at once. Send a message to me. Rebecca's worse now than she was just a month ago. When did you see her last?"

"I'm able to spend an hour with her each Sunday after church."

"Nothing yet on that journal she's kept?"

Eden shook her head. "She's decided I won't have it until she's gone. I've given up asking her to let me see it."

"It's undoubtedly at the convent, in the hand of Sister Marianne. I wouldn't worry too much. Rebecca must feel it's safe there. You'll receive it at the proper time."

"Marianne holds great respect for the memory of Priest Damien. Brother Dutton, too," Eden said.

"I, too, hold them in regard where their sacrifice and good deeds are concerned. Priest Damien was a commendable man of selflessness. However he made some statements that trouble me deeply." Ambrose shook his head. "The most critical spiritual issue for mankind is how a sinner is made acceptable to the one true God who is perfectly holy. The Scripture is clear. Christ's work on the cross is the only deed ever done that can atone for our sins. No man's own deeds of sacrifice and humility are adequate to earn him righteousness or prepare him for eternity. Good works are commendable when done faithfully *for* Christ's glory—such deeds God promises to reward. However, the concept of *earning* forgiveness of sins, or working for God's acceptance, is false teaching. It is a danger. If that were even possible we would never know when we have done enough. Instead we must place our confidence in Christ who certainly has done enough. 'It is finished,' He said from the cross. The work of redeeming sinners was accomplished and paid for *in full*."

Ambrose drew his brows together, concern willing his rugged features. "Here is the danger. When a believer does not know the Bible he is wide open to false teaching."

"Did you know the first Christian minister to help Kalawao

was Minister Forbes?" she commented. "He was a visiting pastor who came with two photographers. They took pictures of the lepers to put in the Honolulu papers to sound the alarm. And the first school on Kalawao was set up through John and Caroline Walsh. The Board of Health hired the couple to build and staff a small hospital, and start a boys' and girls' school."

"Yes. If I remember rightly, both hospital and schools were enlarged, but remained in need. I remember seeing those photographs Pastor Forbes put in the papers. Unfortunately, ministers like Forbes or the Walshes have been bypassed for the glorification of certain others who receive all the publicity. Sometimes history can lose the truth through repetition." She nodded. "I've also heard disturbing talk recently from Aunt Lana about 'witchcraft' here at Kalaupapa," she said.

"True, enough. The sorcerers, or witch doctors, whatever people call them, have a following here. They're called the *kahuna anaana*. There is much superstition. Some satanic power is behind it. The devil is a deceiver. Satan comes disguised as an 'angel of light.' He doesn't necessarily show up with horns, a pitchfork, and hooves— but he probably would if he thought it would snare more frightened souls into following his rebellion."

───❦───

The next morning Ambrose boarded the steamer and returned to Honolulu.

The days rolled along. Without Ambrose and Keno and his cheerful cousins, Eden noticed the evenings were especially quiet. She missed their smiles and laughter.

Dr. Jerome withdrew into the isolated world of his work, and Aunt Lana was busy helping Dr. Bolton. When the candles were extinguished and Kalawao was asleep, the night was as black as coal. Misty clouds blanketed the sky. The sound of the wind and waves wrapped about her, sighing, calling.

Finally one morning when daylight dawned, word came from Bishop Home that Rebecca had died during the night.

At first Dr. Jerome refused to believe the news that the rest of them had expected for two months. When he did accept reality he retired to his bungalow, sobbing. Eden covered her face with her hands.

Suddenly, realizing the stressful situation her father was struggling with, she remembered that he might need help with his heart medication. She hurried inside his bungalow and saw him sitting at his desk with his head on his arms. She searched diligently for his nitroglycerine tablets.

Dr. Bolton came to the open door and entered, going straight to Jerome. He had his bag with him, reached in for his stethoscope, and swiftly listened to Jerome's heartbeat.

"Here's his heart medicine," Eden said.

"Hand it to me."

Bolton bent over Jerome who had slumped in the chair. He placed a tablet under Jerome's tongue and worked on him efficiently. Eden was as grieved watching Dr. Clifford Bolton as she was about her father. It struck her that here was an extremely gifted man who, within a year or maybe two, would be unable to perform his work. Work so much in demand and so necessary.

Aunt Lana arrived breathing hard.

"Anything I can do?" she whispered to her husband.

"I believe he's just had a serious heart attack."

Eden stood, her emotions in limbo, as if she stood on the outside of a window looking in, unable to hear what was being said but watching people moving about urgently.

She stirred, then went to her father's bed and pulled back the blanket.

"Help me get him to the bed," Bolton said to Lana. Eden fell back upon her skills as a nurse. She had thought herself prepared for her father's emotional breakdown, but she hadn't considered it being initiated with a heart attack.

After they'd gotten him into bed, Dr. Bolton continued watching over him.

While Dr. Bolton cared for Jerome, Lana held Eden, whose face was wet with tears. Lana took her to the cottage, and told her to lie down.

"Rest, dear, there's nothing more you can do now," she said, as she left the room to go help Dr. Bolton with Jerome.

In the following days Eden's father remained bedridden and under Dr. Bolton's care. "If only I had access to the facilities at Kalihi," he said to Brother Ira Dutton who'd come by to see if there was anything he could do.

"The schooner will arrive in two weeks," Dutton said.

"I fear we couldn't move him now anyway."

Eden had written Ambrose with not just the news of Rebecca's death, but now Dr. Jerome's illness. The delayed communication with Honolulu was such a trial. It took weeks to send a letter and weeks to get a return message, all depending on the dates the steamer came and went. She was accustomed to writing a note and sending a boy to deliver it within the hour. Now she must wait for weeks to send for Ambrose. As Brother Dutton had said, the schooner wouldn't arrive anytime soon.

She gave the letter to Dutton who handled the mail. He always picked the postal bag up from the general store and brought it down to the beach on the day when the Board of Health steamer arrived.

Aunt Lana was the one who handled her older sister, Rebecca's, funeral. She had the Bible instructor from the small Protestant church meeting lead in prayer and read about the resurrection of Christians from 1 Corinthians 15, followed by the children's choir.

On the morning after Rebecca's funeral, Eden opened her door to step out and found a selection of flowers and ferns in a little woven basket. A piece of paper had ink printing from the press and a drawing of a gate opening toward a rainbow with hovering doves. A bluebird was flying away toward the open gate. "Free at last," was printed below the bird as well as a verse from Scripture: "We are confident, I say, and willing rather to be absent from the body, and to be present with the Lord."

The paper was signed simply *Also waiting, David, 2 Corinthians 5:8.*

⸺ ❧ ⸺

A week after Rebecca died, the *kokua*, Lotus, came down from Bishop House to Eden's bungalow. The girl carried something in her arms wrapped protectively with a blue scarf.

"This is yours, Miss Derrington. Mother Marianne gave it to me this morning to bring to you. She says, may you have peace and the good will of God all your days."

Eden knew it must be the journal Rebecca had told her about. She took it carefully, and thanked her. "And may both of you know the joy and peace that only Jesus can bring."

"Aloha," the girl murmured and turned away.

"Before you go, Lotus, I wanted to tell you that a gift will come to you from Honolulu after I've returned to my grandfather's plantation. The gift is for your kindness to my mother and for your faithful service to her."

Lotus smiled, her eyes shining, and murmured her gratitude. Eden looked after the girl. She had plans for Lotus. Some pretty clothes, some shiny costume jewelry, and enough money to live on comfortably while she waited out her days at Bishop House.

The parcel in her hands shone in the sunlight. The journal, she knew, would reveal pathos and bring more tears. Clasping it, she went back inside her bungalow.

She could begin reading it that afternoon, or perhaps during the evening. She might even wait until she returned to Honolulu. At the moment the larger details of her mother's sojourn on the isle of exiles could wait for a less climactic time.

But there was one piece of information she wanted to know before leaving Kalawao—whose child was Kip? Was there another name for the baby boy Rafe had rescued from the incoming tide that day on the beach?

The journal and its telling content could wait for a sunnier day when her heart was less heavy and willing to be buffeted by its contents. Now, with all that had happened, and her father bedridden, tomorrow's uncertainties were enough without delving into the past.

Chapter Fourteen
Yesterday's Secrets

$\mathcal{A}$s the days turned to weeks, Kalawao's weather worsened. Sometimes the sunshine was absent for days, and the ocean waves were ruthless.

Eden read Rebecca's journal from the beginning to the end. The saga told in descriptive form the numbing isolation of her early arrival at the camp and of her eventual acceptance of "these light afflictions, which are but for a moment."

Then came the shocking mention of a baby boy. When Eden looked at the date, it lined up with Kip's age. Rebecca told of her first *kokua* being violated by a haole visitor on Molokai, resulting in the birth of a baby boy. "He was drinking, and when he drinks he is unreasonable and cruel. Had I not been so far along in the dread disease he would have violated me. But he feared to touch me. He held no fear, however, of a sin against God! Leah was always an attractive woman and she told me later that she'd known him in Honolulu."

So Kip is not Rebecca's child, she thought, feeling neither relief nor disappointment. She'd been ready to accept the truth, regardless. After meeting with Rebecca and seeing how far her mother had deteriorated, Eden had already begun to have doubts before reading the diary. Kip could not be much older than three years old, and conception would have occurred four years ago. Even then, Rebecca would have been into the later stages of leprosy.

Eden read on: "So Leah had the baby," Rebecca wrote. "The man responsible, whose name is well known in Honolulu, came here on a trip with the Board of Health."

Eden gasped and gripped the journal. "What?" she breathed. "Oh no! Oh what can this mean?"

Her eyes rushed through the words to find the name of Kip's father, but she could not find it. Oh! She took in a deep breath to calm herself. Then she went back and read from the beginning again. The name must be there—

"The baby is a beautiful healthy boy who deserves to live regardless of the brutal way he was brought into this sin-cursed world. Leah and I have prayed together of what to do. We could turn him over to the boys' orphanage run by the priest, Damien, but Leah is reluctant. So I have a plan to save him."

Eden went on reading how Rebecca planned to have Leah bring the baby to Rafe Easton, who was on Kalaupapa at the time serving as a journalist for Great-aunt Nora's *Gazette*. Rafe was to take the baby to Dr. Jerome.

As Eden already knew, Rafe had not been able to meet with her father, who had left the area. Rafe had ended up taking the baby whom he'd temporarily named "Kip."

But who was responsible for Leah becoming pregnant? Did anyone at Bishop House know? Priest Damien? Brother Dutton? Would Lotus know? No, probably not Lotus, but possibly Mother Marianne—

Then Eden saw the man's name and her heart jumped. *Townsend Derrington*, powerful member of the Hawaiian Legislature visited Kalaupapa in 1889 with Charles Billings, sent by King Kalakaua and the Board of Health to report on the condition of the hospital.

"Leah had known him in Honolulu," her mother had written.

Eden went on to read that Townsend had recommended that Grandfather Ainsworth send a woman named Leah to become Rebecca's *kokua*.

Eden sat in silence, allowing the shocking information to settle in her mind. What would Townsend have done had he known the baby boy, Kip, that meant so much to Rafe, was a child he'd fathered? Would he have tried to gain jurisdiction over him to hurt Rafe? Of course he would have! And worse, Townsend was probably the one who'd anonymously informed the Board of Health that Kip was taken from Molokai. Oh, she put nothing past Townsend!

She stared at the journal. She was probably the only person alive who knew Kip's parentage.

How would Rafe respond if he knew? Would it change his feelings toward the boy? Had he adopted him yet? But Townsend had blond hair and cold blue eyes; Kip had dark hair and light greenish eyes—which must come from his mother, Leah.

Oh may Townsend never come back to the Islands!

Eden wondered what she should do with the information. Tear it out of the journal and burn it? Safeguard Kip's future and keep Rafe from looking at his adopted son and thinking of Townsend?

Could she keep the diary under lock and key for the next fifty years? If she did, there would always be the chance that someone, someday, would discover the diary.

This must be a matter of much prayer. Whatever I do, I must act in wisdom.

─⦾─

During her days in the little hospital Eden aided the sick by distributing medicine to ease their suffering: protiodide of mercury, half-grains of opium and potassium arsenite, and small amounts of watered laudanum.

Dr. Jerome had improved but was confined to bed rest.

"And if I see you trying to get up again, I'll keep you sedated," Bolton told him gruffly.

Jerome smiled wanly. "As you say, Doctor."

As the days turned into weeks, Jerome manifested severe depression and would hardly eat.

"I wish Pastor Ambrose would arrive," Bolton told Eden.

Ambrose did arrive—not on the steamer as they'd expected, but on the *Minoa* with Captain Keno and two of his cousins who offered their services, including getting Dr. Jerome aboard.

"We'll need to carry him," they explained. "He'll need to be held steady on the whaleboat, and that won't be easy in the rough sea."

"We'll manage," Keno said.

Ambrose, in his old worn frock coat and black hat, had walked into Jerome's bungalow and up to the side of the bed.

"The attack was severe this time," Jerome told him, his voice weak. "Thank you for coming, friend."

He reached a frail hand toward Ambrose who took it between his own tanned hands, and shook his head.

"It's time you went home to Kea Lani." He gestured to Keno and the two young Hawaiian men standing with arms folded across their chests.

"I brought my army," Ambrose taunted. "You have no say in the matter. It's home to Honolulu for a long rest."

"And when you get better you can return," Dr. Bolton said with forced cheerfulness. "Meantime Lana and I will manage your clinic and keep the research going."

"I've every confidence in you, Clifford. Lana, too . . . I don't want to depart, but if I must, I can leave this work to two of the finest researchers in all the Islands."

"We'll try not to let you down."

"I'm the one who's let everyone down—especially Rebecca."

"No, Jerome," Ambrose said firmly. "Rebecca is far better off with the Lord than suffering here in this camp. God called her home.

He never makes timing mistakes. 'My times are in thy hand,' wrote the psalmist."

They left the bungalow to give Jerome some quiet. Eden hadn't yet told Ambrose or Keno that she was also returning to Honolulu. Keno walked with her toward her bungalow. Something appeared to be on his mind. She broke the silence, and asked, "When will the *Minoa* lift anchor?"

"We intend to start for shore in the morning. We have a litter all ready for your father." He reached inside his shirt. "Candace wanted me to bring you her letter." He handed her a sealed envelope addressed in the recognizable flowing hand of her cousin.

"Oh, delightful. I hope she fills me in on all the social news going on in Honolulu."

"Oh, she will, all right."

Something in his response alerted her. She looked at him. He brushed his hair from his forehead and looked up at the sky. "Getting windy. I—I better get you in the bungalow and get back to Ambrose. He'll be over to see you in a little while." He smiled. "See you later on."

Eden watched him with her curiosity afire. He was behaving unusually. What was he uncomfortable about? She looked at the envelope in her hand. "Yes, and thank you—oh, Keno, by the way, I'm returning to Honolulu with my father. For the present, I have accomplished what I wanted here on Molokai."

He turned back and looked at her, and she could not tell if his reaction was surprise or concern.

"Oh," he said quietly. "You are, are you?"

An odd response. Almost as if he were seeing a bunch of new troubles.

"Okay," he said quickly. "I'll have your things brought out first thing in the morning then."

"Thank you."

He walked away toward Ambrose who stood by Jerome's bungalow talking with Dr. Bolton.

Eden entered her bungalow to read Candace's letter:

Dear Eden,

I hope you're surviving on that dreadful place. Ambrose and Keno both have told me about everything that's happened. I'm sending this letter through Keno because, woman to woman, I can best tell you what's happening in Honolulu.

You may know by now, if Ambrose has mentioned it to you that Rafe is back in Honolulu. Remember our 24-hour prayer vigil for him? God be praised. He's all right again. He can see!

He hasn't wasted any time either. He's already rebuilding the burned sections of Hanalei. He's also more involved than ever in the annexation movement. There looks to be a showdown coming over the 1887 Constitution. Great-aunt Nora is afraid there will be a strong move against the queen.

I do not know what happened between you and Rafe after his injury, but the mention of your name angers him. Rafe seems to be a different person than he was before this tragedy struck.

I am not the only one who notices this change. Keno mentioned it to me first. If anyone understands Rafe, it is Keno and Ambrose, yet they agree that he has changed.

Keno says Rafe is a walking thunderstorm ready to hurl lightning bolts. That is not all. When Rafe returned to Honolulu, he did not come back with just Zachary. Celestine and Kip are at Hawaiiana, and Parker Judson is here with his niece Bernice Judson.

Rafe is spending quite a few of his evenings with the Judsons. Bernice gives dinners and balls several times a week with a lot of Honolulu society—including the Hunnewells. Poor little Claudia is extremely angry over Zachary's "passion" for Bernice.

On the other hand, the "bright new star" of Honolulu, Miss Bernice Judson, is making her biggest play yet for Rafe. He appears to be giving her an open door!

And so dear cousin, I would advise you to return as soon as possible. If you do not, I sincerely believe a surprising new engagement

announcement may come in the next six months. The last I saw
Rafe he was riding about Honolulu in a fancy carriage with Bernice.
Your worried cousin, who is also your best friend,
Candace

———

Eden, angry, hurt to tears, and feeling hopeless, grabbed the nearest thing she could get her hands on and hurled it at the cottage door just as Ambrose called out and tapped at the door.

Eden flung her hand to her mouth and stared. *Oh no!*

"Eden? Are you all right?"

"Yes, come in. The door's not bolted."

She placed Candace's letter on her table and pushed it out of sight.

Ambrose entered, picked up the book on the founding of the Hawaiian alphabet by Hiram Bingham, and raised a bushy brow.

"Was this meant for my poor head or for Rafe Easton's?"

So he knew. Of course he would.

"That scoundrel." She turned her back and held in her tears.

Ambrose closed the door. "Yes, he can be one when he wishes. Right now he's enjoying the role."

"Is he," she said bitterly, "how nice for him—and 'Bunny.'"

"Now, now. I hear you're coming back with us in the morning. I am pleased, lass. You've made the right decision."

"Yes, and I'd already decided on going back before getting Candace's letter." She faced him, taking back the prized volume and setting it down gently with her other books. "So no one should think I'm rushing to Honolulu because of Rafe and Bernice."

"It may be a wise idea, Eden, to let Rafe know you do care what happens between him and Miss Judson."

"He already knows how I feel," she said. "Anyway, I don't know why I should be surprised." She looked at him. "About Rafe, I mean. I discussed with you on the ship that Rafe has cared about Parker

Judson's niece for a long time, even before he became serious with me." She thought of the picture and birthday card she had discovered in his cabin aboard the *Minoa*.

"Rafe may, or he may not be serious about seeing Miss Judson. I know he has become angry with you. I believe that's the cause for most of his recent actions."

Angry with me, she thought. *I'm the one wronged, not Mr. Easton.*

"Well, lass, he does have his vision again. God has treated him with loving-kindness in that important regard."

She had to admit she was glad to hear this news.

"I have hope that all these difficult issues can be worked out in due season," Ambrose said. "They can be, if misunderstandings are addressed before even larger ones bring their harvest. And mark my words: they will bring much unhappiness if stubbornness and pride reign in both of you. Regret will come calling in the future. The harvest will be a bitter one."

When Ambrose departed, Eden just stared at the closed door.

A restive spirit had settled over Honolulu, and Eden's emotions seemed to match its turmoil. No sooner had she returned to Kea Lani than a flurry of extended conflicts—of both family and Island politics—knocked at her door.

Now that she'd returned to Oahu, sooner or later she was bound to meet Rafe again. How would she react? She refused to let her heart dwell on their past. What was the good of it? The trial at Hanalei and losing his sight had caused him to confront his heart. In so doing he must have decided what he had previously tried to reject—that he was still in love with Bernice Judson.

What could she do about it? Hate him for the rest of her life? Bitterness over her disappointment could have one outcome: it would damage the rest of her life. She must put her trust in God, who had saved her soul and surely cared enough about her life to provide the way she should walk into the future.

If she longed for a meaningful relationship with a man, the last few months had revealed that the heart-to-heart union was not to be with Rafe Easton, however much she still loved him. Especially telling, he had not contacted her, not even to share the merciful news of how God had restored his vision!

If he could not even share that with her, then what remained of their relationship, and what could put it back together again?

Nothing—except the will and purpose of God. At present, it looked as though it was not His purpose.

Keep walking forward, relying on His love and grace. Underneath are the everlasting arms, she often quoted. *When I stumble—He will lift me up.*

She was also burdened by what Rebecca's journal had revealed about Kip's parentage. That revelation could overshadow Kip all his life. What would Rafe do if he learned the truth about the boy's biological father? The situation was dreadful. Yet, how could she keep such important information from him?

Eden had been home on Kea Lani with Dr. Jerome for several weeks. She was in the process of readjusting her ambitions so she could put her mother's journal into form for publication in a magazine or newspaper or even a book. She hoped Rebecca's experience would stir the conscience of many to do more for the Kalawao leper settlement. Her first step was to discuss her plan with Great-aunt Nora.

Eden, when attending Aunt Lana's nursing school in San Francisco, had spent a summer working as Nora's secretary on the final draft of a history she'd written on the first missionaries in 1820. Nora had written other short books on the Islands as well, and more recently, the Derrington family history. Whether or not Nora ever intended to continue the family chronicle was unknown. Presently she was agitated over the *Gazette* going into bankruptcy. The debts were climbing, and her attempts to get a loan had met with failure.

"Sometimes I believe that rapscallion brother of mine is influencing his banking allies to keep me from getting a loan. You know why, don't you, my dear Eden? We are loyal royalists, friends of the queen whose right it is to keep her throne. But Ainsworth is a rabid annexationist. He's a friend of that mischief-maker Thurston and the other members of the notorious Annexation Club. Vipers, all of them!"

For the most part, she agreed with Nora about Ainsworth hindering a loan, but she disagreed about Mr. Thurston and the annexationists striving for a republic form of government being rapscallions and vipers.

"I might have been able to get a loan from Rafe before this tragedy," Nora said mournfully.

So far, everyone Eden met since returning to Honolulu spoke of "the tragedy."

Eden didn't want to become involved in the problems Nora had with Rafe as a lender, but her great-aunt's countenance was so distraught that she felt prompted to ask about it.

"Why can't you request a loan from him now? From what I hear he's doing well again. He is even dividing his half of Hawaiiana with Keno and expecting no payment until Parker Judson is fully paid for the land."

"There's no doubt of that. You'll excuse me for saying this, Eden, but you seem strong enough to handle these matters—if he should marry the Judson heiress he will become one of the richest men in the Islands."

Eden shrugged, her heart beating with the same old struggle over anger. "Money isn't the answer to all things. Nor is health. Far greater lessons in life have been learned through poverty and illness than by owning Nob Hill mansions and winning Olympic medals."

"Well, all that may be, but money is exactly what I need right now. It would indeed solve my dilemma for the *Gazette*."

"So Aunt Nora, have you contacted Rafe since he's returned from San Francisco?"

"No, I hear he's none too pleasant these days."

Eden kept silent. *Well, I'm not about to contact him for another loan! Not even to save the* Gazette.

Nora returned to Tamarind House on Koko Head in defeat. When Eden heard a few days later that Nora had twisted her ankle while walking on a windy cliff, Eden was concerned enough to step into a dilemma that she would have otherwise avoided.

"She'll be all right," Zachary told her. "Dr. Corlay says nothing is broken. Even so, I want to go to Koko Head." He scowled. "There's something I want to check at the house. I've been thinking about it ever since Townsend escaped. Both Rafe and I think Townsend might have stayed there until he could pay some contact in the gambling cartel to take him out by private vessel."

Eden was interested at once. "I thought something like that myself soon afterwards. Marshal Harper never checked Tamarind."

"No," he said ruefully. "He was too busy with the obvious, checking public steamers. As if Townsend would be dumb enough to go out in public as beat-up as he was." He chuckled at the memory, and then stopped quickly. "I suppose I shouldn't have laughed—well, anyway, I'd like to take a look around the cellar, and all that. Just to see for myself if there's any evidence he was there. Rafe is almost sure of it."

"I'm coming with you," she said. "I want to know, too. And I need to talk to Nora about an idea I have to get a loan for the *Gazette*."

"A loan? You mean from Rafe?"

"No," she said abruptly. "I was not thinking of him."

She thought Rafe was deliberately taunting her. She had received an envelope that morning addressed to her. *Rafe Easton, The Royal Hotel*, was written in the upper right-hand corner. Inside was a bill for the clinic and four bungalows, the use of the *Minoa*, and, as if that wasn't enough: "Soon overdue" was written at the bottom with a bold underline.

Zachary glanced at her. "Just as well that you not ask Rafe. I don't think he'd give it to you. I don't know what's gnawing at him recently, but something sure is. I think it all began at the Judson mansion."

"Yes," she said with determined disinterest. "I'll go pack a few things. When do you want to leave?"

"No time like today, but we'd better have the noon meal first."

She was about to leave the room when she looked back. "Why can't Candace grant Nora a loan? They've always been close. She's at Tamarind now."

"Candace? Oh she would've bailed the *Gazette* out of its muck a year ago if she could use her inheritance. But she can't."

"What do you mean, *she can't?*"

"It's all tied up until she turns thirty. I thought you knew, she doesn't inherit a penny until then."

"By then we'll be sunk."

"All she has is her monthly allowance, but she said she's used most of that on her wedding trousseau.

Eden grew silent. She could have thrust the nasty bill Rafe had just sent her to Zachary to show Zachary how dreadful Rafe had become, but she held back. *No sense upsetting Zachary now.* Eden had wondered why Candace hadn't produced some of her inheritance money to help her future husband secure Hawaiiana. Now she knew why.

Eden did not wish to admit—especially now after the engagement to Rafe was broken and there was no hope of her owning Hawaiiana—that a faint germ of jealousy had lurked within her heart. That smidgen of jealousy nudged her within, just looking for a weak spot to fill her heart with resentment. Rafe had built the plantation house with her in mind. Now it would go to Candace.

Well, my eyes are green, she thought, *but I don't want to let the green-eyed monster of jealousy devour me. I'm happy for Candace and Keno. They're like brother and sister to me. Besides, I wouldn't have lived there often anyway. Rafe's heart was set on Hanalei. And I've let that slip through my fingers, too. Now it looks like Bernice will share it with him.*

"Candace will be wealthy someday," Zachary was saying, with the suggestion of envy in his voice. "She'll receive her father, Douglas's, inheritance and also what Grandfather hands over to her as his chief inheritor. I'll be fortunate if I inherit anything. With

Townsend a criminal and wasting what he did have on gambling debts," he said bitterly, "there won't be much of anything left to me. And even that will be divided with Silas—or maybe he'll get it all. Grandfather isn't likely to leave me much either. I was hoping to eventually get the *Gazette* from Aunt Nora, but that too, looks like it's turning to dust. You probably won't get much either, dear cousin. Uncle Jerome, I understand, can't pay Rafe for the clinic and bungalows."

"Oh, don't even remind me of that loan. The first payment is drawing near." *And if Rafe's mood is any indication, he'll enjoy holding his hand out,* she thought.

"Who's going to pay?"

She hadn't actually worried about the loan until now, since she'd expected to marry the "lender." Now, with her father too ill to work, all of that was left in ashes. The only thing that had survived was the dollar sign of debt.

Eden sighed. "I suppose I'll need to start making payments. I'll need to go back to work at Kalihi." Even with her full weekly pay she could not pay him off quickly.

"But Grandfather has begun giving me a monthly allowance," she said, pleased.

"You should have had that a few years ago, like the rest of us. Maybe we'll both end up in debtor's prison," he said morosely.

Maybe I will, Eden thought. *How much money has he spent on his little "Bunny" lately,* she wondered. Once again she had to nip the bud of bitterness before it bloomed.

Luncheon was served in the pleasant dining salon at Kea Lani before Eden and Zachary left for Koko Head. The doors onto the lanai stood open, revealing a stunning view of white sand and aquamarine sea. She never tired of that scene or took it for granted, even if she saw it every day.

She was weary, however, of the emotional tension crackling between Zachary and Silas. And to add a little more tension, ever since Grandfather Ainsworth had returned from the mainland, he was turning each meal into a discussion of annexation versus the Hawaiian royal throne.

Looking stately, garbed all in white, his small, neat beard glinting, he sat at the head of the long table while luncheon was served. He discussed with great concern the queen's "suspicious dealings" with her chief aid, a Hawaiian named Samuel Nowlein.

"Not proven at all, Grandfather," Zachary said, shaking his head. But Silas nodded. "Absolutely correct, Grandfather."

Ainsworth was lecturing: "And there are plans afloat at this very hour to throw out the '87 Constitution." He tapped on the table for emphasis. "A Constitution that is legally part of our governing system, signed by King Kalakaua. It is nonsense for the royalists to call it a 'Bayonet Constitution.' It's mere rhetoric to stir up the people.

"Liliuokalani, too, understood perfectly what was in the '87 Constitution. She willingly vowed to the legislature and cabinet, before she took the throne, that she would uphold it! But now! Ah, yes, but now! Now, if Thurston is right she plans to revoke it at the beginning of the year. There are secret meetings held in Iolani Palace and in Washington Place," he said of the queen's private residence, "with Samuel Nowlein and others about how to overthrow the Constitution and replace it with a new one that favors her sovereignty.

"If she does, it will be our signal to move. And this time, without backing down as we did with Kalakaua. She wants to go backward to a time in her brother's reign when the throne was absolute—and also corrupt—so she is free to do anything she or her constituents want at our expense.

"Well, we built *this* Hawaii. It was nothing before that. Nothing but grass huts. We planted the trees, introduced the sugar, the coffee, the pineapples, the buildings, and businesses. And we're not going to surrender it all now and have no voice in the way taxes and governmental decisions are made. I say we cannot have that kind of arbitrary rule in the Islands and survive for long. The times are different. We need to form a republic, just the way the colonies did in the United States in 1776!"

Eden was hardly listening. She was thinking of what Candace had told her before going to Koko Head about Rafe rebuilding Hanalei. At present, Celestine and Kip were living at Hawaiiana. After Candace and Keno were married, Celestine insisted she would leave for Hanalei on the Big Island, even though Candace said she could stay at Hawaiiana.

"As you know," Candace had told her, "there are plenty of rooms. So I told her how Keno and I would be pleased to have her stay on with Kip, but she intends to go to Hanalei just as soon as Rafe has the damaged rooms rebuilt. Rafe wants Kip to grow up on Hanalei rather than on Hawaiiana. Right now, Celestine is practically Kip's mother, grandmother, and governess all rolled into one. She's a wonderful woman."

Eden would never argue with that. Celestine had always treated her kindly and had supported Rafe's decision to marry her. What did Celestine think of him changing his mind and seeing a good deal of Bernice? Knowing Celestine, she would stay out of any conflict and support Rafe in whatever he did, just as Celestine had loved his father, Matt.

Thinking of Celestine and Kip brought Townsend to Eden's attention. Eden worried about Kip. What should she do about the startling knowledge of his biological father? Was it right to keep silent? She had still not told anyone. There was no one to gain advice from, since discussion would open the proverbial Pandora's box. She thought about going to Ambrose, but he might feel obligated to go to Rafe. Then, what? How would it affect Kip's future?

Eden realized her grandfather had changed the subject from annexation to his next favorite subject, the marriages of his two grandsons.

"It is past time for both of you stalwart young men to get married." He frowned at them. "I need the Derrington name to grow, and you two sit about and moon over the Judson girl as if she were the only one in all Honolulu. And you, Zachary—Miss Claudia

Hunnewell is the perfect young lady for you. She's tolerant and has nerves of steel."

Silas laughed. "She'll need nerves of steel with Zach's imagination running wild. Anyway, Miss Claudia told me that Zachary wants to marry Miss Judson. Whenever I see her around Honolulu, though, she's escorted by Rafe."

Ainsworth slapped his napkin next to his plate. "That was unnecessary, Silas."

"Zachary," Eden said calmly, "we need to leave for Great-aunt Nora's. I want to get to Tamarind House before the weather changes. The wind seems to be rising."

Zachary looked toward the lanai where the breezes were stirring the large potted ferns. "Yes, you're right." He stood and politely excused himself to Ainsworth who gave a brief nod.

While he ran upstairs to his room to get his overnight bag, Eden tried to smooth things over. "I'm sorry your luncheon was spoiled, Grandfather."

"Not at all, my dear." He shot another severe look at Silas who looked genuinely troubled about his slip of tongue.

"I apologize, Cousin Eden. I wasn't thinking as I should have in your presence."

She managed a smile. "I'm sure I'm not a bit offended at anything Mr. Easton is doing in Honolulu."

Grandfather Ainsworth cleared his throat. "Well you don't speak for me, my dear. I'm offended. I'd speak to Rafe about this broken engagement if I thought it would do any good."

"Please don't," she said, and rose from her chair. "Any hopeful message for Great-aunt Nora about a loan, Grandfather?"

Ainsworth smiled. "You tell my stubborn sister that the best thing to do is to sell the *Gazette*. I won't bail out a paper defending the corrupt monarchy—least of all one through which my own grandson, Zachary, is willing to give his family a black eye with stories of scandal."

Silas hadn't spoken; he stood by his chair until Eden left the dining salon.

Twenty minutes later, Eden met Zachary near the front door. They went down the steps to enter the waiting carriage.

"I should put an article in the *Gazette* about how to escape the Islands," he said stiffly as the carriage rolled away from the house.

"You can't put a story about Silas helping Townsend escape in the *Gazette*," she soothed. "You've no proof of that."

"Not yet."

"Then you can't print it. What will it gain any of us? And if you go against Grandfather's advice about protecting the family name, I believe he'll disinherit you as he warned."

"I've no doubt of that," he said bitterly. "He ran Rafe out of Honolulu a few years back, didn't he? All because Rafe supported the monarchy back then. So Rafe was fired from the *Gazette*. Grandfather could do that because he owned part of the paper then, but he doesn't own it now."

"Neither will Nora if she doesn't pay her debts," Eden said with dismay.

He looked at her, bringing his golden eyebrows together. "Did she mention that she's thinking of taking a loan out on Tamarind House?"

Eden turned her head, horrified. "Oh she wouldn't."

"She says she's considering it."

"Great-Grandmother Amabel's house! Oh, that's a horrid idea," Eden said. "For one thing, Tamarind is all she has. And it's part of our Derrington legacy. What if something should go wrong and she can't pay the loan. She'll loose an heirloom. And its family history means so much to all of us."

"Nora said it would be her last resort."

"When did she tell you this?"

"About a week ago."

"Strange, she never mentioned it to me. I saw her a few days ago."

"There's a reason why she didn't mention it to you." He looked at her, a twist to his smile. "The Judsons are interested in Tamarind House, or rather, I should say Bernice is. She's all but forgotten I'm alive since Rafe went to San Francisco."

"I'm sorry you care for her," she said, "but if you want my opinion—"

"I know you don't like her. But Rafe seems . . . Oh, sorry, I shouldn't be saying that."

"It's all right. He does like her. Very much, I would venture."

"I'm not that sure. Maybe that's why I'm not storming mad at him. He's strange recently. Seems unauthentic, if you follow me. Everyone notices he's different. It's mainly Bernice that tries to capture his attention. She's always having revelries and insisting that Parker Judson go and bring Rafe."

Well no one can force him to go unless he wants to, she thought. She gripped her seat. Bernice again. Stepping in, taking over, daring to push her aside as clutter in the way of her fashionable shoes.

"Bernice had one look at the house and nearly begged Parker Judson to buy it."

"She was at Koko Head? When did she see the house?" she asked curiously.

"Well I don't like to say it, but I think she was with Rafe."

Eden felt a ripple of anger.

"If it hadn't been that Nora wisely hesitated on a sale, the deal may have been signed, sealed, and delivered as they say, by now."

"It isn't right," Eden murmured. "Anything as important as Tamarind House should first be talked over by the rest of the family. Nora just can't sell it!"

"I'm afraid she can," Zachary said, "and she will before she loses the *Gazette*."

"If that's true, she may have something to hold over Ainsworth's head. He wouldn't be pleased if she sold the house. Nor is the *Gazette* worth an exchange for Tamarind House."

"Actually," he said with a sigh, "I don't think so either. But we don't have anything to say about the transaction. Of course, she may not do anything so drastic. Let's hope so, anyway."

"We've got to get Nora a loan," she said. "There must be someone with money."

He looked at her. "Rafe. As I said earlier, I don't think you'll get far, but you can always try."

"But Rafe brought Bernice to Tamarind to try and influence Nora to sell."

"Oh, no, not that, I'm sure that wasn't the reason."

"But you said—" she began.

He looked at her. "I'd better tell you. Rafe came to Tamarind a few days ago with the same intention I have: to see if there's any evidence Townsend may have stayed there until he could safely get to the mainland. I don't know if he found what he was looking for. He hasn't clued me in. Not that I've seen him since.

"I don't know how Bernice happened to be with him. She has her whims, and when she has them, she gets what she wants." He jerked a shoulder with irritation. "She may have run into him accidentally, or pretended it was like that. I can see her coming along, and when she saw the place she decided then and there how much she liked it. Once she liked it—she wanted it."

Eden studied Zachary. His tone and insight took her by surprise. "You don't sound as enamored with her as you once were."

He shrugged. "I'm not," he admitted. "Silas was wrong. Seeing how she'd turn her back on me to track Rafe showed how undependable she really is. Silas made a remark at the table about my interest in Bernice, but he was out of date."

Eden was pleased to hear this. She hadn't actually thought Zachary was truly in love with Bernice as he'd claimed. Eden continued to think Claudia Hunnewell was more adjusted to Zachary's moods and temperament. Claudia loved him, and was a girl who did not easily ruffle. Although a Hunnewell and wealthy, she wasn't spoiled. At least their grandfather was right about Zachary marrying Claudia, even if he'd gone wrong concerning Keno. Now, thankfully, he'd come to respect and like Keno, and wholeheartedly supported their engagement. Their wedding was within three months. As for Ainsworth's support of her past engagement— he was grieving the loss of Rafe.

—◦⌒◦—

The ferryboat ride to Koko Head, where Tamarind was located, was pleasant with calm blue waters and a partially clear sky. The ferry arrived at the landing near Kuapa Pond at Maunalua. Eden and Zachary left the boat, and took the vine-tangled path to the horse road, where a horse and buggy waited for them.

Eden noticed that Zachary was deep in thought as he paid special attention to his surroundings. She believed she knew what was on his mind. This isolated area and the land about it was so thick with wild lantana and palms that it provided an excellent cover for any person who wished to keep out of sight.

The horse road, which had been rough in places, was now level and smooth. As they rounded the bend, the house came into bright view, set on a terraced hillside with a wall of leafy tropical greens— emerald and lime-colored with splashes of crimson, pink, and yellow blooms. A strong structure, three stories high, Tamarind greeted them with memories, both light and dark. The buggy was halted on the familiar lava rock court, and as Zachary and Eden stepped down, Candace came to meet them, smiling cheerfully.

"She's getting better. At first I feared her ankle injury was serious. The doctor assures us nothing is broken, just a mild sprain. She's waiting for us in the parlor with refreshments. Come along."

Neither Eden nor Zachary mentioned their suspicion that Townsend had hidden in the house during Nora's stay at the Royal Hotel in Honolulu.

After refreshments, as the sun was setting, and they were informed that dinner wouldn't be served until eight, Eden saw Zachary slip toward the back of the house. She knew he was headed for the basement or the trash hut in the backyard. She wanted to follow him for she had her own suspicions to satisfy, but after assisting Great-aunt Nora to her room to rest for an hour, Candace drew Eden away.

Eden decided there was no reason to be anything but forthright about the dilemma they faced, and Grandfather Ainsworth refusing to give Nora a loan.

"Tell me, Candace, were you here with Nora when Rafe and Bernice came?"

Candace raised her delicate auburn eyebrows and seemed to measure Eden's mood. She must have decided that she was strong enough for the jolt.

"Yes I was. Bernice is beautiful, but I think she's soulless."

"Soulless? Everyone has a soul."

"Oh, you know what I mean—without a conscience, or any genuine depth."

"What makes you say that?"

"Well, the way she floated about, looking like the cover of a magazine, making over the house as if she were a child insisting on a certain bonbon."

"I don't know her very well. I only saw her one Christmas holiday."

"She lived in Honolulu for a while when we were growing up. I used to play with her sometimes. Even then she had to win at everything, from ball and jacks to hide-and-seek. I can understand what most men see in her. You would too, if you were around her long enough. I'm just glad she never decided she wanted my Keno."

"What I am really trying to learn is whether or not she was serious about gaining control of Tamarind. Zachary seems to think so. He thinks she will talk her father into offering Nora a great amount of money."

Candace lounged on her daybed, twisting a ring of her lovely auburn hair around one finger. The diamond engagement ring from "her Keno" sparkled. Eden rejoiced to see it. Candace had never appeared so contented and happy as she had these few weeks since Eden had come home from Kalawao. Such satisfaction was a long time in coming, and to see her coolheaded cousin finally reap this reward was enough to cheer Eden's heart.

"Yes, I do think Bernice was serious about wanting Tamarind. I know she offered Nora a large price, right in front of Rafe."

Eden tensed. "Did he side with her?"

Candace looked off into the distance. "Well, you know Rafe better than I do. You know how he can be absolutely—what's the word . . ."

"Enigmatic," Eden said coolly.

"Yes. Sometimes it's difficult to know what he's thinking. He's a master at shielding his emotions."

"He said nothing to Nora about doing as Bernice asked?"

"Nothing. Actually, he just wandered off somewhere in back and returned later."

She refused to feel mollified that Rafe had not tried to talk Nora into selling Tamarind. As far as wandering out back, she knew the reason for that—to look for evidence that Townsend had stayed here. She wondered if he'd found anything.

"Candace, we simply cannot let Nora sell this house. Like I told Zachary, it's a family holding, full of history and memories. We must do something to keep her from such an error. She's so worried about losing the *Gazette* she may decide to exchange a real Derrington treasure for a failing news journal. That would be a tragedy, and Grandfather is in a fighting mood."

Eden went on to tell her about the disagreement at luncheon between Zachary and Silas, and what he'd threatened to reveal in the *Gazette*.

"He wouldn't do that. He doesn't know Silas aided Townsend. I understand the cause for tension between them, but Silas is family. Anyway, Nora wouldn't allow that in her paper."

"A loan," Eden murmured, pacing. "I have to find someone who will lend enough money to save the paper."

"There's no alternative that I can see," Candace said. "I'll speak with Grandfather again and try to make him see his family obligation, though annexation always becomes an issue. I suppose the families who lived through the American Civil War faced many of our same problems. Loyalty versus one's divided family."

Eden agreed, still pacing.

"We're left with Grandfather, or Rafe," Candace said.

I shall never go to Rafe Easton! How can I?

—ᗉᘉ—

Though Eden refused to entertain the idea of turning to Rafe to save the *Gazette*, she had a strong motivation to contact him about the information her mother, Rebecca, had revealed about Kip's parentage.

When Eden wasn't in a dilemma about how to help Nora, she worried about how to handle the critical information on Kip without hurting anyone involved. She had prayed about it, and continued to do so.

Meanwhile she kept the journal and diary hidden in her room at Kea Lani until she could begin writing the material into weekly installments for the *Gazette*. Sometimes Eden became so troubled about the facts concerning Kip and Rafe that she pondered destroying those sections of the journal.

When Eden returned to Kea Lani she went straight to her bedroom to make sure the journal remained secure in its hiding place. Not that anyone was interested enough in Rebecca to remove it. The Derringtons had small interest. She had not come from an important sugar-raising or political family with many friends and relatives. Rebecca and Lana Stanhope had been raised by a widowed father who had died years earlier. He'd been one of those gold and silver seekers who had never discovered anything "but an ache in his back," as Aunt Lana had once told her.

He'd died when his horse threw him on a mountainous road. Rebecca and Lana were placed in a Christian home for orphans, and then separated for some years before they tracked each other down in San Francisco. People they didn't know had paid for their upbringing and schooling—Rebecca as a schoolteacher and Lana as a nurse. Through a local church they had heeded the call to missions and had come to the Islands. Everything else about Rebecca was now ancient history, including the Derringtons' unenthusiastic reception of Rebecca as Dr. Jerome Derrington's wife.

So, Eden thought, no one in the elite sugar families would steal a journal of her mother's trials as a leper! Eden's hopes to have the journal in print were directed toward the compassion of outsiders who would want to help the exiles.

Satisfied about the journal, she checked her personal mail and saw an envelope from Rafe's mother at Hawaiiana pineapple plantation. Eden opened it quickly.

The message was in answer to one Eden had sent to Celestine before going with Zachary to Tamarind House. She read: "Dearest Eden, so pleased to hear from Rafe that Dr. Jerome is recovering from his serious ailment, and that you are safely back in Honolulu."

Eden paused. From Rafe? Then he knew about the circumstances in which she had returned. A small pleasure in learning he'd mentioned it to his mother lightened her heart. The optimism fizzled quickly. More than likely Celestine had asked about matters at Kea Lani and Rafe casually informed her of what happened.

Eden read on: "As to your question about our little Kipper, no, sadly, the adoption has not yet gone. Everything was prepared for signing the papers in San Francisco when Rafe lost his sight. I need not tell you about that horrible situation. You understand, perhaps better than anyone, what the possibility of blindness meant to my son. You can appreciate his dilemma about whether to go through with the signing, or to wait for further evidence the adoption was God's purpose. Rafe did not believe his sight would return, and was not willing to take on the responsibility for Kip's sake. Evidently you thought the same."

Eden frowned. *I thought the same? I never implied such a thing. Now where did that come from?*

179

She kept reading: "Rafe decided to wait until he knew he could raise Kip in the way he'd planned. Now there's been a legal delay again, and so we must wait. Meantime, Kipper is quite happy. He calls Rafe 'Da-da' and doesn't know the difference between adoption and biological birth. At least not yet. When he does I'm sure matters will have been worked out and he will become Daniel 'Kip' Easton.

"Do come by Hawaiiana and visit me when you've opportunity. I'll be here until Candace and Keno marry in September."

Celestine's answer had complicated matters. How could she tell Rafe that Townsend had fathered Kip in a drunken spree? Would it be wrong to destroy the information to protect Rafe, and Kip's future?

And yet keeping the facts hidden from him would also be an injustice. Adopting Kip was a grave responsibility. Rafe had a right to know all that was involved.

Another thought troubled her. Since Rafe hadn't signed the adoption papers would he now find it easier to not do so? And the boy himself—how would the shocking story of his parentage affect his life?

And what about the bond Bernice was forming with Kip? Eden saw Bernice's actions as a mere connivance to build a stronger connection with Rafe. What would a woman like Bernice Judson care about an illegitimate baby from a leper colony?

Eden sat down, forehead on her palm, and stared at the restful light blue carpet as if it held the answer to her dilemma.

The complicated matter was too serious to ignore or keep locked away in her knowledge. And perhaps the Lord did not intend for her to carry the burdensome decision on her own. She was no longer going to marry Rafe, and Kip was not her prospective adoptee, but Rafe's.

Eden made up her mind. She would need to tell the facts as they were to Rafe. What he did with the information would be entirely up to him. In fairness to Rafe, it was her mother Rebecca who had first turned Kip over to him.

With the decision made, she felt a load of worry slip from her shoulders and stood to her feet.

She would find out when Rafe was next at Hawaiiana and rally her courage to go there. She hadn't any doubt that he would receive her. Especially when she let it be known that Kip was the reason for the meeting.

Chapter Sixteen
Serpentine Smile

At Kea Lani, Eden hurried downstairs and onto the front lanai facing the carriageway. Yes, her horse and buggy were still there under the shade of the clustered coconut palms. She wanted to get the meeting with Rafe over as quickly as possible. She left the lanai and dashed down the stone steps.

The trip to Hawaiiana was not long, maybe five minutes inland after she reached the turnoff to the mission church near the old Easton pearl lagoon, which had been so long in the greedy hands of Uncle Townsend. Recently the pearl lagoon, along with the Kona coffee plantation, Hanalei, were returned to the rightful heir, Rafe, whose father had developed both.

Eden scanned the distant hills of green foliage among dark boulders.

It was nearing four o'clock when she arrived at the pearl fishery, less than a half mile from the mission church. A new road had been cut and cleared to reach inland toward the mountains. Sitting on the edge of her seat and holding the reins in gloved hands as the buggy bumped along the ungraded road, Eden scanned the land. The mission church stood alone in the field, and the thatched roof bungalow Ambrose and Noelani lived in sat nearby among tropical shrubbery and palm trees.

If Rafe hadn't intervened, Parker Judson would have torn down the bungalow and mission church when the two partners first began laying out the land for Hawaiiana.

On either side of the road the land had already been cleared for planting—land that stretched to an invisible bright blue horizon. The earth was a rich brownish-red, perfect for growing. The direct sunlight was hot, the trade wind refreshing, and she felt a certain pang of loss. Rafe had once meant for her to be a part of this, and even the big plantation house had been constructed with her in mind.

How could she have let it slip through her fingers? And yet she had, a little at a time through her delays in her love relationship with Rafe Easton. For the last two years it was *wait, wait* until finally, she supposed, he had wearied of it all and turned to Bernice Judson.

Now Rafe's half of Hawaiiana was divided between him and Keno, and she would never live in the great house. It would go to Candace. Bernice would have Rafe and Hanalei—plus all of Parker Judson's holdings—to bring to her marriage.

It seemed to Eden that her long-laid plans of going to Molokai to meet her mother and to work with her father had ended with little of blessing in return for her service. She had a fistful of wind, as the saying went.

Since she'd lost Rafe Easton, perhaps another man would be in her future. But if so, where was he? As she looked down the long narrow road, it was empty, just the way her heart felt. She did not think any more love was left in her life to give to another man. It had always been Rafe. Without him there was no one. She would probably end up like Aunt Lana who'd been nearing her fortieth birthday before marrying Dr. Clifford Bolton. And now that they were married, he'd contracted leprosy.

Eden! How cynical you have become. Where is your trust in the goodness and loving-kindness of your heavenly Father? Does He not have the best plans for His children? Those plans may not always seem to be what is desired or expected by the human heart, but in eternity's view, when it comes to reaping eternal rewards, His plans lived out by faith in His provision are more precious than gold.

Why are you cast down O my soul, and why are you disquieted within me? Hope in God.

Eden looked toward Mauna Loa. A haze robed the mountain with mixed shades of charcoal, purple, and green. *How often does a mist come between our vision of trusting God, and the long path we are walking, sometimes struggling, or through barren places? Yet, the Lord knows the way.*

The palms and ferns rustled along the road. Eden stopped the buggy beneath several large crepe myrtle trees in full magenta bloom. With the plantation house directly before her, she dropped the reins, climbed down, and looked toward the entrance.

She straightened her shoulders, took a deep breath, and dashed up the steps to the front porch. She rapped the bronze door knocker.

Noelani opened the door. Surprise crossed her pleasant face and then vanished into an expression of consternation.

"Eden, dear, what are you doing here?" Her voice was lowered and she looked past Eden's shoulder to see if anyone was with her.

"I need to see Rafe. Is he here?"

Before Noelani could reply a voice called from another room, "Who is there, Noelani?"

Footsteps sounded, and Eden, believing it was Celestine, smiled in greeting.

Her smile fell as she saw Miss Bernice Judson.

Noelani stepped aside and Eden came through the door. She removed her sun hat and met the frosty blue eyes of the beautiful young woman with fair hair, and an afternoon dress of expensive embroidered silk, artfully chosen to match her eye color.

"Why, you must be the nurse I've heard so much about. Eden Derrington, isn't it? And fresh from the leper camp—oh my, but interesting. Do come in," she said as if she were the lady of the house.

The voice and words were socially polite enough, but Eden felt the unmistakably condescending attitude.

"I'm Bernice Judson," she continued. "My uncle is Parker Judson, a man you've no doubt heard of."

Just about everyone in Honolulu knew who Parker Judson was. Was she offering a reason for her own importance?

At first Eden's emotions balked. But she reined them in. There was no reason why Bernice could not visit Hawaiiana if she was welcomed, as no doubt she was. Eden reminded herself she no longer had a right to question Rafe Easton's social agenda or what women he preferred for company.

"You may remember me from the Christmas holidays of two years ago when I came from Nob Hill to visit," Bernice went on. "I believe Zachary is your cousin?"

"Yes he is—and Miss Candace Derrington."

For some reason Bernice's smile froze at the mention of Candace. *Now what is this about?*

"Oh yes, Candace. She's going to marry a half-Hawaiian isn't she?"

Her superiority was offensive. "Yes, a wonderfully gifted man, and very handsome, too. Keno Hunnewell. She's a fortunate woman. I doubt any woman alive could take him away from her. He is wise."

The smile was perfect, the social amenities all that were to be expected, but Eden found the blue eyes that measured her to be cold. "So Oliver Hunnewell told me."

So that was the reason she disliked Candace. Candace had turned down Oliver for Keno. Why should that bother Bernice? Perhaps once she had been after Oliver and lost him to Candace? Then, for Candace to turn him down for Keno would sting one whose pride assumed she could win any man she wanted.

Bernice kept smiling, the perfect model of poise and grace, undoubtedly developed from practice at some elite finishing school.

Eden noticed that Noelani hovered in the background looking

concerned. Bernice noticed Noelani, too, for she turned toward her. "That will be all, Noelani. Why don't you go and see if Mrs. Celestine is ready for her tea. I believe she wants it served in her room upstairs."

Of all the nerve, Eden thought. What was she doing playing hostess and giving orders?

Noelani seemed about to speak. Then she must have changed her mind, and with a polite nod of her gray head, took her leave.

Bernice looked at Eden as if they shared a secret. "One must be firm with servants. I've found them to be too inquisitive."

"Noelani isn't a servant," Eden said tonelessly. "She's family to us."

A golden eyebrow elegantly lifted. "Even to Rafe?"

Eden firmed her mouth and kept silent. She could not speak for Rafe Easton any longer.

Bernice kept her smile in place, but didn't budge from her stance in the hall as if keeping the way to the "king" blocked from "the unwashed peasant."

Eden, too, stood her ground—just as graciously, she hoped.

"Can you tell me whether Rafe Easton is here, or in the fields?" she asked pointedly, letting Bernice know she would not be intimidated in Hawaiiana House. To be treated as an unwanted stranger in this home that was built for her pricked Eden's pride.

The tension between them crackled.

"Rafe is upstairs in his office. I'm afraid he can't see you at the moment."

Eden remained silent.

"I'm sure you'll understand," Bernice continued, her voice as warm as honey. "He's been so busy recently. Did you know he is running for a new seat in the legislature? It was Uncle Parker's wonderful suggestion. We made our plans while in San Francisco. So, he's backing Rafe to run for a seat. He'll win. Uncle will campaign for him, and Rafe has asked me to do a little tour with him —nothing too much, you know, just saying a few words to the crowd and pointing out what a fine representative he's been. So I'm sure that as an intelligent woman you will understand that he does not wish to be *troubled* at present."

"Oh? Did Rafe tell you so? I didn't realize you had become his secretary."

Bernice's lips tightened. Eden felt malice in her stare.

"Rafe told me he did not care to be disturbed by anyone. If *you* insist—*he* is a gentleman. So, I suppose I could go up and disturb him."

"Miss Judson, if I cared to insist on seeing Rafe Easton, I would ask Noelani to bring him my message. I wouldn't be asking you."

That must have stung, for Bernice lost her poise and stared at her with an expression Eden could not interpret.

"I'll see him another time," Eden said with a calmness she did not feel, "a more convenient time for the both of us. Sorry to have disturbed *you*, Miss Judson."

Eden turned toward the door to leave. She glanced at the stairway and saw Rafe. He was casually dressed in a loose white shirt, and didn't appear at all as if he'd been hard at work, unable to be disturbed.

The moment Eden saw him, she experienced the same emotion she'd known in his presence for years—only now mingled with vexation. How long had he been standing there, leaning on the banister with arms folded, watching and listening?

The scoundrel! He looked amused, as watching a drama on a theater stage. What was he thinking of two young women locking horns over him?

She tried to keep her heart from running away as their gaze held. She felt a flame of challenge in his dark eyes.

If I were a man, Eden thought, *I'd feel as if he just threw down the gauntlet and demanded I pick it up.*

"Oh, Rafe, I didn't expect you," Bernice said, walking toward the stairs, her dress rustling. She paused in a theatrical pose, one jeweled hand on the banister, looking up at him in a deliberate show of her profile. What would the dramatic Bernice produce next? Eden wondered. A dagger—and threaten to plunge it into her beautiful, tortured heart over this romantic triangle?

"I was telling Miss Derrington you were crowded with desk work and may not wish to be disturbed. I knew we were having dinner with Uncle Parker tonight at the beach house and that you wanted to get as much done as you could before we left."

Eden looked at Rafe. Somehow she expected him to come to her defense in this awkward moment. She couldn't explain why she expected this. Except in the past he'd always been there for her. She'd momentarily forgotten that the situation was far different between them now.

When he said nothing, Eden's pride rose in full force. He was refusing to reach out to her. *Very well, Rafe Easton.*

Eden managed a gracious smile of her own. "Oh that is quite all right, Miss Judson. I would never wish to interrupt such a busy *man—and* his secretary. Nor the dinner at the beach house with dear Uncle Parker. I shall be on my way, thank you. I've other matters to attend."

Eden turned and opened her own door. She was passing through onto the porch when she could not resist the opportunity to turn around with a sweet smile: "The only reason I stopped by was to discuss a matter concerning Kip. But I shall contact Mrs. Celestine in a few days and give the information to her to pass on to her busy son. Good day."

Rafe straightened from his laconic stance but Eden did not wait. She had made her sword thrust, and now she needed to sidestep before he could parry. She snapped the door shut behind her, and dashed down the steps and across the yard to her buggy. She knew him well. She had to get away before he could catch up. She heard the door open.

Hurry! she told herself.

She'd always been quick on her feet when other girls seemed hindered with skirts and fancy shoes. She looked back over her shoulder. Yes, he was coming. He swung effortlessly over the porch rail and was on her track.

Scoundrel! She jerked her skirt up and stepped into the buggy in a flash.

She snatched the reins, hearing his steps coming across the yard. "Away Kona, away!"

The horse moved quickly as if bound for green meadows—

Then Rafe whistled; Kona's ears pricked up, she whinnied, then slowed, prancing to an obedient halt, shaking her flowing white mane.

Eden shouted: "No, Kona! Away! *Hurry!*"

The horse suddenly pulled forward, its mane flying.

"*Good* Kona!" Eden cried with a laugh. Glancing behind her shoulder she saw Rafe standing with hands on hips looking after her. She lifted a hand and waved goodbye.

Back at Kea Lani, Eden was puzzled over Bernice Judson's behavior. Why would she feel such a strong need to hinder Eden's meeting with Rafe? Why would a woman as beautiful as Bernice, with the benefit of a large inheritance in her future, feel the need to be so deceptive to win the man she wanted?

She must still see me as a strong competitor. It's possible she doesn't feel as secure about him falling out of love with me as she likes to pretend.

Eden mused. Maybe she had some hold over Rafe Easton after all.

Chapter Seventeen
Invitation to Iolani Palace

A few days later at Kea Lani, Eden sat at a table under a
canopy on the sloping lawn. She was enjoying morning tea
with Candace. She watched her cousin frown with intensity as she
poured over fine samples of drapery materials.

Eden's mind drifted inevitably to Rafe and his unexpected
silence on Kip. Strange, after two days she would have thought he
would contact her on the matter so important to him. He had
responded instantly on the stairs when she had tossed him the bait,
just as she had expected him to react when anything concerning the
little boy surfaced. Was it possible he already knew?

No, she thought again, *how could he? His reaction at Hawaiiana
showed surprise and concern.*

Then why was there no message from him, wanting to know
what she was keeping back? Could he be waiting for her to contact
him again? Not likely. She had made it clear that she would not,
and the chess piece was in his hand. And it would remain there, she
decided.

Candace was pondering two samples. "The drapes now in the

master bedroom are much too dark. I asked Keno whatever was Rafe thinking of by installing dark blue shades in the bedroom. Keno gave me one word." Candace smiled. *"Sleep."*

Eden also smiled. "I thought the bedroom draperies arrived yesterday?"

"Oh they did. They're upstairs in the linen closet. But I told Keno we should have new draperies installed in all of the upper rooms of Hawaiiana."

Just then, Eden noticed an envelope on the table that had gotten pushed aside by the samples. She saw her own name in Great-aunt Nora's handwriting.

"Nora sent me a message from the hotel?"

"Oh! Yes, I forgot." Candace picked it up and handed it to Eden. "It came in this morning's delivery."

Undoubtedly Nora was writing to discuss any corrections for the first installment of Rebecca's journal. Eden had signed a legal document giving the rights of publication to the *Gazette*.

If "Rebecca's Story," as it was titled, was successful in sales that would help Great-aunt Nora begin paying off some of the paper's mounting debts.

Eden opened the envelope and read a quite different message:

Eden, dear.

July 7th is just two days away. As you know this is the pleasant evening for Queen Liliuokalani's ball at Iolani given for the legislature.

The queen says there will be dancing: lancers, waltzes, polkas, gallops, and a minuet. This will be followed by what she calls "a tasty and bounteous supper" served in the state dining room. I can only say the ball will be most enjoyable.

As a dependable ally of the queen, I have received an invitation. I cannot decline without appearing most ungrateful, and perhaps rude.

However, it is unfortunate, because I find I must decline unless you come along as my guest, which I am permitted to bring. I will need you to assist me. My ankle is much stronger now, but the stairs there can be difficult. Besides, dear, it has been much too long since you gave yourself some pleasant entertainment. I do believe you need to rest your mind from so many worries.

Zachary, dear boy, will serve as our male escort, a necessity, I fear. The queen knows he writes news stories and articles in favor of her rule. She also knows he is the grandson of Ainsworth, one of the instigators of agitation in the Islands. She also understands that you and Jerome fully support her.

Do come, and do wear a special gown, won't you?

Oh, by the by. I have heard that the handsome Oliver P. Hunnewell has returned to the Islands from San Francisco. I was quite shocked to hear this, I must say. Although his father Thaddeus is one of the main rabble-rousing annexationists, Oliver is known to oppose the Hawaiian Annexation League.

Since I am not certain you were ever properly introduced to Oliver, I shall take the opportunity at Iolani Palace to do so.

Great-aunt Nora.

Eden was surprised at the news. Now why would Oliver Hunnewell return to the Islands so soon after leaving for the mainland? Eden understood that his father, Thaddeus P. Hunnewell, had mustered the call to family dignity by forcing his son to leave Honolulu when he did. Oliver had caused a societal scandal by fighting with Keno over Candace. When the men had come to blows in Oliver's garden, he had demanded that the marshal arrest Keno for attacking him. Oliver could not have returned to Honolulu without his father's approval.

Eden glanced cautiously over the edge of the letter at Candace, hoping she was not paying much heed to what it might contain. With relief, she saw Candace remained absorbed in choosing her new drapery. Would it upset her unduly to learn that Oliver was back in Honolulu just three weeks before her wedding? Eden decided it was best not to mention Candace's old fiancé when Candace was having such fun as future mistress of Hawaiiana's Great House.

Whether trouble would spring up depended on Oliver's reason for returning to the Islands. Did it have anything to do with Candace, or was there something else?

In the past, Grandfather Ainsworth had planned, and even *schemed*, to compel Candace to marry Oliver. Thankfully, that battle from a bygone "family war" remained in the past. Candace's tenacity in marrying the man she loved had won the day without a hint of conflict remaining between her and Grandfather.

With the divisive winds of power politics blowing strongly, Eden naturally believed Oliver's motives in returning to the Islands at this time were politically rooted. From a young age he had shown himself adept at politics, winning a seat in the legislature just a year after returning from a British university. He and Rafe were perhaps the youngest men to have held seats in the legislature. While attending a dinner at the Hunnewell house, Candace had overheard a conversation between Oliver and an Englishman in service to the British minister Wodehouse, discussing spying for the British. She'd used this information to get Grandfather Ainsworth to reconsider his insistence upon marriage to Oliver.

Did Rafe know Oliver was in Honolulu? If he did Keno probably knew, even if Candace did not. Keno was not likely to greet the news of his old rival's return tranquilly.

Later that day in her room at Kea Lani house, Eden reread Great-aunt Nora's letter to decipher her insinuations. If Eden's attempt at reading between the lines was in any way correct, it sounded to her as if Nora was suggesting that she, Eden, consider Oliver Hunnewell as a romantic investment now that Rafe Easton was no longer viable.

—⁂—

The evening of the queen's royal dinner was a warm and humid evening in July. Zachary arrived home at Kea Lani early from the *Gazette.* She noted a certain excitement in his otherwise ice-blue eyes that hadn't been there at breakfast, putting her on alert. When she casually mentioned his demeanor, he took her into the library and shut the door. He looked at her nervously.

"I've been a clever hound on the trail of *the* fox."

Oh, no. In Zachary's mind *the* fox could be none other than Silas.

"A big story will soon break in the *Gazette,*" he said.

"Do be cautious. Your good graces with Grandfather depend on not attacking the Annexation League. If your big story concludes with the name of Silas *Derrington,* you know what Grandfather's reaction will be."

Zachary shrugged. "Grandfather just won't accept the truth, but that won't put a hurdle in my way. Even when I try to please him, he has some other reason to criticize me. Did you know Oliver Hunnewell's back in Honolulu?"

She admitted she did, and he went on, "I wonder how Candace is going to take this?" He looked toward the mantelpiece to the clock. "Anyway, that's all I can say now. I'm going over to the hotel to talk to Rafe. Then I'll pick up Nora. Then we'll come by for you this evening for the ball. Oh—I'd better bring my dinner clothes. I'll change at Rafe's."

Later that evening while Eden prepared herself for the elaborate ball at Iolani Palace her concerns were mounting over Silas. She had an impression that he was aware of trouble and was worried. Zachary must have information that would diminish him in Ainsworth's eyes.

Candace had come to Eden's room to help arrange her hair and to share her pearls to match Eden's exquisite gown. Candace got on fairly well with Silas. Eden turned in the chair at the vanity table and looked at her thoughtfully.

"Do you think Silas is behaving—well, sort of strange recently?"

Eden dared ask, knowing that such a discussion could lead to more trouble.

Candace paused with comb in hand obviously surprised.

"Strange? Suspicious! Well, I can't say I've noticed anything as bizarre as all that. Why?"

Eden drummed her fingers on the table looking at herself in the round mirror. "Perhaps it's my imagination. I've thought him pensive and rather worried about something recently. I've tried to get him to talk, but he merely smiles at me, as if I'm a little girl in pigtails."

Candace laughed. "He's a lone wolf all right. I noticed that since the time he arrived. I do think he's beginning to mellow a wee bit, though. I know he does talk a lot with Ambrose."

That caught her interest and brought some hope to her heart. "Oh? How do you know that?"

"I've seen them together walking around the mission church, or on the road to Hawaiiana. I admit, like you, I'm rather taken aback. Silas is such a cynic I wouldn't have thought a man like Ambrose would fit his mindset. But I do see them together."

Eden found the news encouraging. She knew well enough what a praying man Ambrose was, and she admired him for it. Everyone was busy *doing*, but few spent time in the warfare of intercession to God—including herself. She sighed.

"I'm happy to hear it," Eden said as Candace went back to work on her hair. "Ambrose must be answering Silas's questions about God. Silas is so unhappy."

"I don't know why he should be. He is getting more opportunity from Grandfather than Zachary. He's almost in the place of a son rather than grandson. After what happened with Townsend I think Grandfather is overreacting to the loss."

"I wouldn't mind Grandfather making Silas a son, if—"

"If what?" Candace formed the last steps of the popular upsweep, making sure several fashionable curls remained near Eden's neck and temples.

"If I were confident Silas was as loyal to Grandfather as everyone assumes he is."

Candace watched her thoughtfully. "Now that's a strange thing to say, Eden. Why wouldn't Silas be loyal to his own grandfather? Look at all Grandfather's done for him."

Eden did not want to pursue the topic too far. She said simply, "Well he does have some mysterious friends, or maybe I should call them associates, or acquaintances."

She was thinking of the strange couple she had heard Silas speaking with months earlier in the garden. She hadn't given much, if any, thought to the matter with so many other concerns in her heart. But it was surfacing in her mind once more. Was there anything to it?

"I cannot say I've noticed anything unusual," Candace said. "However, don't pay too much attention to my ignorance. You know how absorbed I've become with the wedding next month."

"Oh that's quite understandable." She looked at her curiously. "Candace, you've never told me your views on the annexation issue. Made up your mind yet?"

"Well, I wasn't invited to the queen's ball," Candace said wryly. "That should tell you how the royalists think of me."

"Yes, I suppose so. Like grandfather, like favorite granddaughter," and Eden smiled.

Candace laid the comb down, finished with Eden's hair. "I wish you and Zachary wouldn't keep suggesting I'm the favored one. I am not. I am merely the only child of Grandfather's firstborn son and it's cultural to—" She stopped, and her mouth curved into an ironic smile.

Eden laughed. "It is cultural to favor a firstborn grandchild perhaps?"

"Well—it's not my fault. And anything Grandfather leaves to me, I'll gladly share with you and Zachary."

"Oh you silly thing." Eden was on her feet and hugging her, smiling. "I shouldn't have brought it up. I am not a bit jealous. You've always been generous. Why even tonight, look at the pearls you've brought me—and this gown. Even when I lived in the bungalow with Ambrose and Noelani you were generous."

"Oh I wish it had never happened. It was wrong! Plain sinful, if you want my opinion on how you were treated. You were always a Derrington, and you had every right to share in the family blessings as Zachary and I did. When I was younger I should have done more for you. I should have spoken up and made an issue of it with Grandfather and Great-aunt Nora—but I did not. I'm ashamed of it."

Eden grew serious. She thought of the times as a young girl when she had watched Candace in the role of Grandfather Ainsworth's favorite. Back then, with Eden longing for her father, Jerome, and believing Rebecca dead, she would have given almost anything to exchange places with Candace—just to bask in the approval she had seen Grandfather Ainsworth shower on Candace.

Eden no longer desired that favored position, nor did she need Grandfather's or Dr. Jerome's approval in order to feel whole. She had learned, both on Molokai and in Honolulu that her relationship with her Father God through Christ the Son fulfilled the longing in her heart for acceptance and security. She was a member of the "household of God," as Scripture said, and "accepted in the beloved." She could now reach out to her father and grandfather with love and not expect, or need, their applause. She was content with being who she was—and who the Lord intended to make her in His family of the redeemed.

"Dear Candace, don't feel guilty," Eden told her. "There's no reason. I can look back now and see that God ordered my steps. I thought I was the forgotten one, but He remembered me all along. If it had not been for Ambrose and his knowledge of Christ, I may not have come to God as I did. He's always been an earthly father to me. And now, why, you're like a sister to me."

Candace hugged her. "I feel the same. And yes. There is much to what you say about God's leading in our lives. We do not always see the good that God is working. I wish now, that I'd had more time with Ambrose and Noelani."

Eden looked at the clock. "Oh! We have to hurry. Zachary will be here soon with Nora."

Eden finished dressing for the ball in full attire of satin trimmed with pearls. The dress was stunning, with the finest silvery hue that lightened the pale intermingling colors of blue and green. She sighed when Candace had first brought it into her bedroom. She had never seen such a color before and it went perfectly with her own eyes, hair, and fair complexion.

She was not unaware that she had been born with beauty, but she had always been careful to not flaunt, something Bernice did with great fanfare.

Eden had been taught restraint and dignity. "Better the female heart is adorned with purity and faithfulness. If you want a man to respect you, then you must respect your own body as important, as having value," Noelani had said during Eden's teen years. "Don't grant a young man liberties he doesn't deserve. Only your husband, who has committed himself to you, should enjoy them. Never think you can keep a man by surrendering what belongs to your marriage alone. If he will not consider marriage to you, then he's not worth your time—he is a taker and not a giver of the honor of bearing his name. Nothing would sting worse than trading your value for promises from an uncommitted man. Let him go now, and keep yourself for the man the Lord has for you."

Chapter Eighteen
A Spy Among Us

*I*n his suite at the Royal Hawaiian Hotel, Rafe dressed for the queen's ball. He slipped into the pristine white shirt Ling had handed to him. Ling then picked up the dinner jacket, inspecting it for lint. Finding none, he passed it to Rafe who watched him ruefully.

"You know, Ling, I really can dress on my own. My mother even taught me to tie my own shoes."

"Go to see the queen. Must look very good."

Rafe sighed. "If I must. Ah, for the good old days of my youth."

Ling laughed. "You ancient fellow, right?"

"You should have seen how I dressed aboard the *Minoa*, then you would have something to complain about."

"Prob'ly holes in trousers. Shirt torn."

Rafe hadn't intended to go to the affair at Iolani Palace, preferring a quiet evening in the hotel with newspapers and books to read. He would enjoy the Royal Hawaiian Band—but even then, he preferred classical music, which always made Keno groan, since he liked his ukulele.

"You like to stay home because you lazy fellow," Ling jested.

"You want to keep from people. You still mad at Miss Green Eyes."

Rafe gave him a hard look. "Now where did you pick up that name?"

"Keno say you *always* call her that—"

"Forget what Keno says. Take my word for it; since all he thinks about is his marriage, his mind is twisted. I don't want to hear about *green* or *blue* eyes." He took the tie from Ling's hand. "I'll put it on."

"You bad mood tonight. I leave you put own shoes on, too!"

"Thank you," Rafe said wryly, when someone rapped on the door. He glanced toward the front room. "Answer it, will you? I'm expecting Zach."

"What am I—butler too?"

"Throw in 'cook,' when the dining room is closed. That reminds me. Order more coffee beans from Hanalei. We're out."

Ling covered a smile and went to the door mumbling, "I send for coffee beans two day ago. See what good servant I am? You lucky I not go back to Shanghai."

Rafe caught up his dinner jacket and smiled.

He thought of the evening ahead. He was attending the queen's ball for the legislature for two reasons. First, Eden would be there. He had asked Great-aunt Nora to bring her and keep his request under lock and key. He could have gone to Kea Lani before now, but he'd decided against it. She had probably expected him to go there after that cynical fiasco at Hawaiiana.

Then, there was the surprising news that Oliver Hunnewell was in Honolulu, and would be there tonight. That was curious. With his father, Thaddeus, one of the most dedicated of the men hoping for the removal of the monarchy, why would his son be invited to the queen's festivity? Neither Ainsworth nor Hunnewell senior were invited. Rafe held a seat in the legislature, which accounted for his presence, but why Oliver?

He frowned. Just whose interests was Oliver serving—the British, Liliuokalani, or his father Thaddeus Hunnewell?

Zachary burst into the room carrying his dinner clothes over his arm. He dropped them on the chair and turned to Rafe. Something more important than clothing churned in his troubled mind. Rafe took one look at his tense features and knew it would be a rough evening.

"I've been *the* clever hound on the trail of *the* fox."

Rafe tried not to smile since Zach was so profoundly serious. *The* fox could be none other than Silas.

"This time I've got the information on him," Zach went on. "And I'm going to use it. Right in the *Gazette*." He held up last week's edition and tapped a headline that seemed unrelated to anything that could trouble him.

"Sounds interesting," Rafe said smoothly. "Lay it all on the table."

Zachary's eyes fairly glimmered as he glanced toward the other door as though cautious that someone—Silas himself?—might have an ear at a keyhole.

"Witchcraft," Zach stated bluntly, but in a low voice.

This was so unexpected that Rafe just stared at him. Zach must have thought he didn't believe him because he nodded his sleek blond head. "Yes, you heard me. Witchcraft. That's what it boils down to in the political pot."

"Witchcraft," Rafe said. He folded his arms.

"Exactly."

"Silas practices witchcraft," Rafe said slowly. "Is that what you're saying?"

"He might. He wouldn't need to, though. But he might."

Rafe straightened, hands on hips. "Zach—sit down. Start from the beginning. Ling? Bring us whatever you have in the kitchen, will you?"

Ling was gaping at Zachary.

Rafe sighed. "Ling?"

"Tea," Ling announced. "I have tea in kitchen. Bring from Chinatown."

"On second thought, better order coffee from the café."

Ling started off, but loitered at the door, until he noticed Rafe watching him. Then he went to order the coffee from the café at the hotel garden.

Zach had drawn a wicker chair to the table near the lanai. Leaning toward Rafe he said in a low voice, "I've got the story that will put the *Gazette* at the top of the Honolulu papers."

Rafe had heard this before. "Not without Nora's approval, and Ainsworth won't appreciate an attack on the Derringtons."

"I'll need to convince Nora to let me flame the headlines. If anything will help the sales and save the *Gazette*, the scandal being operated in Iolani Palace should do the trick."

Rafe already knew Silas was involved with the gambling cartel. Silas had admitted as much several months back. But what had this to do with Iolani Palace? Maybe Zach had stumbled onto something.

Concerning Silas and the gamblers from Louisiana, Rafe had kept the knowledge quiet for only one reason—to give Ambrose time to try and win Silas away from the cartel to bow the knee to Christ the Redeemer. Not only was the cartel corrupt, but it could also be a danger to Silas, who probably knew enough to put others at risk of being unmasked for their involvement. Was this what Zach was trying to explain? What any of this might have to do with witchcraft, however, was a puzzle.

"We know the syndicate is involved with members of the legislature," Rafe said. "Maybe with Liliuokalani. Thurston is sure of it, though I'm not convinced yet. The syndicate wants both gambling and opium bills introduced, passed, and handed over by a cabinet member for her signature before she dismisses the legislature in September."

"That's it, all right," Zach said eagerly. "Several men are here in Honolulu from Louisiana. Silas is working with them. And they're working with the Chinese kingpin."

"How do you know that?" Rafe pressed.

Zach looked sheepish. "I've followed Silas a few times since we returned from San Francisco."

"And what did you discover—that he went to a Chinese gambling house in Iwilei?"

"Right. Or Rat Alley, as some call the area. It was the same house I trailed him to in the past. That night, for instance, when I was bashed in the head in Hunnewell's garden, I'd followed him there. There were several men representing the cartel. They all had the same Southern accent Silas has. I even heard one of them mention New Orleans and some place called Gretna, Lu-ze-an-a, was the way he pronounced it."

"Interesting, Zach, and good work on your part," Rafe said, though he knew of the men and the kingpin's gambling joint.

"Spying on the men from Louisiana is one thing, but the home turf of the opium kingpin is another. It's a risky undertaking—too risky. We think Sen Fong was the number two man in the opium smuggling. He became a follower of Christ and was murdered to keep the cartel undercover. We found him with a knife through his heart in the garden at Hawaiiana. I still believe he came there to inform on the big kahunas calling the orders."

"You're right," Zach admitted. "The marshal hasn't been able to bring anyone to trial for the murder either."

"There's a strong chance he won't, or can't. The Chinese cartel operates undercover as a law among themselves."

Zachary gave a shake of his head. "The more I dig into the gambling and opium trade, the deeper the tunnel gets."

"I suspect it leads all the way to China," Rafe said. "Even San Francisco. That tunnel is well connected. The cartels are as intertwined as two snakes. I suspect the lottery representatives from Louisiana came here either to expand in the Islands, or to take over from those already here. It's my guess they'd rather strike a compromise with the Chinese opium kingpin, and keep the lucrative business of the casinos for themselves."

Zach's eyes glimmered. "And that isn't all. One time when I followed Silas I had better luck seeing the person he went there to meet. It was Oliver Hunnewell."

The connection to Oliver captured Rafe's interest; it made sense to him. If Oliver was working to get the lottery signed into law, then the timing was right for him to show up in Honolulu on the verge of the queen pushing underhandedly to get the bill through the legislature.

This might be the connection he'd been looking for. He must move with caution, though.

"The cartel has a witch on their payroll," Zach said with a smirk. "I haven't been able to dig up much on her, however."

"A fortune-teller, though they all hatch from the same egg. I can tell you a little about her."

"You know?" Zach asked surprised.

"I've been suspicious for months. I first saw her here in the hotel lobby with a man. Whether he's her husband or an associate is unclear. I inquired about her at the hotel office, and her name is Wolf. She's a wolf all right, in sheep's clothing, pulling the wool over Liliuokalani's eyes with her trickery."

"And Silas knows about her," Zach insisted. "Oliver mentioned her to him. I heard him speak of 'the witch.'"

"I'm sure he was just being sarcastic. She claims to be a tarot card reader. But whether she calls herself a fortune-teller, soothsayer, or *kahuna*, it's all the same where the Scriptures come down. It's an evil deception, and forbidden."

Zach nodded. "So if she's listening to this tarot card woman, Wolf, what does that say about the queen's spiritual discernment?"

"We don't know her that well, but I suspect someone in her inner circle does know her well enough to take advantage of this as means to deceive her and get her to make certain political moves."

"Who would that be? It wouldn't be Oliver. He has no easy access," Zach said.

"And Silas even less."

"You're right," Zach said grudgingly. "Silas isn't that important to the queen, and he doesn't know enough to pass things on to the tarot card reader."

"So it has to be someone at Iolani who at least has access," Rafe said. "He or she must be trusted by Liliuokalani, and must know some of her schedule and her agenda. If those making decisions on Hawaiian affairs of government are going to be guided through tarot cards, then someone who knows enough of what's going on with the queen has to inform this Wolf woman how to interpret as she flips her deck of cards."

"You're absolutely right. So then . . ." Zach sounded a little disappointed. "Silas is a low-level." He frowned. "Even so, he's in with the cartel. And so is Oliver."

So, Rafe thought, *my suspicions were right all along. The gambling syndicate—and probably the opium dealers—are preying on the queen's vulnerability by influencing her through a soothsayer. When men worship at the altar of greed it motivates the human heart to have no moral boundaries. The tarot card woman is just one more false teacher leading foolish people down the wrong path.*

"I must say," Zach said thoughtfully, "I'm disappointed in the queen. She must be spiritually naïve. If she knew the Scriptures, she would never allow that fortune-teller to waste her time."

"That's one reason men like Thurston and others want a republic rather than a monarchy. If we don't have wise leadership we need the right to vote them out. With royalty, you're stuck with the family for generations. All Europe is a picture of what happens when a royal family must rule."

And just how much was Silas involved in this new ruse?

It's time to talk to Silas, Rafe decided. And it would be wise to have Ambrose there when he did.

Rafe thought of the ball. Tonight Oliver would be at Iolani Palace. Was it a coincidence? Or was he coming to meet someone . . . perhaps the individual who had information for the "Wolf"?

Rafe gripped Zach's shoulder. "Zach, you've been a big help. I believe you've put me on the right track with the information on Oliver. He'll lead me straight to the person tricking the queen to trust the card readings." He smiled. "Maybe you should seek the office of marshal, or start your own private detective agency."

Zachary flushed at the compliment. For the first time he was speechless.

Rafe laughed and pushed him toward his dinner clothes. "C'mon, Zach, we've a lot of work to do tonight!"

The sky behind the feathery boughs of the jacaranda trees was turning from a greenish-blue to lemon and crimson, and the air was sweet with the scent of flowering blooms. The Derrington coach bringing Eden, Zachary, and Great-aunt Nora to the queen's ball rolled smoothly along King Street toward Iolani Palace.

Eden smiled at her great-aunt, proud that she looked so sedate and trim in her dark satin gown. Why Nora had never married in her youth remained a mystery. She had never explained, and no one in the family seemed to know, including Ainsworth.

Nora's reputation as a royalist and friend of the queen allowed for Zachary's presence as their male escort, even though Great-aunt Nora suspected her "dear boy's" interest in attending hinged on his personal investigative activity for the *Gazette*.

"It's true I have my suspicions about tonight, Aunt Nora," Zachary confessed, seated across from her and Eden. "I'm admitting to my masquerade as a good and loyal supporter of Liliuokalani."

"Rubbish, dear boy. Keep in mind we are all royalists here tonight. Away with useless suspicions! There will be no spying on

Liliuokalani." She poked her cane into his chest from across the seat.

"You see what it has come to, Eden?" he jested. "The lady is resorting to threats and physical abuse. Seriously, Aunt! Don't you realize some of the strongest proponents of annexation are members of this legislature? They've come to dine and dance to the music of the Royal Hawaiian Band, not to support Liliuokalani in her wish to burn the '87 Constitution."

"You sound suspicious yourself as a secret annexationist. Be that as it may, I didn't arrange for you to accompany Eden and me here tonight to spy on the queen."

"The *Gazette* would be wiser to allow latitude for more serious undercover work on the queen and her loyalists than printing what kinds of fruits she had for luncheon, or what charitable potluck she went to on Friday afternoon. The *Gazette* must print the truth, Aunt Nora. Otherwise why have a newspaper? Might as well print fairy tales and hand them out on King Street . . . let's see, how about 'The Emperor's New Clothes'? Sounds like Honolulu politics." He laughed cynically.

"By all means print the truth. Let the aftermath fall where it may. I've no interest in covering up the *truth*. But this razzle-dazzle rhetoric coming from the 'Thurston Party,'" she said disparagingly of the Reform Party and its main annexationist, Lorrin Thurston, "is outright poppycock against Liliuokalani."

"Now you're sounding like Grandfather," he complained. "He won't accept the facts on Silas because Silas is a Derrington. What if there are facts?"

Nora frowned. "Any particulars that may arise during this nasty political season in Honolulu must first be fully confirmed. We don't want to soil ourselves by printing gossip and accusations by enemies who will stop at little to get what they want."

"I'll get to the truth," Zachary stated. "Rafe will back me up on it, too."

"Just make sure of your sources, my boy. Remember: In the mouth of two or three witnesses shall every word be established."

Eden remained silent throughout. She had her own suspicions as well. Silas's recent actions did not bode well for him. Zachary was either convinced he knew something detrimental about Silas and was trying to trap him, or he was sifting through what Great-aunt Nora would call "the muck and mire." The way he kept mentioning how Rafe was going to "back him up," caused her to wonder if they hadn't joined forces, at least for tonight.

The coach entered through a guarded gate and stopped at the carriage landing where uniformed footmen came to assist them. Ahead, Iolani Palace gleamed like a Christmas tree with lights and chandeliers.

Eden drew her lovely satin skirt above her dancing slippers, and Zachary helped her step down from the coach to the landing. Her gaze scanned the courtyard. Members from the Legislature were already gathered with their ladies, fraternizing while wondrous music flowed from the famed Royal Hawaiian Band. Benches and chairs were conveniently gathered on the square for any who cared to sit and listen, instead of dancing.

Will Rafe be here tonight? she wondered. If he came with Bernice she must be gracious enough to not let the sight throw her off her spiritual balance.

While waiting for Great-aunt Nora to be assisted from the coach, Eden looked at the other guests. Most of the ladies wore exquisite gowns and full ensembles. Eden was glad her ensemble lacked nothing in comparison, even if the jewelry she wore belonged to Candace—who insisted she wear the blue topaz to complement the undertone of the satin's silvery-blue color.

The men were arrayed in fine evening clothes, but one young man in particular stood out in any masculine crowd. Her gaze struck gold as it stumbled over Rafe Easton.

So, then, he did come, she thought uneasily. *He's bound to ask me about Kip. This won't be pleasant.*

Eden glanced at Great-aunt Nora and felt a bubble of suspicion rise. She wondered if Nora had invited her to be her aide when

Rafe was the real reason she was invited. Nora may have thought she was doing the right thing in bringing Eden to where Rafe could see her.

It wasn't as if Nora sympathized with her loss of Rafe to Parker Judson's niece in the grandmotherly way Noelani did.

"Mooning over such losses is a waste of one's life," Nora had said. "One must arise from the mourner's bench and press ahead to new challenges, new opportunities."

And then, conveniently, along came what Nora called "the handsome Oliver" Hunnewell. "Have you given a second thought to this bachelor who is just waiting to be snatched up by a clever young lady? And such a family, too."

Rich, powerful, feared, and therefore, respected. Not respected due to character but because the Hunnewells carried a symbolic "bullwhip." One of a lesser social class must never cross a Hunnewell. Therefore, any young woman who caught him would be considered fortunate.

Great-aunt Nora may, however, have wanted her here tonight to help her get a loan for the tottering *Gazette* from Rafe Easton.

Well, I'm not about to go to him again over money! she thought for the umpteenth time. She couldn't rest easy thinking of the payment due for all the supplies on Kalawao. What an embarrassing situation to be in! Especially now, when they were no longer engaged.

And how can I worry Father about overdue bills when he's just recovered from his heart attack? Oh, Lord, help me, she prayed.

Rafe noticed her, and their gaze briefly touched. Eden tried to look unperturbed over his presence. She turned her shoulder toward him. She hadn't seen Bernice with him, but Bernice may be elsewhere at the moment. Then again, Rafe may not have brought her since Parker Judson was a known annexationist.

"Ah, look who's here," Zachary said with pretended surprise. "Why it's our old pal Rafe Easton. Let's go say hello to him, Eden, Aunt Nora . . ."

"Nonsense, Zachary," Nora quipped. "A lady doesn't barge into a circle of men—and look at Mr. Cook smoking that odious cigar. Revolting. I can smell it clear over here. Shameful." She drew out a lace handkerchief and fanned it in front of her face letting the fragrance of lavender permeate their surroundings.

Zachary coughed. "Oh, that lavender—too strong, Aunt. Why not try jasmine next time."

"Oh please! Must we carry on like this?" Eden snapped. "Let's go inside!"

"Yes, quite," Zachary apologized. "This way, ladies. I'll bring you into the palace."

Just then the unexpected appearance of Dr. Jerome caught their attention. They stopped and looked at him.

"Uncle Jerome," Zachary mused, scowling. "Now why is he here tonight?"

"Did he mention being invited, Aunt Nora?"

"Dear Jerome, unlike that scallywag Ainsworth, is believed by many at court to be a fair and just man and, by the by, a supporter of Liliuokalani."

"That's the first I've heard of him being a monarchist," Zachary mumbled. "The other day I heard him tell Ambrose that the leper colony on Molokai would be much better off under American supervision."

"Indeed it would," Eden agreed.

"Sure it would. There would be funds for better housing, better food, and well—better everything. America has gobs of money. American officials can spread it around the globe like gold dust and then just tax the rich to pay the bills. And everyone around the globe loves them for it, too."

Nora glared at him. "Sometimes I take you seriously."

Eden did not think her father was a monarchist. If given the choice to decide, he would have opted for annexation—no doubt for some of the very reasons Zachary mentioned in his cynical humor.

Thankfully, Eden's father, stronger after his physical setback, and encouraged by his loyal friend, Ambrose, was recovering from

Rebecca's death to find spiritual purpose for his future. The living seed of God's Word was sprouting anew. Grandfather Ainsworth had suggested that Jerome might run for Townsend's old seat in the Legislature. Whether this was mere hope on her grandfather's part or a realistic possibility, she did not dare guess.

"I don't believe Father's invitation was political at all. His work in leprosy research on Kalawao, though short-lived, is why he received an invitation. He's respected, regardless of his political allegiance," Eden explained.

"Leave it to a woman to straighten me out," Zachary said with a sigh.

"Well said, dear Eden," Nora boasted. "The queen is above petty politics."

Zachary almost hooted his laughter. "Bring out the flag, bring out the drums and flutes."

Great-aunt Nora lifted her walking stick. "Hush."

Jerome walked over to see Rafe. Eden watched as they shook hands. Then her father laid his other hand upon Rafe's shoulder. She guessed her father was praising the outcome of his restored vision during his stay in San Francisco under Dr. William Kelly, though they all recognized the recovery was due to God's grace. Did Rafe know the mission church under Ambrose had held a constant prayer vigil for his recovery? Surely Keno must have told him, she decided.

"Why Miss Nora, how pleasant to see you again," came a voice behind Eden. She turned as a familiar figure in a fine dinner jacket bent over Nora's extended hand as if she were the queen. It was Oliver Hunnewell, and his smile was not only for Nora but also for Eden.

"You know my niece, Miss Derrington, of course?"

"Indeed I do. So good to see you again, Miss Derrington." Once again he bowed slightly in the British fashion as Nora continued. "And this is Mr. Oliver P. Hunnewell, as you know."

For a frightening moment Eden almost laughed, remembering the way Keno and Rafe had made fun of Oliver's continual usage of his middle initial. She struggled to keep a poised expression, lowering her eyes. This may have been a mistake, for when she was able to look at him again he wore a pleased smile, as though he thought his presence had overwhelmed her into girlish retreat from his charms.

She stared back evenly trying to show him otherwise, but that seemed to please him more. Her cheeks flushed. She was sure he also took that as a sign of his sweeping triumph.

"I hope I shall have the privilege of at least one waltz this evening, Miss Derrington?"

"Well Oliver, it's a surprise to see you back in Honolulu," Zachary cut in. "So soon, too, after my cousin Candace gave your engagement ring the old one-two and heave-ho." He snorted.

Eden heard a faint gasp from Great-aunt Nora. Oliver drew himself to full height, which then matched the blond elegant figure that Zachary cut in his dinner clothes.

"I beg your pardon, Mr. Derrington?" Oliver said.

Oh, no. . . . Next Oliver will be hauling out his white glove to flip across Zachary's smiling face.

"Hello Oliver," Rafe Easton said from behind them. Eden let out a breath of relief, something she would not have done five minutes earlier. She'd rather face Rafe's questions about Kip than tolerate conflict between Oliver and Zachary.

"Rafe," Oliver acknowledged.

"Welcome back to Honolulu."

"Thank you," Oliver said stiffly. He turned back toward Eden. "I look forward to our waltz, Miss Derrington."

Eden saw Rafe look at Oliver and then glance at her.

Ah, ha! She turned to Oliver, smiling demurely. "As do I, Mr. Hunnewell."

Oliver smiled, bowed slightly, nodded to Nora, and strode toward the palace steps.

"I've never been so shocked, Zachary," Great-aunt Nora scolded. "Have you no manners?"

"What did he do now?" Rafe inquired. "Forget to use the 'P' in Oliver's royal title?"

Eden swished her fan in front of her face to hide a smile.

Zachary glowered. "That fellow really believes he is a noble. All I said was—"

"All you said was an insult about his losing Candace," Nora scolded. "One never says things like that in proper society. You don't point out that a man's fiancée has given the engagement ring the old 'heave-ho.'" Nora looked at Rafe for confirmation.

Rafe smiled, but Eden caught a glint in his eyes. "Women are good at giving engagement rings the old heave-ho—though some like to keep them as souvenirs."

Zachary chortled. "Or sell them."

Nora groaned. Eden turned away. "Aunt Nora? Are you coming with me? The guests are going indoors. The band is tuning up. I don't want to miss my waltz with such a gentleman as Oliver."

"Yes, of course dear. Come along Zachary, give me your arm, dear boy. I do forgive you—this time. But do behave yourself this evening."

Zachary exchanged glances with Rafe. Eden did not know what it meant. Was it a signal for something? She knew Zachary had gone to Rafe's hotel earlier with news that undoubtedly had something to do with Silas and the cartel, and perhaps Oliver as well.

"Rafe, won't you join us? You did come alone?" Nora asked meaningfully.

"I shall be pleased to join you, Miss Nora," Rafe smoothly replied. As if on cue, Zachary released Eden's arm, and took Great-aunt Nora's. Eden found Rafe walking beside her, and then slowing his step as he took her by the forearm.

"Wait . . . I want to talk to you about Kip," he said in a low voice. "Let Nora and Zach get ahead of us."

"Oh but I can't," she taunted. "You see, I'm so busy. You can get the information from Mrs. Celestine if ever I find time to send it. And until then, Mr. Easton, if you wish to request an appointment,

I'll need to check my schedule. I shall never again go to Hawaiiana to be insulted by that—that awful feline cat-woman you have running your life for you!"

Rafe smiled, looking undisturbed. "Cat-woman?" he said. "Oh you mustn't be so hard on little Bunny."

She didn't believe he called her that, but that he enjoyed making her think so.

His eyes defied. "Ready to talk?"

She dug in her heels.

"Oh I simply can't," she said in a hushed voice. "I shall miss my waltz with . . . Ollie. That's what I call him."

She saw the flicker of anger in his dark eyes.

"Do you indeed, Miss Derrington? How charming. The waltzes come later," he added coolly. "Or did you also want to polka with Mr. P.? I'm sure he'll oblige you with a hop about the floor if you smile at him enough."

Eden bestowed her sweetest smile on him, her heart beating with anger. "My amusements are less dramatic. What about yours, Mr. Easton? Do you like to hop about the dance floor with your little Bunny?"

He tilted his dark head. "A slow romantic waltz is more to my liking. How about you, Miss Derrington, are you willing to oblige my preference?"

Their eyes held.

"I told you, I'm very busy. What did you want to talk to me about?"

He folded his arms. "Take a guess." He glanced about the courtyard. "Let's go somewhere and talk. I won't keep you long. I wouldn't want to make Ollie jealous."

"You forget yourself, sir," she said loftily, snapping open her feather fan and swishing it provocatively. "I don't know about your Bunny, but I never wander off in the twilight with a man unless I've an escort."

His jaw flexed.

"If there's anything detrimental in your mother's journal I want to know exactly what it is. Even if I need to carry you off to the coach and drive to Kea Lani to get the facts. I want to see that journal."

"Rebecca's journal is in my bedroom locked away. I don't think you'll risk arrest by Marshal Harper for break-in and entry."

Their eyes held. His cynical amusement vanished. He grabbed her arm and propelled her toward the carriageway where the various coaches and buggies were parked.

"Are you going to talk, or do we go to Kea Lani?"

"You won't find the journal even if you do."

His eyes snapped. "You're the most frustrating woman I've ever met. The matter about Kip is too serious to ignore. Will you stop playing childish games and tell me the truth?"

"I care about Kip, too. I want what's best for him now and in the future." She folded her arms. "And after the way you've treated our relationship, I don't think you're ready to handle the information my mother entrusted to me."

The air seemed to curdle between them.

Her attack upon his maturity touched the root of his pride—the insult had done its work. She realized she'd gone too far.

Almost immediately she was grieved. She thought of how he'd always been honorable, decent, and strong. He'd helped Zachary, and Keno, and even herself during the years when she'd thought someone in the Derrington family had murdered her mother. But her words were a device to hurt back as he'd hurt her.

Now what? Apologize? Tell him she hadn't meant it? Run to him, hold him, and tell him she loved him as much as ever—and except for the trouble between them over Miss Judson she could not be more proud of him as a man?

His earthy dark gaze grew heated. He began to step toward her, and she stepped back. She caught a breath, snatched up her skirts, and ran toward the court.

At first she heard his footsteps. Then they suddenly stopped. By the time she'd reached the edge of the court where the guests mingled peacefully and the band played soothing music, she paused and turned. He had not pursued—he was too angry.

Then, as she stood in the torchlight, she saw Rafe walk toward the court. She saw Great-aunt Nora and Zachary on the steps of the palace and hurried toward them.

"There you are," Great-aunt Nora said, looking toward Rafe. She seemed to understand that something was wrong.

Rafe walked up. Eden refused to look at him and moved to the other side of Nora, looping her arm through Nora's. "We'd better go in, Aunt."

"Yes, come along, Eden dear."

Zachary looked at Rafe with masked sympathy, as though he also knew something had broken between them.

"The dancing is beginning," he said lamely. "I hope I'm not expected to do a polka with anyone. The last time I tried it my knee bothered me."

Without another word they walked up the steps and into the palace.

Six gleaming chandeliers glittered. Between the doors into the receiving hall hung large oil paintings of some of Europe's royal family members. An attractive amber panel lined the wall. Royal footmen were handsomely attired with gold braid, flanked by royal attendants in full regalia. The Royal Chamberlain led them toward the doorway into an area where the guests were dancing.

Oliver Hunnewell walked up. "My waltz, Miss Derrington?" He looked at Rafe for permission among gentlemen.

Rafe bowed his dark head briefly as though releasing her from his attention.

"Your waltz," he agreed. "If you'll excuse me I wish to speak to someone across the room."

Well, I got my sword thrust, Eden realized as he left. *Now, Rafe cares even less what I do. I've only added more justification in his mind for his behavior.*

She moved onto the floor to waltz with Oliver. A minute later she noted that Rafe was across the room near the long veranda, talking to a man.

Queen Liliuokalani sat in an elaborate chair smiling and watching the others having a pleasant time. Eden saw Great-aunt Nora seated in one of the chairs against the wall talking to a Hawaiian woman. Dr. Jerome sat beside Nora engaged in their discourse.

Zachary, blond and handsome in his dark evening clothes, was waltzing with a young woman who would have made Claudia Hunnewell mourn. Eden thought how much Claudia would have enjoyed being here at the ball with Zachary—but as the daughter of their stalwart annexationist, Thaddeus, she would hardly be welcomed. Eden had no idea who this other young woman was. For that matter, she recognized few in the room.

Eden was downcast. Despite her lush ball gown, elaborate hairstyle, and lovely appearance, she had failed in her response to Rafe.

Drat everything! Eden thought. *I wish I were home at Kea Lani asleep. Maybe I'll get a cat to keep me company.*

Chapter Twenty
The Soothsayer

T he change in Great-aunt Nora took place unexpectedly and mysteriously.

Nora had gone with a group of guests into the courtyard where the breezes were cool, to sit on chairs and enjoy the music played by the Royal Hawaiian Band, which had switched from dance music to a concert.

Eden was with Oliver on the upper balcony where she'd noticed Rafe at the other end with others including the attractive young lady Zachary had danced with earlier. Rafe was leaning on the rail, listening, and occasionally making some comment to the young lady. For as long as Eden could remember he'd preferred large orchestras and classical music, and while the Royal Band did not play classical they were famous for their lovely music.

Oliver was monopolizing her and talking about a dinner he would enjoy taking Eden to on Saturday evening at Hunnewell House. It seemed that a great many elite were going including Miss Judson, escorted by Rafe Easton.

The time hastened onward toward the dinner to be held in the

State Room; Zachary joined Eden and Oliver. Oliver's eyes raked him and he tightened his lips. He slipped his jeweled pocket watch from his silk vest, glanced at the time, then politely smiled at Eden and excused himself. "I'm afraid that even amid times of relaxation business demands my attention. Unfortunately, I must meet an associate in the court. Please excuse me, Miss Derrington."

As soon as Oliver had gone through a doorway Zachary looked in Rafe's direction. He picked up their drinking glasses, commenting that he would replenish them from the punch bowl in the State Room.

When he'd gone, Eden turned to see that Rafe had also slipped away.

They're watching Oliver. Did they expect him to meet someone from the gambling and opium cartel?

About ten minutes later Great-aunt Nora returned. Eden was startled by the change in her appearance. Her face was strained, her cheeks a fevered pink. *Of all things!*

Eden started toward her when Zachary reappeared without the punch glasses. He looked as if he'd been running. He saw Great-aunt Nora and then moved toward her. Eden followed, noting signs of the older woman's weakness.

Zachary took hold of her shoulders. "Better sit down, Aunt Nora."

"I'm all right—" she murmured.

Eden spoke with professional efficiency, "Are you ill, Aunt Nora?"

Nora slumped into a quiet faint.

There was a stir in the room. The Marshal came from somewhere, servants moved in, and Dr. Jerome was hurried in from the balcony. The queen insisted Nora be taken upstairs to one of the daybeds. No one else was permitted to go into the queen's private quarters besides Zachary who carried her, and Eden, as a nurse to assist her father.

Nora came out of her faint some minutes later, murmuring that she was perfectly fine and that she was a dreadful burden to everyone—and that the commotion was such an embarrassment. She wished to go to her room in the Royal Hotel.

"Be still," Dr. Jerome urged. A medical bag was ushered into the room from somewhere, kept by the royal physician, Dr. Trousseau, for emergencies. Eden assisted her father in a swift, cursory examination of Nora's heart condition, for they both feared symptoms leading to heart failure.

Not until the exam was concluded did Eden turn from the bedside and see Zachary on the other side of the room. He was surveying the room and the window, and was looking up and down the corridor.

Eden walked up to him and quietly said, "It's rude to look into people's closets and under their beds. Whatever are you doing?"

"Shh." He glanced toward Dr. Jerome and Aunt Nora, who were talking in low tones, then gestured her over near the open window.

"The queen's expecting a caller to her private living quarters soon after the State Room dinner is over and the guests go home."

"So?"

"Use your head, Cousin! This secret caller is connected with the cartel. Either gambling or opium. Rafe thinks both. You're in this room. A perfect spot to observe the identity of the caller."

"Oh no I'm not— " She turned away.

He pulled her back. "Don't be a goose, Eden! This is important for the future of the Islands! Listen," he whispered, "the queen's apartments are just down the corridor. But the stairway is just below this room. So if people come up, you'll hear them walk by the door. Rafe says all you need do is open the door a crack and look at the caller." He snapped his fingers. "Spiff, nothing to it. It's not as if you're being asked to hide in her closet, or creep under her bed."

"Oh, well, thank you very much. That makes all the difference."

His mouth twitched. "Well, you know what I mean."

"Did Rafe ask you to get me to play spy?"

"No. Fortune turned our way."

She must have looked appalled for he scowled. He glanced again toward the bed to see if Jerome still had his back to them.

"Where's your patriotism?"

"Patriotism!" she whispered hotly. "I'm not an annexationist, remember?"

"Looks like Rafe is right," he lamented.

She narrowed her eyes. "What do you mean?"

"You want to protect Oliver Hunnewell."

She looked at him sharply. "Did Rafe say that?"

He wouldn't answer. "Just see if it's Oliver who shows up at the queen's apartment with a woman in a black veil."

Woman in a black veil? Her interest was awakened.

"Nora and I won't be in this room for very long. If the secret caller isn't likely to show until after the dinner—the dinner doesn't end until one o'clock. It's several hours yet before the guests depart."

"Find a way to keep Nora here."

"I can't do that. She's already recovering. Her heart is all right."

He looked over at the medical bag then at the clock. "Three more hours is all we need. Even if her heart is fine, she still fainted. Poor Aunt. A little nap will be good for her."

"Zachary!"

Behind them Dr. Jerome was saying to Nora: "You'll need to rest for a time, though. I want to make certain your recovery is strong before we take you down to the coach."

Zach nudged her. "You see?" he whispered. "Straight from the doctor."

Eden moved toward the bed where Nora lay.

Her father was saying, "I'll send word to the queen and to the guests from the Legislature that Miss Nora Derrington will be just fine. As far as I can now tell, your heartbeat is normal."

"I told you so," Nora snapped. "Such a fuss, Jerome. I want to go back to the hotel."

"You did faint, Aunt Nora," Eden said quickly. "And we're not sure why."

"You'll need to lie still for a while. Then we'll take you back to the Royal Hotel," Dr. Jerome said calmly, patting Nora's hand. "All is well."

Eden handed her father a glass of water that she'd stirred powder into.

"Yes, a wise idea. Here, drink this," Jerome told Nora. "A couple of hours of rest will do you much good."

"What is it?" Great-aunt Nora demanded suspiciously. "I don't need any medicine."

Eden lifted her aunt's head from the pillow. "It's just a minor calming powder to give you a rest while we wait to go home. I'll stay right here with you."

"Oh if you both insist," Nora complained. "You're enough to wear me out."

"Now, now," Jerome said as if coddling a child.

"You're not upsetting the queen's ball," Zachary spoke up. "The dancing has ended. Next is the dinner, and then we'll go home."

Nora looked at him. "I'd almost think you wanted to keep me here, dear boy."

Zachary plucked at his tie. "Why would you think that?" He nervously laughed.

"Yes, why indeed? I suppose Rafe is involved in this?"

Zachary's eyes met Nora's. A strange moment of silence followed, and then Nora sighed. "So I thought. Very well, I shall lie here until the cat is out of the bag."

She reached for the glass. When she finished drinking, she handed the glass to Eden and said, "There, now you and Jerome should leave or you'll miss the dinner." She rolled over on her side.

Eden had watched this strange interplay with interest. So, then, it's just as she'd thought earlier and Zachary was in this with Rafe. They must think Oliver was aiding this woman in a black veil—

"Eden?" Jerome said.

She nearly jumped, and turned toward him. "Yes?"

Her father showed her the medical bag. "I'll leave this on top of that chest over there. I'm going to the State Room with Zachary.

Shall we have something sent up?"

"No, I'd rather not. I don't think Nora will awaken and want anything either."

"Then I'll check on both of you after the dinner. If Nora is awake and feels stronger we'll leave at once for Kea Lani. I think she should be looked after by Noelani at the house rather than being alone at the hotel tomorrow."

Eden nodded. When they'd gone she went to the side of the bed to peer at Nora. The powder had induced sleep. Eden frowned. What had Nora seen or heard that had upset her so deeply? Had fear or shock prompted her strength to fail? Would she explain later? If Rafe suspected anything he was likely to question her when she returned to the Royal Hotel.

Nora had seemed quite troubled. She hadn't wanted to stay here in the palace even for a few hours. Did it have anything to do with the queen?

Eden paced across the carpet, hardly noticing the rich decoration of the guest room. Maybe Zachary was right in asking this of her. Maybe this all had something to do with the gambling cartel, or granting an exclusive right to some group to sell opium to the Chinese working the cane fields? And why would the queen give such special concessions except for money?

Ambrose was certainly concerned about the selling of opium to the sugar workers. He'd spoken of the evils of making money by harming others. He'd mentioned that King Kalakaua had given a Chinese kingpin the right to sell opium. Walter Murray Gibson, the prime minister, had worked with the king, first promising that exclusive right to one drug dealer, taken ten thousand dollars—to later sell that same exclusive right to another dealer who offered twenty thousand dollars. He never returned the ten thousand to the first dealer.

Now Ambrose feared that Liliuokalani, a decent woman, would also compromise and sign the lottery and opium bills if they were passed in the Legislature.

Just who was this secret visitor that came late, so as not to be seen? What would be discussed at a clandestine meeting at one in the morning? Couldn't the queen have spoken to this individual during the festivities?

Eden could understand the monarchy's need for money. Hawaii was in debt from the reckless living of the past king and his prime minister, who spent as though they were ruling kings on the level of Europe's monarchies. Now Liliuokalani had to try to undo the waste and raise revenue to pay off those debts. Nonetheless, the great debt should not legitimize bringing in more prostitution, more gambling, and more opium. She could see why Rafe wanted to know who was influencing the queen to get corrupt laws passed upon the Hawaiian people.

Eden's heart beat faster. *All right. I'll spy.*

When the dinner in the State Room was over Eden could hear the many guests leaving Iolani Palace in their coaches, and the calls of *aloha* and other pleasantries.

It was time to make her move. She saw that Nora was sleeping soundly. Then she opened the door to the corridor and looked out. She had no idea which apartment was the queen's and she wasn't about to get herself into trouble by snooping in places she had no right to be.

A few minutes later she slipped out the door. Guards were posted, as she knew, at the bottom of the beautiful carved staircase, and also on the upper landing.

Eden moved down the corridor as silently as she could in her satiny skirts. Another door opened ahead and she stepped quickly behind a large potted palm.

A woman emerged from a room that seemed to be dark. She too, seemed as bleak as a shadow, dressed all in black, or a deep midnight blue. She wore a half veil that draped from her hat to partially cover her face.

Eden now remembered where she had first seen the woman. At the time a man had been in her company, a tall, slim man also wearing dark colors—rather unusual for the tropics. This had been at Kalihi hospital months earlier when she'd followed Dr. Jerome to Hunnewell's garden.

She had seen them together again before she went to Kalawao —at Kea Lani the morning after the prayer meeting for Rafe in the mission church. Eden had heard voices in the garden. One of those voices had belonged to Silas—and the others had belonged to this same couple.

Eden was further surprised when the woman walked confidently toward the corridor that Zachary said led to the queen's private apartments. She seemed to know the way. She heard voices as a man greeted the woman. Then she heard a door open and shut. A few moments later Eden heard other voices sounding as if they were coming up the stairway. Eden sped back to the guest room.

Inside with Great-aunt Nora again, she regained her composure. A few minutes later she answered the door to an attendant who had come from the queen. Was Madam Derrington feeling better? Was anything needed, or could anything be done to make them more comfortable? If they wished to stay the night they would be quite welcome to do so. If Madame preferred, the royal physician, Dr. Trousseau, could see her when he arrived early the next morning.

Eden thanked the attendant profusely, but assured him her great-aunt was much better, and they would both leave for Kea Lani plantation as soon as Dr. Jerome came. With a bow the attendant left, and Eden leaned against the door. After being treated so kindly, she felt ashamed she had been sneaking about spying.

Eden bowed her head and did the one thing she could to help. She especially prayed for Queen Liliuokalani, asking that she would be led into all truth and would escape the deceptive lures of the dark spiritual netherworld. "May the queen seek spiritual guidance only from the Spirit-breathed Word of God."

Eden was waiting by the door to the corridor when Dr. Jerome returned. He checked Nora's pulse, listening with the stethoscope.

"Good," he said. "Then for some reason, Nora merely had a fainting spell. Perhaps it was all due to the excitement. Her age, you know."

Where was Zachary? Eden stepped out of the room and looked along the corridor. She saw no one, not even the usual guard near the stairway. She had turned to reenter the room when Zachary came up the stairs.

He drew her away from the doorway.

"We need to be quick. Learn anything?"

"Yes, I recognized her," she whispered.

"The woman with the veil, all in black?"

"Yes. But you seem to already know who she is."

"Yes, but there's been no proof of her contact with the queen until tonight. She's German and called Fraulein Wolf. She went to the royal apartments?"

"Yes." She glanced about nervously, hoping the guard wouldn't appear. "I've seen her before tonight on at least two occasions. Recently, in the garden at Kea Lani."

His eyes gleamed. "Silas, of course. I've got to let Rafe know."

"What do you and Rafe know about her?" Eden inquired.

"Enough to know she's probably been hired by a certain group to influence the queen to sign the lottery and opium bills. Rafe says she's fortune-telling with tarot card readings."

"Yes, but why would Silas—" She stopped.

"You've seen him with the fortune-teller?"

Reluctantly she nodded. "At Kea Lani."

She told him what happened in the garden on that morning when she'd heard voices arguing.

"Ah! Did you hear any of the conversation?"

She told him what Silas had said. "There was a strong disagreement."

Zachary frowned.

"I'd give anything to sit in on the meeting Fraulein Wolf and Liliuokalani are having right now," he said.

Eden was troubled. "I wonder how much Silas knows?"

"Too much, as Rafe puts it. Anyway, Rafe will find out in a day or two. He's going to confront him, but he'll have Ambrose there, too."

Eden was relieved. It was wise to bring Ambrose, and safer for Silas who would have an opportunity for spiritual guidance.

"I say Silas is working with those who are deceiving the queen with tarot cards and advice on who to pick for her cabinet. It's all a ruse to get what they want."

Eden was dismayed. Had Nora seen or heard something about Fraulein Wolf? If so, it could account for the shock that had caused her to faint. What would she do about supporting the monarchy?

Eden believed Nora, with all of her firm moral convictions would be troubled enough to stop supporting Liliuokalani. She was not likely to work for annexation, but she would do nothing for the monarchy either. She would probably quietly withdraw.

Eden now faced her own decision. She knew it would not be pleasant, either way. Truth divides. And in the world of spiritual truth it was the same: "He that is not for me," Christ had said, "is against me." A decision for or against the Savior is required of all.

"You should know," Zachary whispered, glancing down the corridor, "that Rafe is sure Oliver is working with the cartel. He thinks Oliver came tonight to pass information to the soothsayer. She'll then repeat these secrets to the queen who will then be amazed that the tarot card reader could know such private matters about her, as well as events occurring around her."

"But where would Oliver get this kind of information?"

"That's just it, Eden. As Rafe says, there has to be someone else. Someone close enough to the queen. That's what Rafe and I are trying to learn. Grandfather Ainsworth will be devastated because I was right about old Silas all along."

Dr. Jerome poked his head out the door. "There you both are. I almost thought you'd deserted us. Come along, Zachary, I'll need your help. Nora is awake and anxious to leave."

"I can walk on my own," Great-aunt Nora said a few minutes later when Eden insisted that she let Zachary carry her to the coach.

"Now, Nora," Dr. Jerome said firmly, " you may not walk yet. Zachary will carry you. Come now, no protestations."

Zachary came to the daybed and offered her an elegant bow. "Your servant, my lady. Permit me."

Nora smiled weakly. "Oh very well, dear boy. How can I turn down such chivalry?"

*A*fter the Reform Party leader, Loren Thurston, returned to Honolulu from Washington, D.C., his plan on the annexation of Hawaii by the United States—as laid out in a treatise written aboard the steamer coming from San Francisco and then sent to Secretary of State James G. Blaine—was fast sliding downhill. His plan to influence the native Hawaiians to give up their monarchy was a dream. Rafe knew the native Hawaiians were far more loyal to the idea of their chiefdom and their ancient spirits' religion than they were to annexation and allegiance to a republic or a democracy.

Rafe Easton stood with Parker Judson, Thaddeus P. Hunnewell, and a few other men from the Legislature's Reform Party across the street from Iolani Palace. The event of the night before had not changed political viewpoints.

If they knew the queen was listening to political advice from a sooth-sayer with tarot cards they'd be even more determined to end the monarchy, Rafe thought.

All of the men held strong views on the annexation issue. They had left Aliiolani Hale, the government building across the street from the palace, and stood by King Street waiting for the last member of their group to join them for a meeting with Queen Liliuokalani.

Ainsworth Derrington finally arrived from Kea Lani. Rafe was relieved to see that Silas Derrington was not with him. Of late Ainsworth had brought his grandson with him to every important meeting of the Reform Party. Rafe had not commented, however he was now certain Silas was walking a tightrope between loyalty to the Derringtons and to previous commitments to the Louisiana gambling cartel.

Rafe needed more information on Oliver, the cartel, and the soothsayer before he confronted Silas. Until then, it was wiser to say nothing of what he knew to the Reform Party men, especially with Hunnewell's own son, Oliver, involved.

After the greetings, Hunnewell hauled out his gold timepiece. "It's time, gentlemen. The queen expects us. Let's register our disappointment in her choice of new cabinet members. Let's make it clear we won't support certain men."

Ainsworth looked at Rafe. "Do you have the list of our Reform men, Rafe?"

"Right here, sir."

Ainsworth snatched his walking stick and his hat. "Then let's walk over together, gentlemen. We need to show unity in insisting at least one Reform Party member be admitted to her cabinet."

Rafe was uneasy. As they walked it reminded him of a military cadence. *Only drums are missing,* he thought wryly.

Whenever Thaddeus P. Hunnewell was the spokesman for something, Rafe had discovered that the cause would usually end like the nursery rhyme he'd read to Kip the night before—"Humpty Dumpty." Humpty was more than likely to have a great fall. He wished he hadn't shown up this morning. He looked toward the ocean. On this sunny day with blue skies and blooming flowers he thanked Father God for His compassion and for the return of his vision.

But then Eden appeared in his mind as if to remind him he had not come to the throne of grace for help in time of need concerning her.

He frowned. No matter how much she had hurt him, he needed to forgive her, forget the injury, and leave any thought of "getting even" behind him. He must move forward in faith.

Rafe knew what to do. How often had he told others to do the same thing? He understood what was expected of him, and yet anger wrestled within, demanding satisfaction.

Don't listen to sin's demanding voice, he kept telling himself. *It has no more authority over you. You have a new Lord, Christ. He is there for you, on the throne of grace. Therefore, go to Him for help with confidence—*

———

Inside Iolani Palace, the gentlemen waited in the reception hall to be received by Queen Liliuokalani. A few minutes later they were shown into the Blue Room where the Hawaiian queen sat with her skirts spread around her feet.

"Your Majesty," Rafe said and lowered his head with respect.

Liliuokalani appeared pleased with him; her dark eyes softened perceptibly.

Rafe ignored the impatience in Hunnewell's gaze. If Hunnewell expected him to be rude, he must reconsider. Liliuokalani was, after all, the queen of Hawaii. At one time Rafe had supported the monarchy as vigorously as he was now anxious for the Islands to become annexed by the United States. He did not trust men. He could see how in future generations the people and culture would go astray as mankind always did and the strategic location of the harbor becoming a greedy morsel for military usage. The change that Rafe went through from monarchist to annexation had been gradual. First he was overwhelmed with the unfairness of being unable to adopt Kip. If the babies and children born on Molokai were free of leprosy, they should be free citizens of the Islands—not kept behind fences as unadoptable. There was also the problem of having one person on the throne who ruled over all. This was the reason his family had left England in the early 1700s to sail to the American colonies. *Freedom!*

"I remember stories of your great-grandfather, Daniel Easton," she said to him pleasantly. "We learned about the early missionaries at royal school. He was one of the first, I believe, from—" She bounced her fingers on the arms of the chair thoughtfully. "New York. Long Island. That was it, wasn't it?"

"I'm flattered you remember, Your Highness."

"Most early missionaries came from Boston or Connecticut, so your great-grandfather stood out to me as unusual. He was a physician, was he not?"

"He was. He's buried here, in fact, behind *Kawaiaha'o*," he said of the historical church down the street from Iolani, where most of the kings and royal families attended worship.

Thaddeus cleared his throat. "Madame," he interrupted, "we received your summons to meet with you."

She turned a somewhat cold stare upon him, obviously not pleased by his too bold interruption.

"Be seated, gentlemen," she stated. "I have a luncheon appointment this noon and unfortunately I am wanting time."

"Just so," Hunnewell said, clearing his voice again. "This shouldn't take much time, Madame."

Rafe did not sit, but believed he should leave the main discussion to the older men, despite his knowledge or ability or zeal for annexation. He stood to one side near a window that faced the street.

Liliuokalani was accompanied by several men who were her friends and personal advisors. These included Paul Neumann, attorney and a former cabinet member, and Samuel Nowlein, captain of the queen's Royal Guard, and Joseph O. Carter, of Bishop and Co. Bank.

"Madame," Hunnewell began, "I have a list of names the loyal Reform Party has circulated to the Legislature. Several would be beneficial to you as you choose qualified men to serve you and the Islands in your new cabinet." He looked at Rafe, who opened his leather binder and removed the list he had created the night before in his hotel room.

Hunnewell handed her the folder including the list.

At first she did not accept the folder. Rafe glanced at her lap where her hand clenched under a partial fold of her sedate black dress. She was partially lame in one foot and wore dresses that covered the sight.

Trouble, Rafe thought. *Hunnewell is making things worse with his arrogance. Hunnewell has no clue of how to work with her.*

Hunnewell kept holding the papers toward her, his mouth tightening.

Rafe's eyes met those of Ainsworth Derrington, and could tell he was thinking the same thing. Always the most intellectual and dignified of the Annexation Club, he politely intervened. He behaved as though Liliuokalani could not reach the folder. So he slipped it from Hunnewell's rigid hand and with a light bow passed the folder not to the queen but to her ally, the attorney, Neumann.

Neumann accepted the folder, exchanging a brief smile with Ainsworth. Ainsworth knew most of Liliuokalani's allies and he had wealth to shine his self-placed halo.

"Madame," said Ainsworth with quiet dignity, "we of the Reform Party would indeed beseech you to appoint at least one man from our party to your cabinet. When you have time to look at this list of some of the most qualified gentlemen in the Islands—all of them, Madame, second- and even third-generation Hawaiians, and proud to be so—you will find the names of men absolutely trustworthy when it comes to the good of the Islands."

Liliuokalani's round face and solemn dark eyes remained cool.

"Thank you, Mr. Derrington; however the men I will appoint as my cabinet officers will all be sworn to uphold the good of my people and of the Islands of our long and fortunate ancestry."

Rafe saw Hunnewell's broad shoulders stiffen.

"Unfortunately, " Liliuokalani continued, "I cannot think the same for all of those in the Legislature who plot to steal away my rightful throne in order to annex the Hawaiian Islands to a foreign government. Nor do I believe the American president and Congress will safeguard the scheme to do so."

Hunnewell turned white. Rafe saw his hands go behind his back and knot tightly.

"Madame," he said coldly, "if there is discontent among members of the Reform Party and among the haole Hawaiians it is due to the scheme of another making! I speak of the royal intention to over-throw the legal Constitution of 1887 and replace it with a new Constitution that undermines the freedom and security of families that helped build Hawaii into the country it is today!"

Liliuokalani leaned forward in her chair, hands on the armrests. Rafe expected the grand show of her dignified standing and walking out on them, but she did not. From behind them he heard the steady voice of Charles B. Wilson, the head of her security.

"Take it easy, boys," he said. Rafe had seen him enter by a side door a minute earlier. He now stood gazing at Thaddeus P. Hunnewell. Hunnewell turned toward him matching scowl for scowl.

Ainsworth moved swiftly to tone down Hunnewell's frustrated rhetoric.

"Madame, in all due respect, may I say that Mr. Hunnewell is correct in voicing his concerns? Certain individuals among us have heard that you intend to usher in a new Constitution to replace the 1887 laws—laws the High Court of the Islands have upheld since your brother, King Kalakaua signed the document."

Liliuokalani's expression remained inexorable, but Rafe sensed her rage. The pulse slammed at the side of her wide throat. Her fingers curled around the arms of her royal seat. Obviously she saw them as arrogant men trying to steal what was hers by birthright.

"Do you speak of the so-called Bayonet Constitution? In which my brother was all but held at rifle point while Mr. Thurston, Mr. Dole, and others held him hostage?"

"Madame! That dreadful story has been so exaggerated that it's become little more than a fable to rile up the people!"

"I was there, Thaddeus," Neumann spoke up. "The king had no choice but to agree to the demands of Thurston and Dole."

"I was there also," Ainsworth said, with steely gray eyes. "And I say there were no guns and no bullets. Just common sense. It was imperative for Hawaii's good that we stop from sinking the Island into bankruptcy through the mismanagement of Walter Murray Gibson."

Hunnewell turned on Ainsworth. "Better speak the true facts as they are, Ainsworth. You know them as well as I do. Recklessness, that's what it was. Plain recklessness made possible by the king himself, and by that conniving thief he allowed to run his government— Gibson!" Hunnewell pulled a handkerchief from his front pocket, wiping his brow.

Well, Hunnewell's done it, Rafe thought. *He's turned any possibility of working with her into hash by riling a proud woman. The man we need here is Ambrose.*

Nothing is ahead except conflict, Rafe thought as he left Iolani Palace. The meeting with Liliuokalani was over. Little if anything had been accomplished except stirring up indignation in royalists and annexationists alike.

Ainsworth had left with Hunnewell, and Rafe walked across the street with Parker. They paused in front of Aliiolani Hale where the Judson family coach was due to arrive for Parker. Bernice had ridden in with her uncle and had the coachman take her to visit friends.

Rafe was returning to the Legislature for some business he wished to clear up, and later was to meet Ambrose at his bungalow, where Noelani wanted him to come for dinner.

"Well," Parker Judson said, "I think Hunnewell crashed our boat into the rocks today."

"Hawaii and the throne mean much to her. I don't think she'll yield her principles. Men with Hunnewell's temperament only make matters worse. She left angry."

"As did we."

Just then, a horse and buggy came along King Street, slowing at a little building that bore the name, "The *Gazette*."

Eden was the young woman driving the buggy. Wearing a pretty hat and a green dress with puffed sleeves she drew the buggy to a halt and climbed down.

Seeing her again turned up the flame of Rafe's resentment, though he fought against his anger. So! Here again was the little darling tripping about Honolulu as free as a bird. Here was the woman who'd promised him she would always be devoted no matter what.

He narrowed his gaze. No matter what—unless a man is believed to be blind. Then she was quite willing to toss him away. She looked across the street and saw him. He could tell because she stared and then abruptly turned her head away.

Here was the young woman who had refused to give him new information on Kip because he wasn't *spiritually mature* enough to handle the truth! Rafe's heart thudded. He had half a mind to walk over and shake her. The misery and sleepless nights she had caused him in San Francisco—the *heartbreak!* Oh no, he wasn't about to walk back into that relationship again. He told himself firmly *that* Rafe Easton was through with Miss Green Eyes. She could save all her waltzes for Oliver—

Until, Rafe thought coolly, *I get Oliver booted out of Honolulu for working with enemies of any true Hawaiian. She won't get Oliver. I'll see to that.*

The Judson carriage was coming toward them. Rafe glanced at Eden, then at the carriage holding Miss Judson.

Rafe felt a surge of satisfaction. He decided to drag out his farewell a few minutes longer and use Bernice to hurt Eden. Too bad he couldn't have taken Bernice to the queen's dinner the night before. Then again, after gaining Eden's cooperation to confirm who the secret visitor was to see the queen, maybe it was wiser that he hadn't brought Bernice.

─ ⌒ ⌒ ─

Eden saw a coach race down King Street and draw near to where Rafe and Parker Judson were standing.

The uniformed driver opened the coach door and Eden saw a woman's lovely pale skirt. A trace of feminine lace showed above a stylish pair of dressy shoes that emerged from the coach to the stepping platform. Out in full view came Miss Bernice Judson, or "Bunny face," as Eden when frustrated, thought of her. But there was nothing in Bernice's appearance to mock, except her obvious conceit.

Bernice Judson stood in the sunlight like a princess who could wave the wand over Rafe's shattered dreams and heal them. She was clothed as stylishly and expensively as though she were arriving on Nob Hill for a gala, socialite ball.

Rafe walked to the carriage talking to her and smiling, while Kip clasped her hand.

As if she's his mother, Eden thought. At least Kip looked as healthy and robust as ever.

Why, he's deliberately showing more attention to Bernice than necessary. He's goading me. Scoundrel!

His behavior only provoked her to act indifferently toward him, although indifference was the last emotion she felt churning within.

Rafe met her gaze evenly and then turned his fullest charm on Bernice.

Eden's anger simmered. *Have it your way, Mr. Easton. If you can live without me—I can live without you. And Rebecca's journal and the information on Kip will remain with me.*

238

Nor would she give him or Bernice another moment of her time. She turned, straightened her shoulders, and swept up the wooden walk to the door of the *Gazette*. She opened the door and went in, banging it behind her.

Inside the room she tried to calm her breathing.

Zachary was bent over a stack of scribbled papers on his desk with pencil in hand. He looked up and frowned.

"Are you all right?"

"Of course I'm all right."

"You look ill—or angry."

"Well I'm not."

"Are you sure?"

"Stop quizzing me, Zachary!"

"Okay, okay. How's Nora today? I didn't see her before I left Kea Lani this morning. I needed an early start." He patted the stack of papers. "I have a load of information that will make this paper zing with sales." As usual he added the obstacle, "All I need is permission from Nora. But I'm going to wait until my meeting with Rafe at the Royal Hotel tonight. I wonder if he was able to get Silas and Ambrose together yet."

"I've no idea. He's out front now, with Mr. Judson and his niece. Why not go and ask him?"

"Oh. Is he out there?" Zachary went to look out the window. "Sure enough. There's Bunny, smiling at him."

"Nora was up when I left," she interrupted. "She even wanted to come into town with me. Candace talked her out of it for another day. Tomorrow she'll go back to the hotel. Something happened to upset her at the ball, but she's not talking. I don't think we should trouble her about it either. It will only put more stress on her."

"I wasn't going to ask her. I think I already know. So does Rafe."

"As for the information that will make the *Gazette*'s sales zing, I don't believe Nora will give you the permission.

"I've heard that before," he said wryly, returning to his desk, "but when Rafe and I get through with our detective work there won't be a choice. It will be printed in the *Gazette*. Grandfather or not. And probably no inheritance either." He went on working, his sleek blond head bent over the desk.

And that's why the Gazette *must be saved,* she thought. Nora's already promised the paper as his inheritance.

"I'll be working for an hour or so in Nora's office," she told him, and went into the small room, shutting the door behind her, also shutting the door of her mind to Rafe.

She sat down and produced a working installment on the first section of the journal. It covered her mother's heartbreak when she first discovered she was a leper. She went to work writing and rewriting until the edition was presentable to give to Nora for her first read-through. When she looked at the clock again, she decided it was time to go back to Kea Lani and give the installment to Great-aunt Nora. Naturally, there was nothing in this section on Kip. Nor would she ever put the truth about his parentage in the *Gazette* for strangers to read.

She grew uneasy. *But did Rafe believe that?*

She was sure he was still in a hard, cold disposition over her insult last night. She felt miserable. There was so much wrong everywhere. She needn't look for it in Iolani Palace or Washington, D.C., or on Kalawao or in the darkest regions of the world. She had only to search her own heart to find the sin of disobedience.

She massaged her aching temples. *Savior, I desperately need You. Help me.*

———⟨∘⟩———

When Rafe arrived at Ambrose and Noelani's bungalow he was in the mood for Noelani's mothering ways offered in the form of delicious food. After dinner, dessert, and some of his own coffee from Hanalei, he discussed the morning's meeting with Queen Liliuokalani.

"Naturally, everything was left in ruin. But old Hunnewell went on his way patting himself on the back for standing up to the woman ruining Hawaii."

"You're beginning to sound as if you're leaning again toward the monarchy," Ambrose said.

Rafe shook his head. "No, not that. Just weary of seeing everything come to a fruitless conclusion. I believe the men are correct when they say she's out to destroy the '87 Constitution. The very throne expected to rule by law and right is being corrupted by the big money interests. They're coming in quietly, but their ambition is to influence the queen to rule in their favor. I see a nightmare coming if we don't stop it. Soon, I fear it will be too late."

Rafe told him of the ongoing battle in the Legislature. Certain men were pushing for the queen to grant an individual right to one opium supplier, who, in turn would then pour money into the Hawaiian treasure chest—alleviating some problems for Liliuokalani to pay the Island bills.

"The trouble is that the treasure chest was looted and spent by Kalakaua and Walter Murray Gibson in their time, and there's no reason why new and greedy hands won't loot it again. So Hawaii is left teetering on a crumbling foundation of debt," Rafe told him. "The queen is dancing around the issue. She's claiming she doesn't support the opium law, that her cabinet supports it, but in her next breath she's asserting her sovereignty to make a new Constitution.

"You can't have it both ways. But as we know, crying crocodile tears is the way of all politicians—and queens, by the way. Her supporters are pushing for the passage of the opium bill, and members of the Reform Party are fighting to stop ratification. We were able to vote it down again last week, but they'll be back in their huddle with the queen, trying to find new tricks to wiggle it through the Legislature."

Ambrose's frown deepened. "I've been a quiet supporter of the Hawaiian monarchy."

"I know you have," Rafe said with a wry smile.

"I'm not one for removing the old landmarks, or overthrowing governments unless—well, that is a difficult decision, isn't it? After the fact, however, I support the American Revolution against the British Government. However, at the time?" he pondered, and rubbed his chin. "I wonder if I would have done so. Then, the Civil War of 1860—a nation divided with sound arguments on both sides. Well, sufficient unto the day is the evil thereof. We have enough to plague us now, and a revolution on the wind. I feel that I must decide based on my best interpretation of Scripture. Nora has nudged me for months to take a public stand for Liliuokalani, and so have Noelani and Eden."

Eden. Rafe drummed his fingers on the table. "And are you?"

Ambrose paused. "I don't know yet, Rafe, and that's the truth. Nora called on me just a few days ago. I told her my concerns on this question over opium and gambling. She insisted it was a lie hatched by Thurston's gang of annexationists."

"I suppose I'm a member of this gang?" Rafe said.

"Nora didn't mention you but she is upset you're in the Reform Party. She continues to mourn the old days when you worked for the *Gazette* and wrote articles in favor of the monarchy. So, Rafe, I cannot in Christian conscience support a monarchy that looks the other way over opium. Hawaii can't know the blessing of a righteous God if we embrace vices contrary to His wisdom.

"I've told Nora and Noelani that for now I'm staying out of the political fight. I'm reserving the pulpit for teaching God's Word, as the pulpit is meant to be used."

Rafe nodded. He respected this decision.

"I'll keep you informed on the opium bill," Rafe said. "And now I must get back to my hotel room. Keno is coming over to sign some papers on Hawaiiana. Then I need to take them to Parker to get his signature."

Ambrose walked with him to the door. "I won't ask about you and Eden."

"Good," Rafe said. "Because there's no chance of that, Ambrose."

"When will you tell me what it's all about? What happened

between you two? An angry man is toying with fire, Son. You know that."

Rafe hesitated.

"I can't talk about it," he said. "Don't ask me. I'm not ready . . . goodnight—see you tomorrow. Tell Noelani thanks again for the wonderful supper."

Ambrose looked after him thoughtfully. The impenetrable armor was back in place more secure than ever. Rafe had worn it for years when growing up under Townsend, and it had taken even more years for Rafe to put it aside. What had happened between him and Eden that had hardened him?

Neither of the two would talk about it with him, which was unusual. Both Rafe and Eden had often sought his advice in their own way and now, Rafe avoided the old chats they used to have. Ambrose frowned. He missed them. He hated to see his nephew like this. Satan had gotten some strong jabs in recently, beginning with Townsend. Rafe even avoided discussions with Keno.

Eden, too, merely changed the subject or busied herself when he spoke of Rafe. But Ambrose was not fooled. They were hurting deeply.

Ambrose thought about Miss Judson. There'd been nothing but contention since that young woman showed herself in Honolulu. Nor did Ambrose believe Rafe was in love with her.

He walked thoughtfully to his little study to read Scripture and pray for God's intervention in the lives of two of his most cherished spiritual "children."

—◌◌—

Great-aunt Nora was sitting at a desk in her room at Kea Lani when Eden arrived from the *Gazette*. Her thin, pale hands clutched a pen, and she had some papers in front of her. She put them aside in a folder when Eden entered the room.

Eden leaned over to plant a kiss on the wrinkled cheek. "How is your health, Madame?"

Nora smiled wanly. "Hello dear. Oh, I'm fine. I've a room at the Royal hotel again. I'm working up courage to call on Rafe. Perhaps this evening." She looked at Eden. "Care to accompany me?"

"Not if my life depended on it."

Nora's silvery eyebrows climbed. "Oh, my, and here I was prepared to share some unpleasant news ... I think I shall wait until we have tea."

"I don't want any more unpleasant news, Aunt. And I do not want to hear anything about Rafe Easton."

"No, of course you don't, poor dear. He can be a scoundrel, can't he? However, I believe with Candace that he's deliberately acting his part."

"Oh I'm sure he is. He finds the part fits him so well that he's enjoying it," Eden said. "He was out across the street near the government building this morning, paying homage to the Princess Bernice."

"Well, as you say, never mind that now. But I do need a loan or it will be the end of the *Gazette*. I've held out financially for several years, and I've come to my empty flour barrel. If the Lord doesn't help me get a loan, no one can. And now! Enough of my lamentation. What have you put together on Rebecca's journal?"

Eden sat down to read it to her. The dramatic part of the personal saga was in telling how her mother's own husband had broken the news to her.

Later, when Eden stopped reading, Nora wiped her eyes and shook her head, looking into the distance. "I never knew the cost, never stopped to consider how much pain those two young people went through. I'm afraid I was willing to stand aside and keep my emotional distance. It's all coming home to my heart, Eden. I feel ashamed of myself."

"Don't hurt yourself, Nora. You could have done little anyway."

"Perhaps . . . then again, perhaps I could have done something that would have brought blessing. Ah, life. So many mistakes, regrets, and wishing otherwise."

"Only God knows. But let us go on. '*Forgetting those things that are behind, and reaching toward what lays ahead.*'"

"At least I can put her journal in installments in the *Gazette*. This story may do so much to help others. We shall do what we can today. Today," she repeated. "Today is really all we have. Tomorrow is not ours yet and may slip away. While yesterday is already lived, for better or for worse."

Eden made up her mind to do all she could to save the *Gazette*. No, she wasn't going to Rafe, but there was one last man she could see about gaining help for her great-aunt. He had authority, money, and he was polite. The man was Parker Judson. Yes, she would brave the lion's den and confront him over his niece desiring to buy Tamarind House in an exchange for a loan to Nora.

The whole suggestive offer from Bernice was selfish and even cruel. If Parker Judson was the man she had always been told he was, he would not let Bernice own Tamarind, and he would offer Miss Nora Derrington, a fine elderly lady, money to save her little news journal.

It was a last-ditch try, but she was in the mood to try. What had she to lose? As Martin Luther had once said, "One with God is a majority."

If she failed, if this deed perhaps was not God's purpose, then she could at least go to sleep with a clear conscience, knowing she had done all in her power to help her beloved Aunt Nora. Just sitting and doing nothing while Nora withered away seemed an awful expenditure of time. What was that verse? "*Redeeming the time because the days are evil.*"

They were indeed.

*T*he sound of the sea and the breakers washing ashore filled the night. A billowy cloud of silvery-white briefly effaced the full moon.

Eden turned her horse and buggy aside from the path to park in an area surrounded with wild lantana. A gush of warm, damp wind from the surf greeted her. She climbed down from the buggy and secured her sweet mare, Kona—that Rafe had given to her the previous year—to a wooden rail beneath a *hau* tree, where a profusion of yellow blossoms sprinkled down like drops of rain.

"You be good and stay here," she murmured. The horse shook its mane and rolled a big eye.

Eden felt the wind stirring the lantana about her. She looked toward the Judson beach house. The house was near Sans Souci and the Kapiolani park grounds on Waikiki Road. Some of the wealthier beach homes and bungalows, like Hunnewell's house, were also nearby.

Eden recalled a night when she had trailed her father from the Kalihi hospital to Hunnewell's, and discovered a secret meeting of the Annexation Club with Grandfather Ainsworth, Silas, and Rafe in attendance. There'd been much trouble that night—including insulting words and fists exchanged over Candace between Hunnewell's son, Oliver, and Keno.

Now Candace and Keno would be officially engaged in a week. Eden was pleased that Grandfather Ainsworth had cheerfully accepted Candace's love for Keno. The news that Keno's biological father had been a "Hunnewell" had greatly benefited Keno's status among the elite, such as her grandfather. The idea that Keno was an actual cousin of Oliver Hunnewell was a thorn to Keno, but as he'd said, "Something good came of it. I got Candace."

Eden agreed. They were getting married soon and that was a victory. That was more than she could say for herself.

Eden looked from the road and saw the moonlit grounds of the Judson house. She would not have come except that Candace had assured her that Bernice Judson would not be with her uncle Parker. Bernice was attending another fine ball, this one at the Walsh home. Candace was also dragging Keno there, much to his exaggerated howls of misery, "Oh for the deck of the *Minoa* and the shoreline of the Caribbean!"

Eden imagined that Rafe—handsomely dressed and catching the appreciative eye of other young women there—would be Bernice's escort.

The Judson house was one of several such abodes Parker Judson kept around the Islands. It was pleasantly situated with Diamond Head in view, and its many windows faced west toward Waikiki.

A curving drive began at the wrought-iron gate, and wound up to the steps for the large front lanai. *Kiawe* trees sheltered the house from the road, and some *ti, bougainvillea,* and *kolomona* veiled the tall fences that cordoned off the property. The windows were aglow with yellowing light from the lamps, and she saw another coach parked on the drive—the horses flipping their tails.

Don't tell me Parker Judson is entertaining, too! I should have checked first. How disappointing! I must get in to see him.

Nora and the *Gazette* were worth the effort, despite the possibility of being turned away, though she did not think this would happen. She was a Derrington, after all, and her father was a highly regarded doctor. His return from Kalawao, ill, had merely served to elevate his reputation among those who knew him. Some were saying that if he recovered his strength sufficiently, he should enter the Legislature to win Townsend's seat and overcome the whispers about Townsend Derrington's odious reputation.

Yes, she was almost certain that Parker Judson would talk with her, if only out of surprise that she had called. Eden knew if Noelani realized she'd come here without an escort, she would be frowning for the next month.

At the front door she was received by the butler and shown into the parlor. He told her Mr. Judson was busy in his study, but that he would inform the master of the house that Miss Derrington waited in the library to speak with him. The butler asked if Miss Derrington cared for some refreshment while she waited, but she politely declined.

─◦◦─

In the next room, the private study of Parker Judson, Rafe Easton was gathering the legal papers he and Parker had just signed. The document allowed Keno to buy into a substantial portion of Judson's remaining rights to the Hawaiiana pineapple plantation. The financial loan to Keno to be able to pay Parker had come from Ainsworth Derrington who'd kept his promise of some months earlier to help Keno buy good land. It had been Rafe's idea to allow Keno to buy a fair portion of Hawaiiana. Now that Keno was soon to marry Ainsworth's granddaughter, the loan had been even more generous and appropriate.

Rafe was putting the documents into his satchel to bring to his lawyer, whom he'd seen that evening at the hotel, when the butler announced, "A Miss Derrington to see you, sir. She's waiting in the next room."

248

Rafe paid little heed. He assumed that "Miss Derrington" was Candace, who'd come by the Judson house on some business detail concerning Keno and Hawaiiana. Rafe had known Candace for some years now, and she was a coolheaded, self-reliant woman inclined to take the lead, despite her staid upbringing. He smiled as he thought about Keno. He was in for it, all right. Then he thought of Eden and his smile vanished. He'd never met a more frustrating woman. Not even Candace topped her!

"Oh, sure. I'll be in to see her in a few minutes," Parker told his butler, a man better suited to England than Honolulu, and who'd impressed Ling so much that to Rafe's amusement, Ling tried to copy his professionalism, even down to the wardrobe.

Parker turned again to Rafe. "Well Rafe, that about settles things. I'm pleased it all worked out as it did. Keno is a fine young fellow. I think he'll make a big success of his share of Hawaiiana."

"I'm certain he will, sir. He's not only dependable but of excellent character."

"I'm also sure of that. Ambrose did a fine job with both of you. Too bad I wasn't smart enough to turn Bernice over to him, too."

Rafe extended a hand. Parker Judson firmly shook it.

"Settled," Rafe said. " I'll go out the back way if you don't mind. I'm rather in a hurry to get back to the hotel."

"Don't forget the dinner tomorrow evening. Bernice is expecting you."

Parker walked across the room and opened the study door. It entered into the library. Rafe stepped back so Candace couldn't see him. The last thing he wanted was to spend another hour outlining the partnership he would soon have with Keno. Let her "sweet, handsome Keno Boy," as she called him, explain. But first the lawyer would need to explain everything to Keno at the hotel.

Rafe gathered the final document and placed it in his satchel. He was about to leave, when he heard Parker say, "Why Miss *Eden* Derrington, isn't it? This is a pleasant surprise. Won't you be seated? Can I offer you something? Fruit juice, tea?"

"Thank you, no, Mr. Judson. I do hope I'm not interrupting your evening."

"Oh, nothing of the sort. A bit of business concerning your cousin, Miss Candace, and the young fellow she's going to marry."

Taken off guard, Rafe wondered that he felt such vexation. *Eden! What can she be doing here?*

"I'd have thought you'd be attending the Walshes' ball tonight, Miss Derrington . . . their daughter, Miss Margaret, is a close friend of yours, is she not?"

"I believe you may have confused me with my cousin, Miss Candace Derrington. I've not been involved in Honolulu's festivities for some time. I only got back from Molokai with my father two weeks ago."

Rafe stood with hand on hip debating his response to her unexpected entrance.

The study door to the next room was a few inches ajar so he could hear Eden's voice. He knew her so well that he could read how tense she was, even if her words were socially correct. He narrowed his gaze. She wouldn't have come to talk to P.J. about Bernice? Not a chance. She had more pride than that. Could she have known he was here? No. If she'd known he was meeting with Parker, she would have stayed far away.

"Oh yes, I've heard about Dr. Jerome's work on Molokai," Parker was saying. "How is your father doing?"

"He's recovering—although not well enough to return to his research clinic in Kalawao. I doubt he'll ever be able to return."

"And his clinic?"

"It's been turned over to Dr. Clifford Bolton and his wife. She is my aunt. They make an excellent team. She's a loyal and good woman. She yielded her own life to marry him and become his *kokua*. You know Dr. Bolton is a leper?"

"Yes, a tragedy. Mrs. Bolton sounds like a wonderful person."

Rafe's anger pounded in his temples. Lana had stood fast with Clifford—but Eden had deserted him in his darkness.

He folded his arms and leaned against the wall near the door. His decided to eavesdrop on what his ex-fiancé wanted from old P.J.

"You're in medical research, also?" Parker was saying. "Your mother succumbed to it recently. A pity. You were able to see her, I understand? Well, that accounts for something meaningful."

"Yes . . . I'm still working in research at Kalihi. But I'm very involved in a task that means a great deal to me. I'm bringing my mother's story on Kalawao into print. I have her journal to draw from."

Rafe straightened. Rebecca's journal! He drew his eyebrows together.

Eden told Parker about the journal and of her plans to have it printed in the *Gazette*.

"The first installment will come out next month. That's why I'm taking such an interest in my great-aunt Nora Derrington's journalistic enterprise, the *Gazette*"

So that's her motivation. The Gazette.

As he realized that Eden had come to Parker Judson hoping to get a loan, Rafe grew more concerned. More was at stake than just saving Great-aunt Nora's newspaper. What was revealed in Rebecca's journal and diary? The consequences of certain revelations could damage the innocent.

"Unfortunately, my great-aunt is deeply in debt and unable to get a loan. The *Gazette* is about to go bankrupt. It's why I've been bold enough to come to see you, Mr. Judson. I've learned from Mr. Easton that you are a resourceful man, interested in branching into new businesses."

Mr. Easton! Rafe folded his arms again.

"I'm speaking for Miss Nora, and myself, when I request your consideration in the hopes of getting a loan—"

Well, there it was out in the open—a loan for Nora.

Rafe tapped his chin considering what he'd heard. For one thing, Nora had retaken a room at the Royal Hotel. He knew of her debt dilemma on the *Gazette* long before this evening, and he'd expected the same kind of visit from her about a loan as Eden was making to Parker.

So whose idea had it been to come here to Parker?

Undoubtedly Eden's. Rafe believed Nora knew next to nothing of Eden's boldness to come here tonight. If Nora had realized Eden's plan, she wouldn't have allowed her to come here alone, even if Parker was trustworthy and old enough to be her grandfather.

Rafe wasn't surprised that Eden came up with a plan different than Nora's to borrow the money. Eden would find the task of coming to him humbling. She had reason enough to avoid him, after walking away when she believed he would remain blind.

Absorbed in what he'd heard about a journal, he wondered how much her mother had revealed about her life at Kalawao. It must unveil a great deal of misery that had occurred in the early days of the detention colony. More importantly what did it reveal about Kip? If it revealed what he thought it did—

Abruptly now, he came to the decision he'd mulled over for weeks. It was important to speak to Nora and make a deal with her about the *Gazette* before Eden told her she'd seen Parker Judson. If he knew P.J., he'd offer the loan. Tonight was good timing since his lawyer would be at the hotel.

Within minutes Rafe's horses were trotting along the road toward the Royal Hotel on King Street. He pulled out his watch. It wasn't yet six o'clock. There was time enough to accomplish his purpose. If all went as he anticipated, when Eden showed up at the *Gazette* tomorrow to work on the installment from Rebecca's journal, he would pay a surprise visit, and he would hold the key to the *Gazette*.

—⌒⌒—

Early the next morning Eden arrived at the *Gazette* before Zachary or Great-aunt Nora did, anxious to continue editing the first installment of "Rebecca's Story," as Eden named the series. She left her buggy under the shade of some palms and came to the door with her key, only to find the door unlocked. Odd, she hadn't seen Nora's carriage, and she usually did not arrive until noon. Zachary came in at nine o'clock. She pushed the door open.

She heard someone in Nora's office, went there, and opened the door wide. She stopped.

Rafe Easton was behind the desk, his feet up on a chair, and his hands behind his dark head. There was the suggestion of a smile, but hardly a pleasant one.

He surveyed her. "The perfect employee. Arriving with the early rays of sunlight and going steadfastly to her work. When you came to Hawaiiana about Kip, what did you really want? More money? This time to bail the *Gazette* out of bankruptcy?"

She tightened her mouth at his provocative mood.

Perhaps if I try to be pleasant . . .

"We never did thank you adequately for your help, Rafe. The printing press is working wonderfully well. We were able to train a boy named David to use it, and he's very ambitious to get Scriptures to the children there. Ambrose is looking into the possibility of printing Scriptures into Hawaiian."

"So Ambrose told me," he said. "Did you come about more money?"

Her temper snapped. *All right! I tried!*

"No, Mr. Easton, I am obviously not seeking a loan for the *Gazette*. Nora's loan will come from a man known to be a gentleman." She lifted her chin triumphantly.

"You used Kip as an excuse, but you did come to Hawaiiana for a loan," he persisted.

She was about to hotly deny it when something in his eyes alerted her. She didn't think he believed that at all. He was urging her on to insist that she had gone to see him about Kip so he would then ask why she did not want to tell him *now*.

So she kept silent.

He put his feet down and stood. He smiled. "So here we are.

There's no one to interrupt us. There's no Bunny muddying the waters. It's a nice day outside; the breezes are soothing, the birds are trilling . . . so now, in a calm and reasonable way tell me about Kip. What did your mother write in her journal? How much did you tell P.J. last night?"

She surveyed him in his handsome white linen shirt and dark trousers. She smiled too, but controlled her notebook and the journal. "How did you know I went to the Judson house last evening? I haven't mentioned it to anyone."

His gaze dropped to the journal. "I was there at P.J.'s when you called. We'd just signed a contract about Keno and Hawaiiana. I listened."

"Of all the nerve!"

"Quite easy, actually. The occasion fell into my hand like ripe fruit. I then knew I'd better act quickly on behalf of the *Gazette*."

His gaze tested her. "Speaking of the *Gazette*, we may need to delay printing the first installment of Rebecca's story. The content will first need to meet my approval as chief editor."

She had nothing to say for a moment. More than three years ago when Rafe had first planned to enter journalism, he'd written well-researched articles for the *Gazette*, all of them fully supporting the Hawaiian monarchy. But what could he mean now?

"You mean you've become chief editor?" she demanded.

He smiled. "Nora hasn't told you yet? No, she wouldn't have had time." He folded his arms across his chest. "Our little business transaction only took place last night in my hotel room under the direction of my lawyer."

Business transaction! She searched his eyes and saw a gleam of triumph. Despite her bewilderment, his rousing gaze drew her. How dreadful if those warm eyes should have remained sightless.

She flushed, realizing he'd noticed her wayward thought. Still holding the journal and her notebook in her arms she marched to the window and said over her shoulder, "I'm sure I don't know what you mean."

"Oh I think you do. After your meeting with Parker, I decided it was past time for Nora and me to have that little talk she's wanted. So we made a deal."

She turned. "*You* gave Nora a loan?"

"I didn't exactly say I'd given her a loan."

"You just implied—"

"I said we settled on a business transaction with my lawyer."

"You can't do that."

He smiled tolerantly. "No? Why can't I?"

She hurried back to the desk where he sat on the edge, arms folded, apparently enjoying himself.

"Because Parker Judson told me he'd grant Nora and me the loan to save the *Gazette!*"

"So he did. However, dear old P.J. is a few hours too late. Nora *sold* me sixty percent of the controlling interest in the *Gazette*. I now control this nostalgic little newspaper."

Eden sank into the hard-backed chair. "Oh no!"

"So you would prefer Nora to be indebted to Parker Judson. When Nora dies then the paper would be neatly swallowed into all the other Judson assets. Then what would happen to Zach? This paper means a great deal to him. We're all surprised just how talented he is as a journalist. He's not a planter like Ainsworth, but he does have an inquisitive mind. That works to his advantage. I aim to keep Zach secure despite your grandfather's cantankerous mood."

His answer surprised her. It sounded as if he had acted to protect Great-aunt Nora and defend Zachary's inheritance. This action sounded like the old Rafe Easton she'd known and loved most of her life. If what he suggested was true, she would have no qualms with his preempting Parker Judson.

"Nora would never *sell* the *Gazette*."

"She did. It brings me great satisfaction. I remember three years ago when your dear Grandfather Ainsworth marched over here with Townsend and fired me for an article supporting Liliuokalani. That wasn't enough; he wanted to run me out of Honolulu, and Townsend helped him by backing him."

"Please I don't want to talk about Townsend. Anyway, you've nothing to complain about." She turned toward him. "If Ainsworth hadn't fired you, you wouldn't have sailed to French Guiana where you located the new variety of pineapple slips."

"Wrong, again. I had planned a voyage. Forget that, however. I carry no old grudge against Ainsworth. I have a strong affection for him, actually. About my new journalistic venture, I intend to oversee what's published in the *Gazette*. Nora, dear heart that she is, has agreed."

"I don't believe it!"

"Ah but she has. And she's turned your project over to me. First read-through, editing . . . all of it." He looked at her evenly. "With that much clear, I'll need to read Rebecca's journal for myself before I agree to publish your installments." He smiled, but a flicker of anger came to his eyes. "Since, as you say, I'm not man enough to handle the truth about Kip, I'll cling to Bunny's hand while I read it."

"So that's it. You did *all* this just to get control of the journal!"

"I wouldn't agree I did it *all* for that purpose. I considered Nora and Zach. You may not believe this since you prefer to think the worst of me, but I had a loan in mind for Nora even before the fire at Hanalei. Naturally all that happened afterward interfered. I told her this and she's convinced of my purposes, even if you are not."

Her mind was running. She had already signed a contract with the *Gazette* giving the paper the right to publish the journal on their schedule. The decision may have been hasty, but she'd been dealing with her beloved great-aunt at the time when Nora owned the paper. She'd never imagined that Rafe Easton would end up in control.

"Are you telling me you paid off all Nora's debts for the *Gazette?*" she asked.

He took out his watch. "Her debts are, or will be, by this afternoon at three o'clock, paid in full. She is a very happy lady. If you don't think so, ask her. She will sleep well tonight. So will Zach. The last thing he needs is to agonize over Ainsworth cutting him out of Derrington assets. Ainsworth has held money over the heads of his family members too long. I think his refusal to give his sister a loan for the *Gazette* was uncalled for. True, the *Gazette* supports the queen, but we needn't destroy one another over politics."

She couldn't argue against his reasoning.

"So," he said, putting his watch away, "everything is securely in the hands of my very smart lawyer. I'm sure you're extremely pleased."

Their eyes met but the gaze held none of the old romantic spark—just a test of wills.

If she felt anything, it was caution. And yet . . . the spark was not yet cold, dead ash. As their eyes held, some warmth grew. As though he felt it, and the experience frustrated him, he stood abruptly and walked to the window, looking out for a moment. He turned his head toward her again. He looked pointedly at the leather notebook she continued to grasp.

"You can leave that on my desk, and be on your way, Miss Derrington. Also, leave the first installment. I will need to see that as well."

"I'll do no such thing. This journal is mine."

"If you want her story printed, as I wholeheartedly agree it should be, you will leave the material on my desk and trust me to do what is right."

"The journal was entrusted to me, and I'm to have control over its contents and what's revealed to the public."

"Then Rebecca did write about Kip."

"Yes, but do you actually think I'd include anything about him in the *Gazette* for every stranger to read? If that's what you're worried about—"

"That isn't my concern, Eden. I'd never expect anything that low of you where Kip's concerned. But I can't take risks with the boy's future. I need to know all the truth to safeguard his future.

When you threw that bait at me at Hawaiiana saying you had information on Kip, you knew it would prompt me to take action."

She turned her back because he was right.

"So why did you even mention Kip since you refuse to share the information?"

She walked to the open window.

"Because," she said defensively, "I did intend to discuss certain matters with you at Hawaiiana. It was you who—"

"Never mind all that. Let's get serious. For Kip's sake. We'll discuss these 'certain matters' now," he insisted.

"No, because afterwards I saw I was wrong. I won't do it now."

"Eden I'm not in the mood for one of your tantrums," he snapped. "The debate over revealing to me the truth, is over. You signed away the rights to Rebecca's journal to the *Gazette*. Those rights now belong to me. I intend to have the truth, as I told you at Iolani, and it won't do you any good to run away this time."

She sucked in her breath, consumed in withstanding his argument.

"I'll destroy the journal first," she challenged.

"Is the truth that bad? You merely turn up the heat telling me that!"

She started to head for the door, clutching the materials. He calmly moved to the door and leaned there.

She stopped.

"Be reasonable, Eden, will you?"

She saw her hopeless quandary. There was no getting around him. He was deliberately out to make matters difficult for her. Frustrated by her defeat she dropped the notebook and journal on the desk.

"There! You win! You always have to win don't you? Then go right ahead, read it." She pointed at the journal. "Learn about Kip's father, and be sorry you didn't *trust me*."

It was as if something inside him exploded. The next thing she knew he stood, blocking her, grasping her forearm.

"Trust *you*? You're the last woman I'd trust again with anything precious to me."

He released her. Stunned, she drew back and found herself against a chair. She dropped into it, staring at him.

His rousing eyes refused to let hers go. Leaning over her, a hand on each of the chair arms so she could not escape, he said, "You expect me to trust a woman who claimed to love a man and then abandoned him upon believing he was going blind? I'd sooner play Russian roulette with the rest of my life as to risk my heart with you again."

"That's a lie, Rafe Easton! *You* were the one who thrust *me* away. *You* wouldn't trust *me*. Oh I know all about how you loved Bernice all these years you said you cared for me. Even when you were willing to marry me it was Bernice your heart truly wanted."

He drew back. "What are you talking about?"

She sprang to her feet. "You know exactly what I'm speaking about!"

"No, I don't!"

"I saw the card and photograph in the captain's cabin."

"What card? What photograph? What captain's cabin?"

She hurled the words at him. "The *Minoa*. The card and photograph Bernice sent to you. Treasured by you and kept in a secret place. Asking you to admit—as you'd done before— that you loved only her!"

"There is no card. No photograph of Bernice. If I wanted to keep a photograph of her around, I'd set it out so I could look at it, not stash it in my desk. Besides, what were you doing snooping in my cabin drawer?"

"I'll admit I snooped. And I'm glad I did. I discovered the truth about Rafe Easton and Bernice Judson."

"You wouldn't know the truth if it landed in your lap."

"I know the truth!"

"The only thing in my ship desk suggesting a woman among my private mementoes was a jade comb from the Caribbean."

"Oh, yes, I saw it. Very lovely. For my fair Bernice."

"No. Not then. When I bought it I had you in mind. But I decided against giving you a gift back then. You were attending that nursing school of your aunt's and I wasn't ready to get serious, and it wasn't proper to give you something personal—blame that on Ambrose's lectures. I'd forgotten all about it."

She looked at him. She was beginning to feel her foundation cracking. Though angry, she believed him about the jade. Instead, she refocused on the obvious betrayal: *But I did see that card and picture. I'm not hallucinating.* "But you were seeing Parker Judson's niece at that time."

"What of it?" He showed no guilt or shame. "Yes, I saw her a few times. You and I weren't engaged then. Neither of us had made a commitment about caring for each other. That's why I decided against giving you the jade piece. It was too soon. It was also the same time you saw Kip aboard the *Minoa* and jumped to the conclusion I'd kept a mistress!"

"I did not!"

"Of course you did."

"What was I supposed to think? You were too proud to tell me the facts."

"You could have asked me. Then believed in me when I told you the truth."

"I did, later."

"It took you long enough."

"It did not! Anyway, where did it get me?"

His eyes narrowed. "What do you mean by that?"

"You were still carrying the torch for Bernice! That's what I mean!"

"Hold on," he said tersely. "You're the one who threw me overboard! *He's blind! Poor Rafe. Well, goodbye Rafe. You don't fit into my big plans any longer. We'll just forget everything, just as if it didn't happen. You go your stumbling way in the darkness and I'll carry on my life's ambition on Molokai. Well, so long Rafe.*"

She sucked in her breath, knotting her hands. "So that's it. That's what you believed about me? I would never say such a thing, ever. What happened to you, to hurt me so deeply? If you knew how much—" She stopped.

"Oh, very touching."

The disdain in his voice nearly drove her to haul off and slap him.

"Cad!" she threw at him. "Scallywag! Rogue!"

"Anything else?"

"How dare you! I never said anything so venomous to you in your life. You know it."

"Are you willing to stand there and lie about the letter?"

"What letter? You wouldn't even see me, or write to me, or even tell me to go drown in the pearl lagoon! Yet you stand there after all I've been through, and dare say—and dare say—" She began to cry, but corrected herself. *Oh, no. No tears in front of him! He'd claim that was a dramatic ruse.* "And you dare say I abandoned you in your blindness?"

"I suppose your abominable letter just formulated itself and dropped down from the sky," he said with derision.

"What letter?" she repeated, fuming.

"Why do you keep asking 'what letter?' That treacherous letter you sent to cheer me up in one of the worst trials of my life."

"I sent you no letter."

"I couldn't read your loving words for myself, so Bernice read them to me—"

His sentence came to an abrupt halt. He stared at her.

Eden stared back, glowering at him. But her glower quickly faded. Rafe looked as though he'd experienced an intense jolt. She grew confused, then worried. Was it his head again—she took a step toward him.

"*Bernice read them to me,*" he repeated.

He slowly sat on the edge of the desk again and put a hand against his head.

She continued to wait, breathing hard from her pounding heart, her hands cold and damp, surprised by his odd expression.

"Rafe? Are you—are you well? Is your head . . . ?"

He sighed. "The only thing wrong with my head is that I've used it to play the fool."

His manner had so drastically altered that she was dazed.

He looked at her for a long moment. He groaned, got up and walked over to the open window and leaned there. He murmured to himself as he shook his head in vexation.

"Rafe—"

He turned, studying her. "You *did* get my letter from San Francisco?"

"No. There wasn't any letter, I told you that. There was nothing from the time you rode away from Hanalei."

"I wrote to you from San Francisco."

"You wrote to me?"

"I want to hear this again. Did you write to me from Kalawao about ending everything between us?"

She gasped. "You got a letter? But how?"

"Eden, please, just answer the question."

"No. I didn't write you from Kalawao or from anywhere else. Your silence was confusing, but it also made your feelings about me clear enough. Then when I found the evidence in the captain's cabin I understood why. So I was waiting for the right time to send the ring to you at Hanalei. It's safe. Bernice should like it—"

"No, don't." He came back to the desk again, absently moving pencils, papers, and a clock.

"I've got to look into this," he murmured.

"I want to know about this letter," she said. "The one you say I sent to you. I don't understand."

His gaze held hers. "Nor do I, yet. But I aim to find out. I should have done so a long time ago. To be clear—you never received my San Francisco letter."

"No."

"And you never wrote to me at the Judson Mansion, Nob Hill? Or at the Palace Hotel?"

"No. Why should I, after what I found in your cabin?"

"You keep talking of that, when I said I never kept a photograph of Bernice aboard the *Minoa*, or anywhere else. There's some mistake."

"There is no mistake. I saw them."

"You could have written and asked me about them."

"And you could have written *me* about my walking away in the midst of your trial. I've been in Honolulu for weeks. You might have contacted me with questions. Instead, you've—"

"Yes, I know." He ran his fingers through his hair. "You're absolutely right. I could have contacted you. I admit it. I didn't wish to get involved again. It wasn't easy to hear you say in your letter that I was now worthless to you because I was blind."

Painful shock overwhelmed her. She sat down and turned her head away. "I'd *never* say that to you, or even think it—"

She wanted to say something more that would end their estrangement, but sensed it would be unwise just then. Although his anger toward her had apparently taken flight, he was not readily responding. He looked weary, even discouraged, not with her, but with himself. She wanted to reach a hand to touch, but dare not be presumptuous. She saw the flexed jaw. He remained inaccessible. He'd just admitted how he did not wish to get involved again. He meant it. She would respect the distance he wanted to uphold for now.

"Anyway," she murmured, "I didn't have the address of Nob Hill. Nor would she have given my letter to you if she'd known about it."

It was a bold thing to say to him, but she believed it. He was silent, pensive, as if he knew as much.

"Nor did I have the time to write anyone from Kalawao. It was dreadful there—and what would I say? The mail there is miserably slow, as you know. It took weeks after my father's heart attack to get a letter to Ambrose. Then, two more weeks before he arrived on the

Minoa. Kalawao is like a prison."

"What about the message I asked your father to tell you before I left on the steamer? I knew you were going with him to Molokai. I asked him to say that I'd write you when I knew the outcome from Dr. William Kelly."

She hesitated. Then there had been a message. She wanted to wail in frustration.

"No." Her voice was barely audible.

He looked at her.

"I guess," she added, looking away, "he was too taken up with going to Kalawao to bother about such things."

Her voice was bitter.

He stood and moved aimlessly about the small office-room. Then he walked to the window, hands shoved in his trouser pockets. He looked onto King Street. People walked by. Horse-drawn buggies trotted down the street. The palm trees rustled their dance.

After a minute of tense silence he walked to the door, and opened it. He started out. He stopped, and looked back at her. Their gaze held.

"Eden, I have some important matters to straighten out."

She laid her hand on Rebecca's journal. "Aren't you forgetting this?"

"No, I haven't forgotten. Right now there's something else more important."

She looked at him. Her heart skipped.

"I'll be in touch with you about it at Kea Lani."

He departed, shutting the door behind him.

Eden watched through the window. Had he nothing more to say? Or was there too much to say it all now? Her heart was telling her that there wasn't just one step back—not a quick embrace, or a long kiss—but perhaps a thousand steps were needed, and much forgiveness.

Rafe must feel more strongly about it than she did. Their trust in each other had been breached and trampled on by lies, deceit, and pride. She, too, had been proud, refusing to seek the deeper reasons why Rafe had suddenly turned from her. Yes, there'd been the incriminating evidence in the cabin drawer, but she could have insisted on an answer.

She could envision broken pieces of what once was theirs, stretching out before them like a great wilderness through which they must journey before they could reach the goal

No, it would not be an easy journey. Perhaps it was not even a journey Rafe wished to start out on again. She too, felt weary, betrayed, bewildered.

As Eden gazed out on the sunny warm morning, she wondered whether Rafe believed women in general sought him not for who he was, a Christian *man*, reborn in Christ, but because of his indisputable looks.

Man looks on the outward appearance, but God looks on the heart.

If Rafe believed this about women, then Eden's own supposed rejection over his blindness would have convinced him he was right. He was angry because he wanted to be loved for who he was, not just a handsome, strong body. He had once believed that her love went much deeper because of their belief in Christ, and it did.

But then, along came the dark trial beginning with Townsend and the fire, and ending with a letter of cruel and hurtful lies.

━━⟡━━

In his hotel suite Rafe searched his trunk and baggage for the letter he'd received from Eden in San Francisco. He called for Ling who hurried into the bedroom. Ling flung his hands to his head in despair when he saw the clothing and goods spread out on the floor. Rafe faced him.

"That letter I received from Eden when I was at the Judson mansion. What did I do with it, do you remember?"

"Long time ago. You expect me know everything?"

"Think. It's important. I suspect that letter didn't come from

Kalawao at all but from Judson Mansion. Written upstairs by the pretty hand of a treacherous woman."

"You think so? I think so all along."

"Why didn't you say something?"

"You no listen to me. Very stubborn man sometime."

"All true. And see where it got me? Take heed Ling. Now think. What did I do with it when I came back to my room?"

Ling rubbed his chin. Rafe glowered at the clutter, hands on hips, thinking.

"We in library. Miss Judson there, watching you. Mr. Zach come. Then I think you put letter in dinner-jacket pocket—black one."

"Yes, I remember. Then where's the coat?"

"I send to be cleaned long time ago. You wear others. Black one still over here now, in good closet." He pointed. "But no letter inside pocket. Was none when I send to be cleaned in Chinatown. Pockets all empty. Always check before laundry. Pocket empty," he repeated. "Strange."

Empty. Nevertheless something in Ling's voice roused Rafe's interest. He saw the familiar sly look Ling used when he wanted Rafe to ask more questions because he had something to tell. Before he would tell, he must be prompted and made to look as though it were his honorable duty to tell what he knew.

"All right, Ling. Why do you say that?"

"Say what?"

"The pocket was empty."

Ling looked uneasy. Then, embarrassed. "You change mind and give letter to Miss Judson?"

"Not at all."

"Okay. I tell you, Mr. Rafe. Very bad. I catch lady in your bedroom at Judson Mansion. She laugh. She say you spill something on black jacket. Say you ask her to bring jacket to room to give me. No sound good, but how I ask question of fancy daughter of Mr. Judson? And, jacket was wet, like she said. But I remember. Think she put something behind back and hold in hand when I come in bedroom."

So that's how she did it. The deceitful little wench!

He'd been ripped apart by what he thought was Eden's rejection, immaturity, and selfishness.

Rafe recalled how in the library Bernice was going to take the letter but he'd insisted she leave it with him. Naturally she saw him place it in his pocket, while he'd been blind to her scheming intentions.

"I do remember," he admitted, angry with himself as much as he was with Bernice. As a man, it was his responsibility to be wise in these matters and not to let his decisions be influenced by someone like P.J.'s spoiled niece. Again, pride had interfered with wisdom. He thought he knew best, but his determination had gotten him into the tragedy with Townsend and now Eden.

Rafe thought back to what had seemed a minor incident. When they'd gone into the salon to meet the other guests she'd spilled something on his jacket. Then she'd apologized profusely and insisted on taking his jacket to Ling. *She must have come directly to my room and removed the letter to get rid of it.*

"I think she took the letter, left my room, and destroyed it."

"Think same thing. I say very strange woman."

He looked at Ling who fidgeted with the silvery buttons on his fancy jacket.

"All right. You know something more. What is it?"

"I think letter you write Miss Eden never go to postman. I put on hall table. Then I see Miss Judson at table short time later. Now I know. She write lying letter from Miss Eden. I think she take your letter away. It never get to leper island."

Bernice had read what he had written in confidence to Eden, and answered it the way she wanted Eden to reply. Then, knowing he couldn't see the handwriting, Bernice was able to pretend the letter had arrived from Kalawao.

"And like a fool I swallowed it all."

"Not your fault. Miss Bernice woman with tricky fishnet. She like you too much. She catch if can."

"No thanks," Rafe said. "Character is all-important, Ling. Wealth, beauty, and influence are death traps in the wrong hands. If someone can cheat and lie to reach their goals, you'd better not have your back to them when they don't want you anymore. I'm going out. I'll be back late tonight."

He went out the bedroom door.

Ling looked around at the clutter. He sighed, shaking his head. Slowly, muttering in Chinese, he began to put things back—one at a time.

Chapter Twenty-Three
The Long Way Back

*E*den drove the buggy along, thinking. If Bernice could lie so easily to get her way, there was little reason to trust her words on the card. If Rafe had kept a photograph of Bernice on the *Minoa* he would have admitted it. He hadn't tried to excuse himself where Bernice was concerned. Then, since Rafe hadn't put them among his personal papers, who did?

Her hands tightened on the reins. She was remembering something . . . Keno standing by the captain's desk. Keno glancing her way before slipping something into the drawer. Could it be? But how? Where had he gotten it?

She moaned and tears prickled her eyes. How ashamed she was over the spiteful things she'd believed about Rafe. During all these miserable months it had been nothing but another lie.

Lies. Lies ruin, destroy, kill, and maim. And who did Jesus say was the father of lies? Satan was a liar and murderer from the beginning.

She must talk to Keno at once!

When Eden arrived back at Kea Lani, Candace was coming out the front door carrying a large bundle, followed by one of the serving girls, who also carried a large bundle. Candace waited until Eden stopped her buggy and turned the reins over to the stable boy.

Eden walked up, holding a hand against her pretty green hat.

Candace smiled. "That horse is totally spoiled. She might as well be your baby."

"Kona? Well, she is!" Eden said, laughing. "I won't make any excuses. I loved that horse the moment I saw it at Hanalei. She was one of Rafe's colts, but he gave her to me."

"Don't let Bernice know. She'll insist he give her a horse next."

"Now that you mention Bernice . . . I need to speak to Keno. You wouldn't know where to find him I suppose?"

Candace tilted her auburn head. "Yes, surely, but why would you want to talk to him about Bernice? What do the two of them have in common?"

"Not a single thing. I need to ask Keno some questions about what happened on the *Minoa* when he captained the ship to Molokai. Could you bring me to him?"

"I was just going to Hawaiiana with these new drapes. Keno is there."

Eden halted. "Hawaiiana? Oh, no. That's the last place I want to go. Bernice is there visiting with Celestine."

"I don't think so. I heard something about her going with her uncle and some friends to another of the Judsons' summer homes. One isn't enough, you know," she said with a half-smile. "Bernice is easily bored. This house, I think, is on Maui. Come along, then. I've had new draperies made for our bedroom. I don't think I could endure those dark blue ones. They're of wonderful quality, but so dark! Noelani says they were chosen to make the room better for Rafe's sleeping habits, but Rafe's tastes are not mine—" She stopped. "Anyway, these new ones," she said of the bundles she carried, "are a pale blue and ivory brocade. They're simply lovely. I hope Keno likes them."

"Keno will like anything if you're included with it."

Candace paused and hugged the bundle, her eyes looking into

the distance, as if she saw a mirage. "Lucky, aren't I? To have a man like my Keno Boy?"

"No."

Candace looked at her, stunned. Then Eden laughed. "No, not lucky, silly. Blessed! Blessed by God."

Candace smiled and brushed a dark curl away from Eden's throat. "How right you are. What would I do without you? Anyway, climb in. I've much to do in the plantation house before dinner."

Eden was happy to see Candace so enthusiastic. Her upcoming marriage had put a twinkle in her eyes and a glow to her cheeks. *I've never seen her this happy, and I couldn't be more pleased for both of them.*

Once they were seated, and the reins were in the driver's hands, the horse trotted down a lane lined with feathery green. Eden glanced toward the horizon where billowing clouds churned restlessly.

Eden glanced at Candace. "There's a reason for the way Rafe's behaved." And she told Candace what happened that morning at the *Gazette*. Candace broke into a smile. "Why, Eden! You should have told me immediately. Why this is the best news possible."

"I don't see it quite that way."

"Oh but you simply must. He doesn't love Bernice. If that snake did all of this to come between you two, you and Rafe can come back together again. It was all a fabrication. Rafe must know that by now. He's too smart to marry a woman as empty as Bernice. She couldn't be a Christian and live in such deceit. Her conscience apparently doesn't bother her. It will mean the end of anything between them. Oh this is absolutely wonderful!" Candace repeated, bringing her palms together.

"You may not see how all of this is working out for good, Eden, but it is. Rafe knows the truth now, and so do you. My faith is refreshed. I truly believe you two will marry after all."

Eden kept a grip on her feelings. Candace may believe the matter solved, but Eden wasn't as optimistic. She thought she understood Rafe better than Candace.

"You're sure Rafe isn't anywhere near Hawaiiana?" Eden asked cautiously. The last thing she wanted was another meeting.

"If he left the *Gazette* office in the mood you described, then Bernice is the one who should worry about a confrontation with Rafe. She's off to Maui, though, and I don't think Rafe will go all the way there. I suspect he'll wait until she returns to Honolulu."

Eden smiled. She would like to see Bernice's face when Rafe stood in his confident stance and told her he knew all about her "magical letter" arriving.

Then, she corrected herself. *No. That isn't right. As God's child I do not seek vengeance. That's the way the world's children behave. I'm going to follow the steps of Ambrose. I'm going to pray for Bernice Judson.* There was always hope for such a person.

When they arrived at Hawaiiana, Keno was coming from the field. He was walking with his shirt open and the wind blowing against him and his hat. He saw their carriage and buttoned his shirt, walking forward to meet them. He opened the carriage door and his first smile was for Candace. He bowed. "My *sweet* Lady."

"New drapes," she announced pushing bundles into his strong arms. Then she turned toward Eden. "Eden needs to talk to you about Parker Judson's niece."

Keno exchanged glances with Candace and then stepped back, hand at chest. "Now wait a minute, ladies, I've nothing to do with the wealthy heiress from the Bay City, believe me!"

"So you know she's a wealthy heiress do you?" Candace asked tilting her head.

"Well, who doesn't?"

Candace laughed. "I'll bring these bundles into the house and meet you for refreshments on the lanai when you've finished. With Noelani's help, we're going to tackle those horrid blue-black drapes today."

Keno walked with Eden to the shade of a jacaranda tree. He wiped his brow and apologized for his soiled condition. "We've been working in the mountainous field south of here. New pineapple plantings."

"I remember when you and Rafe put the first slips into the ground. They're doing well I suppose?"

"Oh, excellent. You won't believe the sweet, juicy taste of these new pineapples. They'll be the talk of the mainland. I can see the finest restaurants in California serving our pineapples—and Kona coffee."

She laughed. "You needn't convince me. I had a sample of one of those pineapples on the *Minoa* in San Francisco. And I'm addicted to Hanalei coffee!"

A breeze blew against them.

"I can't understand Rafe," he said thoughtfully. "He's not walking the pattern of his old footsteps, a way I know as well as my own. It troubles me. I told him so, too. He just gave me that steely look of his and went on as if I hadn't said anything. Well, he can see again, thanks to our Lord. But if he'd give you up for Bernice, then my old pal must have lost some of that wit he's known for, even if he's regained vision."

She turned and faced him. "Keno, that's what I need to talk to you about. I think there is a reason why Rafe has been so, well, difficult."

"What do you have in mind?"

"I talked with him this morning at the *Gazette*."

His surprise was evident. "He knew you would be there," he stated, with a hint of suggestion in his voice.

"Oh, he knew all right." She explained about Rafe buying sixty percent of the *Gazette*. Keno whistled. "Smart move," he said thoughtfully.

She went briefly over what it was likely to mean about supporting the monarchy in the editorials, but Keno was elusive about whether he supported the monarchy or annexation. Also, she told him about the vigorous "discussion" they had engaged in, and that she and Rafe had stumbled onto some very disturbing facts.

"What kind of facts?"

She told him that Bernice had apparently made a counterfeit letter from Eden breaking off with Rafe.

Keno groaned. He put a fist to his forehead. "Fool that I am, I didn't have a clue. No wonder he behaved as he did."

"How could we know? We've all been tricked."

"But I should have guessed the problem was something so painful he couldn't talk about it. Even Ambrose missed it." He shook his head miserably, and looked down at the ground. "Ambrose and I both failed him."

The depth of Keno's friendship with Rafe comforted Eden's heart.

"No wonder he's been so angry, with that chip on his shoulder," he said. "Okay, then. Bernice wrote this crazy letter to Rafe in your name. He believed it and everything crashed. Now, you suggest he's on to her. Well, that ends it then, right?"

"There are other problems." She tried to sound casual. Rafe wasn't the only wounded one. She, too, felt so hurt.

"Maybe so. There are always other problems. Look how many Candace and I had."

"I know," she said gently. "But it did come together at last."

"My point. And these matters with Rafe can be straightened out."

"I don't believe Rafe's ready yet. He's been hurt enough recently with everything that's happened—Townsend—"

"Who's still roaming free."

"The trial of believing he would go blind, the betrayal by the woman he thought he could trust above—it's not easy to just pick up where we left off."

"You're right there. Broken bones need time to heal. I had a friend once who broke his arm. But he kept messing with the sling. Even took it off sometimes. Said it was too tight. When he did heal, his arm was crooked.

"You're a wise girl. I guess that comes from all those years with

Ambrose. Let Rafe heal and come to his decisions on his own timing."

"Keno, there is something more. And I'm the one who needs convincing on this. Do you recall the morning my father had his angina aboard the *Minoa?* There was an envelope—"

She could see he was gripped by what she was bringing to his remembrance.

"I confess I went through his drawer," she said, blushing. "Rafe knows I did, too. Because I brought up the photograph and the card."

"I knew you'd found them," he said. "And I knew it meant trouble."

"Rafe denies that the card was there," she said. "After the false letter he received, I can't help thinking he's right. But I can't understand how they could have been planted in the captain's cabin."

Keno ran his fingers through his hair. "I've wondered the same thing. Bernice wasn't aboard the *Minoa* that's for sure. But if Rafe comes out straight and says he didn't stash them away as a secret memento, then he didn't.

"At the time I just didn't know. I was surprised. It didn't fit what I knew about him. And while he saw Bernice in San Francisco a few years ago, most of the entertaining was done at the Judson Mansion by Parker Judson who often had Rafe go there to talk business and meet other associates. Men like Spreckels. I don't ever recall him cooing over Bernice. But like you, I couldn't see how the photograph got in the cabin unless he put it there. So I tried to guard him. I didn't want you to find it. But I knew you saw me. There was just that one moment when you looked over at the desk and I was putting it in the drawer."

"But I can't understand how it got out of the drawer to begin with," she said.

He looked at her sharply.

"You did find the envelope outside the desk didn't you?" she asked quickly, intently. "I was almost sure I saw you pick it up . . ."

"Eden, that's what must have happened! It was on the floor by your father's medical satchel when I saw it and picked it up. And I'm the one who dropped it there!"

"You!"

"Sure. Looking back it's plain enough. I was rushing to find his heart tablets in the bag. I couldn't find them, they weren't in the bag, but I didn't know it. So I practically ransacked the medicine bag. That's when the envelope must have fallen out. There might have been some other envelopes, too—mail, I guess, just sort of stuffed inside. So you see the envelope wasn't in the drawer with Rafe's private papers. I'm the one who put it there thinking it belonged there. I wanted to get it out of your sight." He slapped his forehead.

Eden almost laughed. "You're sure, Keno?"

"Certain as can be. But why would your father be carrying that sort of thing around in his medical bag?"

The tension returned. Yes, why indeed? She wondered.

"My advice is to talk this over with Ambrose. Then bring him with you and chat with Dr. Jerome. He should know how it got in his medical bag."

Eden agreed. What's more she wanted to pursue the "investigation" at once. "Would you explain to Candace that I went to see Ambrose?"

"I'll tell her. Want to borrow one of Rafe's horses? He has half a dozen here in the stables."

"Thanks Keno, but the bungalow is not far from here, I'd like to walk."

The brisk walk revived her. When she neared the church by Ambrose and Noelani's house she heard men's voices followed by laughter floating out the open window. She had no trouble recognizing Ambrose's hearty laugh. She didn't recognize the other. When she entered through the open church door she was surprised to find that Ambrose was with her own father. Perhaps not recognizing his laughter was a reminder of how driven he'd been all these years. But his quest was now over, the door had shut, and she prayed the laughter might grow to replace his obsessiveness, like a strong, stately tree bearing spiritual fruit. Free, at last—and so was Rebecca.

They were sitting on one of the benches down front, talking together like two old friends. She'd already noted they'd been together a great deal lately since he'd recovered enough to leave his bed and take slow walks. She loathed breaking in on their camaraderie. Especially when her reason for coming would renew old tensions. Nonetheless she had to discover the truth.

Ambrose saw her first and stood. "Come on and join us, lass."

Her father smiled his welcome and got to his feet, putting an arm around her shoulder. Jerome had lost much weight and he remained sallow, with his cheekbones showing. Nevertheless he had survived his attack and, by God's grace, it appeared that he would live for some years

"Jerome feels well enough to want to teach the men's Bible class this evening," Ambrose told her.

"Splendid, Father, there'll be a nice crowd I'm sure."

She sat on the bench where her father and Ambrose had been confiding, and admitted that she'd come for a specific reason.

Again, she told of how she'd met with Rafe Easton at the *Gazette* and of the loan he'd arranged with Great-aunt Nora.

"She had to do something to save her paper, and I'm pleased Rafe came to the rescue," Jerome said.

Ambrose added, "There's no other man I'd rather have Nora working with than Rafe. True, he's been up a tether recently, but I believe that is winding down. Now what's this troubling you, Eden? Not Rafe buying the paper?"

She came straight to her quandary and told them about Bernice Judson's letter found on the *Minoa*, and how Keno now believed it had fallen out of her father's medical bag.

"Do you know anything about such an envelope being in your satchel, Father?"

Jerome rubbed the bridge of his nose, then his dark eyebrows shot up with enlightenment.

"Ah, yes! There were several letters that came into the medical ward for Rafe Easton. I'd forgotten all about them. I believe there were two letters from San Francisco—one from his mother, Celestine, and while I can't be sure, another one from Miss Judson. I had intended to take them to his room that day at the medical ward and to read them to him. But I was in a desperate hurry and forgot about them. I do deeply regret it. Rafe departed soon afterward on the steamer, while I must have carried the mail aboard the *Minoa*."

Jerome fastened his apologetic gaze upon her. "I'm sorry my dear. Does that help the matter any?"

Chapter Twenty-Four
Heart to Heart

I will need to go back to work at Kalihi, Eden thought as she sat at the desk in her bedroom at Kea Lani. Several days had passed since she'd spoken with Keno at Hawaiiana.

She sorted through the papers her father had signed for the loan from Rafe Easton to enable the work on Kalawao. She couldn't possibly burden her father with these bills now! When he more fully recovered, then he, too, was likely to return to work at the Kalihi hospital. Just this morning her father had visited Kalihi where he'd seen old friends in the medical world. She wanted to keep him free of worry for at least a few months longer.

Returning to her previous position as research assistant would not be the same as it was under Dr. Bolton and Aunt Lana. She decided she would apply as a regular medical nurse. The new doctor who had taken Bolton's position was a Frenchman named Dr. Traevonne.

Adding up the overall debt, she was embarrassed when comparing it with her finances. She wondered how she would pay it off. She'd decided she could quite easily do without some new clothes.

Even without the debt to pay she had intended to return to work at Kalihi, but not until work on the journal was finished.

Rafe had implied the story should be printed, but the matter remained as unsettled as their relationship. She persisted in her caution over what would happen, and when. Only two days had passed since their confrontation at the *Gazette*, and things had remained quiet. He hadn't contacted her about the journal and the information about Kip, but she had no doubt that he would. She was prepared to tell him the truth!

It was through Great-aunt Nora, who had extended her stay at the Royal Hotel, that Eden learned Rafe had been away from Honolulu. "He told Zachary he needed to visit the Parker Judson house for a day or two."

Nora had the first installment of Rebecca's Story, and was excited about publishing it, "just as soon as Rafe returns from Maui so we can sit down together and discuss it."

Eden smiled. She knew the real reason Rafe went to Maui. Then she sobered and pondered the bills strewn across her desk. Rafe had been generous, but paying it all back in monthly installments would not be easy. After the trouble she'd gone through trying to procure the money to bail out the *Gazette*, she wasn't a bit eager to seek more financial help from *anyone*, including Grandfather Ainsworth.

Besides, her grandfather had been clear about his disinterest in Jerome's leprosy work all these years, and he wouldn't have much interest in paying the debt when he'd denied Jerome money for the project from the beginning.

Now that Jerome's health forbade his return to the clinic, her grandfather would consider payment for equipment and supplies a business risk. It would not matter that Dr. Bolton and Lana were doing research, or that Eden had met her mother and received a journal that she hoped to see printed.

Indirectly, however, Grandfather would help pay off the loan. Eden would use the money he allocated to her as a monthly bequest to help make the payments. She had written a draft on her account intending to have it delivered to Rafe's mailbox at the front desk of the hotel when she went to see Great-aunt Nora that afternoon.

She paced her bedroom floor, then made up her mind. She went to her jewelry box and carefully removed the engagement ring, and slipped it into her bag, while keeping Rebecca's journal locked away.

It was then the message from Rafe arrived from the Royal Hawaiian Hotel. She opened the seal and read: *It's important we meet in private before your visit with Nora. I'll wait for you in the hotel garden salon at 3 p.m. R.E.*

Now how did he know about her visit with Great-aunt Nora? Nora must have told him.

⟨๑๑⟩

Eden wore an ivory brocaded silk with a velvet trim of ribbon, the trim also adorning the rim of her summer hat. She looked fetching and knew it.

She drove her buggy along narrow King Street toward the hotel, wondering if he would explain what happened in his head-on confrontation with Bernice. Somehow she did not think he would share the details. Eden could only imagine, from knowing Rafe, what must have been said between them. Even though their own relationship was wounded, he would not look well on a woman who had played him for a fool. Reading a letter of lies to a man who was unable to see was at the very bottom of the character scale.

Unless she was wrong, Bernice would be an angry woman about now, and spoiled enough to pack her trunks—or rather, have a servant pack her trunks of beautiful, expensive gowns—and head back to Nob Hill society. She would leave a trail of seething smoke and ill will!

Changing the direction of her thoughts, Eden marveled that Nora refused to stay at Kea Lani because she was "miffed," as she put it, with her brother Ainsworth. She wouldn't stay at Hawaiiana, either, because Keno and Candace would soon marry and set up their living there.

"Aunt Nora, we'd love to have you when you're in Honolulu," Candace had protested. Even Rafe's mother, Celestine, wrote to Nora. Still, Nora remained at the hotel. "I relish my independence. Tamarind House is getting too difficult to get around in with my weak ankle. Here, I can ring for help easily, and Rafe, dear boy, is just minutes away."

Eden wondered over that statement. Why was there nothing except affection for Rafe after he had bought out most of the *Gazette?* Surprisingly, they were on affectionate terms, and Nora went out of her way to defend Rafe's decisions. Maybe what Rafe had told her about why he'd bought most of the *Gazette* was gen-uine? If so, her heart warmed toward him. Once again he had reached out to defend Zachary and to show he really did have a nephew-like affection for Nora.

Eden turned her buggy over to the hotel worker with: "Be sure my mare is put in the shade."

Eden entered the carpeted Royal Hawaiian Hotel lobby. Ahead of her, farther down the lobby, the open area leading out to the trop-ical garden gave a wide, scenic view of palms, flowering vines, and other shrubs, while the blue-gray sea graced the horizon. There were large and small dining tables, some were screened and others had attractive canopies. Customers and guests were taking refreshments in the warm, breezy shade. Waiters in pristine uniforms, carrying their trays with smiles, circled in and out and around the tables as if waltzing.

Eden's gaze collided with Rafe Easton, waiting near the garden entry, very good-looking in the well-tailored clothing he wore when working in the Legislature. He looked at her for a moment and then walked forward.

She was almost breathless at the change in him. The anger had vanished, as had the challenge in his manner. Arrogance had been set aside, but she still recognized his inaccessibility. The armor was back, however politely polished.

The impenetrable eyes that refused to let her into his thoughts were still stimulating as they held her. She could almost feel they embraced her. Then she realized what she took for distance was merely restraint while he tried to analyze her reaction to him.

"Hello Eden. I suppose I can still call you that in private? Or is it back to Miss Derrington?"

"Eden will do nicely. And do you wish me to call you Mr. Easton?"

Unexpectedly, an amused smile broke through. "I would prefer Rafe. I've a table," he said. "Tea or coffee? Or do you want luncheon? You won't meet Nora for an hour."

"Is it Easton coffee?" she asked. To find herself back in his presence with the cynicism gone cheered her.

He smiled. "No such success yet, but matters are looking in that direction. Management is on the verge of signing just to get me out of their office, where I incessantly talk about the famous brand."

He drew out the chair for her and quickly gave their order to the waiter.

Again their eyes held. Again she felt the old stirring of excitement.

"We need to face the truth—the foundation to build upon. Nothing else will do. I confess I should have done it before now. Instead I allowed room for the deception to grow and fester. I've no one to blame but myself. Pride got in my way. Perhaps it's more honest to say pride was the mountain I had to climb before getting back on the right God-given path. I believe I'm there again, thanks to the prayers of Ambrose and Keno."

Her heart was energized by his words, but she wasn't certain where his present intentions were taking them. Perhaps, as he was saying, he was laying the foundation first. She thought his reference to truth meant the revelation about Kip's birth in Rebecca's journal.

"Yes, you're right. And I'm going to do what I should have done earlier. I apologize about the journal. I was stubborn. It's at Kea

Lani, whenever you decide to come for it." But she was again taken off guard.

"The journal, for now, is not what I want to talk to you about."

Not the journal? What then did he have in mind?

"Oh. Yes, but I've not forgotten." She removed the first bank draft from her bag and slid it across the table toward him.

"What is this?" Rafe picked it up and looked at it.

"I can make a payment on the fifth of each month. And I'll probably be going back to work at Kalihi in September."

She looked with surprise as he folded it and pushed it back across the table.

"What are you doing?"

"Returning it."

She pushed it back. "At the *Gazette* you warned me that—"

"I didn't believe you'd take me seriously. I want you to forget this debt. And from what Ambrose tells me, the clinic and bunga-lows are being put to good use by Doc Bolton and your aunt."

She smiled. She reached over to retrieve it and he grabbed her hand. Her heart raced at the warm, strong touch.

"Did you really think I wanted your money?"

"You made it clear."

"It begins to look as if we didn't know each other as well as we thought. I was tricked into thinking you wrote me that terrible rejec-tion, and you believed I wanted your monthly allowance. The truth is, I was viciously locked into deception. After that, I wanted to rile you."

"Well you did."

"Looks like we riled each other. It's time to end all that."

She looked at the folded bank draft and tried not to show too much pleasure.

"Shall I allow myself to be relieved, or am I being presumptuous?"

He pushed the rejected draft closer toward her. "In this partic-ular matter, you can be as presumptuous as you like. Keep your allowance for a new dress, or two, though the queen isn't likely to give the Reform Party members another ball anytime soon. Not after what happened at the last one."

"Did Zachary tell you I saw the tarot card reader keep a secret appointment with the queen?"

"Yes, he told me everything. But let's not discuss that issue yet. There is one thing I'd like to know before we go on." He studied her. "The Hunnewell ball is coming up on Saturday. Have you made an appointment with Oliver?"

A surge of excitement filled her. She might easily ask, "What about Bernice?" But that would be utter folly now that it looked as if he might be moving in the direction she longed for him to go. She tried to act sober and casual, though her heart was beating wildly.

"No, I'm not interested in Oliver. I think you know that as well. I've been learning from Zachary that Oliver's involved with the gambling cartel. It's going to devastate his father when he finds out. I'm just relieved Candace escaped the unwise marriage Ainsworth had arranged. Is that what you wished to talk with me about, the ball at Hunnewells?"

"I'm asking you to the ball. Though that is my spontaneous response to how lovely you look, not the reason for our meeting." He scanned her. "Before you respond to that compliment, I'll tell you: I need to talk to you about Bernice."

Eden frowned.

"Not a pleasant subject, I agree," he said.

Eden remained cautious. Rushing forward may be the wrong response.

"She was in Maui with Parker. I went there and spoke with her about the lies she formulated. She had denigrated your priceless character, and like a fool, I took the poison wine she offered. You might like to know that when I was through bragging about your virtues she slapped me not once, but twice." He rubbed the side of his tanned face. "It's still bruised."

Priceless character. Eden's heart took wings and soared. He believed in her again! She was vindicated in his sight, the sight of the only man whose belief in her mattered.

"Eden, I wanted to meet with you here alone to apologize to you."

His gaze held her more tightly than any embrace.

She had always reasoned that in due season there would be, of Christian necessity, the need for both of them to apologize to each other, since she likewise, had not trusted him, and accused him falsely. That he realized an apology was needed brought courage, and hope.

However, once again, instead of rushing forward to claim the prize with gushing tears and open arms, she felt it would be wiser on her part to remain calm, regardless of the storm brewing in their hearts. This was a time for reason, not just emotion.

"I've unraveled the facts about the lost letters," he commented. "She brazenly admitted to it all. The deceptive way she worked it out was clever. It's as though she's in the league with Townsend when it comes to being devious. Look, Eden, I want you to understand there was never anything serious between Bernice and me. Not even three years ago in San Francisco. The fact that I was so deceived by the letter shows a weakness in me, not a weakness for Bernice. I don't know you as well as I thought I did. That's why I've been such an impossible—'cad' I think was your word for me."

"Cad, scoundrel, *and* let's see . . . what was the other one? Oh yes, scallywag," she said with blithe intention.

"I won't argue that. I want you to understand, though, that I did go through Dante's inferno over that ruddy letter!"

She winced. "I never sent you that letter, Rafe! Those cruel thoughts didn't come from my heart."

"I understand that now," he said gently. "In San Francisco, for nearly two months, I believed you did. Even Celestine assured me the letter was from you. So I accepted it."

"Celestine?" she murmured, disappointed.

"She didn't have her reading glasses on," Rafe said wryly. "Bernice planned well. I thought I was thrown aside because of a physical infirmity. The idea was as bitter as gall."

"Oh, Rafe—" She couldn't restrain herself. She clasped his hand, her eyes reflecting her heart.

He brought her hand to his lips, ignoring the public.

He smiled ruefully. "I've a lot of learning to do. I attributed to you some of the feelings I felt for my predicament. The thought of losing control, of being dependent on other people, even you, was a threat. I've always lacked confidence in others, except for a precious few like Ambrose and Keno and, more recently, you. Finding myself in a helpless condition—well, I could go on, but it's apparent. Maybe you'll want to stay as far away from me as possible—not that I promise to leave you to your decision in peace."

"We both have a lot of learning to do. I don't want to stay as far afield from you as possible. If you'd care to know my response to the tragedy when it happened, Ambrose can tell you. He brought me word at Hanalei after you'd been taken to the medical clinic."

"I spoke to Ambrose. I know what happened, now. He made it plain enough. It's evident I'll need to work on our relationship."

Our relationship. The words were warm and wonderful.

Despite her relief, Eden found her cup of joy mingled with sadness that their love had been badgered by such a test. Though she said as much, Rafe disagreed.

"As Ambrose said, better to have our tests now," he said with a smile. "We'll have plenty to keep us busy through the years. Nothing can touch God's own unless it passes through God's permission. Ambrose pointed how the American Puritans had a saying we should appreciate: 'When all we have is God, we learn that God is enough.' I hope I'm beginning to learn what that means."

"Something meaningful came to me through my experience," he continued. "Not only did I learn again the danger of anger and pride, but I have a new appreciation for those bound by a physical affliction. My hours of darkness, fear, and loss were not in vain. Such trials have sent many spiraling headlong into discouragement, then defeat. I've talked to Ambrose and Dr. Jerome—"

"You talked to my father?" She couldn't help being pleased.

"Yes. We're thinking that after things have settled down, we'll get together at the mission church and see about coming up with some way to help people who've had to overcome serious hurdles in their lives—those who've lost their sight or have become crippled. It's a deep and dark valley to go through. I think it's especially difficult for someone like me who had previously been so independent."

Eden warmed to the idea. "A way to reach out to the blind . . . a place for them to go for instance."

"That's the plan."

"I think the idea is exceptional, Rafe."

"As I mentioned, I've spoken to Ambrose about you. He made your innocence plain enough." His eyes softened as they studied her face. "He told me you'd wanted to marry me before I left for San Francisco so you could look after me. Would you really have done that?"

"Yes. What if I'd been the one who lost my sight?"

"I think you already know the answer."

"Yet you doubted me."

"I should have known you'd never betray me. Any woman with grace and mercy enough to care for a deformed leper would not shrink away from the man she loved . . . your lips told me so that night at Hanalei."

"I meant it."

"Ambrose was right. I'm still stinging from his rebukes. It worked, though. I'm back in fellowship with the Lord, and hope to be with you."

"He rebuked you?" She smiled, deliberately. "*Dear* Ambrose," she teased.

His mouth turned. "So you like the 'visit to the woodshed' aspect of it, do you?"

"Yes, a nice firm hickory stick."

"I've been odious, I'll admit. The worse thing was to malign your character. So, how do you like your contrite man to make his amends? On bended knee or in poetic language published in the *Gazette* for all to see?"

Eden wanted to sob, but she didn't wish to overwhelm him with her emotion. He was calm, watching her with a steady interest.

"What would it take for you to want to forgive and 'comfort' me? Or maybe you need to cuff me about first, like Bernice did."

She smiled, and a wave of joy swept through her. She laid her hand over his. "You've had trials enough, I think. I'm now in the mood to comfort."

"Are you then satisfied the photograph and card in my desk— thanks to old pal, Keno—was also part of her exaggerations?"

"Well—almost. Dr. Jerome told me how it was brought aboard the *Minoa*."

"Almost! But not quite? So, then, what still remains of this ugly doubt?"

She watched him uneasily because there was something personal she wanted to know, something that was not altogether her right to know. When he lifted an eyebrow of invitation, urging her to ask, she took in a breath and charged ahead.

"Even if we weren't engaged at the time, did you ever tell Bernice you loved her the way the card implied?"

"In the years we've known each other, Eden my fairest, when did you see me collecting women and convincing them of my captured devotion?"

She smiled. "You always were about as impossible to catch as a slippery eel."

"So you admit it. Then when would I have spent so much time with Bernice in San Francisco as to form this undying love affair she claims took place?"

"Then you never told her you loved her?" she persisted.

"No. Because I didn't love her. You're the one girl I've ever loved enough to marry. To say it politely—our little Bunny fibbed."

"Have you—well—have you kissed her—recently? She is very beautiful."

His warm gaze lowered to her lips. "No. I can't say she didn't try hard enough to make me give in though. Astounding fellow that I am, I managed to avoid the trap. There. You have it. The truth. Are you now satisfied?"

Yes," she whispered, "I'm satisfied."

His relief was obvious.

"If we were only alone, Darling, I would show you what it's like when I really *want* to kiss a woman. As for beauty, you've always dimmed her star of vanity, and haven't half tried. More importantly you outshine her in virtue. Your character first attracted me when we were growing up. 'Who can find a virtuous woman, for her price is far above rubies.'"

Eden couldn't help it. She was so happy, so full of excitement and thanksgiving to their heavenly Father that a few warm tears slipped past her guard. "Then you *do* still love me, Rafe?"

"Darling, I've never stopped loving you. Not at the *Gazette*. Not at Hawaiiana when I played the rogue, and not for all the tomorrows awaiting us. I am forever yours, if you take me. *Now*, how about a little reciprocation?"

Eden smiled and her eyes twinkled. "I still have the engagement ring—"

"That ring! I believe it's jinxed. I think I'll buy a new one!"

She laughed. "Oh no, Rafe Easton, not on your life. That precious ring has too much story connected with it to get rid of now. I'm going to be wearing it someday and telling my daughter and granddaughter just how much of an adventure I went through before I actually married the man of my heart!"

His warm gaze searched hers. He reached over and took her hand into both of his. "Then what are we waiting for?"

Her heart seemed to pause, then beat faster. "What?"

"You heard me."

"You mean . . . you don't mean *now*?"

"Why not? Yes, as a matter of fact, I definitely mean *now*. Before something else pops up! Let's go see Ambrose." He pushed back his chair and stood, looking down at her, this time in romantic challenge. He grasped her wrist and helped her up. "Well, Eden?"

"Now?" she said again.

He smiled. "Now."

"But . . ."

"*Eden . . .*"

"What about Candace and Keno and their big wedding?"

"They have my sympathy."

"You don't want a big wedding service?"

"Not if I can get out of it." He sighed. "I suppose you do, though."

"Well . . ."

"Why not have a celebration *afterward?* It can be just as big as it takes to makes you happy."

"So then, just go get married right now?"

He smiled and edged her out of the garden. "Exactly, my sweet. Just go and get married. Where is the engagement ring?"

"You'll never believe this!"

"You couldn't possibly have it with you now!"

"I do. It's in my bag. I was going to offer it back to you with the bank draft."

"Sublime. You shall see what yours truly is going to do. We're going straight to Ambrose. Just as soon as I retrieve the ring's mate from my suite. But come along—and no protest. I'm not letting you out of my sight until the vows are finished before God."

"What about Great-aunt Nora? She'll be waiting for me."

"All Honolulu can wait. This time we come first! I'm claiming my lost bride."

"And I, my runaway bridegroom!"

"You're even dressed in white. What more could we want?"

She laughed. "A honeymoon in Hawaii?"

"It's yours. Including the finest hotel in Honolulu. I just happen to have a suite there all ready to welcome you."

They soon arrived at the mission church with the warm breezes dancing in and out of the bushes and palm trees as if in celebration of their decision.

Eden was laughing as Rafe picked her up and carried her into the church. Ambrose was just coming out of his little office at the back and saw them, with Eden in Rafe's arms. Ambrose halted. A look of surprise flooded his sun-bronzed face that soon broke into a humorous smile.

"And what is this?"

"I've captured her at long last. Bar the door, Ambrose! It's *I do*, or die!"

Ambrose laughed. "And what do you say to this tyranny, lass?"

"I say, 'I do!'"

"Well! Then what are we waiting for? Let me get my Bible and the wedding book."

"And Noelani," Eden called after him.

"Indeed! If I forgot our Noelani in the moment of your marriage, I'd sooner not face another sunny day."

Ambrose went off to prepare and call for Noelani. Rafe set Eden on the floor but did not release her. They exchanged smiles.

"Together, at last." He swept her into his embrace. She willingly fell into the cloister of his strong arms. She lifted her lips to meet his in a time-consuming kiss.

"I love you, my precious Eden."

She was thrilled from head to toe. "And I love you . . . forever."

His lips took hers again, and promised many more kisses to come. As much as it depended upon him, they would never again part for long. Eden's heart and response echoed the same.

Chapter Twenty-Five
At Long Last . . .

The news of Rafe and Eden's quiet marriage exploded. Friends, family, and associates celebrated, while others writhed with disappointment.

"So that's the reason Bernice is returning to San Francisco so abruptly," Parker had commented when Celestine described her son's marriage.

"It's far better this way, Parker. Eden is a lovely girl. My son's been in love with her for several years."

"Well," he said in a quiet, meaningful tone, "sometimes love must wait for the right time to have its way. It does seem sudden, though, doesn't it?" He frowned. "Those months in San Francisco. Why, I was under the impression from Bernice that Rafe was about to propose to her."

Celestine sighed. "I'm afraid Bernice behaved in a shameless way, Parker."

He looked at her sharply. "Shameless? Coming from you, Celestine, this is extremely worrisome. I understand Bernice is spoiled. However, I always thought she was a good girl. Maybe you'd better explain. Looks to me like I don't know as much about what's going on as I thought."

Celestine informed him of the letter his niece had forged as from Eden.

Parker groaned. "If this is true, and I don't doubt your word, this is despicable."

"I'm sorry to say I was also tricked into believing the letter came from Kalawao. Bernice assured me the letter was from Eden. The contents brought a terrible rift between Rafe and Eden. And much heartache. They were on the verge of marriage just before the fire at Hanalei and Townsend's escape. Suddenly everything was torn apart."

Parker looked sickened. "So that was how she worked it. I'll admit to you that she's done such things like this in the past. I haven't been much of a father to her. She needed discipline while growing up, and I was too busy with my work. I sent Bernice to a finishing school hoping better company would alter her ways. It looks as if the only thing my money bought was charming manners to deceive the unwary. Well, she met her match with Rafe. She barked up the wrong tree when she took him on."

If Parker Judson was disappointed over Rafe and Eden's marriage, Grandfather Ainsworth was jubilant. As Zach later explained to Great-aunt Nora, "Ainsworth beamed upon me and Silas as if we'd struck gold. Grandfather could have passed for 'King Bullfrog' who'd just swallowed his rival from the competing pond."

Nora had laughed, finding anything that put her brother in a humorous light refreshing. "King Bullfrog. That's splendid. You should think of starting a comic in the *Gazette* about King Bullfrog and his constant quest to overthrow the queen! I don't doubt you could think of many comic situations. The readers would be sure to catch the political satire."

But Zachary wasn't laughing when Grandfather Ainsworth jubilantly pointed out to him and to Silas that he was enthralled with the two stalwart additions to the Derrington family: Rafe Easton and Keno Hunnewell.

"Strong and productive! What an asset to me. The Hunnewells are a great name in the Islands," Ainsworth stated. "Thaddeus is following Thurston's footsteps in leading the way to annexation. And Oliver, while he's made mistakes in the weak way he courted Candace, is nonetheless a worthy man. And what have you two lax grandsons of mine been accomplishing to promote the Derrington name?"

Zachary exchanged a dour look with Silas. Silas looked down at his plate hiding a smile.

"That's it! Revert to silence and long countenances," Ainsworth scolded them both. "The answer is ready at hand, is it not? *Nothing.* That's what you've both accomplished! I tell you this is a grand day, boys. At last I've got the young man I've wanted in the family for years."

"Not *years,* Grandfather," Zachary cracked. "It wasn't much more than four years ago that you and Townsend pooled resources and ran Rafe Easton out of Honolulu, Keno with him. Rafe's only just become the 'strong and productive asset' you mention because he brought back the famous pineapple slips from French Guiana."

"Exactly." His silvery eyebrows rose. "It was Rafe's ingenious success that showed me how wrong I was about him. I've wanted him in the family ever since I saw his innovative ambitions."

"Well, I'm glad Rafe and Keno are successful," Zach mumbled.

Silas looked over at Zachary as if he sympathized.

"Well I guess we know where all this celebration leaves us, Zach. We've been relegated to the back pantry to peel potatoes and skin the onions. I'll be gracious, little brother; take your choice."

Grandfather Ainsworth chuckled at Silas's glib retort.

"Now, now my boys, nothing so drastic as that. Zachary, pull yourself out of your self-incrimination. The more you four young men can all join shoulder to shoulder to work for the Derrington name, the more success will benefit all of us."

"Don't forget the Easton name," Zachary said. "Rafe happens to think well of that name, too, and of the man who gave it and Hanalei to him. Work over there is proceeding furiously. Rafe and Eden may be able to move there from the Royal Hotel in another month or so. Then what, Grandfather?"

"Then what? I'm not about to forget the Easton name," Ainsworth said in a mild voice. "The two good names of Derrington and Easton will benefit both."

"What about the name Hunnewell?" Silas asked.

"Ah, that name, too," Ainsworth said. "It's time you began paying attention to the Hunnewell daughters."

Zachary bristled. In the last month or two he had realized that Silas was spending time with Miss Claudia Hunnewell. What a decent young woman like Claudia would see in his gambling brother, Zachary couldn't guess. He was going to find out, though, and soon. He would ask her!

Zachary hadn't thought he cared much for Claudia until after the debacle over Bernice Judson. His interest had recently been tweaked when he discovered Silas was now a frequent dinner guest at the Hunnewell beach house. Claudia had even told him what a fine gentleman his older brother was.

Zachary suspected that his grandfather would not care which of his grandsons married Claudia as long as one of them captured a Hunnewell.

Silas isn't going to get Claudia, Zachary decided. He looked at him with an even stare. *She's not beautiful like Bernice, but she can be trusted.*

Claudia was different. He could love her and respect her. And unlike Bernice, Claudia bowed the knee to Christ and sang in the choir at the mission church. She had a fine voice. What's more, he could see in her eyes that she meant what she sang about: loving, trusting, and honoring the Savior.

Yes. He must go and see Claudia Hunnewell before Silas stole her away.

Just wait until all the truth comes out in the *Gazette* about Silas, Oliver, and Fraulein Wolf. He had enough to unmask the queen, too. He and Rafe were going to use the *Gazette* to turn the light on in the rat-infested cellar of the gambling and opium cartels. All he was waiting for was the appropriate time to call on Rafe at the hotel.

He smiled. From what Candace told him, Rafe hadn't taken his bride back to the Royal Hotel. He didn't want interruptions. He'd taken *Mrs. Easton* to some secret hideaway on one of the other islands. He wouldn't be back for another week. What a honeymoon those two must be enjoying!

———⌒⌒———

When Mr. and Mrs. Rafe Easton did return to the Royal Hawaiian Hotel the room was filled with flowers and well wishes from friends. The news of the Derrington luau on Kea Lani came as no surprise to Rafe and Eden, though the size of the celebration Ainsworth was giving for his granddaughter did.

After Rafe carried her over the threshold and set her down, he stared at all the containers of lush flowers filling the floor, tables, and lanai.

"Leave it to Ling to store all the congratulatory flowers here."

Eden lifted her skirt and stepped over one more container of white gardenias with their heavenly scent. She laughed. "I'll send them to Kea Lani for the luau. When we're able to live at Hanalei, I'll bring the best to be planted in the garden . . . as a reminder of our honeymoon."

"You won't need honeymoon flowers in the garden to remind you that I'm a romantic man. The honeymoon continues."

"It does, does it?"

He pulled her into his arms and bent to kiss her when someone rapped on the door. Releasing her, Rafe maneuvered around pots of flowers to reach the door.

"Welcome back to reality, old chap," Zachary said cheerfully. "Unfortunately, I've got to see you. It concerns—"

"Don't tell me, let me guess." Rafe ushered him into the room.

"Don't trip. Let's see, could it be about our friend Silas?"

"How did you know?"

Rafe shut the door. "Just got lucky, I guess."

"Hullo, Eden, dear cousin—" Zach said. "Just look at the flowers! Say—maybe I can take one of these pots to Claudia when I see her later."

"Take as many as you like," Rafe urged smoothly.

"By all means," Eden said, but quickly removed the gardenias and orchids she wanted to keep. "Let me collect the name tags first, too. Otherwise I won't be able to thank the people who sent them."

"Yes, and don't forget the big hullabaloo on Saturday," Zach reminded them. "That's another reason why I came. Grandfather wants to make sure you'll show up early since the party is to honor you."

"*Hoolaulei*," Eden corrected with amusement.

"Sounds the same to me," Zach said.

"Maybe they are," Rafe commented lightly. "This *hoolaulei* is better suited for one of the hullabaloos of Kalakaua's heyday."

Zach laughed.

"If I don't show, do you think anyone in the huge crowd will miss me?" Rafe asked Eden.

"Yes." Eden smiled. "I will."

Zach, standing behind Eden caught Rafe's eye and smiled faintly. *Lucky you*, the look seemed to say.

"Oh another thing," Zach said to Rafe, reaching into his pocket. "Ainsworth asked me to give this message to you. He said it was in answer to the one you'd sent a day or two ago about a meeting with him."

Eden, unaware of any meeting between Rafe and her grandfather, looked at Rafe as he took the message and put it in his pocket. She wondered what it was about.

Eden went to send for coffee to be delivered since she was unfamiliar with the workings of the small "kitchen" Ling had set up. Ling was spending time with his family on Hanalei.

When the coffee was served, and good-natured small talk over, Zachary began to talk about Silas. Eden, however, did not care to hear any new information until later when she would hear it from Rafe.

She went into Rafe's bedroom for the first time, now her bedroom as well—she was still a bit dazed about the tremendous change, and unloaded her smallest traveling bag. She wanted to change from her traveling clothes into a cooler afternoon dress. As she did, she thought about Rafe. She had thought she knew Rafe well in the past, but each day was a new experience in learning new things about him. Especially how romantic he was, his sense of humor, and his patience with her. She would not have thought he was patient during the miserable time of their misunderstanding, but he was.

She also discovered his great love for reading in the evenings, that he had a lovely singing voice and could play the guitar. He was captivated with the study of the universe. He liked to take her outdoors on a clear night and tell her about the planets and constellations.

He also spent more time studying Scriptures than she had known, and prayed often. At the first light of dawn he would fling back the drapes or bamboo blinds to watch the sunrise. Eden would cover her head with the sheet and he would tease her about what she was missing. He would always hold her in his arms and pray a brief prayer aloud for them before they would begin the day, either together or apart.

These were only a few interesting things she had learned since becoming his bride. If possible, she loved Rafe even more now than before they were married.

Rafe is the most wonderful man in the whole world, she told herself. *Now he is mine.*

So far, marriage was exciting. She was not the least disappointed in anything marriage offered or demanded.

All those lonely nights she had spent on Kalawao, and now, she could sleep contentedly in his arms, with her head on his strong chest and depend upon him. Marriage to the right man like her darling Rafe was *thrilling*. She looked forward to many years of happiness with a large family and life on Hanalei.

Part 3

Stars and Stripes Forever

*A*fter Zachary left the hotel suite, Eden entered the living
room and found Rafe at his desk leafing through what
appeared to be legal forms.

"Was Ainsworth's message about the celebration on Saturday?"

Rafe glanced up at her. He hesitated, and then came to a decision. He stood from the chair with papers in hand.

"We have no secrets now." He snatched the message on the desk,
and passed it to her.

"It's about Kip."

Her light mood vanished. After Ambrose had performed the
marriage ceremony, she had returned to Kea Lani to pack for the
two-week honeymoon. She had intended to leave all serious concerns behind and think of the exciting time before her. Then, aware
that such a serious matter as Kip's parentage would not disappear
just because she'd become Mrs. Rafe Easton, she had packed
Rebecca's journal at the bottom of one of her bags and later told
Rafe she'd brought it along.

"This is our time alone. Everything else must wait."

He had not mentioned the matter any further until the day before their return to Honolulu.

On that morning when she arose, she saw that Rafe had taken the journal with him on his usual early morning hike. She had worried and prayed about his response to the disappointing facts surrounding Kip's birth, and when he returned that noon she could see the truth had soberly affected him. Even then, he had set aside any discussion until they were back in Honolulu, where he was obligated to return to the Legislature for an important vote.

The fact Ainsworth had sent a message about Kip through Zachary told her that Rafe had made a decision about the dilemma facing them. She found his action surprising, since Ainsworth would surely seek control of his blood grandson, and Kip meant so much to Rafe.

Eden read Ainsworth's message:

> *"Rafe, I must say this crisis you allude to with Kip comes as a shock to me. I have no knowledge of why your decision to adopt him should pose a quandary to me, or to any future Derrington. I will discuss the matter you bring up Saturday at the luau. We should be able to get off from the throng without being noticed.*
> A. Derrington

Eden looked up from the message.

"Then you're going to tell him?" she said anxiously. "Darling, are you sure?"

"The truth is always best. Ainsworth must be told the facts."

She took hold of him, her eyes searching his. "If he learns Kip is his grandson, you'll lose him."

"He'll do everything in his power to claim him. I know that. He's received Silas, and he'll certainly want a young boy to bring into the Derrington family, especially after losing Townsend. Trying to hide Kip will harm rather than protect."

Yes, she could see Rafe's reasoning. Lies and secrets would bring a harvest of trouble.

"It's Townsend who seems the great risk," she protested. "What if he seeks control of his son just to hurt us?"

"After his crimes? He won't dare show his face in public soon. If he does, he'll be arrested. As we know, it's Ainsworth who will want control of his grandson."

"Then, what will we do about Kip?"

"I don't know yet. I'll need to talk to Ainsworth."

"I should have burned the journal when I had a chance. Then no one would have known."

He enclosed her in his arms. "No, you did the right thing, Eden, my love."

"Did I? Do you sincerely believe that?"

"Yes. I sent a letter to Ambrose before contacting your grandfather. Ambrose asked point-blank whether I could raise a boy, knowing Townsend had fathered him."

Eden, too, had worried about that aspect of proceeding with Kip's adoption.

"I told him it didn't matter. Zach and Silas are Townsend's sons, too. That doesn't provoke my dislike."

"What did Ambrose say?"

"Ambrose agrees with my decision to let the truth prevail, to allow God to work out His purposes with Kip and with the rest of us. When Kip grows up he will face his parentage the way many of us face our problems. He'll need to find God's calling in his life's circumstances. It will be up to us, to his Grandfather Ainsworth, and the rest of the family to see that he is raised in a way that prepares him.

"If he is raised to trust in Christ then, when a young man, he'll be able to confront the giants. I have a feeling he'll be strong enough to handle it. And so," he said calmly, "I'm going to have a talk with Ainsworth. He has blood rights because Kip is a Derrington. I won't fight him if he insists on bringing Kip to Kea Lani as his grandson."

She supposed he was right. It was wiser to put everything on the table now.

_____

At Kea Lani, Hawaiian music rolled along the expanse of lawn, while frothy-tipped waves from the Pacific curled onto a stretch of white sand near the dirt road leading to the Easton pearl beds. Thanks to Rafe, the historic church founded by Eden's parents remained, and the Sunday morning sermons continued to be faithfully preached by his uncle, Ambrose Easton.

The nearly one thousand adjacent acres reaching toward the Koolau mountain range now made up the new Hawaiiana pineapple plantation, of which Keno now held his share. Keno was also managing Hawaiiana during Rafe's term in the Legislature, and the rebuilding of sections of Hanalei on the Big Island. Rafe was adding to the plantation house to make it even grander for Eden, as its new mistress.

It was late afternoon and palm trees rustled as if swaying to the music. The sun was low in the cloudless sky as Rafe walked with Ainsworth across the lawn, away from the crowd of the merry guests, where they could discuss Kip without interruption.

"I'll be forthright, Rafe. You provide my family with something that I didn't recognize during the years you were growing up at Kea Lani. I always thought you an intelligent boy, but headed for trouble. You didn't seem able to accept your father's death or your mother's marriage to Townsend." He looked at Rafe. "Of course, now I know why. Back then I hadn't accepted the truth. I thought you had a chip on your shoulder. Ambrose insisted otherwise, but I was stubborn. I shouldn't have permitted Townsend to bully you and treat your mother cheaply. The older I get, the more ashamed I am about it."

Rafe wondered that Ainsworth was apologizing at this late date.

"I never held that against you. It was Townsend." He could have said more—but what good was continued resentment?

"There is one thing," Rafe said. "Have you heard anything about Townsend?"

Ainsworth's face melted into troubled bewilderment. "Not a word, Rafe. I thought he might come to me for money soon after his hideous deed, and I alerted the marshal, who had a few fellows on watch. Needless to say, he didn't show up. I have no idea how he managed to escape the Islands." He met Rafe's gaze squarely. "He received no help from me. I hope you believe me."

"I do, sir. I've not always agreed with the decisions made about his actions—"

"I know that."

"But you were always honest about your intentions. Now I prefer to move forward in life. I have what I've wanted most, Eden, Hanalei, and thankfully, my sight. I'm married to your granddaughter and I happen to be a contented man. And I anticipate a good relationship with my new grandfather. After all, I never had a grandfather until now."

"I'm humbled," Ainsworth said, looking pleased. "But before we leave the subject of Townsend, where do you think he went, and how did he get away?"

Rafe hesitated. "He received help from the gambling and opium cartels. He went first, with a woman's help, to Tamarind House to recover and then boarded a smuggling boat to one of the Islands. Then a ship took him either to California, or the Oregon coast. And he's either gone to the Caribbean, or he remains somewhere on the mainland."

Ainsworth looked amazed. "I think you're right, Rafe. He may be waiting for my death, thinking he'll inherit some big piece of the Derrington pie. If so, he's in for a tremendous shock. He's not inheriting a single penny, pineapple, or stalk of cane from me!"

"You may be right about his believing he'll inherit money. He knows he won't get Kea Lani. He could never come back and live a normal life. As I told Eden he'd be arrested and he knows it. But money sent to him through a lawyer? Yes. I think, sir, you've added the final dot and period to his plans."

"Well, he's not getting a thing, Rafe. Now." He smiled. "Let me surprise you by saying that I would rather have my other grandson Kip raised under your proven character, and subject to your uncle Ambrose's biblical guidance. Silas and Zachary are fine young men, but Silas has a failed life, partly because of Townsend, and Zachary is a good enough lad . . . but unfortunately, emotionally troubled."

Rafe stared at him, at first unable to believe what he had heard. "Are you saying, sir, that you want me, and now Eden, to proceed with adopting Kip?"

"I understand your surprise, but yes, that is what I am saying. I'm an old man. I won't be around many more years. Kip is what, two or three? My departure will come in his youth when he will still need strong guidance. I would much rather have this boy in capable hands from the beginning. I can see him all I want, I'm sure. You'll let him come and spend time at Kea Lani. I'd enjoy having him call me 'Grandfather.' But everything else, Townsend included, let us keep among the three of us—I assume Eden knows since Rebecca left her the journal. When Kip is grown and I am gone, I'll leave it to your discretion as to whether or not he ever learns about Townsend and Molokai."

Rafe was speechless.

"You might have destroyed that journal and no one would have been the wiser. Yet you came to me with the truth. That impresses me, Rafe. What better father could this little fellow have? The thought occurred that for *once* something coming from Townsend will grow up to honor the Lord. What better legacy could a Derrington have than that?"

He put a hand on Rafe's shoulder, and his eyes twinkled in the setting sun. "And may you have many *Easton* sons and daughters."

～ ⌘ ～

The full moon was rising as Eden joined her father and the members of the Derrington family. Jerome smiled at his daughter and stood, pulling a chair closer for her to sit near him. "Well, what do you think, Ambrose? Did I get a fine son-in-law?"

Ambrose looked across the lawn to where Rafe, Keno, and Zachary stood. Keno said something and Rafe laughed.

"If there ever was a marriage I wanted to take place, it was this one. Of course, I could add Keno and Miss Candace to that list as well. By the way, isn't it a little past time for that big event to take place?"

"Two more weeks, Uncle," Eden said, laughing. "Candace has pinned a calendar above her mirror. Every day she enjoys marking off one more day."

"I thought I would never see the day when that marriage would happen," Great-aunt Nora said. "I'm so relieved Candace isn't marrying that dreadful young man, Oliver."

"Now Aunt Nora, not so long ago you told me the handsome Oliver was a fine gentleman, worthy of my consideration," Eden said.

Nora looked uncomfortable. "So I did, dear. That was before I understood the rapscallion is a friend of the gambling and opium ruffians. I shall feel pity for Thaddeus Hunnewell when he discovers his firstborn son is one of them."

"It does seem to me," Ambrose said, "that the opium cartel has a rather free hand on Hunnewell lands to intimidate the workers. What's your opinion, Jerome?"

Dr. Jerome stroked his chin, his green eyes sharp in the firelight. "I'll admit I'm a trifle suspicious of their foreman. He appears to bully his own countrymen."

"When we went there on Thursday to hold the service?" Ambrose asked, drawing his bushy brows together.

"Yes. I think his name is Wong. He said nothing to me, but he did intimidate the group of men and ladies walking to our cabana near the field."

"I'll speak to Rafe about it," Ambrose said. "He'll see Thaddeus Hunnewell in the Legislature on Monday. I don't think Hunnewell senior will approve of the foreman's behavior. Perhaps the fellow is being paid by the kingpin to intimidate. The last thing the opium cartel wants is to lose their addicts to the freedom of knowing Christ."

"They won't stop us," Jerome said. "The work will go on unless Thaddeus orders us off his land. I don't think he will. He doesn't come to the mission church as often as I'd like to see him, Ambrose, but he does revere God."

Ambrose seemed to agree. "Maybe I'll call on Thaddeus this week. It's been some time since I saw him. I'll invite him to our men's Bible study."

Great-aunt Nora stood. "Well, dear ones, it's time I went indoors. Tonight I expect to go to bed early. I hardly slept a wink last night. I rarely do when I come to Kea Lani. That dreadful old mattress Ainsworth keeps in my room hasn't been exchanged for a new one since King Arthur discovered the magic sword."

Everyone chuckled. To Nora, everything was the fault of her "cantankerous brother."

"I'll walk back with you, Aunt Nora," Eden said.

Inside Kea Lani house, Eden accompanied Nora into the large library, while Nora looked for a book to read.

"It always aids my sleep, and digestion," she said. "I usually fall asleep because the book is boring."

She settled her pince-nez and leaned forward to read some of the titles. "Let's see . . . leave it to Ainsworth to have ordered *this* dreadful one: *Inside the Political Mind of the Royal Family*, by B. B. Rothersfield. Posh! It's about England and King George the some-number-or-other. Well, that should make me drowsy. Come along, dear. Will you and Rafe be staying the night?"

"Yes, we're so close to the mission church, we can walk."

"Good. I believe Candace is having Keno to Sunday dinner, and it will be delightful to have the two of you joining."

Eden went with Nora to her bedroom where Nora gouged her walking stick at the mattress. "That's the rascal. Look at it—old and lumpy. Why, I had that same mattress as a girl. Imagine! I believe he refuses to buy me a new one just to keep my visits here brief."

Eden struggled to keep her laughter down. "I'll make it a point to order a new mattress for you. A goose-feather mattress. How will that be?"

"Sounds marvelous. Hand me my medication, will you dear?"

Eden did so. "Aunt Nora, there's something I want to ask you."

"For a goose-down mattress you may ask anything you like."

"I'll be straightforward. What did you see in the court of Iolani Palace at the ball that caused you such distress you fainted?"

Nora stared at her. She walked over to the brocaded wingback chair and lowered herself with a sigh. "Did Rafe suggest you ask me?"

"No. I've wondered about it since then. I was on the balcony when you came in from the court where the band was playing. You looked as though you had seen the unbelievable. Then you fainted."

Again, Nora sighed. "Well Eden, I did see something that shocked me. I suppose it caused my fainting. Close the door. I'll tell you. I suppose you'll repeat it to Rafe?"

"Well, we don't wish to keep secrets from each other."

"Wise decision. It doesn't matter. I think he already knows well enough. In fact, he knows even more, and so does Zachary."

Eden closed the door and sat opposite Nora. She leaned forward, hands folded on her lap, watching Nora.

Nora looked up at the ceiling as if gathering her thoughts into words and then began quietly.

"I feel like a Benedict Arnold, but when the truth must be spoken what can one do but speak? I discovered something that night that is most dismaying. It alters my opinion of Queen Liliuokalani."

Eden took her hand. Did this have anything to do with the late night visitor? "Yes?"

"It's shameful, really. I was convinced Oliver was a gentleman, as you know. But Oliver Hunnewell is a spy. He's mixed up with the powerful gambling syndicate from the American mainland."

Eden wasn't surprised. In fact, she knew that to be the case, as did Rafe and Zachary. But why did Nora believe this?

"What happened to convince you, Aunt Nora?"

"First of all, the scoundrel met a woman who entered the court by way of the royal guardhouse. And how could she get through the guardhouse area without someone high up helping her? Otherwise, she would need to come by the civil gate, like the rest of us."

Eden asked quietly, "You saw her then? Do you know who she is?"

"Oh, yes. I've seen her before at the Royal Hotel. She's a sooth-sayer."

The facts seemed to be straightforward enough. Nora had actually seen the tarot card reader arrive, and Eden had seen the woman as she came up the stairway into the private living quarters.

"Her name," Nora said softly, "is Madame Wolf—actually *Fraulein*, since she is of German ancestry. I don't know whether she is married or not, but I've seen her at the Royal Hotel twice since I've been there, and both times with a man. I don't know his name. I'm sure Rafe has seen her as well."

"Yes, and I saw the couple speaking with Silas in the garden here at Kea Lani."

"A dreadful revelation. My suspicions about Silas now appear to be certain. You've told Rafe of course?"

"Yes, but he already knows enough about Silas to show that he, like Oliver, was involved with the cartel out to influence the queen."

"Well I'm grieved to say this, my dear, but it seems clear that Liliuokalani is being influenced, whether she knows it or not. They are out to get those horrid gambling and opium bills passed by the Legislature and then signed by her into law."

"And they are using the tarot card reader to influence her?"

"Yes, that is what shocked me. I would never have believed it if

I hadn't seen her arrival and the queen looking in her direction with approval."

"And you saw Oliver, too?"

"Oliver and another man meeting Fraulein Wolf. Oliver handed her some papers. Then the three of them walked back into the palace through another route, the man showing the way."

"Who was he?" Eden begged.

"Well that's it, dear, the frustrating thing was I couldn't see the man's face. But I recognized the woman, as I said. By shuffling tarot cards and drawing from the pack, she supposedly reads the past and predicts the future. It is all nonsense, quite absurd. And very reckless of the queen to listen to her. Imagine! That is what had me so upset. It still does."

"And rightly so," Eden soothed.

"To think that my friend, the queen, would trust what she is told from cards!" She put a hand to her forehead.

"We don't know for sure if she does listen to her, Aunt Nora. We mustn't rush to judgment."

"No, but I fear that she *does*. The odious question is: Who decides what information will be given to the fortune-teller?"

Yes, and who was the man with Oliver Hunnewell who gave her the papers? And what role did Oliver hold in this dark scheme?

"I fear the queen may secretly meet with this Fraulein Wolf often. I am most disappointed. Ainsworth is right about some of his beliefs concerning the queen. Whereas I—" She looked pained. "Whereas I have put too much confidence in frail human flesh. 'Put not your confidence in man,' Scripture teaches us, and I've unwisely put too much in the monarchy."

Chapter Twenty Seven
Seeds of Deceit

*T*he evening lights were coming on in Kea Lani plantation house, golden against a darkening sky. A silvery star winked down.

Rafe watched guests conversing with each other on the front lawn of the great white house, discussing everything from sugar prices to politics. He stood with Keno and Zachary behind the chairs where Eden, Candace, and Claudia Hunnewell were talking.

"If she tries to banish the Constitution of '87, we won't stand for it," someone announced.

"Careful how you speak of the queen," Zachary commented sarcastically, "you might be accused of treason and hanged from the downtown coconut trees."

"Treason, bah! They're the ones who want to commit treason against us planters. We are all first-, second-, and third-generation Hawaiians, but you wouldn't know it to hear some of them talk. What do they call us, reformers? The 'missionary party,' and you can hear the scorn in their voice. They say we're thieves and robbers, too."

"If the truth were known," another said, "we're the men who built Hawaii."

"Absolutely."

"Quite so, quite so," Ainsworth said.

"We made it what it is today, everything from Easton pineapples to Spreckels and Derrington sugar. We brought the good hotels, established the schools and hospitals. Now that the Islands are productive, we're not going to have our rights taken away. If they think they can now control our harvest by claiming we stole it from them, then they're the thieves!"

A strained hush of voices followed. Ainsworth frowned. "Now, Sam. Let's not get too riled. There won't be a new Constitution. No one is taking away our rights. The Legislature just won't allow that to happen."

Zach leaned toward Rafe. "How can he say that? Whoever is feeding information to the soothsayer has one goal: getting the queen's pro-lottery and opium cabinet approved by the Legislature. Once that's done, the next step is the new Constitution."

"I know that. So does Ainsworth. We need to be cautious what we say here. There's bound to be individuals who will report anything Ainsworth says to the queen."

"Silas! Who else? Have you seen him tonight?"

Rafe smiled and said, "The culprit is standing by your elbow, just behind Claudia's chair."

Zach turned and looked at his half brother as if a viper had slithered its way beside his ankle. He moved away from Silas and sat down beside Claudia, who smiled sweetly.

"Once again I'm *persona non grata*," Silas murmured to Rafe.

Rafe said, "At least you've convinced him to declare his intentions to Claudia."

Silas chuckled. "My real intent. I'm surprised you noticed—no one else did."

Rafe looked at him with an easy smile. "Looking out for your little brother?"

Silas stared back. "If I were that charitable, I'd board the next steamer to the mainland. That's the only way Zach will be content."

There was wearied cynicism in his tone, as if he would prefer a mended relationship with his brother.

"Let's just say Miss Claudia is a fine Christian girl; too good for me. Besides, she's in love with him. The trouble with Zach is that he is dense on matters like Claudia, but sharp when it comes to the danger he's rousing with his snooping."

Rafe looked at Silas. "Better explain that."

Silas shrugged and looked at the guests milling about.

"If anyone knows what I mean, it's you. He's snooping too close to big names in the cartel. Where big money is at risk, the sharks come out to protect their feeding ground."

"If anything serious happens to Zach the sharks will wish they'd never ventured into these waters. You can tell that to dear old Oliver the next time you meet with him."

Silas stared at him.

"Yes I know about Oliver and about Fraulein Wolf duping the queen. Listen Silas," Rafe said in a low, even voice, "you're a bigger fool than I thought if you keep marching to their drumbeat. The march ends at the cliff's edge. They're going over one of these days and you'll go with them unless you get out. Ambrose has warned you. We've said nothing because we're giving you time to act wisely. And I know you helped Townsend escape."

Silas's fingers moved compulsively up and down the buttons on his shirt. He looked ashen.

"I had no choice. I didn't want to help him. I tried my best to get out of it but they threatened to go to Ainsworth. That will be my ruin, and they know it. They know I like being part of the family."

"So that's the method they used to arm-twist you into helping Townsend?"

He gave a nod.

"We need to talk elsewhere," Rafe told him. "C'mon, let's walk toward the road."

Eden, back with the guests after helping Nora to bed, noticed Rafe and Silas walking away from the lawn. It was difficult to maintain her smiling attitude as various people came to impart their well wishes for her marriage to Rafe Easton. Eden was anxious for the evening to end. She wondered how Rafe's conversation over Kip had ended with her grandfather, and now, her cousin Silas would have to tell him about the cartel.

When the evening of celebration ended and Eden stacked their wedding gifts on her dresser in the bedroom, she lingered with amazement over the diamond necklace and earrings Ainsworth had bestowed upon her as a family heirloom.

In a lovely little ceremony at the height of the party, her grandfather had presented Eden with her great-grandmother Amabel's diamonds from South Africa.

"My dear granddaughter has joined her life with one of Hawaii's best treasures, Rafe Easton," he had announced. "And now Eden deserves some of the best treasures of the Derrington family legacy."

The tears had filled Eden's eyes and she'd almost fainted at the surprise and joy of the honor.

Now as she looked at the diamonds, she wondered where her great-grandmother Amabel had gotten hold of these treasures. Great-grandmother had probably received them from her great-grandfather. But where had he gotten them? Had he been to South Africa when a young man?

"Pondering your own diamond mine in the Transvaal, my sweet?" Rafe asked as he entered the bedroom.

"I'd much rather hear what Silas and Ainsworth told you tonight—and I've something interesting from Great-aunt Nora."

He removed his jacket and looked around for a place to hang it. He opened the wardrobe and what seemed like a hundred dresses, hats, and shoes seemed to take up every inch of available space.

Eden noticed none of this as she hurried to tell him the details of her meeting with Great-aunt Nora.

Rafe looked at his jacket again. He tossed it on the chair and poured a cup of coffee. He drank it, watching her. She explained about Oliver Hunnewell meeting the soothsayer at the ball.

"Of course," he said. "The insider!"

"Oliver? But—"

"Not Oliver. The Hawaiian who brought Oliver to meet the tarot card reader near the royal barracks."

She searched his face. "You simply *can't* mean—?"

"I *do* mean. Samuel Nowlein, captain of the queen's Household Guards and a resident at the Royal Barracks. He's a solid royalist, known to be working with the lottery's foreign promoters. He'll do whatever he needs to secure Liliuokalani on the throne."

Perhaps Rafe was right, she decided. From what little she knew of royal society Samuel Nowlein was a dependable friend to the queen. "But was he the man Great-aunt Nora claims to have seen?"

"I can't be sure, but I believe he's the mystery man within the walls," he said.

"It's true that he, above some others, would understand the queen's mind. He would know her daily routine, too."

"Giving him ample opportunity to pass on private information to Fraulein Wolf for good usage in her card readings. Silas assures me the queen has fallen for Fraulein Wolf's deceit."

Evidently she could use some wisdom from the Scriptures, Eden thought. King Saul lost his kingdom by going to the witch of Endor. Was the queen of Hawaii any better than the king of Israel? She knew the queen was not.

"Unfortunately she doesn't see through these shrewd individuals taking advantage of her," Rafe said. "Nowlein supports one of the queen's main goals—to introduce a new Constitution in January. If she can do so, she'll have regained the sovereign control over Hawaii that Kalakaua lost in '87. In the minds of the royalists, the money offered by the lottery and opium dealers will end Hawaii's debts. They think it will supply a huge bank account from which to draw funds, and grant complete independence from the haole Hawaiians."

Eden's hopes spiraled. She was almost sure now there would be a revolution as there'd been in 1887. When the unwavering Great-aunt Nora became disillusioned with the monarchy, matters were serious indeed.

"Sit down, sweet. Let me tell you just how much money the dear boys from the Louisiana gambling clique have dangled under the nose of the queen and her allies."

Rafe pulled a sheet of folded paper from his pocket.

"Where did you get that?" she asked in a low voice.

"Silas. And don't ask me how he got hold of it; he wouldn't explain."

Eden was surprised. "He's helping you? May I ask, why?"

"I put him on the spot. It was either cross the line and come clean, or he was going to be hung out to dry. He admitted tonight, as he has to Ambrose, that he spied for the cartel."

"I was convinced of it," she told him. "The couple in the garden at Kea Lani were threatening him about something."

"It was about getting him to help Townsend," he said flatly. "Silas aided his escape."

Eden stood. "That evening after I left the Kalihi hospital where I spoke with Lana." She shuddered. "Townsend was in the boat-house?"

Rafe drew her into his arms, his hands reassuring as he stroked her soothingly. "No. Townsend wasn't in the boathouse. He was at Koko Head waiting for the cartel to get a boat and take him to the other side of Oahu, to Rabbit Island. From there, a ship eventually picked him up. He's probably somewhere on the mainland."

"And Silas?"

"He took care of him at Tamarind House. I always suspected Townsend was hiding there. What better place, with Nora keeping a room here at the hotel? Silas helped him aboard the boat. Do you remember when I went to Tamarind?"

"Yes, you took Bernice there. I was very disappointed."

"I didn't take her there to suggest she buy Tamarind. In fact, I didn't take her with me at all. She invited herself along. I went there to see if I could find evidence of Townsend's stay."

"And did you find anything?"

"Yes. He always was a heavy smoker of Cuban cigars. He left bits all over the cellar. I knew he'd been there. If the marshal had gone—well, he didn't. Zach went there with you, didn't he?"

"Yes, but I don't think he found anything."

"Regardless, Townsend's reckoning awaits the proper hour. Silas told me tonight that he's going to work on our side while appearing to serve the other cause. Ambrose has made an impression on him."

"Is it safe for him to be a spy?"

"They may continue to trust him. Remember, his name was in the *Gazette*, not Oliver's or any of the others. They may think they're still in the shadows."

"What did Silas write on the paper you have?" she asked.

Eden listened, surprised, then amazed as Rafe explained the lottery scheme as Silas had explained it in his report.

"Fraulein Wolf read her tarot cards and convinced Liliuokalani that a certain man with the initials 'T.E.E.' would call on her the next morning, July 8, at ten o'clock. The man would bring a packet of papers. If the queen cooperated she would receive a large amount of money from across the waters. The fortune-teller told her she must have the Legislature accept the lottery bill. If they did, the gambling franchise would bring one million dollars!"

Rafe paused in his reading to look at her. "A million bucks."

Eden shut her eyes. "Wait until Ambrose learns this."

Rafe read on: "The fortune-teller came back to Iolani the next morning, arriving at nine o'clock. She remained until she *felt* the presence of T.E.E. in the palace and then left. The queen said, 'Sure enough, he showed up just as she said he would.'

"T.E.E is an unknown. He came as a lottery promoter for those who were forced to stop their operations in Louisiana. I,

Silas Derrington, know this because I was one of them. We came to Hawaii to interest several powerful men in Honolulu to seek a gambling franchise.

"Queen Liliuokalani told T.E.E. to send her a copy of their proposal.

"In payment to gain the gambling franchise, the cartel offered to give fifty thousand *each* for building railroads on Oahu, and the Big Island of Hawaii. And they said they would also improve Honolulu's harbor. There would be another $175,999 to urge industries to come to the Islands, and $25,000 for tourist travel and immigration."

Rafe paused and Eden said, "No wonder the queen, Samuel Nowlein, and the others are so determined. She must have been stunned by their offer—"

"Stunned enough to swallow the bait. This offer must look to her and the others like the solution to all of Hawaii's financial woes. All they do in return," he said, "is to sell to the highest bidder the right to turn the Islands into a gambling paradise. After all, who cares about the degradation of culture? A leader's responsibility to rule under God, for the betterment of the people doesn't enter their consideration. Along with attracting gamblers, the kingdom can make even more money by having brothels well supplied with prostitutes. And don't forget to sell a franchise to dish out opium and more alcohol. After all, we're doing this to *save* Hawaii from going down in debt."

Eden stood. "And she said she would do what was best for Hawaii. How easy to make excuses when one's heart is bent on having its way."

Rafe said, "It's hard for me to reject the notion that there hasn't been some promise of private booty to be passed around as well. Not to the queen, but to some of the others. There's no evidence of that, but personal greed and a lust for power are ever with us, and are often garbed as angels of charity for the masses. Underneath, they don't care about the 'masses,' but their own pockets."

꧁꧂

A week later when Grandfather Ainsworth sat at the breakfast table enjoying his morning coffee and waiting for the platter of various sweet fruits to be brought in, he opened the morning *Gazette*.

Silas stopped pouring coffee into his cup and watched with startled amazement as his grandfather's face went from a peaceful tan to two ruddy blotches on his cheeks and then fading to a pasty white. Ainsworth gasped so loudly that it startled the man who was entering with the platter of fruit. He tipped the platter, and half of the mango and kiwi plopped onto the floor.

Silas stood. Was his grandfather having a heart attack? He started around the table to reach him when Ainsworth exploded with temper.

"Where is that Benedict Arnold?" He slapped his hand against the table causing the dishes to rattle. He rose. "Is he too much of a coward to meet me face-to-face?" He turned and stomped out of the dining room, into the hall, and to the bottom of the stairway. Silas followed.

"Zachary! Come down you traitor!" Ainsworth grabbed his walking stick and thumped it on the stair.

Silas cleared his throat. "He's not here. He left an hour ago. Mind telling me what's wrong?"

Ainsworth whirled on him. "Wrong? Read it!" He pushed the *Gazette* into Silas's hands and continued shouting at the empty stairway.

Silas stared at the bold black headline: "Derrington Grandson Involved with Mainland Gambling Cartel."

The article began, "Silas Derrington may be a newcomer to the Islands, but as a gambler from Louisiana he knows how to wield political power and rake in the winning chips.

"Silas is the elder son of once respected legislator Townsend Derrington, who is now wanted by the Honolulu police for numerous crimes. Credible sources insist that Townsend's son, Silas, is involved in a fortune-telling scam with the gambling and opium deal-ers to influence the queen to pass the lottery and opium bills . . ."

Ainsworth called for his hat, coat, and carriage.

"From this moment Zachary is disinherited. He is not permit-ted to set a foot in this mansion! I thought Rafe owned sixty percent of the *Gazette*! How could he permit Zachary to print this rub-bish?" He snatched the *Gazette* and shook it. "And Nora! My sister! Allowing this kind of rabid gossip to be spread all over the front page! I'll take them to court. I'll make the three of them eat their words. Daring to attack you like this. Dragging the Derrington name through the mud. Pay no heed, Silas. I'll see the *Gazette* ruined for this."

Silas groaned and slumped down on the stairs.

The next day, Zachary hung his golden head, staring miserably at the carpet in Rafe and Eden's living room of their suite at the Royal Hotel.

"Now he's struck me from his will. I'm not even allowed in the house. All of my belongings were taken from my room and dumped on the lawn. 'And don't come back,' Grandfather shouted, shaking that walking stick of his like it held magic to turn me into a toad."

"We may all be toads before this ship passes in the night," Rafe commented. He was frustrated over the action Zach had taken. He'd blown the bugle before the charge was ready. Now Oliver knew they were on to the scheme to influence the queen.

Zach hadn't just hurt himself. The reputation of the *Gazette* was on the firing line, as was Rafe's, and Nora's. While the infor-mation Zach disclosed was primarily fact, he'd forged ahead inde-pendently and ruined Rafe's plans.

Zach ran his fingers through his hair. "Nora won't speak to me. Candace says she can't wait to get away from Kea Lani to live at Hawaiiana. She doesn't want me coming over. She's even thinking of moving into the plantation house alone before the wedding. Keno's mad at me because Candace is upset. I'm done for, Rafe. I'm skinned, gutted, and deep fried. You're the only friend I have left."

"Don't count on it. I'd like to throw you over the lanai if I could get by with it," Rafe said.

Zach went on moaning out his mistreatment. "I'm living on my boat now—and everything inside is cracked up."

"Get it fixed. Send me the bill."

"What about my inheritance? It's gone. I'm a pauper. Who would marry me now?"

"I don't know," Rafe said.

"No Derrington inheritance," Zach moaned again. "Not even a bag of marbles."

Rafe's thoughts turned back to Silas. Rafe was now writing a report to alert the Reform Party movement of what was ahead so they could plan their own offensive to stop the passage of the lottery and opium bills. Silas had told him the queen was working on a new Constitution. "If the queen's supporters in the Legislature can get the lottery and opium bills passed, she'll sign them and close the Legislature in September. Then, next January, she'll introduce the new Constitution to replace the 1887 one."

If she does, Rafe thought, *there will be a revolution.*

"You blew it all right," he admitted. "Why didn't you get my approval before rushing to print?"

"Because I knew you wouldn't give me approval," Zach confessed. "Nor would Nora."

"We know why Nora would never break the story. But I intended to, as you know. We even planned it out. The first breaking headline wasn't to be about Silas, but Oliver."

"I know, I know, but he's slippery. We won't get much on him."

"It so happens I have new information on him."

Zach looked up. "What is it?"

"So you can put it in the *Gazette* tomorrow? I know you hate to hear this, Zach, but Silas is the lowest catch on the totem pole."

"It was the way Silas acted at the *hoolaulei* last week. He was out to impress Claudia. Well, now she knows what he's really like."

"You'll be astounded to know he's not the least interested in Claudia. He was forcing your hand. You won't accept this, but he had your best interest in mind. He knew Ainsworth wanted you to marry her, and he thought he'd help you along."

Zach snorted.

"Whatever brotherly feelings were beginning to sprout," Rafe suggested dryly, "you've now ripped to shreds. You've smeared his sins all over the front page."

"He deserved it," Zach grumbled.

"If we all got what we deserved, I shouldn't want to say where our final destination would be." He drummed his fingers pensively. "We've got to move on and see what we can do to give an emotional sedative to your grandfather."

"Before that happens we'll have a snowstorm in Hawaii for Christmas," Zach lamented.

Rafe smiled. "Thinking about the *Gazette*, I need to see Nora about getting Eden's first installment of 'Rebecca's Story' printed. We'll do it this week." He looked over at Zach. "Think that's possible?"

"The next edition? Sure, why not? Maybe it will even soothe the feelings of Honolulu citizens toward the *Gazette*."

"Then go talk to Nora about it today, will you?"

"I'll go now. Is she here in the hotel?"

He nodded. "We saw her at breakfast. Tell her to get Eden going on the second installment right away. I've got to go meet Hunnewell and Thurston at the Legislature."

Chapter Twenty-Eight
The Announcement

*I*n the days after Zachary's disclosure, people in Honolulu
seemed much less upset than Grandfather Ainsworth. There
were angry letters to the *Gazette* office from the queen's supporters,
and mockery from other newspapers over the "astute journalism
practices of the mighty *Gazette*," but nothing from either Iolani
Palace or those in the Legislature supporting the lottery bill.

Zachary and Ainsworth did not know Silas had turned his back
on the gambling cartel and promised to help Rafe thwart the cartel
plans. With Zachary disinherited, and Ainsworth fuming at Rafe
because he "hadn't kept a closer eye on that volatile nincompoop
Zachary," Rafe decided to risk a meeting between the offended parties. He asked Ambrose to encourage Silas to confess the truth
about his past to Ainsworth. And he was pleased when Ambrose let
him know that Silas was willing.

Although hoping to go to Hanalei on the Big Island for the rest
of the summer, Rafe was obliged to remain at the Royal Hotel for
the long session of the Legislature. The queen had refused to permit
the customary yearly dismissal.

"It's part of the opponents' plan to keep us in session until they can bribe enough legislators to vote for the approval of her new cabinet, containing supporters of the lottery. So far, Thurston's Reform Party has managed to vote down the names the fortune-teller told her. Each time we send several trusted names, she refuses to add them," Rafe told Ambrose.

"How does the vote look?" Ambrose asked.

Rafe shook his head. "It's just a matter of time before the bribery tactic wins. She wants men like Samuel Parker and Wilson for marshal."

Ambrose raised his brows. "Wilson? Charles Wilson? Not Percy Harper?"

"Wilson and his wife are friends of the queen. He's also more willing to make some arrests and use a curfew, if necessary."

Ambrose studied him. "What are you suggesting, lad?"

"Silas has learned that when the queen gets her cabinet and her votes in the Legislature, the next step is to call for a new Constitution. If she does go through with it Thurston's Reformers will raise trouble. The queen has confidence in Wilson to do what is needed. So, she needs these men confirmed before the Legislature is dismissed."

"I see. Well a person can't run a country and expect blessing by selling gambling, opium, prostitution, and liquor franchises to raise money for the government coffers."

─◌◌─

When Eden heard the bill was going to pass and the queen would sign it, she and Candace mobilized the Christian women's groups in Honolulu to call on Liliuokalani and plead with her not to sign the bills. Although the queen kindly received them and understood their concerns, she was determined to "do what is best for Hawaii."

"I can tell her what's best for Hawaii," Ambrose stated to Rafe one evening soon afterward when he and Eden had gone to visit with him and Noelani.

Eden was developing a closer relationship with three-year-old Kip, now that she knew they would adopt him, and she would become his mother. At present, Kip was attached to Celestine since she'd cared for him for most of his young life. Celestine was also attached to Kip, and because she was a fine woman with strong Christian principles, Eden thought Kip should stay as near to her as he wished.

The next big event for the Derringtons and Hunnewells was the marriage of Candace and Keno Hunnewell. Candace had a grand wedding with Eden and Claudia among her bridesmaids.

"Be sure now to toss the bouquet to Claudia," Eden whispered to Candace.

Looking beautiful, as all brides do, Candace came forth down the mission-church aisle on the arm of Grandfather Ainsworth, beaming with pride.

Keno was handsome but nervous, and Rafe stood as his best man.

Silas was there, in the background, silent and unobtrusive, waiting for the meeting to be set up with Ainsworth. So far, Ainsworth refused to see Zachary, but after the festive schedule centering on Candace's marriage was over, Rafe believed Ainsworth would relent.

"I'm the one who decided we needed to delay the meeting with Ainsworth," Rafe told Eden.

She was surprised. "But you were the one who planned it. Why a delay? Zachary has been terribly depressed. He wasn't even free to attend the wedding because Grandfather refused to see him sitting in the pew."

Rafe explained that he was giving Silas more time. "He needs to establish a favorable record of activities for the Reformers. Ambrose and I will be his witnesses. When your grandfather learns Zach was correct, though unwise, in his newspaper column, Silas will be able to produce activities of true repentance, to show he's switched sides.

He'd better have something in his basket or your grandfather won't show Silas any grace either. He'll be ready to disown, disinherit, and otherwise boot them both out of Honolulu."

Eden smiled. "Clever, are you not?" She kissed him.

When the meeting was at last held in the Kea Lani library, it was a quiet gathering of the five men: Ainsworth, Ambrose, Rafe, Silas, and Zachary.

Zach stood stiffly on one side of the room staring at the tips of his polished shoes, looking tall, slim, and golden in his stylish white suit.

Silas stood facing the window. Ainsworth paced over the carpet, hands behind his back, looking down. Ambrose stood by a section of leather-bound books.

"Well?" Ainsworth snapped. "You wanted this meeting. What have you to say for yourself?"

"I didn't ask for this meeting," Zachary grumbled. "I told the truth about the queen, the cartel, and those helping and deceiving her." He looked at Silas as he added, "By bringing in a witch!"

"If that were all you did I'd commend you. You disgraced our name before the people of Honolulu. You brought shame to Silas!"

"He brought shame upon himself—"

Silas turned and gravely looked at his grandfather.

"Zachary is right this time, Grandfather. Everything he wrote in the *Gazette* had a foundation of truth."

Silence enveloped the room.

"I first came to Hawaii as a spy for the gambling rackets in Louisiana."

Ainsworth sucked in a breath. Zachary gaped at him.

"When I first saw that I was going to be accepted into the Derrington family I tried to worm out of the syndicate—not because I cared for the Derringtons, but because it looked as if I might inherit money. Money was all I wanted. I spied for Oliver Hunnewell as far back as the night at Hunnewell's beach house when Oliver planned to steal the Annexation Club's manifesto and send it to the queen.

Oliver is with the gambling cartel because he plans to become rich through the passage of the lottery bill. His father, Mr. Thaddeus Hunnewell, knows nothing about his son's deceit. The gambling hierarchy hired the 'witch,' who is a supposed tarot card reader. Her work is to influence the queen to stand firm and get those bills passed, signed, and into law."

Silas looked at Rafe. "Ask Rafe and Pastor Ambrose. They know all of this. I've already confessed it to them. I'm afraid this is only news to you," he said sympathetically to his grandfather. "You're the one who believed in me. I'm sorry to say your confidence was misplaced."

Ainsworth stared at Silas, transfixed. Zach was shocked, obviously wondering why Silas was vindicating him at his own expense. Rafe and Ambrose had been praying for this in order to break down the wall between the two brothers.

"One reason I've confessed tonight is because of Zachary. My conscience won't let me uphold a lie that injures him. He shouldn't be the one who leaves Kea Lani, or loses his place in the family. I'm the one who should pack my bags and get out. And I've decided to do just that."

Rafe shot Silas a glance. Was he serious? Rafe saw that Ambrose was also taken by surprise.

"I'll leave Honolulu for the mainland next week," Silas told Zachary. "You were right. I've been a gambler all my life. But I'm through with the cartel, gambling, and deceit. And if you care to know why this change, Ambrose can explain that."

"Silas accepted Christ as his Savior a month ago. For various reasons we kept it between us to divulge at the right time," Ambrose explained.

"Ambrose has patiently put up with me and my insolent questions about Christianity until I became convinced Jesus is the Way, the Truth, and the Life. Rafe is my witness, too. He and Ambrose have been protecting and advising me for months. Rafe asked me to take the first step of my new life tonight and declare myself. I've tried to do it. For Zachary's sake, and for his reputation."

Ainsworth remained speechless. He felt for the arms of his leather chair and eased himself into it, shaken.

"Silas took a big step tonight, Ainsworth," Ambrose announced. "It took courage and faith in God to risk himself and salvage Zachary's reputation."

"That's not the end of Silas's story," Rafe spoke up. "For the last month Silas has served our cause. Whatever he's learned about their plans he's told me. And I've told the Reform Party leaders. The information he's given us is strengthening our cause to secure Hawaii's future as a territory of the United States. Tonight, Silas discovered the queen has already drawn up a new Constitution. If she gets it passed, everything we've built for generations is likely to be taken away."

"She's what?" Ainsworth responded for the first time, leaning forward.

Rafe looked at Silas. "Why don't you explain what you heard."

Silas nodded. "The queen's been working on a new Constitution for some time now. I even know the names of the men she's been meeting with to write it."

"Astounding!" Ainsworth mopped his brow and fumbled around the top of his desk. "I've got to get a message to Thurston—"

"No, sir, don't act yet," Rafe interrupted. "This must be handled on her time schedule, not ours. We must wait. Let the details come unraveled one at a time at her own pace. In this situation we can't instigate a rebellion. We must react to her actions."

Ainsworth gave a reluctant nod. "Maybe you're right, Rafe. Go on, Silas. Who are these men you mentioned?"

Silas looked cautiously toward Rafe. Rafe nodded.

"She's had meetings with her lawyer, Paul Neumann, and also Samuel Parker. And Samuel Nowlein, captain of the Royal Guard. Also, Charles Wilson. The Constitution they've drawn up was turned over to Arthur Peterson, I suppose to see if it will hold up in court. Tonight I heard that she will call for an important meeting in early January, and read the new Constitution."

Ainsworth was on his feet. "By George if she does, Thurston and the Reformers will seek to have her step down from the throne. Mark my words."

"She did swear an oath to uphold the 1887 Constitution when she came to power after her brother's death in San Francisco," Rafe agreed.

"We won't go back to the ancient rule of the old arbitrary Hawaiian chief," Ainsworth continued, pacing again. "We've built what we have; we didn't steal it. In 1820 Hawaii was little more than some grass huts and unclothed people steeped in pagan worship practices. Why, the first missionaries nearly starved because there was no food. They tried farming and the land hardly produced! You can read these facts from the early missionaries themselves. Even Nora has written about it. We will not have Kea Lani or Hanalei or Hawaiiana or any of the plantations taxed into poverty or taken from us.

"We Derringtons and Eastons have been good Hawaiians since we arrived a few years after the first dedicated missionaries. We're not going to be robbed of our birthright here in Honolulu just to please a queen who wants to reign by ancient customs."

"You're right," Rafe said firmly. "We were born here. We've done our part to make the Islands prosper. We're going to stay, and we're going to be free."

───◈───

After their honeymoon, Mr. and Mrs. Keno Hunnewell invited Rafe and Eden to dinner at Hawaiiana. Celestine had quietly moved into the hotel taking Kip with her before Candace and Keno returned as the new master and mistress of the Great House. Celestine's presence at the hotel worked out well because Eden could easily bring Kip to their suite each afternoon for supper and playtime, while Celestine visited with Great-aunt Nora.

Zachary was also invited to the Hawaiiana dinner—forgiven

and back in Candace's good graces. Much to his delight Claudia was there to comfort his woes, though most of Zach's woes had taken flight recently, thanks to Rafe and Ambrose's meeting with Grandfather Ainsworth.

Ainsworth had decided if not to forgive Zachary's article in the *Gazette* against the Derrington name, to at least turn his back to the "abysmal blunder."

"Truth doesn't always give a man the right to blare it out for all to read," he had lectured.

Silas, too, was mildly embraced back into favor. "Ainsworth's exuberant that Silas is spending time at the mission church with Ambrose and Jerome. And Zach's sudden devotion to Claudia Hunnewell has Ainsworth whistling as he walks, thinking no one notices the new energy in his step."

Eden smiled. "Candace always did see through Grandfather's vinegary ways, but I guess it took the rest of us a little longer. I'm still awed that he's letting us adopt Kip."

"He prefers that we adopt him."

"That's quite a compliment."

Perhaps it was the crumbling divide between Zach and Silas that amazed Eden the most.

"They actually talk to each other," she told Rafe one afternoon. "Candace says she saw them walking together down the road to Ambrose's bungalow. She heard Silas say something, and Zachary laughed and put a hand on his shoulder."

Relationships did appear to be on the mend, at least in the extended family.

"I wish Hawaii was that amenable to breaking down the barriers of conflict," Eden said. "Instead, the bulwarks are going up. It's been a year of repeated crises and clashes between the Legislature and the queen."

"Wishes rarely come true, darling," Rafe responded. "Some things in this life are worth fighting for and dying for. Compromise is often for those who have no genuine convictions, and find it easier to withdraw from legitimate controversy.

"I don't want my life and property left to the fickle whims of a royal family. History bears out what happens when such people retain control of power for too long. The old sin nature is too corrupt to trust with so much power passing from one carnal monarch to the next. I want a republic with individual rights and personal freedoms protected by adequate checks and balances to limit power of any corrupt leader. Power in the hands of a king, a queen, or a president is only as secure as the ruler is both wise and trustworthy. When there is a dearth of wise leadership, that, according to Scripture, is a judgment from God upon a nation.

"Hawaii ultimately does not belong to the self-appointed royal family, but to the Sovereign of the universe who has the right to bless or to judge. How did Liliuokalani's family get the Hawaiian throne? By conquering the smaller leaders of the other Islands. Royalty was seized by force. Absurd! There is one true royal family—the family of King David of Israel. Why? Because the Lord God chose David. Jesus came through that line. And one day the whole earth will bow the knee to the true King of kings."

"I love you," Eden said with a smile. "Maybe you should think about becoming a king."

"Yes, and you'd make a beautiful queen."

Rafe pulled her into his arms.

—◌◌◌—

Christmas season was drawing near. Eden had completed "Rebecca's Story" in the *Gazette* and as a result, she was asked to speak to ladies' clubs. But Eden had not been feeling well and turned down the invitations.

When Rafe asked about her lack of energy, she responded, "I'm fine. I just don't care to travel to the other Islands alone and you're too busy to come with me."

"You know, your story on your mother was so well received that maybe you should turn it into a book that could also circulate on the mainland."

"Yes, that is an idea. I'll think and pray about it."

He walked over to her, held her, and kissed her several times.

The next day Eden received her usual letter from Aunt Lana on Kalawao who wrote to her every six weeks. Dr. Bolton, surprisingly, had not progressed with his leprosy and was doing well running Dr. Jerome's clinic.

Eden always sent extra gifts of food, clothing, and private necessities by way of the steamer. She and Rafe had also set up a special "blessing" fund for Lotus, her mother's faithful *kokua* at Bishop House. Eden slept better knowing Lotus was well provided for and enjoying treasures such as pretty dresses, shoes, and books to read.

David, the young man running the printing press at Kalawao, was doing quite well, so Ambrose told her. He had printed the Scriptures in Hawaiian and was giving them out to all who could read.

One day near Christmas Zachary burst into their Royal Hotel suite to tell Eden and Rafe that he was engaged.

"And we're not even waiting for the typical year's engagement. Claudia's afraid her father may come between us. Old Thaddeus isn't too keen on having me as a son-in-law. He'll come around, though. Grandfather says he'll have a long talk with Thaddeus. We're thinking of following in your footsteps. Just surprise everyone and go to Ambrose to get married."

"When you do," Rafe said smoothly, a flicker of humor in his dark eyes, "we'll be sure to give you and Claudia a big hullabaloo after your honeymoon."

"Whatever we call it," Zach said, "is good enough for me. This is the happiest I've ever been. I think I've loved Claudia all along and didn't even know it."

"Just as long as you know it now," Rafe said.

"And be sure she knows it, too," Eden added. "Tell her so more than once. Words of love and well-chosen words of praise build a contented relationship."

When Christmas came around Rafe surprised Eden with red rubies that sparkled in candlelight. "You know what you can do with them, don't you my love? What women always do with their fabulous jewels. Keep them locked up in a dark safe. Then, when you're silver-haired and old you can unlock the safe and show them to your granddaughter. Then she can have them when she gets married and put them back into the dark safe with Amabel's South African diamonds."

Eden laughed. "That's where you're wrong. I'm going to wear them whenever I want. Rafe, they're so lovely. And I've a Christmas present for you, too. Actually, two presents. One you can see under the tree when we go to Kea Lani tonight. The other—" and she deliberately took his hand and rested his palm against her womb.

He drew in a light breath, his gaze holding hers.

"You don't mean what I think you do?"

"A baby," she said. "We're going to have our own baby."

He held her tightly as their lips joined in celebration.

"When?" he asked, sounding a bit uneasy.

She lifted a brow. "Not worried about it?"

"Actually, yes."

"June."

"June," he repeated thoughtfully. "Hanalei is ready now. I suppose the trouble here will have settled by then. The situation will probably explode in January. I'd rather you were with Noelani on the Big Island. It will make me feel easier. Celestine can go with you, maybe Nora, too."

"Trouble?"

"The revolution." Rafe told her how Liliuokalani had called in the British Commissioner, James H. Wodehouse. "I believe she did this to try to frighten the Reformers. She needed British advice, she told him. The queen wonders if she should call all the representatives of other countries to Iolani Palace to be safe in case of violence!"

"Violence," Eden repeated, "from the Reform Party?" She smiled ruefully. "I think you're right. It was an act to intimidate men like Mr. Thurston. What did the British Commissioner tell her?"

"He was cool and calm. He told her no, he didn't think it was necessary. Did she expect danger? She told him there might be."

"Oh Rafe, I wish it didn't need to come to this."

"There's no stopping it now, honey. The differences are too great. History will bring us one way or the other, or perhaps I should say God's providence will have the final vote." He looked at her long and intently. "*Our* baby. Maybe I should send you and Nora and my mother to the mainland."

"Oh no you don't, Rafe Easton. I appreciate your wish to wrap me in safety, but I'm staying where I belong. At your side. I'll go to Hanalei and stay when you're dismissed from the Legislature, but when the time is near for the baby to be born I want you with me. *Promise?*"

His lips met hers tenderly. "A promise, darling Eden."

After Christmas nearly all of the Hunnewells and Derringtons celebrated Zachary and Claudia's "elopement" to the mission church where they were married by Ambrose. Only Oliver was grim at the news of his younger sister's wedding.

"I cannot believe my good fortune," Ainsworth cried, "Derrington-Easton-Hunnewell! Oh, Hawaii! What great things lie in store for you in the coming generations."

Rafe and Keno burst out laughing with the others joining in.

In January of 1893 there was little to laugh about as a mood of anticipated trouble hung over Honolulu.

The queen and her allies proved capable of ridding themselves of their last remaining obstacle: the Wilcox Reform cabinet. Rafe had expected it all along. Several men who had cooperated with Thurston's party were not Reformers at heart. They had believed by cooperating they would receive even higher positions of authority. When this did not happen, they moved back across the aisle to vote in harmony with the Liberal and National parties.

Then with the aid of some Hawaiian nationals, they all joined political forces against the Reformers. Holding a "no confidence" vote, they removed the Reform Party majority rule. This enabled the queen to appoint Samuel Parker as chief of her new cabinet.

Samuel Parker was a likeable gentleman who supported Liliuokalani's goals. Within days, the lottery and opium bills were again brought to the floor and passed. The queen now had what she believed was crucial to introduce her Constitution of 1893.

When Saturday morning, January 14 arrived, all the preparations for the closing of the Legislature were in place. At 10 a.m., Liliuokalani called her new Samuel Parker cabinet together in the Blue Room. She told them she would abolish by sovereign authority the 1887 "Bayonet" Constitution and announce a new one.

Meanwhile, outside Iolani Palace hundreds of native Hawaiians waited for the queen to come to the balcony and tell them the news they waited for, that supreme authority in the Islands was now back in her hands.

Across the street at the Aliiolani Hale building Rafe watched the members of the political association *Hui Kalai'aina* out on the lawn, dressed in colorful garments.

"Look, isn't that Peterson and Colburn?" Zachary said to Rafe.

The two men from the new cabinet came out of the palace and hurried toward Judd Street, as if late for an appointment.

"Interesting," Rafe mused, watching. "I'd expect them to be smiling victoriously." He narrowed his gaze. "I don't believe what I'm seeing—"

"Neither do I. They're headed straight for Thurston's office. Everyone is there waiting for the queen's announcement. Hunnewell, Ainsworth—"

Rafe and Zach dashed off after the two cabinet members.

When they caught up with the men, a crowd was gathering outside Thurston's office. Within a short time, the news spread among the Reformers, and soon larger crowds began gathering trying to find out what was happening.

Inside the small room, men packed against the walls and around the tables and chairs. Arthur Peterson, John Colburn, and Paul Neumann, the queen's lawyer friend, looked out of place among the annexationists.

Rafe and Zach pushed through to where Lorrin Thurston, Thaddeus Hunnewell, Ainsworth, and other leaders gathered around a table talking. The two cabinet members and even the queen's attorney, Paul Neumann, explained to Thurston and the others what had happened in the meeting. In the Blue Room, the queen had stated she was going to introduce her new Constitution on the balcony before the native Hawaiians. The trouble came when the Samuel Parker cabinet become cautious of the political consequences, and even though they had supported the lottery and opium bills, they had respectfully but firmly refused to endorse her Constitution!

At first Rafe was as surprised as Liliuokalani must have been.

"Are you telling us the Samuel Parker Cabinet is not endorsing her Constitution as now written?" Rafe asked.

"We are not. We have politely declined. What do we do now?" they repeated to Thurston, their faces strained with worry. "You know her temperament, gentlemen. She is a determined woman."

Rafe could hardly believe his ears. This was almost ironic, he thought. For the long 172-day legislative session, Thurston's Reform Party had fought the lottery bill and the Samuel Parker cabinet from coming to power! And now that very board had opposed the queen's Constitution!

Peterson and Colburn told their audience how they had argued in the meeting to let the present Legislature terminate without having the Constitution bomb thrown in their faces. If she were patient, there would be a period of time after the lottery was enacted and money coming in, for a stronger chance of getting her new Constitution. She would do better now to support men who shared her desire to abrogate the '87 Constitution, and work to see them compete against the seats now held by Thurston's party.

"She threatened to denounce us before the native Hawaiians on the lawn. Shall we resign?" they asked.

"No!" Thurston said. "We will stand with you in this, even if we must declare her in revolution and work to unseat her."

Zach had crawled upon a ledge looking down on the crowded room and was scribbling notes furiously.

Just then, Silas pushed his way through the outside crowd and squeezed into the room. He shook a folded paper at Zach and then pointed at Rafe.

Zach snatched the paper and passed it to Rafe.

Rafe read the warning and passed it to Thurston, who read it to the group: "Big trouble. Marshal Wilson urging queen to arrest all of you. He has been gathering extra policemen. Also, queen may ask British warship to land men on shore for her aid."

"I put nothing past Wilson," Hunnewell snapped.

"Nor do I," Rafe warned. "If the street fills with people it will be the perfect excuse for old Charlie to follow through. If he's already gathered policemen, you know this action of the Constitution was secretly planned well before today. Silas Derrington has turned out to be a worthy spy."

"Indeed!" Ainsworth said, and Hunnewell nodded. "Well, men?" he said.

"If the plan is to hold us somewhere, they'll win the day," Rafe warned. "We need to act at once. Maybe we should split up."

"I think we'd better form a Committee of Safety," Thurston said firmly. "Quick. Get a message to Stevens," he said of the American Minister. "He's already promised to land soldiers from the U.S.S. *Boston*, if necessary, to protect Americans."

By afternoon the Committee of Safety was organized at Thurston's house and controlled by responsible members of the Annexation Club.

"Gentlemen," Ainsworth stated gravely, looking older and weary. "We of this committee have decided it's time for the monarchy to come to its inevitable end. We will seek annexation negotiations with the United States. We desire liberty, personal freedom, and laws of fairness and justice to protect our property and lives."

There was applause. Someone called out warily, "On what grounds do we overthrow the monarchy?" Hunnewell stood up. "By determining to overthrow the bona fide Constitution of 1887, signed into law by King Kalakaua, and upheld by our supreme court. By planning to restore supreme rights to the throne at the expense of citizens who have been Hawaiians for three generations. When she came to the throne in 1891 she swore to uphold the present Constitution. So now she wants to throw it in the wastebasket and declare herself supreme? We, too, are Hawaiians, and we say it shall not be!"

Thurston said firmly, "The solution for the present is annexation by the United States."

Rafe thoroughly agreed.

Meanwhile, the native Hawaiians who gathered on the palace lawn wondered why their queen had not yet come out on the balcony with the expected news. Liliuokalani appeared later that afternoon to their cheers. Looking calm and as determined as ever, she spoke to them in Hawaiian, telling them not to be disheartened but to return home "with good hope."

"Within the next few days," she promised, she would proclaim the new Constitution *they* so desired.

_____ ჟა _____

The Constitution of Liliuokalani never materialized. Instead, "the next few days" saw the landing of American military from the U.S.S. *Boston*. Coolly and deliberately she resigned from the throne and returned with a guard of twenty to her home, Washington Place. As one of its first acts, the new provisional government annulled the lottery and opium bills.

While the new provisional government under Sanford Dole governed Hawaii as a republic, Liliuokalani and her dedicated followers planned a revolution of their own.

A shipload of rifles were smuggled to Diamond Head. Native Hawaiians, *hapa*-haoles and haoles alike, created a small army to overthrow the government and arrest Sanford Dole.

The rebellion, the many guns brought in, even bombs to be set off in Honolulu, were all foiled by the stronger forces of the provisional government. After years of anger, frustration, and bitterness, the destiny of the Hawaiian Islands was settled in peace.

The long-awaited ceremonies and celebration came on August 12, 1898, when Hawaii was formally annexed by the United States. Two years later it became an official U.S. territory.

Rafe and Eden, with their sons Kip and Rory Easton watched the raising of the Red, White, and Blue over the government building. The Hawaiian Islands were now a territory of the United States.

Keno and Candace with their daughter Dianna and another baby on the way—sure to be a "lad," Keno insisted—stood with them, as did Zachary and Claudia Derrington with their son, Bradley.

Silas Derrington, recently married to Claudia's cousin, Margaret, stood on the walkway near the *Gazette*. Great-aunt Nora came out of her office, as sprightly as ever, to behold the political spectacle, shake her head, and return to her desk.

"A lot of noise and silly firecrackers," she murmured. "They should outlaw those noisy things."

Grandfather Ainsworth stood as straight as his now stooping shoulders would permit. He had recently buried a son at sea. After the rebellion of 1895, led by Samuel Nowlein for Liliuokalani, a body was discovered on Diamond Head—the man had slipped, while smuggling rifles among the rocks, and fallen to his death. It was Townsend.

Now Ainsworth had tears in his eyes as he stared at the American flag with Pastor Ambrose standing beside him.

"The earliest missionaries would be proud and pleased," Ambrose commented. "We knew it had to be America—otherwise it almost certainly would have been Japan, Russia, or England."

"Quite so." Jerome nodded his graying head. "The scare over that Japanese warship intimidating Hawaii some time back was enough to convince me these Islands needed some strong U.S. backing."

"I'm assured of that," Ambrose added soberly. He stood with Noelani who, like others with *hapa*-haole ethnicity, was somewhat undecided on the annexation.

"It is done," she had said. "I accept it. I think it will be better for all of us in the future."

Celestine, now a widow, stood beside Parker Judson. He was a happy man today, and not only politically. Bernice had married Oliver Hunnewell in San Francisco, and Celestine had told him just this morning that she would marry him in a year. Rafe approved, so did Ambrose, now that Parker was attending church every Sunday and coming to the men's Bible study taught by Rafe and Keno on alternate weeks.

As they stood on the balcony of what had once been Iolani Palace, Eden smiled at Rafe, her green eyes reflecting happiness. She was expecting their second child and told him she knew it would be a girl this time. She had already chosen her name, Allison.

Rory pulled at Rafe's sleeve and pointed to the flag. "Look Daddy, look."

He was, as Eden suggested, so much like his father that she was sure he would be another Rafe Easton. Kip's personality was nothing like Townsend's. He was calm, intelligent, and liked to study books about the solar system.

"Not me," Rory would say. "I'm gonna be a big planter like Daddy. I like sea and ships, too, like Daddy."

The sea, Rafe thought, *and ships.*

For years he had been certain that someday people of these Islands would be thankful that they were under the strong protection of the United States military. He looked thoughtfully toward the old Pearl River, now Pearl Harbor, and envisioned American naval ships at anchor in its calm Pacific waters.

I am satisfied. I worked steadfastly for annexation. No decision is perfect, but becoming a territory of the U.S. is the better destiny.

As Rory kept tugging and pointing, the flag seemed to tell Rafe that this grand old flag of freedom would fly there for many years to come. The tropical wind carried both shouts of joy, and some quiet tears, as all the Hawaiians joined to face whatever the future would hold.

Eden laughed at Rory. Rafe had lifted him up to see the parade of American flags. Rory clutched Rafe's neck with both little arms, but still pointed to the bigger flag waving in the breeze.

Thank You, Lord, she prayed. *Thank You. . . .*

DID YOU READ BOOK ONE IN THE DAWN OF HAWAII SERIES?

THE SPOILS OF EDEN

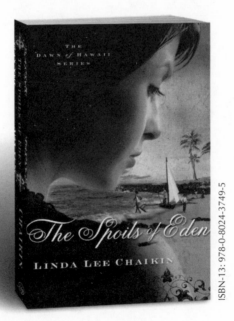

ISBN-13: 978-0-8024-3749-5

The waves lap dangerously close to the abandoned baby— abandoned by the Molokai leper colony of the late 1800s.

That baby will be at the center of an alternately tense and bittersweet romantic struggle between Eden Derrington and Rafe Easton. Eden and Rafe are in love, but Baby Kip may very well endanger their future together.

MOODY
PUBLISHERS

moodypublishers.com

river north

FICTION FROM MOODY PUBLISHERS

River North Fiction is here to provide quality fiction that will refresh and encourage you in your daily walk with God. We want to help readers know, love, and serve JESUS through the power of story.

Connect with us at www.rivernorthfiction.com

- Blog
- Newsletter
- Free Giveaways

- Behind the scenes look at writing fiction and publishing
- Book Club

MOODY
PUBLISHERS

www.MoodyPublishers.com

A Morgan Family Series

CAPTIVE TRAIL

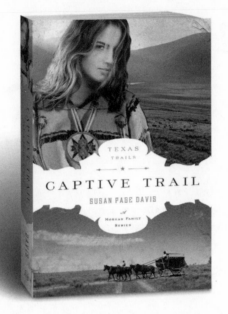

paperback 978-0-8024-0584-5   e-book 978-0-8024-7852-8

Taabe Waipu has stolen a horse meant for a dowry and is fleeing her Comanche village in Texas. While fleeing on horseback she has an accident and must complete her flight on foot. Injured and exhausted, Taabe staggers onto a road near Fort Chadbourne and collapses.

On one of his first runs through Texas, Butterfield Overland Mail Company driver Ned Bright is escorting two nuns to their mission station. They come across Taabe who is nearly dead from exposure to the sun and exhaustion. Ned carries her back with them and begins to investigate Taabe Waipu's identity.

MOODY
PUBLISHERS

MoodyPublishers.com   TexasTrailsFiction.com

A MORGAN FAMILY SERIES

THE LONG TRAIL HOME

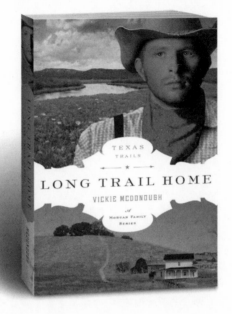

paperback 978-0-8024-0585-2   e-book 978-0-8024-7876-4

Riley Morgan returns home after fighting in the War Between the States and there is nothing he wants more than to see his parents and fiancée again. He soon learns that his parents are dead and the woman he loved is married. To get by, Riley takes a job at the Wilcox School for the blind.

At the school Riley meets a pretty blind woman named Annie, who threatens to steal his heart even as he fights to keep it hidden away. When a greedy man attempts to close the school, Riley and Annie band together to stop him and start falling in love. But Annie has kept a secret from Riley. When he learns the unwelcome truth, Riley packs his belongings and prepares to leave the school that has become his home.

MOODY
PUBLISHERS

MoodyPublishers.com   TexasTrailsFiction.com

A MORGAN FAMILY SERIES

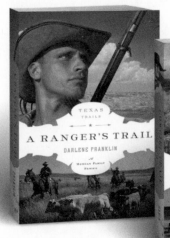

paperback 978-0-8024-0587-6

e-book 978-0-8024-7907-5

paperback 978-0-8024-0586-9

e-book 978-0-8024-7877-1

paperback 978-0-8024-0408-4

e-book 978-0-8024-7892-4

Calling all book club members and leaders!

visit

TexasTrailsFiction.com

for discussion questions and special features

MOODY
PUBLISHERS

MoodyPublishers.com   TexasTrailsFiction.com